SEXY SIX

A BENNETT BROTHERS NOVEL

ISBN-13: 978-1544109879
ISBN-10: 1544109873

Editing: Kendra Gaither at Kendra's Editing and Book Services
Cover Photo: Scott Hoover, Scott Hoover Photography
Cover Model: Nic Palladino
Cover Design: Shanoff Designs

Table of Contents

Grace & Nick

First Date, 2 Years Ago

Whoosh... Thump, Thump, Thump... Whoosh

My heart rate starts accelerating frantically as soon as his door shuts. There's an excited rush pounding in my ears. I reach up to smooth my hair and notice a small tremor.

The entire night has been like something out of a dream. An unbelievably wonderful and surprising dream, starring Nick Bennett.

Play it cool, Grace...

Get yourself together...

I take a split second to enjoy the view as all six-feet-four of Nick's muscular frame is illuminated by the headlights, sending my heart into overdrive again and making my insides twist and twirl. If I don't calm down, there's a high possibility I'll pass out.

Or throw up, which would be the ultimate humiliation.

"Get a handle on it. Monroe women don't lose their cool, Peach Princess. Take a breath and calm down." My grandmother's words ring in my head, barely calming my nerves.

I have to wonder if she'd be able to take her own advice if she was on a date with Nick Bennett.

Most definitely not.

"Here, let me help you." He swings the door open and offers me his hand, helping me to my feet.

"What a gentleman," I tease, surprised at the surge of confidence.

"My mom taught me well, what can I say?" He shrugs, stepping closer and moving me slightly to close the passenger door.

I do an all-over body shiver when my chest rubs against his, our hands still linked. We stay this way a few seconds—close, connected, and locked in a stare. Lost in his gaze, I'm mesmerized as his eyes go soft and start to glow a bright blue. His pupils grow wide before he breaks the stare and looks to our hands.

My confidence wavers as I suck in a deep breath and make a decision, speaking before I lose my courage. “Would you like to come in?” It comes out in a breathy whisper, my stomach knotting.

“I’d love to.” His eyes crinkle in an adorably cute way.

Wait, cute isn’t the right word. It’s more like a sexy glint.

I give him a small grin and lead him up the stairs to my apartment, praying my roommate isn’t home. My prayers are answered when I open the door and see her keys and bag missing from their usual spot.

Letting go of Nick’s hand, I go to turn on a few lamps, dropping my purse on the kitchen counter. When I turn back to him, he’s scanning the picture frames on my bookshelves. He picks up one and looks from me to the frame a few times.

“This has to be your family. You and your mom could be twins.”

“I get that a lot. That’s my mom, dad, and brother, Logan, last year at the fall festival in my hometown.”

He nods, putting it back, and continues to look over the rest of the pictures. I get a little nervous at his silence and walk to him slowly. When I’m close enough, he grabs my hand again and pulls me the rest of the way to his side so I’m pressed against him.

“You are beautiful.” He points to a picture of me and some friends at the beach over spring break a few weeks ago.

My face heats a little as I glance at us in bikinis, toasting margaritas and laughing at the camera.

“Thank you,” is all I can sputter with his close proximity. The warmth of his body seeps into me while a mixture of cologne and laundry detergent fills my nose and becomes my new favorite scent.

It’s all Nick—masculine and earthy, yet soft and inviting at the same time.

He guides us to my sofa, pulling me to sit beside him with only inches between us. "Tell me more about you, Grace. We've spent most of the night talking about me. I want to know more about you."

I'd like to argue, tell him he's much more interesting. But mostly, I love hearing him talk and learning more about him. It's still unreal to me that I'm on a date with Nick Bennett, the same Nick Bennett who has his name on the back of jerseys and a whole campus in love with him. He's a superstar in his own right, and he's sitting on my couch holding my hand.

In case tonight turns out to be a one-time thing, I don't want to waste even a minute boring him.

"Grace?" He leans up, placing his face into my line of view.

"Sorry." I snap out of my head and smile.

He raises an eyebrow expectantly, and I try to think about what to tell him. "Well, I already told you I'm from a small town in Georgia."

"And?"

"I'm going to graduate in a few weeks and start grad school in the fall. I want to do something with my art degree, maybe even work in a gallery one day. I'm pretty sure my brother thinks I'm crazy. He's a very business oriented guy with a plan for everything. It drives him a little crazy that I have this artistic brain. He questions my parents all the time if they brought home the right baby from the hospital." I giggle softly, picturing Logan's scowl when I told him I was going to pursue a degree in art. "To him, it's a hobby and a dreamer's path, but he's coming around."

Nick laughs, shaking his head. The sound is comforting, instantly relaxing me.

"Brothers are a pain in the ass, but I wouldn't trade mine for anything."

"I feel the same way." I laugh along with him and lean back, propping my head on my free hand.

I don't know how long we sit like this, talking about nothing important, just trading stories of our families and growing up with older brothers. He mentioned his brothers earlier at dinner, explaining one was a lawyer and one was in medical school. He goes on to tell me about his best friend, a girl named Bizzy, whom he met when he was a freshman in high school. The way he talks about her is like she's more than a friend. She's his family.

He has no problem sharing openly, and I find myself hanging on to his every word. He may not realize it, but he's a great storyteller. More than once, I'm on the verge of tears with laughter at his reminiscing. Somehow, we move back to the subject of over-zealous brothers and his plans for the future, with his oldest brother, Shaw, leading the way.

"Mine are constantly in my business, and I'm beginning to think I'm insane for allowing Shaw to be my agent. But, then again, he's the only person in the world who I'd want handling my career."

Apparently, being the baby of the three boys comes with its own set of challenges.

"Well, my brother isn't exactly going to manage my career like yours. You're going to be a household name. The football world is about to be taken by storm. Sounds like Shaw Bennett has his work cut out for him."

Nick's smile dies a bit, and he squeezes my hand, making me wonder if I've said something wrong.

"I didn't mean—"

"No, it's okay. But sometimes it's nice to forget all that and chill, just knowing that I'm still a regular person, the same Nick Bennett. One thing about my family and Bizzy, they don't treat me like anything special. I'm still me."

"I didn't mean—" I try again but don't get to finish when he reaches up and runs his fingers over my cheek, leaving a tingling trail. He tucks a piece of stray hair behind my ear then cups my jaw tenderly.

"You didn't, and that's one reason tonight is so awesome. You treat me the same way. I'm just Nick."

There are no words, so I nod quietly.

The air around us heats as we gaze at each other, his eyes roaming over my face. I wait in anticipation, hoping he'll lean in and kiss me. He parts his mouth slightly, his tongue rolling over his bottom lip. This simple action starts a slow burn in the pit of my stomach.

He slides forward, gently urging me to do the same. When our mouths are inches apart, and I can feel the warmth from his breath coating my lips, his phone starts ringing.

The trance is broken. He cusses under his breath, dropping his hand and reaching into his pocket.

"I'm sorry, Grace. I need to answer this."

"Of course." I try to scoot away, but he doesn't let my hand go, forcing me to stay.

"What's up?" He answers so coolly, I wonder if he's nearly as affected as I am. My heart is now beating in overtime, but he seems calm and collected.

The sound of a male voice travels through the line, but I can't make out what he's saying.

"Okay, I'll be home in a bit and we can talk about it then," he tells whoever is on the phone.

More rumbling.

"No, I'm not out drinking. I'm actually on a date."

More rumbling.

"Fuck, Shaw, don't you ever quit working? I said I'd be home soon and call you back."

He doesn't give Shaw time to reply before hanging up and letting out a loud sigh. I watch as his eyes drift closed, not knowing what to say. The thought of him kissing me is long gone.

His eyes come back to me, and he gives me an apologetic grin. "I'm sorry, but I probably should get home."

"It's okay." I try to hide my disappointment.

He stands, bringing me with him, one arm wrapping tightly around my waist.

"Tell me you're free tomorrow night."

"I'm free tomorrow night." There's no hesitation because, even if I was busy, I'd drop plans to see him again.

"Can I pick you up at six?"

"Yes."

He gives me a genuine smile, his face lighting up. He leads us to the door, holding me to him. "I had a great time tonight, but don't think I didn't notice your trick."

"Trick?"

"I fell into talking about me again. But tomorrow night, it's all about you."

He doesn't give me a chance to speak but leans in and runs his lips across mine. My knees go weak as I suck in a breath.

"Sweet Grace, I'll see you tomorrow night," he tells me, stepping back and opening the door.

"Okay, Nick," is all I can force out.

He gives me one last smile and leaves, waving from the bottom of the stairs.

I wave back and cringe at the goofy motion. After a full minute, I close the door and skip back to my couch, plopping down with a giddy squeal.

My fingers move to my mouth and skim over the spot where his lips just were. Excited energy buzzes through my body as I think about the events of the night.

The instant I opened the door to see him standing there, leaning against my doorframe with his all-American smile, I almost melted in a puddle of girly goo.

It was all I could do to remain standing and form a coherent thought, which is completely unlike me.

But with Nick Bennett, I'm lost in a haze. Tall, dark, and handsome doesn't come close to describing him.

Without seeing him fully, I'd bet my life's savings his body is chiseled, just from the way his muscles bulge and stretch in his t-shirts. His hair is dark and wavy, cut short on the sides, and has the 'just jumped out of bed' thing going on. His look is boyish and manly at the same time, something unexplainable.

The clincher is his eyes. They are the clearest, deepest shade of blue topaz I've ever seen. They have a constant gleam, making them shine brightly.

Sexy... Erotic... Claiming... In all my life, I've never seen anything so captivating as the capturing look from those eyes.

"Stop being such a girl, Grace! He's only a guy," I tell myself unconvincingly.

"Only a guy? You can't be serious? When in your life have you ever been affected this way? When??? Oh, that's right! Never!"

Great! Now I'm totally freaking out and having full arguments with myself.

There's a muffled buzz coming from my purse, and I remember my phone is on vibrate. My heart lurches. Is he calling me on his way home?

Is it normal to get excited over the thought of a phone call from a guy you've only known a few days? The same guy picking you up for another date in less than twenty hours?

Am I a lost cause?

Hell yes!

I rush to dig my phone out of my purse right as it stops. Immediately, it starts again, and Mom's name flashes across the screen.

"Hey, Mama." I frown, realizing she's calling really late.

"Grace." Her voice is shaky and broken as she openly weeps into the phone.

"Mama? What's going on?"

"Grace, I'm sending a car for you tonight. You have to come home. There's been an accident."

I barely comprehend the rest of her scattered explanation as my head fills with fear.

Heartfelt thoughts of Nick vanish as I am forced to prepare to go home.

Chapter 1

Nick, 2 Years Later

This is going to be fucking perfect! I slap my hands together and resist the urge to laugh out loud. My brother, Mathis, starts to chuckle under his breath.

"He's going to fucking kill you. Why you chose tonight to screw with him is beside me. You know he's going to go out of his mind."

I stare at the table where Shaw sits with his boss, my coach, and the owner of my team. They're wrapped in what looks like a serious conversation, which is a perfect distraction. Shaw's wife, Bizzy, is sitting so close, they could be fused together.

This is normal between Shaw and Bizzy; he rarely lets her more than a few feet away from him when they are together. To say he's possessive would be an enormous understatement. He's obsessed with his wife, and I'd have it no other way. She's absolutely one of the most important people in my life.

Shaw has managed me since I was allowed to have representation when I declared eligible for the draft. I can't imagine my career in the NFL without Shaw on my side. He's the best in the business, and with his help, I've carved a pretty kickass reputation as the number one quarterback in the league. He may be my agent and lawyer, but he's still my brother. And I fuck with him every chance I get.

"Tell me again why you insist on riling him up tonight?" Mathis hands me a cold beer. "You'd think the Labor Day fiasco would have taught you a lesson."

"Because it's fun. And because it serves him right, taking Bizzy away for the weekend."

"You're being a bit of a baby, don't you think? It's technically the second game of the season. He promised to be in Indianapolis by the time you kick-off."

"It fucks with my mojo. Call me superstitious, but I don't like to mix things up."

"So tell him that."

I swing my head to Mathis and squint my eyes in disbelief. "Are you crazy? I can't tell him that. It's not how it's done."

"So, instead, you're going to drive him to the brink of madness in front of all these people, including both your bosses?"

"Shit yes, and I can't wait." I nod. "And for the love of God, it's not like I'm kidnapping her. He'll get over it."

"He's going to get you back."

"Maybe, but it'll be worth it to see the look on his face. You still in, or you gonna pussy out because you're scared of him?"

"I'm not fucking scared of him. I just like having two brothers, especially one that sets records on the field. It's going to suck to watch you sit on the bench after he whips your ass."

"Like that would ever happen."

He gives me a knowing grin and tips his beer to me in a conspiring motion. "Let's get this show on the road."

I drain my bottle and hand it back then jerk my head to the emcee on the stage. He says a few words to the band then steps up to the podium.

My eyes scan the room to ensure everything is still in place as I run my hands down my suit jacket and walk toward the table at the front of the room.

"Ladies and gentlemen, welcome to the sixth annual Greater Miami Foundation Dinner, hosted by the reigning Super Bowl Champions!"

Loud cheers and applause erupt around the room, with the loudest coming from the team, which takes up an entire section.

He goes on to mention the numerous local charities that will benefit from this year's donations and reminds all patrons of the silent auction in the other room. He also thanks the vendors for all their help in making this night a success. Finally, he straightens and gives the band the signal to get ready.

"We've had a special request tonight. Nick Bennett has asked to kick off the festivities by leading the first dance."

The room goes quiet; most of the players are in on my plan. I stop beside Bizzy's chair and watch her eyes grow wide in recognition. Her face starts to heat as a small smile slips across her lips.

"Mr. Bennett has requested that his, and I quote, *'favorite girl in the world'* join him."

Bizzy starts to giggle as I extend my hand, and she slides hers into mine. Shaw's body goes stiff, and he audibly growls. Fire blazes in his eyes as I tuck Bizzy's hand in my elbow and lead her to the dance floor.

The song plays, and we spin around as we have so many times to the chords of "My Girl".

As we dance, players, coaches, and trainers cheer us on. The one person not cheering is Shaw. His lips are sealed tight, the vein in his forehead bulging.

I make a point to wink at him again before twirling Bizzy.

"Why do you do this to him?" She does a poor job of hiding her own amusement. "You'd think the prank on the boat would have taught you a lesson."

"Let's not talk about that. Besides, he needs a dose of his own medicine."

"You know we'll be there before you even run onto the field. I made him promise."

"That's not good enough. I want to enjoy the morning with my family. It'll help settle my pre-game nerves."

"Since when?"

"Since I decided about ten minutes ago."

She throws her head back laughing as the last chords of music die down. Shaw's on his feet in a flash, but his boss is faster, rushing to the dance floor. I kiss her quickly on the cheek then deposit Bizzy in his arms as the next song starts.

He spins her like a pro, bringing her back to him and leaning close to her ear to say something.

Her eyes land on mine and grow in surprise as she realizes I've orchestrated this whole thing.

She shakes her head, still smiling. I slink to the side behind a few of my closest players who shield me as I watch man after man cut in and dance with Bizzy. Even my coach takes his turn.

She graciously accepts each dance, knowing most of the men. The dance floor fills with others as the band keeps the music going. Everyone seems to be having fun except Shaw. He's glaring at every man with a tick in his jaw. Finally, Mathis breaks in as my little prank comes to an end.

I almost fall on the ground when Shaw finally sees his opportunity and stalks to Bizzy, slinging Mathis to the side and gathering her in his arms.

She tosses her head forward, leaning their foreheads together, and kisses him lightly, whispering something. Tension visibly leaves his body as he holds her tight and slides her down his front, swaying with her.

"Thanks a lot, asshole." Mathis comes to my side, rubbing his arm. "Next time, it's your ass getting the tail end of that."

"You okay?" I slightly sympathize because I've been on the receiving end of Shaw's stronghold many times.

"Yeah." He gives me a cocky grin. "You were right. That was worth every second. I thought he was going to come out of his skin."

"Hang tight." I go to the bar behind us and order two whiskeys then carry one back to him.

He takes it readily and raises his hand in a toast. "To another kickass season with a ring and a championship!"

We tap glasses, and I swallow down the liquid. Feelings of content and happiness wash through me as I scan the room. Everyone starts to let loose as the real party begins.

My body freezes when my eyes land on the woman in the corner. She's nearly glued to the wall, standing next to an enormous painting of the city skyline. When our gazes meet, I inhale deeply… It's her.

Those violet eyes pierce into my own as my heartbeat quickens. Her lips part as one hand covers her chest. All the noise, all the people, the entire celebration going on around us disappears as I stare at the woman who touched my heart and then disappeared without an explanation.

A look of recognition washes over her face, and I swear her eyes shimmer. I blink slowly, trying to regain my senses. Every nerve ending in my body lights on fire knowing she's here. So many scenarios run through my mind, but they all come to a screeching halt when I open my eyes and she's gone.

I shove my glass at Mathis and start to move until he latches onto my elbow, turning me to him.

"Man, what's happening? You're pale."

"She's here. I saw her. She's here," I repeat in desperation.

"Who?"

"Grace. My Grace…"

He stills, blowing out a deep breath. "Oh, fuck," is his only response.

Oh, fuck is right. It's been two years, but I'd know those eyes anywhere.

Grace

It was him. GOD, after all these years, it was really him.

I race through the long hallway to the elevator and pray I can hold it together until reaching my car. My heart thuds against my chest as I run for my life.

STOP BEING SO DRAMATIC, GRACE! I chastise myself and force my movements to slow, getting into the elevator and smiling at the lady perched on a stool running the elevator service tonight.

When we get to the ground floor, a security guard insists on escorting me to my car and smiles sweetly when I thank him, locking myself in.

Only when he walks away do I let the true internal freak-out take over.

This is your fault, you idiot! You knew he'd be here! His team is the main sponsor! He's a celebrity in this town!

I should have left after the band announced his name, but I couldn't tear my eyes from him. The second he stepped onto the dance floor, I stopped breathing. He is still the most handsome man I've ever seen. Watching him on television is nothing compared to seeing him in person. He's taller, broader, and more muscular than he was. His dark hair is longer, but his eyes... his eyes cannot be denied. They are still the most piercing blue topaz I've ever seen in my life. And until they landed on me, they were glowing.

Tonight was a huge night for me, for the gallery. My job was simple yet so important. It was the chance for me to impress some of the wealthiest patrons of the city and dazzle them with my knowledge of the art on display.

I did a damned good job, too, until the dancing started. Then I sunk into the closest corner and watched the man who stars in my dreams take the dance floor. Envy rushed through me seeing him with Bizzy.

I know they are only friends, but I wished it were me in his arms as he laughed and spun her around the room. He openly shared his close relationship with Lizbeth Hastings, so it shouldn't have been a surprise to see them together.

I read online that she recently married his brother, and by the looks of the man wrapped around her on the dance floor, they are very much in love.

My mind wanders to Nick again, wondering if he has a woman in his life. From what I saw, he was alone tonight, but that doesn't mean anything. Men like him have women flocking to them. Rich, famous, successful... it's the perfect combination for a Miami socialite to latch onto.

He was opposite of me in every sense of the word, but I still found myself drawn to him. But what about now? Would we have chemistry? Are we even compatible?

Then again, I haven't seen him for two years—two long, agonizing years. It seems I've lived a lifetime since he walked away from my apartment that night.

That night... memories swarm my head, and the feelings come crashing back to me. Images of a younger Nick Bennett pop into my mind, and I'm transformed back to the twenty-two-year-old girl who'd had the best date of her life and the promise of more to come.

Time doesn't matter. The puttering of my heart tells me as much. It's amazing what the mind suppresses and how, with only one glance, all the feelings return.

The touch of his hand on my cheek, the brush of his lips, the cocky wave as he left...

I lay my head on the steering wheel and try to calm my panting breaths.

Tears sting my cheeks as I start the car and force myself to drive home.

Pain sears in my chest as I remember the way he looked at me the last time I saw him. Then the sound of his messages for three weeks after I went home. His voice changed with each message, going from concerned and sweet to finally resignation.

I thought a quick text would help explain I was in the middle of a family situation. It was a stupid move and a lame excuse, but at the time, it seemed like the best course of action.

I never heard from him again.

Chapter 2

Nick

I walk through Shaw's office and stop at Gail's desk, lifting her out of her chair in a bear hug. She slaps at my back, mumbling something into my shirt as she tries to squirm away.

When I put her down, she straightens her blouse and pinches one cheek roughly. "Such a showboat."

"Not at all, just glad to see you."

"Glad to see me or trying to gain an ally?" She slants her head with a knowing twinkle in her eye.

Gail has been Shaw's assistant since he started at the agency. She's an extended part of our family, and he couldn't make it one day without her. Even if she doesn't admit it out loud, I'm convinced I'm her favorite.

"Nah, he's already cussed me out, but it was worth the verbal beat-down to watch him. You should have seen it!"

Her face spreads into a wide motherly smile. "I wish I could have been there."

"Is he busy?" I glance over my shoulder at Shaw's closed privacy blinds.

"Never too busy for you. He was on the phone, and I suspect it was with Bizzy because he closed the blinds on his own." She winks, and I grab my stomach in disgust.

"Stop! I don't even want to know what that conversation could have been about. Those two are ridiculous."

"Being in love is not ridiculous. Still, you should probably knock first," she warns, pushing me toward his door.

I knock then poke my head through when Shaw yells to come in.

"Got a second?" I close the door and go to his sofa.

"This is a surprise. Everything okay?" He stands and comes around the desk, leaning against the edge.

"I need a favor. An off-the-books, keep your mouth shut, don't breathe a word type favor."

He raises an eyebrow, crossing his arms. "I'm listening."

"I need to find someone, someone special."

"Anyone specific or are we talking blind date type of thing?"

I jerk my head at him, wondering what the fuck he's saying. Then it hits me. "No, you dumbass. It's someone from my past, someone I lost touch with, and I think she's in Miami."

"Oh."

"You thought I'd come to you to find me a date? Are you insane?"

He shrugs. "Stranger things have happened."

"Well, this isn't like that."

"What is it like?"

I fall back and tilt my head to the ceiling, knowing I'm going to regret this. "I met a girl in college. We had a great date, and then she disappeared. Something happened, but I don't know what. I never saw her again until the Foundation Dinner a few nights ago."

"You want me to find a girl you had a date with? Is that code for fucking?"

"No, asshole! This is different. We met at a party and spent the whole time talking. By the end of the night, I asked her out. The second night, I took her on a date, and it was much the same. The chemistry was insane. You know I didn't date, but she was the exception. She was incredible. When I left her, we had plans for the next night. Except, I never saw her again. She didn't answer her phone, and by the third day of not hearing from her, I learned from her roommate there was a family emergency. I received one text then not another word. Then came the draft and graduation, and I got caught up in the hype. But I never forgot her."

"Why would she be in Miami?"

"I don't know, but I saw her. It was a brief second, but there's no doubt it was her."

"It's been a while since you left Tallahassee, and you were drinking. Are you sure it was her?"

I raise my face to him, trying to calm my irritation. He's asking logical questions, sane questions, but there's only one way to make him understand. "Usually, I'd agree with you. Her hair was different, her clothing was different, and she looked professional, more mature. Regardless, I knew the instant I saw her. It could be two years or ten. It was the eyes… She had violet eyes that can't be forgotten."

"Jesus the eyes…The fucking eyes."

He knows exactly what I'm saying, considering he's obsessed with Bizzy's ice blue-grey eyes. "I guess us Bennett brothers have a commonality."

There's another knock at the door, and Mathis strolls in without waiting for an invitation.

"This is a private meeting," I grumble.

"Now, it's a party of three. I couldn't miss this." He goes to the chair facing the desk and turns it so his focus is on me. "You tell him yet?"

"Most of it."

"Wait? Mathis knew and I didn't?" Shaw questions.

"Yeah, I told him after it happened. When nothing came out of it, I never talked about it again. Besides, you were busy."

"Mathis was in medical school. Can't get much busier!"

"I'm the cooler brother." Mathis doesn't skip a beat, egging him on.

"That's fucking questionable, considering I worked a miracle to keep his ass in Miami so Mom and Bizzy didn't kill me. Not to mention, you received the largest—"

"I get it." I raise a hand to stop his impending tirade. "But seriously, I knew you had other things on your mind, and it actually slipped one night while I was drunk."

Mathis slaps his hand over his heart and leans back dramatically, adding to my growing aggravation. Shaw bursts into laughter, going to sit.

"We're kidding with you, Nick. Mathis gave me a head's up you may need something." He glances at his watch then back to me. "And it's been almost forty-eight hours. I've been waiting for you."

Now, it's their turn to exchange a look that I don't like one bit. Before I can say anything, Shaw starts firing questions.

"For one, I need more to go on than her eye color. What's her full name? What do you know about her? Age? Height? Overall description?"

Everything comes rushing back. "Her name is Grace Monroe. She's somewhere around my age… twenty-five, maybe twenty-four. I'd guess she's about five-five. Her hair was a rich shade of brown with streaks of auburn shining through. It was long, straight, and silky, going to the middle of her back. To say her eyes were violet is an injustice. They were so many different shades of purple.

"She had a southern accent, not from around here. She mentioned living close to Tallahassee, a small town in South Georgia. I didn't get too many details, but I believe she was an Art Major. The two times we were around each other, our conversation was all over the place. We joked about the stupidest stuff, everything mindless. She took my mind off the upcoming draft and all the pressure I was under. More than once, I found myself wondering what—" I stop talking and see both my brothers staring at me, their jaws hanging.

"Holy shit." Mathis whistles and leans on his knees. "You have it bad."

"Nah, I'm very observant." I try to sound nonchalant but fail miserably. Replaying my words in my head, I realize how much of a sap I sounded like. "Okay, I admit, this girl got under my skin."

"So why didn't you approach her the other night?"

"I looked away for less than a second and she was gone, but I think she saw me, too."

"She saw you and ran? Maybe that should be your first clue."

"Don't be an asshole."

They both glare at me with shit-eating grins until I start to squirm in my seat. "You both need to stop fucking looking at me like that. I'm regretting my decision to ask for your help."

"Give us a break. I personally have been waiting for this day for a very long time, even more so since I fell for Bizzy. All your comments are going to come back to bite you in the ass. I can't wait to tell her."

My body stiffens. "You can't say a word, Shaw. You neither, Mathis." I point between them. "No one can know until I find Grace. I'd like to talk to her first. She may not remember me. Hell, she may be married. This has to stay between us until I get more information."

Shaw raises an eyebrow at me questioningly. "You're not going to tell Bizzy?"

"Not yet. She knew about Grace and our date, but when Grace disappeared, I blew it off, pretended it didn't bother me. If Bizzy knew how often I truly thought about Grace, she'd have scoured the campus searching for answers."

"This doesn't seem like a bad thing, and I thought you two didn't have secrets."

"We don't, well, not usually." I try to think of how to explain. "You're married to her, so this shouldn't come as a surprise, but she's a bit protective of me."

"No fucking shit," Shaw and Mathis both mutter.

"But it's more than that. You both know she thinks I've always been too focused on her, especially in college. So, I never told Bizzy because it would be another reason for her to feel guilty. She always said I paid too much attention to her and not enough on me."

"I get it completely," Shaw agrees.

He, of all people, understands how Bizzy's mind works. Even all these years later, she'd likely find a way to feel guilty about Grace's disappearance.

"So, do you think you can help me?"

"Already on it. Should have a lead for you by tomorrow morning at the latest." Shaw sits back and crosses his arms in satisfaction.

"That was fast."

"I started working on this when Mathis called me. So far, I've requested the guest list, actual attendees, and full vendor roster. If Grace was there, we'll find her," he assures me confidently.

"I hate to sound like Captain Obvious, but have you searched for her online?" Mathis takes out his phone and starts to type something.

"Nothing there. She has no digital footprint—no Facebook, Twitter, Instagram, snapchat, Tumblr—nothing. I've looked."

Mathis's eyes snap to mine in surprise.

"What? Told you I'd been curious about her. I search every few months." I shrug. I also lie. I've searched every single week in hopes that something, any clue as to what happened to her, would pop up.

I'll keep that tidbit to myself. No need to tell them I've been hung up on this woman for years.

"Nick." Shaw sits up, dropping his hands to his desk as his face grows serious. "Is there something you're not telling us here? This seems a little deeper than a crush."

"Like I said, curiosity."

His eyes pierce into mine, and a few beads of sweat roll down my back. As my big brother, he's always been able to read my thoughts, but I hold his stare, trying to remain cool.

There's a flash of understanding in his eyes, but instead of questioning me further, he looks at Mathis then to his computer.

"My calendar is clear for the rest of the afternoon. The first round is on you." He points to me. "It's the least you can do for that bullshit the other night."

I chuckle as images of his face flash through my mind. "It's your fault for being such an easy target."

I expect some sort of irritated comeback, but he shakes his head as he packs up his computer.

"I can't wait to meet Grace Monroe. If she's still single, maybe she'd like to meet Darren Jackson. He'll be in town in two weeks."

There's his comeback.

My humor fades as a growl rumbles from my chest. "Don't you fucking dare."

I don't find anything amusing when they both roar in laughter.

I bolt awake at the sound of Shaw's ringtone. My eyes refuse to focus as I dig around for my phone. By the time I locate it, my brain hurts and my head is pounding from the noise.

"What?" I barely croak, still unsure of where I am. One thing is for certain; I'm not in my bed.

"You alive?" Shaw fucking chirps in my ear.

"No," is all I can force out. "I'm not even sure where I am."

"Damn." He whistles, the sound sending my head spinning. "Maybe I shouldn't have left you two at the bar."

"Jesus, keep it down." There are a few seconds where all I hear is the clicking of his typing.

"Listen, you're at Mathis's condo. He said he dragged you into his guest room last night."

I'm finally able to crack open one eye and recognize the room in my brother's place. "That's good."

"Well, it's about to get better. Grab some coffee and call me right back. You have five minutes."

"What's going on?"

"You're going to need coffee. Mathis is already at the hospital, so you have the place to yourself. Five minutes. Move your ass!" He hangs up before I can tell him to screw off.

I hardly ever drink heavily during the season because it fucks with me too much. But with the reappearance of Grace, last night I decided to break my own rule and drank more than I'd like to admit. Jack Daniels pounds through my head, staying with me every step as I make my way to the bathroom and splash water on my face. My eyes finally clear, and I cringe at my reflection.

Wrinkled clothes, bloodshot eyes, and hair standing straight on top of my head. What a fucking winner.

I finish in the bathroom and head to Mathis' kitchen, grateful for the simplicity of his coffee maker.

In exactly five minutes, Shaw calls back as I sink onto the couch.

"You feeling better?"

"Getting there." I take my first sip and lean back. "Want to tell me what's got you so worked up?"

"Mathis said his iPad is on the coffee table. Can you find it and log into your email?"

"What the hell is wrong with you this morning? Did you wake up with extra bossiness? If you don't tell me what the fuck is going on, I'm hanging up and turning off my phone."

"Get into your email, Nick, now." His tone changes, and I suddenly know what this is about.

"You found her."

He's quiet as I grab the iPad and log into my email. The instant I open his message, my heartbeat speeds. Grace's beautiful face appears on the screen.

"It's her. This is Grace." I tell him what he most likely already knows.

"Figured… Jesus, Nick, I can totally see it now. She's stunning, and the eyes…"

Tinges of jealousy prickle my skin. "Watch it, Shaw."

"Whoa, I'm obviously not a threat, but I can appreciate this woman's beauty. She's exactly as you described her."

"Yeah, she is. How'd you find her?"

"The information came through early this morning. You obviously haven't used Google in your searches, or you'd have found her, too. Grace Monroe is part owner of Monroe Gallery in South Beach. The gallery provided all the pieces and artwork for the event the other night."

"That explains why she was there."

"Monroe Gallery is owned by her and her brother, Logan Monroe. He started the process of opening the gallery eighteen months ago and has since made quite a name for himself in the art community. Grace joined him here a few months ago."

Months? She's been in Miami for months? Why didn't she contact me? Maybe she's not alone or she's married. Maybe she's involved in a serious relationship. The little sip of coffee starts to roll in my stomach.

I realize I'm being completely irrational. Two years is a long time. *How stupid am I? What exactly was I expecting here?*

"If she still goes by Monroe, I'd guess she's not married." Shaw answers my unspoken question. "You were right about her not having a social footprint. She's nowhere online except her biography on the gallery's website, which was only added last week."

A week... Google... If I'd have just looked.

I click on the Monroe Gallery website and find her. It's the same picture Shaw attached to his email with a brief bio on her, written by a PR Group in what appears to be a press release.

Grace Monroe graduated with a Masters in Art History this past spring. While she strives to understand the business aspect, she admits her passion lies within the Art World. Her flare for contemporary work has made its mark in the area as she specifically seeks local artists. In the short time she's resided in Miami, Grace has made a reputation for herself among the artist community with her own work displayed in the Monroe Gallery.

Grace, along with her brother and business partner, Logan, have a deep-rooted love for the Arts and have made it a mission to bring exposure to all local artists, regardless of their specialty. For more information...

The rest of the article lists the contact information for Monroe Gallery and displays a few pictures of the building.

"Impressive," is all I can say.

"It really is. This gallery has a stellar reputation, which is a challenge in this area. Art galleries are common, but Monroe is landing more and more special events around the city. That's another thing I wanted to mention."

"What?"

"I called the Foundation Coordinator this morning. According to her, Logan Monroe fought hard for the opportunity to land the event."

"Is that odd?"

"No, but I have a feeling it wasn't a coincidence you saw her that night."

"Are you saying?" My heartbeat speeds again, thinking maybe, just maybe…

"It's a gut feeling."

"I'm going to the gallery." I close the iPad and stand, ready to get the hell out of here. Knowing she's close erases the looming hangover from last night's overconsumption.

"Already taken care of. You have an appointment tomorrow morning at nine a.m. I tried for later this afternoon, but she's out today."

"Damn, tomorrow's a full day of practice and videos." My mood sinks.

"I've handled that, too. I took the liberty of sending a message to your coaches that you're researching a charity project, and you'll be late tomorrow."

"You lied to my coaches?" I ask, surprised.

"I stretched the truth. There's a huge difference."

"Thanks, man. I owe you."

"One more thing, I made your appointment under the name Mr. DeSeis. Didn't want to alert her that you're coming in."

"What the fuck is that? DeSez?"

"No, you dumbass, D-E S-E-I-S is how you spell it. The Seis means six in Spanish."

"Do I even want to know where you came up with that shit?"

"I was trying to keep your identity secret. Not like I could say Mr. Bennett. If she remembers anything about you, that would be a dead giveaway."

"Good call, but couldn't you have thought of something more easily pronounced?"

"I thought it was clever on the fly. Show some gratitude."

"You're right. Thanks." The name grows on me a little.

"Want me to dig a little deeper, see what I can find out before tomorrow?"

The hair on the back of my neck stands at his question. This is where there's a fine line between being my brother and being my lawyer. He's programmed to go into protection mode. I'd bet he's ready to run a total background check on her now that he knows where she works. He'd likely request her and Logan's business permits and tax records to build an entire profile on her life the last few years.

Remembering the small amount of time I spent with Grace, she was a bit shy. She deserves her privacy.

"No, I'm going into this blind. Let me talk to her. Like I said, she may not even remember me."

"Okay, Nick, I'll put my agent role on hold for now. As your big brother, though, I'm going to tell you something. This woman made an impression on you that obviously stuck. I'd bet you did the same to her. Good luck."

We hang up, and I drop back to the sofa, opening the iPad again. Pathetically, I read the bio three more times before doing a search to find anything I can on Monroe Gallery.

Then I start the countdown of the hours before I see Grace again… and can find out exactly what happened to her.

Chapter 3

Grace

There's an unusual buzz in the air as I walk around the gallery to ensure everything is perfectly in place. Logan is impeccable in his business and development sense, but when it comes to the actual art, he lacks the fine-tuning skills for display.

For example, he's placed one of our new glass-blown vases in the corner where its beauty isn't portrayed as it could be. I shake my head as I find a more appropriate spot for it in the middle of the storefront window where the colors sparkle in the natural sunlight.

One day, I'm going to design extravagant pieces like this and sell them all over the world.

As each day passes, it seems everything is falling into place. Art isn't only a passion of mine; it's a piece of me. For as long as I can remember, I've wanted to create beautiful things. It's hard to explain to people, but I think my family finally understands it's what makes me truly tick. It brings me happiness, and most of all, Logan is one hundred percent on board. No longer is he teasing me about being a dreamer; he's now helping me make these dreams come true.

I do one more inspection of the front room before going to get ready for my appointment. Logan said this could be a big time client who has several interests in both finding pieces for his home and his office. I don't know much more except he must have money because Logan insisted that I needed to *'be ready for anything'.*

Usually, I'm a tad bit nervous with client meetings, but this morning, the butterflies are in overdrive as I check my hair and makeup one more time in the small bathroom.

The soft sound of the wind chimes I hung out front indicate someone's here.

I smooth my sundress once more and plaster on a smile, ready to impress this client.

"Welcome to Monroe Gallery." I walk to the front room and stop dead in my tracks, the rest of my words dying in my mouth.

Nicolas Bennett is standing in the middle of the room, his hands in his pockets with his signature boyish grin. Seeing him the other night from a distance didn't do him justice. Now, being this close, it all comes rushing back.

Slight stubble covers his face, but I can still make out the small dimple in his cheek and cleft in his chin. He's even more handsome than I remembered. His eyes meet mine, and I suck in a deep breath. The look triggers a memory, his blue-green eyes shining so brightly they glow.

"Nick..."

"Grace." My name on his lips sounds the same as the millions of times I've played it over and over in my head.

To this day, I still have his messages saved from when I left school without an explanation. The thought sends a burning pain to my chest, and I bite my tongue to try to keep my emotions under control.

He sees it, his eyes flaring as he takes a step toward me, his hands coming out of his pockets. Without thinking, I rush to him, throwing my arms around his shoulders and hugging him.

His arms wrap tightly around my waist, and his head sinks into my neck. "God, Grace, it's so good to see you."

"You too," I mumble into his shirt and inhale. Cologne, laundry detergent, and something new. Something even more masculine.

He keeps me close, as if knowing I need a second to compose myself. When I know I'm not going to cry, I step back and drop my arms to my sides.

"This is a surprise." I try to hide the tremble in my voice.

"A good surprise, I hope," he says softly.

"Of course, it's a good surprise," I rush to say then remember my appointment. "But I have an appointment showing up any minute."

His grin grows wide, making my heart flutter again. “I’m already here.”

“Wait? You’re Mr. DeSeis?” I narrow my eyes in suspicion.

“Guilty,” he admits, laughing. “But in all honesty, it was my agent who set up the appointment under Mr. DeSeis.”

“Shaw did that? Why?”

“I guess he thought it would be funny. Seis is six in Spanish. Six happens to be my nickname on the field.”

Anyone who knows football knows he’s referred to as Sexy Six. The nickname has been around for a while now, but I don’t dare let him know I’m aware. It was a great choice for Shaw, and pretty funny.

“Are you looking for artwork?” I change the subject.

“No, I’m looking for you.”

His words send a jolt to my system. “Me?” comes out in a squeak.

“Yes, you. I caught sight of you for a split second the other night. Then you were gone.”

My face starts to heat, and I look down to avoid his stare.

“Why’d you run?”

Humiliation slams into me at the way I left the event. I’m a grown businesswoman now. What was I thinking, running away like that? I knew he saw me, but I figured he didn’t remember me.

“I… I…” My brain refuses to produce a good excuse, so I close my mouth and twist the ring on my finger.

“Hey.” His hand moves under my chin and gently raises it so I’m looking at him.

“I didn’t know if you’d remember me, and I was in shock seeing you. It was a reflex to leave immediately.” Admitting the truth sounds pathetic, and I bite my tongue again to quit talking.

“Remember you? I’ve never forgotten you.”

Sincerity is written all over his face. “I’ve never forgotten you, either,” I blurt out without thinking.

His grin from earlier returns, and he drops his hand from my chin only to grab my hand. "I'm glad to hear that, Sweet Grace, because I came prepared to catch up." He kisses my knuckles, lowers my hand, and walks out the door.

I stand frozen as I watch him through the front windows. He opens the door to the black SUV parked out front and takes out a drink carrier. I recognize the logo as the coffee shop down the street where Logan and I visit almost daily.

Nick comes back in, pointing to the drinks. "I brought morning cocktails."

"Cocktails, huh?"

"Is there somewhere we can sit?"

I can't stop the tear that spills down my cheek before I can swipe it away.

"I'm sorry, Grace. It was stupid of me to assume you'd—"

"No! Nick, I love it! Standing here with you, in my gallery, after all these years, I think I'm just in shock. Come with me." I motion to the back and use the ten steps to get myself together.

When we get to the break room, he sits quietly, setting the drinks out. "The owner happened to take pity on me and made your favorite when I told her I was meeting you this morning."

I sit and take a sip of the raspberry mint tea. "Oh my God, this is so good."

"She said you loved it."

"She would know. I've become an addict since moving to Miami." I giggle. "This tea is right up there with wine on my daily consumption list."

"I'll have to remember that." He winks and sits back. "How have you been, Grace?"

That's a loaded question, laced with curiosity. To most people, it's a common conversation starter, but to me, it's an opening to tell him what happened in college. Instead of delving into the details and ruining the mood, I decide to skim over the details.

"I've been okay. I had a rough few years, but I was able to go back and finish school. Now, I'm living the dream of owning a gallery with my brother."

"It's a great place, from what I see and hear. You two have an excellent reputation."

"That's all Logan." I point to the large office across the hallway. "He's the brains. I'm still the artsy girl who loves the actual pieces."

"It sounds like you two make a great team. I'm glad to hear he came around. Last I remember, he wasn't on board with your long-term plans. Seems like he found a way to monopolize on both your talents."

"He did, but I'm not the only one with a brilliant brother who's also my agent. Look at you, Mr. Football Star. I hear you've done well for yourself."

His eyes grow wide, and I realize my mistake immediately.

"Football Star, huh? You been following me, Grace?"

Heat creeps up my cheeks as I shrug, trying to play it off. I take another sip, trying to shield my face and failing. I sense his stare and glance up to see his eyes dancing with humor.

"I may have heard a few things. Not to mention, my brother loves football."

"Uh-huh… well, I guess you could say I've done well. Shaw's the best. He's truly got my best interests in mind, but he's still my brother, which means he finds a way in my business. A lot."

"Tell me about it! Logan and I have worked our asses off to get this gallery up and running. Even with me finishing school, I've been involved in every decision. But at the end of the day, he still plays the big brother role."

"Well, I have a really great token on my side. Do you remember my best friend, Lizbeth Hastings? We call her Bizzy?"

"I do remember her." *How could I forget?*

"She's Bizzy Bennett now. She married Shaw. It came out of nowhere, too. One minute we're all having dinner, and he invites her on a business trip. Then BAM! They come back in love and completely ridiculous, so anytime he gets out of hand, Bizzy is my buffer."

Even though I knew Bizzy married Shaw, I act shocked and laugh along with him. "A business trip led to love? Who knew?"

"I guess the signs were there if we'd paid attention. She admitted being in love with him for years but never wanted to chance their friendship. But the way he explains it is crazy. He says it literally rocked him to his core. It hit him hard out of the blue, and the trip was his way of getting her alone to see what would happen. There were a few bumps in the road, but they are sickeningly in love. It's actually nauseating to see sometimes. Imagine your very best friend and your brother. He's not only in love, though. He's a madman when it comes to her, so it's my duty to give him shit every chance I get."

He talks more about Shaw and Bizzy, and I'm reminded of the fierce love and loyalty he showed in college when he talked about his family.

I almost ask about his prank at the foundation dinner but thankfully stop my big mouth. He doesn't need to know I'd been watching him like a creeper.

"I think it's sweet. How's your other brother?"

"He's awesome, doing his residency in Pediatrics at the same hospital Bizzy works. They spend a lot of time together. Actually, we all do. I may give Shaw a lot of shit, but he and Mathis are still my best friends.

"Enough about me. Tell me about you. Miami is a long way from home, isn't it? I remember you lived in South Georgia."

Usually, I shy away from talking about myself, but with Nick, it comes easily. "I'm amazed you remember that. Yes, I'm from a little town called Thomasville, not too far outside of Tallahassee. My parents still have our family home there, but Logan and I wanted a more booming metropolis for our gallery. We could have gone to Atlanta, but the beach life was more appealing to us both, so we made it happen."

He's quiet for a moment, and I get self-conscious. He stares at me intently, his eyes blank.

"What?" I ask, wondering what exactly I said to change his mood.

He sits back up and reaches for my hand, cupping it in his own. "I can't believe I'm sitting here with you after all these years. You have no idea how many times I've thought about seeing you again."

"It's surreal." My voice is barely a whisper.

"Yes, it is." He glances at his watch then mutters something under his breath. "I'd like to do this again, but first, I have to ask you something."

My heart stops as I prepare for him to ask why I left and never returned his calls or messages. Why I basically dropped off the face of the earth, never to be heard from again. Sitting here now, seeing him again, my reasons for becoming invisible seem stupid, so I brace for his question.

"Are you seeing anyone?"

This is the last question I expected, and I almost choke as I shake my head.

"Good, because I want to take you out to dinner. Unfortunately, we have an away game this weekend, which means I'm leaving tomorrow. We're not scheduled to return until Monday. Are you free Monday night?"

"Won't you be tired? Indianapolis isn't an easy trip."

His lips tip up in a knowing grin. "How'd you know I'd be in Indy?"

Busted! Shit, I'm terrible at this secrecy thing. If I don't learn to shut my big mouth, he'll know exactly how much I've followed him throughout the years, which makes me pathetic. I try my best to act nonchalant and once again blame it on Logan.

"I told you, my brother likes football."

He doesn't hide his amusement, standing and taking me with him. I was too preoccupied earlier when he hugged me to notice, but he still towers over me, even in my heels.

My chest bumps into his, and I catch myself by bracing my hand on his stomach, feeling the ripples under his shirt. Involuntarily, my fingers grip the material, and I hold tight.

His hands move down to mine where he links them together. I draw in a breath and peek up, locking eyes with him. The air in the room changes as he licks his bottom lip. "I'm glad your brother likes football. Maybe he'll come to a game sometime."

"He might like that." I fight hard not to stutter over my words. He knows I'm lying, but I'll be damned if I admit it. I've given too much away already.

"I hate to leave, but I've got to get to the stadium. Can I call you tonight?"

"I'd like that."

He gently removes my hands from his stomach but keeps one firmly in his grasp and leads us to the front of the gallery. When we get to the door, he turns to me and pulls his phone out of his back pocket.

"What's your number?"

I rattle off my new Miami number and hear my phone ringing in my purse in the back room. He puts the phone to his ear and waits.

"Hey, Grace, it's Nick. I'm standing here with you, so I know you'll get this message. I'm heading to work, but I'll call you around eight. If I miss you, call me back." He hangs up and drops the phone back into his pocket.

"I'm standing right here, you know?" I say playfully, my butterflies returning. Two years is a long time, but he still has the ability to make my heart flutter.

"Yes, but I wanted to give you a reminder."

"I see you haven't lost your charm."

His face takes on a new expression, one I've seen once before, and I fight to keep the tears at bay.

"It's been a long time, Grace, since anyone has called me charming. I've gotta say, it feels good."

"Nick, I'm sorry," is all I can get out before his finger crosses my lips.

"Not now, Sweet Grace. Not now. I'm dying to know what happened, but not when I have to leave and you have to work. We'll talk about it later. But promise me something."

"What?"

"Promise me you'll answer this time when I call."

"I promise," I respond immediately.

He leans in and brushes his lips across mine in a wisp of a kiss. Then he kisses my forehead before stepping back and letting me go. "It's really good to see you, Grace."

I don't get a chance to respond before he's gone and climbing into his truck with a wave. As soon as he's driven away, I place my fingers to my lips and am transported back to my apartment two years ago when he did the same thing. That was one of the single greatest moments of my life at the time.

Chapter 4

Nick

"Stop riding my ass!" I throw a shirt at Mathis's face. "I told you, it wasn't the time."

"I don't get it. Why not? Couldn't you just say, 'Hey, Grace, what happened?'" He tosses the shirt back, and I fold it to pack in my suitcase.

"You really need some friends… Or I do, one or the other. I can't believe your ass is here drilling me about this. Don't you have babies and children to heal?"

"Ha ha ha… I'm on call, so I'm free to badger you until I get a straight answer. Why didn't you ask her?"

"Because it wasn't right. I can't explain it." I raise my eyes to see him watching me with contempt. Out of the three of us, he's the most level-headed. He dissects situations until he's made sense of them. I'm more of the hothead, and Shaw is the lawyer—type A to the finest degree. My parents are saints. I realized that as soon as I made the Pros. Thank God for Bizzy to level out the testosterone in my family, or my mom may have gone crazy.

"Can you try? Walk me through it."

There's no way I'm going to tell Mathis how I arrived early enough to watch Grace open the gallery and walk mindlessly around rearranging things, or how I snuck out and ran to the coffee shop hoping they knew what Grace liked to drink.

Lucky for me, it was a very quiet morning and no one recognized me. The coffee shop owner was a bit stand-offish when I walked in. As soon as I mentioned having an appointment with Grace, she thawed, and I knew then Grace was still the same. Once you met her, you couldn't help but like her.

"I can't describe it. It was too much and not enough at the same time." I walk across my bedroom and slump into a chair. "To say she was gorgeous isn't right. It's not good enough, but it's more. She was the same girl and yet so different. I knew immediately that something bad happened. No words were shared, but when she practically leaped into my arms, I felt it. She was trembling, so I watched my words carefully and tried to keep the mood light. When I brought her tea inside, she actually shed a tear. It threw me for a loop."

"She cried over tea?" He cocks an eyebrow and bites the side of his bottom lip. "That seems weird."

"I thought so, too, until we started talking. But I couldn't push. She needs to tell me what happened in her own time."

"So, I hate to sound like Bizzy or Mom, but was it there? The attraction you've held on to for two years, is it still there?"

I half-groan, half-laugh, nodding my head. "Fuck yeah, it was. But this time it was stronger. This woman is amazing. She's humble and shy, but she's not fooling me. In the few seconds I wasn't staring at her, I saw some of her work. She's talented, but it's more than that. She's dedicated.

"I'm going to regret telling you this, and I swear it's going to bite me in the ass, but only one time in my life have I ever felt this connection to anyone. Let me give you a hint; that woman is now our sister."

He rolls off my bed and leaves the room, coming back with two bottles of water. I take the water he offers with a quiet thanks.

"I get it, and I respect it, so good luck." He pats me on the back. "But I have a condition… If this thing gets serious, promise me there's not a baby mama in the wings to stir shit up."

I hold in my laughter until it bursts out of me. Together, we tap the tip of our waters in cheers. "I can promise you, without a shadow of a doubt, there is no baby in my future."

Only we can joke about this since Shaw's situation knocked everyone for a loop. He found a way to fuck things up royally, but luckily, it worked out with Bizzy.

"So what's the next step?"

"I'm gonna call her tonight, take it easy for a few days, but when I get back into town Monday, it's on."

"Do you have an actual plan?"

"Besides instilling myself in her space every chance I get? Not yet, but it'll come."

"That sounds like an awful plan. Have you ever actually dated anyone? Women like to be wooed, swept off their feet, treated like royalty… all that shit. Getting in her space seems a little creepy."

"What the hell do you know about dating? Wooing? Sweeping off feet? Are all those women you work with rubbing off on you?"

Heat creeps up his cheeks, and he tries to hide it by flicking me off. "No, I'm saying maybe—"

"Stop right there. I'll save you any more embarrassment. Grace already thinks I'm charming. She said so herself. I'll turn up the Bennett charm and see what happens. It can't be that hard. Look at Shaw."

"Shaw took Bizzy to a beach resort and put her in a thousand dollar a night suite. Their love story is the talk of the fucking nurse's lounge on a daily basis, so I've heard more than I ever wanted to."

"That's kind of my point. Shaw spent four hours away from her and never let her out of his sight the entire trip. I'd say he got in her space. Seems like a good plan."

"Jesus." He runs his hand through his hair, shaking his head. "You two are ridiculous. No wonder Mom loves me the best. I'm the only one with any sense."

"Hey! I take offense to that. I'm the favorite!" I throw my water cap at his head, which he easily sidesteps.

He laughs, watching me closely. "Did Grace really say you were charming?"

"Absolutely. Does that surprise you?"

"No, it makes me wonder about her sanity. Maybe I need to meet her soon, determine her mental stability and see if she needs medical care."

"Maybe you should try working your own charm and make a move. You're not fooling anyone. I see the way you look at Claire." It's a dick thing to change the subject off of me and focus on him.

His face changes, going from fun-loving to serious, something I'm used to seeing when it comes to Claire Dixon.

"Not cool. My situation is completely different." He turns his back to me and goes to sit on the edge of my bed.

"Why are you holding back, Mathis? She's obviously into you, too."

"I'm not talking about Claire. It's complicated."

"How?"

He stares at me long enough for me to think he's actually going to talk about his feelings for Bizzy's best friend, who's also a fellow nurse at the hospital. Then he leans back and ignores the question. "Tell me about your game strategy this weekend. I'm pretty sure the defense has a bulls-eye on your head. You embarrassed the shit out of Indy last year, and they're aiming for revenge."

I let the conversation about Claire drop, knowing he'll talk when he's ready, and fill him in on the basic overview of the game plan. We spend the next thirty minutes talking about football until he gets up to leave.

"Good luck, man. I'll call you Sunday morning before the game. Keep your head straight, your eye on the ball, and be safe." He gives me a quick fist bump and walks out. I hear the door shut a few seconds later and grab my phone, noticing I have five minutes until eight.

A text dings, and my heart sinks when I see the message.

SG: This is Grace. I'm so sorry, but I forgot about a work event tonight. Can we talk tomorrow?

Well, fuck! I sit for a minute, thinking of a response when my phone dings again.

SG: I know it sounds lame, but I have to attend a street fair in South Beach tonight. It's loud and rowdy, and sometimes cell service doesn't work. I promised to meet a professor from

UM who has some graduate work to show. The students are excited. This was set up a few weeks ago.

I smile to myself, and the tension eases. My Grace is rambling, and it's adorable even through text. I inwardly pat myself on the back for my 'SG' contact entry because, to me, she is Sweet Grace.

It sucks she's busy, but it eases any doubt knowing she's thinking about me and not blowing me off again.

Me: Don't' worry about it. I'll call you tomorrow morning. Good luck.

I hit send and wait, wondering if she'll respond. She doesn't disappoint.

SG: If I forgot to tell you today, thank you for the tea. It was really great to see you. Looking forward to tomorrow morning.

With those few words, my mood soars, and tomorrow morning can't come soon enough.

"So what do you do for the next two days? How does this work?" Grace's curiosity gives me a feeling of warmth as I find a secluded seat at the edge of the terminal.

A part of me was apprehensive about what to expect this morning. After I finished packing and got into bed last night, I thought of how crazy this whole situation is—me finding her after all this time and basically barging into her gallery to see if my memories were figments of my imagination. The instant my eyes landed on her, I knew I felt something, but what?

And how did I plan on proceeding? I've never dated, and there's good reason. Casual hook-ups were few and far between, especially after seeing what happened to Shaw. No psycho woman was coming after me with an unintentional pregnancy. Without knowing it, Shaw became the best form of birth control.

So I laid there thinking, wondering the best way to move forward. I didn't lie to Mathis; I plan to be in her space, but until next week, what could I do? This is uncharted territory for me, and the one person who could help me is Bizzy. But I still kept my mouth shut, deciding to navigate through these new waters alone.

I didn't know what to expect when I called this morning, but Grace surprised me by easing right into a conversation.

"It's pretty basic. Once we arrive, we go to the hotel and get settled. Later this afternoon, we'll go to the stadium, walk the field, and maybe run a few drills. Tonight is an in-house strategy meeting. Tomorrow's more of the same, except late tomorrow afternoon when the team rep has set up a meet and greet with a local fan group. Then Sunday, we get to the stadium early for pre-game prep. The game is at four, then afterwards, hopefully there'll be a celebration before heading home early Monday."

"Are any of your family coming?"

"Yes, Shaw and Bizzy will be there."

"That's nice."

There's a small pause before she speaks again. "Nick, I'm so sorry about last night," Grace apologizes for the second time since I called.

"Stop worrying about it. I understand."

"The street fair slipped my mind. By the time I remembered, it was too late to cancel."

Knowing that she even considered canceling for a phone call from me gives me encouragement. Her words are full of sincerity, which is something else that triggers memories of her.

"How did it go?"

"Okay, I guess. It's crazy to know my decision is what gets people recognition."

"You have an eye for art. If I remember correctly, it's always been your forte." I think back to how passionate she became two years ago when she described her love of art.

"You remember that? It was so long ago."

I want to tell her I remember everything about the time we spent together, that I've relived our conversations in my head more times than I should admit, but it seems like too much. "It was hard to forget."

"Well, thank you for understanding. I felt terrible."

My teammates swarm the area as boarding is announced, and I spot two planes ready for us.

"Hate to do this, but I have to go."

"Good luck with the game. Logan's having a game party on Sunday, so I'll be watching."

"Pressure's on then. I need to make sure and perform for the pretty lady watching in Miami."

Her breath hitches, and I grin as someone yells my name to get going.

"I'll call you later, Grace. Have a good day."

"Okay, Nick, have a safe flight." She hangs up, and I pocket my phone with a smile on my face.

A few guys give me a sideways glance as I get on the plane and take my seat, not talking to anyone. Eddie Jarvis, our number one wide receiver, sits next to me and gives me a quick shoulder bump before putting on his headphones and settling back in his seat. The flight attendant comes through to make sure everyone is buckled in and all overhead bins are secure. She stops at our aisle and asks if there's anything we need. Both of us shake our head, and she eyes me with disappointment before going to her own seat for take-off.

Once we're in the air, I grab my iPad and log into the in-flight internet. Usually, I take this time to lock out of general everyday life and mentally prepare for football—getting my head in the game for the upcoming weekend. However, today, I have a mission.

When Mathis left last night, I fought with the decision to try to find out more about Grace and her life. Shaw would be the obvious choice to do some digging, but it feels like a betrayal to ask him to do it.

So I'm going to go the amateur route and see what I come up with.

I start with basic searches in Google by using her name only.

Articles pop up with recent stories highlighting the gallery and events around town. A lot of them refer back to the gallery web page for more information.

I do another search for Grace Monroe + Thomasville Georgia.

The screen loads with tons of articles on the Monroe family in Thomasville with highlights to the name Grace. I start with the most recent.

Holy shit! The Monroes are royalty in the small town of Thomasville. I click on story after story and learn several men in Grace's family have served as elected officials, most recently her Father, Carl Monroe, who was elected Mayor.

Pictures in the local papers show Grace, Logan, and her parents at several events, and I zoom in as close as possible to see her. She's smiling in every shot, her beauty shining.

There are a few mentions of her family farm on the outskirts of town, which specializes in peach orchards and pecan trees. There's a large shot of their home, which appears every bit a sprawling southern mansion, with large columns framing a wrap-around porch on the three-story brick home.

It's gorgeous, with classic southern style, and I curse myself for not asking her more about herself. Grace Monroe was a popular name in searches, but the Grace Monroe of Thomasville is an encyclopedia of useful knowledge.

The flight attendant returns with two bottles of water for Eddie and me. He takes his with a thanks and lays his head back, closing his eyes again. I reach for mine, and she wraps her hand around my fingers, placing a napkin in my palm.

"I'll be in Indy for a few days if you'd like to meet up," she tells me in a seductive whisper, winking.

"Thanks." I practically snatch the water and let the napkin fall into Eddie's lap. It lands face up with her number and a large red lipstick kiss. She watches expectantly to see if I'm going to pick it up.

I don't move, not trying to be rude but having no interest in her number or meeting up with her.

Eddie picks up the napkin and flashes a smile at her. "Sorry, sweet cheeks, he's off the market, but I'll gladly take this if you're looking for a good time."

Her face flames as she rushes away, and I drop my head to hide my chuckle.

"Thanks, man. I owe you."

"Don't mention it. You gonna ever get to the good stuff, or are we going to read about this girl's family the whole flight?"

"What are you talking about?"

"Six, we've been in the air for thirty minutes, and no shit, you've almost put me to sleep reading about this southern girl's family. Where's the good stuff?"

"Once again, what are you talking about?"

"Spotted it the minute you walked into the terminal on the phone. You were talking to a chick, and it wasn't Bizzy. We all know the Bizzy look. This was different. The second clue was when you boarded and didn't give that attendant a second glance when she shoved her tits in your face. Then you took out your iPad in stealth mode, searching for information on this girl."

"I think you may have taken a few too many hits on the field." I shield the screen, slightly embarrassed that I've been caught. "Why the hell are you spying on me?"

"Not spying. It's common curiosity. So let's see it. Grace looks like a hot piece. Want to tell me why you're combing through her history?"

Him calling her a *hot piece* sends a spark of anger through me, and apparently, I don't hide it well.

"Calm down, I ain't going to close in on your girl unless you tell me it's okay." His lips twitch, waiting for my response. He's goading me, which is common among most of the players.

Watching the other guys get riled up is usually hilarious, but not now that the tables are turned.

"It's not okay," is my only response.

"Who is she, Six?"

I think about lying and blowing him off with a simple explanation, but he's probably my best friend on the team. We've worked in tandem and developed a level of trust from day one. He may give me shit, but he's always got my back.

"She's a girl I met in college and recently ran into again."

"You hittin' that?"

"Eddie, she's not player pussy material," I warn him dryly.

"Obviously. She's more of the 'belle of the ball' type, from what I can tell."

"We're done with this conversation."

"I'm only pulling your chain, man. Chill. Let's get back to the good stuff. This time, maybe you can angle the screen so I don't get a crick in my neck trying to read."

"You're a nosy motherfucker," I mumble, typing a few more keywords into the search engine, focusing on two years ago.

Tension fills my body at the top three results. All of them caption a picture of a family dressed all in black, Grace clutching onto Logan tightly, her face buried in his chest. My eyes scan the titles, one immediately catching my eye.

ENTIRE COMMUNITY MOURNS AS KAYLA MONROE IS PUT TO REST IN THE MONROE FAMILY CEMETARY

Yesterday, the town of Thomasville gathered together to pay respect to the Monroe family as they buried their beloved Kayla Rae Monroe in the family cemetery at Monroe Gardens.

Citizens from all over came to mourn the loss of the incredible woman who touched our town for all of her life. Kayla, or Kayla Rae as her friends called her, was a lifelong resident of Thomasville and the founding member of so many of our beloved town traditions.

Last week, our community was shaken to the core when news of Kayla's death spread following an automobile accident on State Road 8. According to the local authorities, details of the accident are still under investigation, but they have confirmed the accident did not involve another vehicle.

Kayla was survived by her husband of fifty years, Roy; Son, Carl; Daughter–in-law, Sharon; and grandchildren, Logan and Grace Monroe.

Our thoughts and prayers go out to the family. The Monroe family has been a staple in the community for many generations…

The article goes on, giving details of the family and their legacy in Thomasville. I skim, scrolling down and stopping at a collage of family portraits. My heart stills when my eyes land on pictures of Grace with her grandmother at several community events.

In every shot, they are laughing or smiling with identical smiles.

There's another small article at the bottom of the page that catches my attention immediately.

Remembering Kayla Rae— from the desk of Grace Rae Monroe

First and foremost, my family and I would like to thank you from the bottom of our hearts for all your heartfelt prayers and kind words during this difficult time. Even in the darkest of hours, the outpouring of support has been a guiding light. We could not have asked for a better community to lift us in these times of sorrow.

As most of you know, Kayla Rae was more than my grandma; she was my inspiration, my cheerleader, and my best friend. From as early as I can remember, she was by my side every step of the way, always supporting every decision I made and encouraging me to follow my dreams. And for that I am grateful.

Referred to as the town Matriarch, Grandma reminded me often of the importance of family, friends, and community.

She loved her life here in Thomasville and loved each of you for what you represented of 'her' town.

Many of you have reached out to my family with personal memories of Kayla and how she touched your life in some way. Every one of these stories has brought a smile to our faces, and I encourage you to continue to share.

I will not pretend there isn't a giant void left by Grandma's death. We are all still reeling with shock and sadness, but we will persevere. Kayla would have it no other way.

With great consideration and thought, I have decided to take a leave from college and stay in order to help my family. My mother, Sharon, and I will be assuming all philanthropic duties to help transition so many of the town's beloved traditions.

Once again, thank you all for loving Kayla Rae Monroe and helping us heal.

~Grace Monroe

"Fuck, that's rough," Eddie hisses beside me, reminding me he's been reading as well. "Sucks to lose a family member, but looks like she really is small town royalty. Did you see they have a cemetery in their name?"

"Shit."

"Did you know?"

I shake my head and close the iPad, dropping it in my bag. "Had no idea, but why wouldn't she tell me her grandma died? We didn't know each other well, but I'd have been supportive."

"Reading that tells me so much more than what's printed in black and white. That story drips monarchy, timeless traditions, and southern obligations. If I had to guess, there's a smokescreen there, hiding a few real reasons Grace stayed home."

I think about what he's said and let the words sink in. Maybe it wasn't a simple case of losing a grandmother. Maybe he's on to something. It did seem as if her family had deep roots. But why didn't she just tell me?

"What's the deal with this woman? Who is she really?" He lowers his voice.

I glance around to make sure no one's listening and find most of the guys with their headphones on and heads laid back. Quietly, I explain my brief history with Grace and her reappearance a few days ago. I skip over my endless search after she disappeared, partly trying to keep some semblance of manliness and partly because I'm embarrassed.

How did I know so little about her? I rack my brain and realize she directed most of our conversations back to me, always listening to me talk about my family, Bizzy, or football.

Back then, I thought I had more time. But I was obviously wrong, and fate had other plans.

Eddie listens, and more than once, I catch his sympathetic gaze. By the time we land, I can't wait to get through today's activities.

Tonight, I'm going to start rectifying my ignorance about Grace Monroe. No more side-stepping her life. Now, I'm more determined than ever to know all I can about this woman.

Chapter 5

Grace

The application on the screen taunts me as I try to find the right words to describe why I am the perfect choice to attend the program. It's easy to fill in the blanks of the normal questionnaire, but when it comes to promoting my own self-worth, I'm useless. Everyone applying for this program is dedicated, talented, and unique in an exceptional way.

You'd think after all my years of schooling, I'd have something to brag about myself, but nothing comes to mind. I'm Grace… the girl who loves art and wants to make blown-glass pieces as a career.

Rarely do I allow myself to think about how things would be if Grandma were still alive. But today, I'm feeling nostalgic as I sit at the computer and glance longingly at the beautiful piece on display in the window of the gallery.

I want to create pieces like that and extend my knowledge to more intricate designs. At one point, the goal seemed out of reach because I knew where I was needed—first at home, now in Miami. It sounds cliché to say this was a dream I shared with my grandma, or that I swore to my crotchety grandpa I'd follow through with the application.

Last week, Logan walked in and handed me a padded envelope with information on an apprentice program, where I could learn the intricacies of the true science and techniques behind designing the world's best glass. All the excitement from years before came rushing back to me.

If accepted into the program, I'd be learning from the top designers in the country, the crème de la crème to say the least. This goes beyond high manufacturers and ventures into the depths of the timeless pieces on display across the world.

It's an unbelievable opportunity, one I never thought possible until now.

I stare at the last question, an essay, and swallow hard, searching for a way to put my thoughts into words. '*What is the single most occurrence, so far in your life, that has shaped your future?'*

The alarm beeps in the back, and I lean to see Logan walking in with a relaxed smile. For so long, he's been stressed, opening the gallery alone and building the business while I popped into town for brief periods of time. Now that I'm living here, he's been able to take some time off and actually enjoy his new life in Miami.

"How's it goin', Gracie Pacey?" He pats me on the head like a family dog then tousles my hair.

"Stop." I swat at his stomach.

He jumps to the side, so I miss, and then he reaches back to mess with my hair again. He's in a great mood, one I rarely saw while visiting because of the pressure he was under. I love seeing this side of my brother.

Tall with a muscular build, jet black hair, and deep blue eyes, there was never any denying he was Carl Monroe's son. Aside from age, he looks exactly like my dad. And as a big brother, he acts exactly like my dad too often to mention.

"Tell me what's been happening around here."

"You only took one day off."

"A lot can happen in one day."

"Well, I didn't burn the place to the ground, I scheduled two events in the upcoming weeks, and I may have found our January showcase with the UM students last night. All in all, I think I did well," I boast because I'm pretty proud of myself.

"Awesome! And...?" he questions by wiggling his eyebrows.

"And what?"

"And you had an appointment at nine yesterday morning. How'd it go?"

"Fine." I close my computer and gather my notes. "He wasn't really a buyer. It didn't go anywhere."

"It didn't go anywhere? Did he show up?"

When I meet his eyes, I see a flash of disappointment and immediately become suspicious.

"Logan?" My instincts go on alert.

"Did he or didn't he show?"

"Who are you referring to?"

"Nick fucking Bennett! Did he show?"

I swallow slowly, realizing my brother set me up. "You knew it was him?"

"Of course, I knew it was him."

"You didn't think to warn me?"

"Hell no! Why would I do that?"

"Why wouldn't you warn me?"

"Warn you? Are you crazy?"

"What are you talking about?" I screech, surprising myself at the outburst.

"You never could hide much, Grace. I knew there was a guy. I just didn't know who until shortly after Grandma died. You did a terrible job disguising your crush. "

"You're wrong! There was no guy, no crush. You imagined it." My lies sound pathetic and weak. Suddenly, I regret all those games I watched with Logan.

"Really, is that why you took a sudden interest in Miami Football after Nick Bennett was drafted?"

"Once again, you're imagining it." I flick my hand in the air, waving him off.

We stare at each other for a few seconds, and he starts to laugh, his stomach shaking until he bends over to hold himself. I try to remain aggravated, but the sound is infectious and I giggle along with him.

"God, it's great to have you here. I forgot how much fun it is to tease you."

"And I almost forgot what a jerk you can be."

His hand covers his heart where he grips it dramatically, feigning hurt. Then his face grows serious. "It's okay for you to have your own life now, Grace. You've earned it. Grandpa's okay, Mom and Dad are okay, and our hometown is running smoothly. You did what you needed to do. Now, it's time to live for you. If Nick Bennett makes you happy, go for him."

I wait for the suffocating guilt to claw at me, but it doesn't happen. Instead, I feel happy… and maybe a bit confused.

"But just because we laughed doesn't mean you're off the hook. You should have warned me."

"Did he show?"

"Yes, he was here."

"Spill." He stands upright and gives me 'the look'.

"First, explain yourself."

He sighs and walks around to the other side of the table to sit. "I worked hard to get the Foundation Dinner gig, not only for the prestige but also because of you."

"Why in the world?"

"I mentioned I knew you had a secret crush, but what I didn't say is it was Mom who tipped me off. She told me you met a boy and had a date. She was so excited, but then Grandma died and everything went chaotic. I wanted to ask you about him, but the time never seemed right until I saw your phone one night. Then things fell into place when we went to clean out your apartment, and your roommate said Nick Bennett stopped by to see if you were okay. The look on your face said it all. You had a massive crush on the school football star."

"That was a long time ago. Things have changed."

"Well, I took matters into my own hands. When the opportunity arose, I wanted to put you in the same room with him, to see what would happen. Never did I expect to find what I saw the next day. I thought it was a little infatuation, but when you walked in here on Monday, I knew. You were completely tweaked."

My face blazes with heat. I was sure I'd done a great job of masking my feelings.

"Then fate stepped in. When I answered a call from a Crenshaw Bennett on Wednesday requesting a private appointment with Grace Monroe, I knew. Everyone who follows Miami football is familiar with Shaw Bennett. Not to mention, caller ID gave the name of the agency. I scheduled the appointment, hoping my instincts were right."

"Once again, why did you keep it from me?"

"Because I didn't want to set you up for disappointment in case he didn't show."

"He came in, shocked the shit out of me, and made me cry. Then he proceeded to be equally as wonderful, and now I'm giddy like a schoolgirl when I think of him. You satisfied?"

His face morphs into anger. "He made you fucking cry?"

"Yes! Because he was so sweet. He brought me a tea, a fucking tea he bribed Marla at the coffee shop to tell him my favorite. I was already on unstable ground with him showing up, so when he gave me the tea, I cried! They were tears of surprise."

The anger disappears as a satisfied grin crosses his lips. "Smooth."

"I'm done with you! I shed tears, looked like a fool, and totally humiliated myself! Why are you grinning?"

"Because I may like him."

"You already like him! He's your number one draft quarterback!"

"Winning me money and dating my sister are two entirely different things."

"We're not dating!" I sound more and more like an irrational dingbat. I need to get my emotions under control and not let him get to me.

"Yet." He gets up and goes to the coffee maker, pouring himself a mug.

"There is no yet," I reply with narrowed eyes. "And stop playing matchmaker."

He raises his hands in defeat, but I can't miss the glint in his eye. "I've done my part. The rest is out of my hands."

"When did you become such a girl? This is very uncharacteristic of you. If I remember, you threatened my half of this gallery if I didn't break up with my last boyfriend."

"That guy wasn't your boyfriend. God, Grace, have some sense! He was a—"

"I get it. No need to relive it. I think he finally got the hint when Grandpa shot out his taillights."

"Lucky his ass wasn't shot. Who the hell shows up for a town function smelling of booze and cheap perfume then proceeds to make out with another woman?"

"It wasn't that bad! It wasn't like we were exclusive." I try to defend the poor schmuck I dated twice last year.

In all honesty, I never wanted to see him again, but pride made me invite him to the end of the season Pecan Picking last year. It was a mistake, but I was sick of all the town ninnies trying to set me up. So I instead invited Paul? Peter? Pledge? What was his name? Even I try to forget.

Pledge! That's it.

"Pledge was a nice guy but completely misunderstood. He wasn't used to our southern style and traditions."

"Jesus, Grace, he was a total dick. And who's named Pledge?"

Watching his face turn red delights me more than it should. Pledge truly was a douchebag, but I was backed into a corner.

My dad may be the Mayor, but he's a father first. He cheered on my grandpa while videoing the whole thing when Pledge sped off our property with shots booming in the air.

Dad waited until the festivities were over before I was subjected to yet another family lecture about the importance of choosing my friends more carefully. My plan to rebel backfired enormously, but it did stop the meddling for a while.

Thinking of Grandpa pulling his shotgun out when he caught Pledge with another woman in the barn is enough to make me giggle. Pretty soon, we're both laughing again at the memory.

"You want to know the best part of that total experience?" I ask through my laughter.

"What?"

"Later that night, Mom cornered me, and she wasn't mad at all. She thought the situation was hilarious and told me Grandma would have loved every minute of it, from the way the town nosy nellies were gossiping under their breath to the way Sheri Cobb was caught with her skirt bunched around her hips. Mom said I was a true Monroe woman."

"Really? Mom would be the first person I'd think was mortified."

"Logan, you'll never understand, but we Monroe women have a trait. It's more of a gift. That night, I knew it was time for me to come here and join you. It finally felt right."

He looks at me in disbelief, his eyes growing wide. "I won't even pretend to understand, but whatever the reason, I'm glad you got here."

"It does feel right, doesn't it?" Even after all the planning and time it took, I want to hear he's glad I'm around.

"More than you'll ever know. Having you has been a Godsend."

My insides warm at his statement. He is more than capable of handling the business on his own or hiring someone with true artistic knowledge. But he's been patient with me, understanding my obligations.

"Tell me something, though. Is he the reason you wanted to open a gallery in Miami?"

No use in lying. "It crossed my mind, but he's not the reason. That would be highly stalkerish. This seemed like the best location out of the two we narrowed it down to."

"I agree but had to ask."

"I didn't know if our paths would cross."

He nods quickly, satisfied with my answer. "With that being said, let's get back to something important."

"What's that?"

"You need to get that application done in the next week, Grace. It's time you follow through. At this point, there is nothing standing in your way."

Hearing this from him fuels my enthusiasm to get into the program, but that enthusiasm quickly fades when Nick's face flashes through my head. How would he feel about me leaving for a few months?

It's way too soon to worry about that. Who knows what the future holds?

Logan's townhome is filled with people when I walk in on Sunday afternoon. I drop off my appetizers on the dining table, which is overloaded with party food, and join the crowd in the living room.

Logan has set up an additional television, and most men are watching with intense interest as the early games come to an end. I give a universal, "Hey," to everyone and get a few grunts in response. A woman I recognize from a few of these parties scoots next to me.

"Hey, Grace, how are you?"

"I'm great, Melanie. How are you?"

"Things are going well. Busy with work, but nothing I can't handle. I was excited when Logan said you'd be here today."

Her statement puzzles me. Why wouldn't I be here? I try to attend all his gatherings, not only because he's my brother but also because I haven't met many people in Miami. He's my only outlet for socialization outside of the gallery.

I must do an awful job of hiding my confusion because her face starts to turn pink. "I-I-I mean, when he mentioned his sister was coming. It's always nice to have another girl in the mix."

I do a quick survey of the room and see only two other women who look bored out of their minds. It clicks that besides those two—who are girlfriends to Logan's friends—and me—the sister—Melanie is the only other woman here.

I look at Logan, who glances up, his eyes darting between her and me. It's then I sense it. There's something going on between Logan and Melanie. I shoot him a wink and turn to Melanie, now determined to confirm my suspicions.

Her cheeks are still tinted when I smile at her.

"I agree, Melanie. These parties can be filled with way too much testosterone. It's always nice to have another woman to chat with."

Her smile returns, and she seems to relax. We make small talk, mostly about the gallery and my experience so far in Miami. I decide after a few minutes that I like her. She's easy to talk to and a lot more down to earth than any of the other girls Logan has dated.

We're interrupted by the ringing of my phone, and I excuse myself, walking into Logan's room when I see the caller. My stomach flips, and I grin goofily, glad no one can witness my reaction.

"Don't you have a game to prep for?" My question comes out giggly, and I want to slap myself.

Nick laughs, the line filling with the fun-loving sound. "Yeah, actually. I only have a few minutes, but I felt bad about having to jump off so quickly this morning."

"Don't mention it. I told you I understand. This is your job, and you're busy."

I mean every word. I know he's busy, and every time he's called we've only had brief conversations lasting a few minutes. What I don't dare say is that those few minutes have been highlights of my day.

"Are you at Logan's?"

"Sure am! Ready to cheer on those Colts! Even wearing my blue and white," I joke.

"Not funny, Grace," he rumbles.

"I'm kidding!"

"What are you wearing?"

"Shorts and a t-shirt. Why?'

"Because I'd be a lot happier if I knew you were at least in my team colors."

I glance down at my shirt and bite my lip. "Would it help if I said my shirt was teal?"

"It helps a little."

There's a loud noise and muffled voice on his end of the line.

"Listen, Eddie just came in and told me it's time for warm up. I'll call you tonight."

"Good luck, Nick. I'm not sure of the proper lingo, but I'll be cheering for you."

"That's all the luck I need. Well, that and the fact that there's a beautiful woman in Miami watching."

Flutter, flutter, flutter… I'm pretty sure my heart is about to beat out of my chest. "Charmer."

"Only with you, my Sweet Grace. Talk soon."

He hangs up, and I fall back on Logan's bed looking at my phone screen.

"Was that him?" Logan pokes his head inside and asks.

"Who?"

"Don't play coy. I saw the look on your face before you disappeared.

Damn!

"Seems like you already know the answer to your own question."

"Well, what did he say? Does he have a strategy? Is he going to do a pocket offense, or is today a throwing game?"

I scrunch my eyebrows, not having any idea what he's talking about. "I have no clue."

"He didn't say?"

"No, why would he?"

"Well, what did he say?"

"Nothing really." I think about our brief conversation and realize we didn't talk about anything. "I did wish him luck."

Logan looks at me with a horrified expression then shakes his head.

"What?"

"You had the Sexy Six on the phone before a major division game, and you said good luck? Grace, this calls for a 'KICK SOME ASS'."

"Well, excuse me. I'm not familiar with the protocol. I'll do better next time."

His face stays blank for a quick second before he grins widely. "Yeah, next time, do better."

I realize I've insinuated there will be a next time, which gives Logan more ammunition to harass me.

"Whatever, we should probably get back to your guests. I'm sure Melanie is lonely."

His grin slips, and I spy his eyes flash at the mention of her name. He grumbles something incoherent and turns to walk away.

A thought jumps at me, and I type quickly, hoping Nick will see the text.

I've been schooled that 'good luck' isn't proper. So instead, I'll say 'kick some ass'. Hope you can hear me cheering all the way in Indy.

I press send and roll my eyes. But I do it smiling.

Chapter 6

Nick

It feels great to be back in Miami, especially after the ass whooping we delivered to Indy yesterday. Airline employees cheer for us as we deplane, with shouts of 'congratulations' and 'great game'. Usually, this would be the motivation to go straight to the stadium and watch films while the game is fresh in my head. But today, I have another destination in mind.

"You want a ride home, Six?" Eddie offers as we wait for our bags.

"Thanks, but Shaw has a car waiting for me."

"That's stupid. I pass your place on my way."

"Maybe I'm not headed home." I raise an eyebrow at him and watch his face split into a wide grin.

"Grace Monroe?"

"You got it." I reach for my bag and slap him on the back. "See ya later."

"Good luck, man. Can't wait to see how this plays out. Sexy Six has a crush."

"Crushes are for boys. I'm all man, and it's time for me to pull out the stops. Not called Sexy Six for nothing."

His laugh roars all the way outside as I head to the waiting car. Once I give the driver directions, I send a few quick texts to my family, letting them know that I've landed and will touch base later. Then I let my finger hover over Grace's number. The thought of surprising her at the gallery was my goal, but she didn't answer my call this morning so she may not even be there.

I don't have to make the decision because SG flashes on my phone as it starts ringing.

"Hey there. Your ears must be ringing."

"I'm sorry I missed your call. I left my phone at Logan's last night," she answers in a rush. "He just now brought it to me. Congratulations on the win."

"Thanks. I think it may have been the last minute message that gave me the extra motivation."

"That was the goal." She gives a light laugh, and the image of her smiling face fills my head.

"Where are you?" I ask.

"Work."

"You busy?"

"Not yet, I'm getting a few things ready for a new display."

"Okay, I'll be there in fifteen minutes. You can congratulate me in person."

"Really? You're coming here?"

"Is that okay?"

"Sure! I mean, of course." Her voice goes squeaky. "My brother's here. Is that okay?"

"Why wouldn't it be?"

"Well, I don't want it to be weird... and he's a little, um, I mean... Well..." The more she tries to explain, the more flustered she becomes, which is completely adorable.

"Grace, it'll be fine. See you soon."

The rest of the drive, I go over in my mind how I've decided to handle this. Grace is an expert in the art of diversion. In the brief time we had two years ago, I didn't notice because I had no idea she'd disappear. But now, I'm wiser.

The last few days, even though our conversations have been short, she's actively kept the subject on my trip, the game, or me. The two times I've asked about her, she's responded quickly and deflected.

That stops today.

We pull up to Monroe Gallery, and I wrestle with an unusual feeling in the pit of my stomach.

Is it nerves? What the hell?

"Mr. Bennett, would you like me to wait here?" The driver turns to face me.

"Yes, but I'm not sure for how long."

"It doesn't matter. The other Mr. Bennett requested my service for the day."

Shaw is really aiming for the favorite brother award today.

"Thanks. I'll be back in a while." I shake his hand and get out, straightening my jacket.

I walk into the gallery with the unusual feeling rattling around my gut. As soon as I enter, I stop dead. The place is completely different than my first visit, and not in a good way. Boxes are piled everywhere with large crates lining every wall. There's plastic covering the floors and the storefront windows.

All of that flies from my mind as soon as Grace steps into view. She's wearing short cut-off jean shorts with denim fringe framing her legs. Her oversized t-shirt is hanging off one shoulder, exposing a bright blue tank top. Her hair is on top of her head with several small braids tied back off her forehead.

She's staring at me with those violet eyes wide, biting her bottom lip.

On instinct, I hold out my arms, and she doesn't hesitate, flying into them. I pick her up and hug her tightly as she squeals, *"Congratulations,"* over and over.

It feels natural to have my arms around her, holding her close. My head drops to her neck, and I inhale. The scent of body wash and lotion assaults my senses. It's all Grace, sweet and intoxicating, and I hope like hell it's soaking into my clothes.

She stops talking but doesn't try to get loose. Her warm breath hits my cheek, and my cock starts to twitch, growing tight against my briefs. I try my best to clear my mind, but it's impossible. It's everything I can do not to start kissing on the soft skin under her ear.

"Jesus Christ, Grace, let the man go! He survived a field of men trying to take his head off. It'd suck for him to suffocate because you've squeezed him to death." A deep voice comes from behind her, and she lets go, almost falling as she lands.

I recognize Logan Monroe standing in the archway with an undeniable smirk on his face. "Not to mention, you probably ruined his suit."

"Oh my God, I'm sorry."

She makes an effort to step back, but I circle my arm around her waist, keeping her close. "Don't apologize."

"I'm covered in dust and spackle."

My eyes roam over her again and don't see any evidence of dust or spackle. "You look pretty clean to me. In fact, you look terrific."

A blush creeps up her cheeks as she holds my stare. Neither of us moves until a throat clears and I'm forced to once again face her brother. This time, the smirk is gone and replaced with a full on smile.

"Grace, you want to introduce me to your friend?" He emphasizes the word friend as if it's an inside joke.

"Nick, this is my brother, Logan. Logan, you already know this is Nick Bennett." She waves a finger between us.

He moves first, coming to me with an outstretched hand. Wisely, he offers the hand that doesn't require me letting go of Grace's waist.

"Nice to meet you," I tell him.

"You too. Quite a game yesterday."

"Thanks. We were pleased with the outcome."

"Think you can pull that shit off this coming Sunday? I've got fifty bucks on the line."

"LOGAN! That's rude!" Grace gasps.

"It's okay, Grace. I'll do my best."

He nods his approval, and I notice he's dressed casually as well.

"What's happening in here? It looks a lot different. Are you moving?"

"Today is a reset of the entire gallery. We've actually closed down until Wednesday. It's going to take some massive manpower to get this place ready," Grace answers on a sigh. "Logan forgot to mention he promised some prime viewing space to a new sculpture artist, and unfortunately, this doesn't mesh well with my fall display plans. So we have to redo all the walls and add a few shelves to get everything in."

"That seems like a lot of work."

"Yes, and I didn't know about it until this morning. Seems it was a bright idea not to tell me with a house full of people last night, so I didn't kill him." She shoots a glare his way.

"It'll come together. I have faith in your skills. This is what it's all about," he tells her sincerely. "You always make it happen."

"Well, start getting those pictures in the back corner wall down. I'll wrap for shipping later."

"You now have an extra set of hands. What can I do?" I say with no hesitation. It's obvious my plans to steal her away for a few hours are not going to happen. But I'm hell bent on spending time with her, even if it means manual labor.

Both their heads swivel to me in disbelief. "Nick, you're in a two-thousand-dollar suit," she points out.

"My bag is in the car. If I can use your bathroom to change, I'll be ready to go."

"Great! I could use the extra muscle. Grace is a beast when she gets going. There's a bossiness only a mama could love."

"LOGAN!" This time she shouts, and I know immediately that Logan and I are going to get along great. He reminds me so much of my own brothers.

"No problem. Give me a second, and I'll be right back." Without hesitation, I kiss her forehead and head to the car to get my bag.

The driver jumps out and rushes to the back door, opening it as if we're ready to leave.

"What's your name?"

"Rodney, sir," he answers so professionally I fight the urge to roll my eyes.

Even if I am a celebrity in this town, I prefer normalcy.

"Rodney, my name is Nick, not sir."

His mouth forms a slim line, and I remember he's probably required to act with a high level of professionalism at all times.

"Or, if you want, you can call me Six, but we can drop the formalities."

His lips tip up in a small grin as he nods. "Got it."

"Okay, there's a slight change of plans. I'm going to be here a lot longer than I originally thought. If you'd like, you can go, and I can call you when I need a ride home. I'd hate for you to sit here bored out of your mind."

"Your brother mentioned your plans might be sporadic, so I'm prepared for anything. Just tell me what you need."

As if on cue, my stomach growls loudly, reminding me it's time to eat. I've been up since five a.m. with little sustenance, which is a bad idea after a game like yesterday.

He starts to chuckle and looks at his watch. "Would you like me to grab you some lunch, Six?"

"Do you mind? There's a café down the street. If I remember correctly, they have a full lunch menu."

"Not a problem. What would you like?"

"You can bring back an assortment, a little of everything. But make sure you pick up one of their specialty teas. It's raspberry something. Ask for the owner and tell her it's for the Monroe Gallery. She'll know what to make."

"Okay."

I take out my wallet and hand him a wad of cash. "Get anything you want as well. We're going to be here a while." I scoot behind him and get my bag.

He goes in the direction of the café as I turn back to the gallery. Even with the plastic over the windows, I can see a silhouette of Grace with her hands flying as fast as her head is bobbing. Logan is standing in front of her with his arms crossed, drumming his fingers on one bicep.

Once again, I recognize this stance. It may be evil of me, but I tamper down my delight that she's worked up. I like it. Maybe I'd be a little more apprehensive if she didn't fly into my arms as soon as I stepped toward her, but there was no denying it. She was excited to see me, too.

Now, it's time to start the process of getting in her space. Without knowing it, she's given me the perfect opportunity.

I walk back in casually, and their conversation comes to a stop. She wheels around, her face red, and Logan gives me an exasperated look.

"Nick, you really don't need to stay. This is going to be a dirty job that will most likely end up with me threatening my brother a dozen times before it's done. I'm sure you have better things to do."

"I'm going to get a few measurements from the office and start loosening the bolts in the back wall. Nick, good luck with this one. If she chases you away, promise me you'll still win my fifty bucks on Sunday."

Grace draws in a deep breath then turns, punching him in the arm. He fakes hurt and walks away whistling.

She hisses and starts shaking her hand back and forth in frustration. "Jerk!" she screams to his back.

I force myself to hide my smile and go straight to her, taking her hand in mine. Gently, I rub the knuckles and bring them to my lips, kissing each one. Her eyes go soft as she watches me.

"Sweet Grace, you shouldn't resort to physical violence with your siblings. It never turns out well," I tease her.

"Gah! I should have known you'd be on his side. Boys!"

I throw my free hand over my heart and toss my head to the ceiling. "Boys? That hurts. I'm pretty sure I left the boy category at about fourteen."

"You know what I mean."

"No, babe, I don't." I close in, bringing her hand to my chest. "But if you want me to leave, I will. I thought I could help today and hang out. If I get in the way, kick me out."

"I feel guilty asking you to stay."

"There's nowhere I'd rather be. You can direct me, boss me around, and busy me with grunt work. Whatever it takes, as long as I can spend time with you."

Now her eyes take on a new kind of heat, the kind that makes me want to slam her against the wall and kiss her until she doesn't know her own name.

"I'd really like that, Nick," she finally responds.

"Okay, point me in the direction of the bathroom. I'll change then be at your beck and call."

She shocks the shit out of me by going up on her toes and brushing a soft kiss across my cheek. "You may regret being at my beck and call, but I'll take it."

Without another word, she twists and pulls me behind her, leading me to the bathroom.

"Grace, I'm not kidding, if you make me move that picture one more time, I'm walking out the door," Logan protests loudly.

"It's not right, but I think if we put that awful sculpture next to the landscaped marsh, it will look much better."

Rodney snorts, turning his back, and I take a sip of my water to conceal my own smile. Watching the two of them for the last few hours has been the best entertainment I've had in a long time.

At first, Grace was very reserved, trying to ease me into the work. But when Logan tore a baseball size hole in the front wall trying to remove a bolt, she lost her shit. That's when the gloves came off. They started in on each other like only siblings can do, and I sat back to enjoy the show.

Rodney joined us after returning from the café and offered his help as well. He took off his own suit jacket, rolled up his sleeves, and together we had all the outgoing paintings neatly piled exactly where Grace instructed. Then we went about spackling and sanding the walls.

In the last five and a half hours, we accomplished almost everything on Grace's to-do list until Logan's hole-in-the-wall debacle.

He argued he was food deprived until she pointed out the three large sandwiches he ate.

Then he tried to say it was a faulty bolt until she corrected him about the other forty removed during the day.

Finally, he relented and walked out, only to return fifteen minutes later with a twelve pack of beer in a cooler and a chilled bottle of wine.

She forgave easily and started hanging the new shelves. All was right again until now. Tensions are starting to run high again.

"Hey, man, you want to sit for a few minutes? I'll take over the placements," I offer, getting to my feet.

"Gladly, let's see if she yells at you." He goes to the cooler and twists open a beer.

"Of course I won't yell at him. He's being nice, and he's our guest. Poor Rodney is probably going to quit his job because he's been forced to spend the day with us crazies!" She wags a finger at her brother.

"No, Grace, I can promise you this is the most fun I've had in a while," Rodney assures her, coming to us. "Give me the measurements. I'll finish the shelves."

"See, Peach Princess, I've always told you I'm fun to be around. It's you who's the insane creature of the family."

Grace's head snaps toward Logan, and her eyes narrow. "Rodney probably has a contact high from the paint. That's the only explanation for thinking this is fun. And don't call me that."

"Peach Princess?" I raise an eyebrow in question.

"It's a silly title from home. Logan thinks it's hilarious to make fun of me."

"Hardly, our little Grace is the town Peach Princess. It's her moniker when we're at home. No one really calls her Grace."

Finally! Here's a chance for me to ease the conversation to her without seeming too invasive. "I'd like to hear this story."

"It's boring and completely embarrassing," she tells me.

"I'll tell it," Logan offers.

"No, you won't."

He ignores her and starts to talk. "In our hometown, the Peach Princess is a very big deal. The title—"

"Stop!" She throws out her hand in the air at him. "You've already messed it up."

"So, you tell it then."

She looks at the three of us and sighs. "Fine, but y'all get back to work."

I go to the wall and remove the picture she wanted down. Rodney and Logan pick up paintbrushes and start to work on the far walls, touching up where the holes were patched.

She hands me the new picture she wants replaced and instructs me what to do next. Once we're all busy, she starts talking.

"It's really a silly story. Before I was born, my family was convinced I was a boy. Grandma was the only one who disagreed, so for the full pregnancy, she secretly prepped for a girl. My mom went into labor on the first day of the Peach Harvest. There were workers all over our property, and she sent Logan to find my dad. Well, he got sidetracked and forgot his mission. So Mom called down to my grandparents' house. Grandma took charge and found my dad, grandpa, and eventually Logan.

"As the story goes, the minute I was born and announced as a girl, Grandma screamed 'I knew it!' She held me close and declared I would forever be her Peach Princess. Pretty soon, the name stuck and the entire town called me that."

"Well, that and she resembled a peach. She was a fat, round little thing with fuzz all over her head," Logan adds with a chuckle.

Grace's face heats again, but instead of getting irritated, she starts to laugh. "That's true. Not to mention, after all those months of Grandma stockpiling girl things, I was dressed in pink and peach the entire first year of my life. Grandma had strong faith in her beliefs on my gender."

I watch her face for any sign of sadness at the mention of her grandmother. Instead, she beams, keeping her eyes on Logan as something passes between them.

The last few nights of research on the Monroe family may have given me an insight into their background, but it's stories like this that will tell me about Grace. I hold in my laugh, thinking about her being known as the Peach Princess to everyone in her hometown.

Seeing her today in action has shown me a new side to Grace. She may be sweet, but she's also a ball of fire. I like it. No… I more than like it.

Sweet Grace may just be my undoing.

I'm coming for you, Sweet Grace. And this time, you're not getting away.

Chapter 7

Grace

This is not a date, Grace. Get your head on straight.

I pin my hair into a bun and check myself one last time in the mirror. Usually, during resets, I don't put a lot of effort into my appearance, but when Nick announced last night he was picking me up and spending the morning helping me, I decided to change up my choice of outfits. Instead of ripped shorts and a t-shirt, I chose a comfortable romper.

It's not quite as casual, but still appropriate for the labor involved in today's work.

There's a knock at the door, and I instantly feel the flapping in my stomach.

Nick's here...

At my apartment...

To pick me up...

To spend the morning with me...

Nick Bennett... The Nick Bennett...

I swallow down my nerves and go to answer the door, hoping that by the time I get there, I can form a complete sentence without stuttering.

This doesn't work because, when I open the door, he's leaning against the frame with one hand holding a bottle of wine. He's wearing shorts and a t-shirt, with his hair still damp from his shower. The smell of his cologne drifts in, and suddenly, I'm transported back to the night he picked me up for our first date. The same nerves assault me, sending my butterflies into a tailspin.

Speaking coherently flies out of my mind, and all I can squeak is a high-pitched, "Hi."

His eyes rake up and down my body, leaving a trail of invisible heat on every inch of my skin. When he finally meets my eyes, I'm frozen in place, lost in the deep blue depths of his stare.

"Hi to you."

It takes a few seconds for my brain to kick in, and I finally step back and signal for him to come in.

He walks past me into my living room and sets the bottle of wine on my coffee table.

"For your daily consumption," he explains, remembering what I said when he brought the tea.

Without another word, he's in front of me again. In a flash, I'm in his arms. Instead of our usual hug, he wraps his arms around my waist and drops his forehead to mine.

"I didn't think it was possible, but you're more beautiful each time I see you. Even at six in the morning, fucking gorgeous." His voice is husky and deep, loaded with intention.

A ripple of heat rolls through my veins as my skin starts to tingle. The air in the room changes as he leans back a few inches and his eyes pin mine.

Slowly, never breaking our stare, he moves in until he's so close I can feel the warmth of his breath. I close my eyes and tilt my head, bracing my hands on his chest.

He grazes his lips over mine until I part them, allowing his tongue to slip inside. The first taste of him takes my breath away. It's everything I've imagined. That damn cologne takes over, invading my senses, and I sink into him, opening wider.

One of his arms skims up my back until his hand is cupping the back of my head. He holds me in place as his tongue strokes against mine, me following his lead. I'm pretty sure I stop breathing and take my air from him as he deepens the kiss.

Silently, I beg him never to stop, soaking in the best first kiss I've ever had. He's gentle yet controlling as his fingertips start to massage my scalp. Our mouths move together, finding a rhythm so perfect I melt.

I was wrong earlier. This isn't what I imagined… It's more.

So much more.

Kissing Nick Bennett has my entire body drowning in a way I never thought possible. It's all-consuming, the kind of experience that can never be forgotten.

He starts slow, withdrawing his tongue and kissing tenderly along my lips.

"Two years, six months and seventeen days. That's how long I've thought about this moment," he whispers against my mouth.

"Really?" I reply faintly, my knees starting to wobble.

"Yes, Sweet Grace. I'm almost tempted to kick my own ass for walking away that night without getting a taste of you. I can tell you right now, if I'd had a taste back then, there's no way you could have disappeared like you did."

"Nick..."

"Shhh—" He slides his hand from my scalp around to my face, his thumb caressing my cheek. "I know why you left, and I understand. But I wish we'd had more time to get to know each other back then. I would have been there for you."

"You know?" I ask, surprised.

"I know your grandma died, and you went home to be with family, which seems like a logical decision. What I don't know is why you didn't think you could talk to me, tell me what was happening. We may have only known each other a few days, but I'm pretty sure we'd established we were friends, maybe headed for more."

"I'm sorry."

"Don't be sorry. It's over."

I nod and suck in a deep breath then lean back and raise my eyes to his. "I'd like to tell you now if you're interested."

"I'm interested."

I release my hold on his chest and take his hand in mine, leading him to the sofa. Once he's settled, I sit close, facing him. He puts our joined hands on his thigh, giving me an expectant look.

"First, can I ask how you know about Grandma?"

His expression turns to shame, and he tosses his head back, keeping his eyes on the ceiling.

"Would it make me a complete tool if I told you I'd Googled you?"

"You Googled me?"

"It wasn't my intention. After you left school, I tried a few times to find you, but realized quickly I didn't know much about your life outside of college, so all my attempts were a dead end. But when I came to the gallery last week to see you and finally learned more about where you were from, I tried again."

He turns to face me, and I hold back my giggles. He resembles a boy about to be scolded. If only he knew how many times I'd actually looked him up throughout the years.

"Well, what did you learn?"

He explains briefly the articles he read, and I remember them word for word, mostly because I co-wrote some of them. My mom and I agreed we wanted to try to control what was printed following the death and the accident. Then he tells me about discovering my dad is the Mayor.

"Is that it?"

"Yes."

"Well, first of all, I need to explain a few things. It's a bit of a story, but when I get to the more recent events, I think you'll understand."

"Take your time. I've been waiting a long time to hear this."

"My family is very established in the town of Thomasville. Our roots are planted deep. The Monroes go back generations. It wasn't always the orchards or the pecan trees either. We've had almost every area of agriculture in our family. In 1942, a family from a neighboring county came to town. They bought some of the abandoned land the town had written off as useless. This was the Rae family.

"For years, The Raes worked their fingers to the bone to get the land cultivated and pretty soon became recognized as elite tobacco farmers in the area. The Monroes didn't like this at all and started a petition to take back the land and run the family out of town. It became an all-out war, but what they didn't count on was Kayla Rae and Roy Monroe falling in love. An even bigger surprise was when Kayla and Roy showed up one night, married. They eloped the minute Grandma turned eighteen.

"It was the talk of the town for quite a while, with rumors flying that Grandma was knocked up. That wasn't true. Well, things were rough for my grandparents. All their lives, they'd lived under their parents' rule, but they were determined to make a life for themselves. Both sets of my great-grandparents were livid and tried everything just short of disowning them to break up the marriage. Nothing worked. The only saving grace was that my great-grandpa Monroe was a stubborn son of a bitch and wouldn't have his son working for anyone but the family. So my grandpa was able to keep his job on the farm and moved them into the loft over a barn."

Nick squeezes my hand gently. "It sounds exactly like those movies my mom and Bizzy love watching."

"Oh, yes, it was the love story of the ages. Eventually, everyone came around. During that time, the boys were enlisting in the service to serve their country, but Grandpa decided to stay behind and tend to the land. He'll tell you to this day that it was the best decision he ever made because he was scared Kayla's dad would convince her that Roy Monroe wasn't good enough for her. So he stayed to prove him wrong.

"The feud between the families died the instant Grandma was pregnant with my dad. All the rifts went out the window. As the story is told, it was a miracle. Suddenly, the Monroes and Raes were a joined unit and unstoppable. Together, my great-grandparents invested and brought the newest and best agricultural practices to Thomasville. Peace was finally found."

"It's a really cool story, Grace. Sounds like you're part of an aristocracy."

I let out a little giggle and nod. "You have no idea. But it's not as grand as you'd think. My mom and dad raised Logan and me normally. I've never had a silver spoon in my mouth. As a matter of fact, when I refused to be a debutante, I thought Great-Grandma Rae was going to have a stroke. But Grandma Kayla openly applauded my decision. She was my partner in crime. I had girlfriends, but Grandma was truly the best. Mom may have had some jealousy of our relationship, but she never spoke up because she loved her equally as much."

"Sounds like an incredible woman."

"She was so much more than incredible. That's why her death turned our world upside down."

"Grace, you don't have to explain any more. I get it. It sounds like she was an exceptional woman. I can see how her death would make you re-evaluate your priorities for a while."

"You have no idea. She may have been exceptional, but she was a stubborn nut! Her death could have been avoided, but she was a Rae to her bones and no one was going to tell her what to do."

He squints his eyes, clearly confused at the change in my tone. This is the part of the story where I always get fired up—and usually emotional. I suck in a deep breath and continue.

"Grandma shouldn't have died the way she did, and to this day, we've been successful in keeping her entire story from anyone but immediate family. For a few months, she was acting off. Grandpa finally insisted she see a doctor and then a specialist. They found several spots on her brain that were pressing on her sensory nerves. Her speech problems and vision were the most affected. Instead of sharing with the family, she made my grandpa promise to keep it quiet until they could get a full diagnosis and make decisions on treatment. Logan was finishing his own MBA. He wasn't the farming type, and my parents were supporting his quest to start a business. I was close to graduation with my own plans to attend graduate school. That was an expectation Logan and I never argued. We knew our education was non-negotiable, and we respected it. So her reasoning was to keep on with life as normal until they had a plan of action. One evening, she took off to the back of the farm to check out something. Stubborn ass wouldn't wait for Grandpa to get out of the shower. On her way, she blacked out and ran her car into a tree. She was killed instantly."

"Jesus!" He lurches forward and twists into me, folding our hands to his chest. "I didn't see that coming. That was her accident?"

"Yes, but it was what happened next that changed the course of my life. I got the call about ten minutes after you left that night. My mom had someone come for me and would only give me basic details until I arrived at home. It was my grandpa… he was inconsolable. She was his life. My time was no longer my own. Every moment I was awake, I was with him. It became obvious I couldn't return to school for the near future, so we made arrangements to finish school while staying in Thomasville. Being a Monroe has certain advantages, and one of them was the influence my dad had in making it so I didn't have to withdraw. Then by the time things settled down, you were gone. Hell, almost everyone I knew from school was gone."

"God, Grace, that's a lot of pressure on you."

"No, Nick, no one pressured me but myself. You can't understand this, but Grandma Kayla and I were so much alike, and Rae-Monroe women have a characteristic. We excel in the face of adversity. Grandpa needed me, and I wouldn't change a thing in the world. He's much better now. Hell, he was better within two months. He's the one who kicked my ass back into gear with graduate school, and he's the one who helped Logan and I follow our business plan through. It was he that backed our gallery. The only caveat was I had to promise to finish my MFA. Once again, non-negotiable. So I worked my ass off and did it then got down here to help Logan."

"I wish you would have told me. If anything, I could have been a friend during that dark time. But what's done is done, and I'm really fucking glad you're here now."

"Me too." I give him a small smile. "Miami has been good to me. It's a dream come true."

Suddenly, in one quick motion, he has me transferred from my spot next to him to directly in his lap. I let out a little squeak that dies in my throat when he releases my hand and frames my face. Gently, his thumbs rub my cheeks as his eyes lock with mine.

"Glad to hear it, but I was more or less referring to right now. You and me, here in your apartment at this ungodly hour of the morning. I'm not lying when I tell you that I thought of you often, more than one person should admit. Seeing you again was a jolt to my system. I'm pretty sure I'm getting a second chance here."

Oh my God! My heart starts to pound so fast that I know he can feel it. He watches for my reaction, which would probably be to leap in the air screaming if I wasn't anchored to his lap. Without words, I lean in slowly and stop only inches from his mouth. Taking a page from his book earlier, I whisper against his lips.

"I'm suddenly a huge fan of second chances."

My intentions to kiss him sweetly are gone when he crashes his mouth to mine. Unlike earlier, this isn't sweet and slow, where he takes his time to explore. Now, he's kissing me like a man kisses a woman he hasn't seen in two years, six months, and seventeen days. The same woman he just admitted to thinking about often.

His hands glide around my neck and tangle in my hair as he folds my body flush against him. My own hands are trapped between us, so all I can do is grip his t-shirt.

I let him control this, hoping he can feel my range of emotions as our tongues swirl together in perfect rhythm. He shifts us, bracing me with one arm as he lays us on our side, him partially on top. The kiss continues, and I'm internally begging for it never to end. Being in his arms is unlike anything I've ever experienced. He starts to slow and break away, nibbling lightly on my bottom lip.

"Grace, remember when I mentioned I was tempted to kick my own ass for not kissing you sooner?" He lays his forehead against mine and captures me again with his eyes. They are burning with the same desire searing through my body. "This afternoon at practice, I am willingly going to get my ass kicked. I deserve it for being a dipshit."

I start to giggle, shaking against him, and feel his own chest vibrating.

The connection from all those years ago just exploded, and one thought crosses my mind.

Logan was wrong. So, so, so wrong. This isn't a crush on Nick Bennett. In this instant, it becomes so much more.

There's no hiding my dreamy mood when Logan walks into the gallery mid-afternoon. He takes one look at me and rolls his eyes then glances around, taking in all the work Nick and I accomplished.

"I hardly recognize this place," he says approvingly.

"It's turned out gorgeous."

"What do you need me to do?"

"You can help me with more of the staging, and then you can take pictures for the website."

"We're that close to being done? We scheduled three days for this."

"Yes, and thanks to Nick and Rodney's help yesterday, and Nick's help this morning, we're way ahead of schedule."

"Where is Nick?" He glimpses toward the back.

"He had to get to the stadium. We were here by seven thirty this morning."

"That was cool of him, especially coming off such an aggressive game on Sunday. He's got to be exhausted."

"I know. We owe him for helping us. It was completely unnecessary."

"Somehow, I don't think he'll agree that we owe him something. Just being around him for those few hours, I could tell he wanted to be here."

The gooey feelings return as I picture Nick's face when he kissed me goodbye earlier. He was hesitant to leave, but after the third call he received and the incessant beeping of his phone with messages, I practically had to force him out the door. I can almost still feel his lips on mine.

Memories of the morning come flooding back. Each time he hung a picture, he took the opportunity to pull me to him and kiss me. Every time our mouths touched, desire scorched inside me. It's hard to believe it's been less than a week since he walked into the gallery to find me.

"Hey! Get out of Grace Space." Logan snaps his fingers, bringing me out of my thoughts.

"Sorry." I shrug unapologetically.

"Did you hear anything I said?"

"Nope."

"Mom called this morning."

"And?"

"She'll call you tonight. She's making sure we're coming home in October."

The Fall Festival! I completely forgot. "Logan, did you mention we have a business to run? Now that I'm here full-time, it's going to be really hard for us both to travel at the same time."

"Yeah, I mentioned it, the same way I've mentioned it the twenty times before. But that's the beauty of being a business owner. We can set our own schedule. I did tell her the holidays are going to be tricky. She agreed to compromise."

"What kind of compromise?" My suspicions rise.

"We'll have to see. I've already signed up to participate in the Small Business Saturday street event on Thanksgiving weekend. So maybe they'll come here."

"Seems reasonable."

"I'm going to do a few things in the office, and I'll be ready to finish this up. Fifteen minutes, okay?"

"Sure." As if on cue, my phone rings, and I can't help my grin when I see it's Nick.

"Better yet, come get me when you're off the phone." Logan walks away.

"Hello," I answer a little too chirpy. *Cool it, Grace!*

"Hey, Sweet Peach."

"Sweet Peach?"

"I came up with it on the way to the stadium. It's a combination of Sweet Grace and Peach Princess."

My chest spasms. "You gave me a nickname?"

"Oh yeah, and considering you always smell like peaches, I think it's perfect."

"I like it," I mostly whisper.

"Are you planning another late night?"

"Actually, I think we'll be through in a few hours. Logan just arrived, and if everything goes as planned, I'll have all day tomorrow to crate and ship the old pieces to their owners. It'll be a great reset, thanks to you. They've never gone this smoothly."

"What do you mean?"

"In the past, we've worked until the last minute to get this place ready."

"You've done this before?" he asks, his tone switching.

"A few times over the last year."

He's quiet, too quiet, the entire mood changing.

"Nick?"

"I'm here, trying to figure out how you could have been in Miami and not called."

There's nothing I can say. How do I explain that I was sure he wouldn't remember me? Or, after the way I ignored his calls after Grandma died, I was ashamed?

"You know what? Don't answer that. It's over. What's done is done." He may speak the words, but he's not very convincing.

"I'm sorry, Nick, really sorry."

"Two years, six months, and seventeen days, Grace, and this morning you changed all that so let's not go back there. We're moving forward. I'm taking my second chance."

"I'd like that."

"I'll be here a while longer, and then I'll come back by the gallery. Anything not done, I can help. Then I'll drive you home."

"You don't have to. Logan will take me home. You have to be exhausted."

He sighs into the phone, then repeats what is becoming my favorite phrase. "Two years, six months,—"

"Okay, okay! I get it," I break in. "I'll see you when you get here."

"That's better, Sweet Peach. See you soon."

He hangs up right as Logan walks over with an expression of excitement.

"Guess what came in my email this morning?" He waves his phone at me.

"I have no idea, but it obviously made you happy."

"A reference request for Grace Rae Monroe from the Art Institute."

My heart starts to race as I rush to him and snatch the phone out of his hand. "How can this be? It's been less than a week since I sent in the application."

"You've impressed someone, which I knew you would." He gives me a one-armed hug. "Good job!"

"It's not an invitation, but it shows they may have interest."

"Of course they're interested. I had no doubt."

I dance around, waving my hands in the air. After all this time of feeling like my life was on hold, I finally feel like it's really starting.

Chapter 8

Nick

"I LOVE it! This is absolutely the most brilliant display we've ever created!" Grace's overly excited voice fills the gallery as soon as I walk in.

Logan's back is to me, snapping pictures as she wiggles excitedly behind him. I stop in my tracks and take the split second to admire her before she turns to face me.

Her face grows brighter as her smile widens. "Nick!"

My feet move fast with one goal in mind. Her eyes grow wide when she realizes my intentions. As soon as she's close enough, I tag her to my side and drop my mouth to hers in a gentle yet firm kiss on the lips. Too quickly, I pull away, aware her brother is watching.

"Sweet Peach," is my greeting, and I like the way her face grows soft at my new term.

"Hey."

"Logan." I acknowledge him with a chin lift, and he does the same, not fazed by my affection. "It looks amazing in here." I peer around the rooms that have taken on a complete transformation since yesterday morning.

"It's all Grace. She may have wanted to kill me when I told her we'd be displaying the sculptures, but she's made it flawless," he praises her.

"It's a group effort." She leans into me and squeezes my waist. "We have you to thank, too. If it wasn't for you, I'd be living here tonight to finish. So thank you."

"My pleasure."

"Seriously, Six, we appreciate your help. I owe you dinner." Logan offers his hand.

"I'll take you up on that."

"I'm going to upload these and start working on the website changes. Be in the office if you need me." He gives a wave and turns to leave, but I catch the grin spreading across his lips.

"I owe you dinner, too. Are you hungry?" Grace asks, twisting into me.

My chest tightens at how natural she feels tucked to my side. Less than twelve hours ago, I showed up at her apartment, planning to let her set the pace. But when she answered the door, all thoughts flew out the window with one glance.

Without answering, I lift her so our faces are close. Her eyes scan mine quickly and land on my lips, knowing what I want. She gives a small smile and lowers her mouth to mine, wrapping her arms around my shoulders.

Our mouths move urgently together, different than any other time I've kissed her. This time, she meets my tongue stroke for stroke, almost fighting for power. My dick grows hard at the thought.

My Sweet Peach may have a wild side. She proves me right the second she adjusts her hips and wraps her legs around my waist, tightening her grip on my shoulders.

There's no doubt she feels my hard cock through my shorts. I fight every impulse I have to grab her ass and grind against her. I give up control, letting her own the kiss. She doesn't disappoint, sliding her hands into my short hair and scraping her nails along my scalp.

She lets out a faint whimper, and I'm done. My dick throbs, jerking as ringing starts in my ears. I squeeze her waist and start to slow down, nibbling on her bottom lip as I break away.

Pride surges through me as I watch her eyes clear and see the faraway look on her face.

"Babe, I'm starving, but not necessarily for food. I have a newfound craving for the taste of you."

Her cheeks flush deeper, and she bites the side of her mouth. "We can leave if you're ready. I can finish my work tomorrow."

"Sure, but first, give me a tour." I'll need the few minutes to get my raging hormones under control, and I say a silent prayer her brother doesn't walk out.

She nods, unlatching her legs and slipping down my body. Her hand slides into mine, and she starts guiding me around the room. She tells me about the artists as she points to their work, but her words jumble in my head. With each word, I'm more drawn to her.

Her voice is full of spirit and excitement, pulling me even deeper under her spell.

When we come to an entire shelving area of glass art, her expression changes. "This is probably one of my favorite displays ever."

"It's beautiful," I tell her honestly. The pieces are all different colors, shapes, and sizes. I immediately see a piece that catches my eye. It's a cylinder shape that branches out at the top with wild, crisscrossing glass. A few of the thin branches have bulbs. "But this piece specifically is incredible." I point, scared to touch it.

Her hand tightens in mine. "Really? You think so?"

"Absolutely, my eyes were drawn to it. Are these going to be for sale?"

"I'll make you one," she replies sheepishly, and it's my turn to be shocked.

"You did this?"

She nods. "I did. It's not as professional and perfectly symmetrical as the rest, but I'm proud of it."

"To me, it's better than the rest of them by far. It actually jumps out at me."

Her eyes dance with happiness, and I catch glimpses of the girl I remember. Then a memory comes barging into my mind. She loves glass sculpting. She mentioned it several times in the few snippets she shared about her art goals.

How could I forget?

"I'm so proud of you. This is what you loved, and you did it," I say softly, running my free hand along her cheek.

She inhales sharply, her eyes starting to shine. "You remember?"

"I do now."

"No one but my family truly knows my love for glasswork."

Her statement seizes my heart. This moment feels intimate, not in a sexual way but in the way that she's let me in on a secret only shared with those who mean something to her.

"Does it have a special meaning?"

She starts to look around nervously, and I step in closer, leaving only inches between us. "Grace?"

"It's supposed to be a peach tree. I made it shortly after Grandma died. I never thought anyone would see it, but it felt right to put it in this display, it being my first real show as part owner. She would have loved to be here, and in a way, she is. I put it here as a reminder of her."

It isn't so much what she's said but the meaning behind it that erases any unresolved feelings of why she never contacted me again. At this moment, something clicks, and I understand so much about this woman that couldn't be explained in her words. It's her actions.

I've been riding on the assumption she lost her grandmother, a woman she loved and admired. But she lost a woman she worshiped, a woman who raised her with values and beliefs.

And now I feel my own loss for not ever meeting Kayla Rae Monroe.

"You didn't answer me. Are you going to sell it?" The thought sours in my stomach.

"I don't think so."

"Good, I think you should keep it."

"I'll still make you one."

"Thank you. I'll treasure it."

"Are you ready for dinner now?"

"Sure, how do you feel about take-out?"

She gives me a questioning look, probably because of my earlier comment regarding craving the taste of her.

"Let me clarify. It's rare I can enjoy a low key dinner. Most people are very respectful, but I still get recognized.

Tonight, I don't want the interruptions. I want to spend time with you."

Her face dawns in understanding, and she gives me a playful smile. "It's easy to forget you're a celebrity in this town. Let me get my purse and tell Logan goodbye. We can get something and go back to my place if that's okay."

"It's not hard for me because I don't think of myself that way, and your place sounds great." I lean in for another quick kiss. "Go get your stuff."

"Here's that charm thing again. Although, I'm beginning to understand the nickname Sexy Six…" She slides out of my arms and walks to the back office.

I watch her sway away, her words ringing in my ears.

Sexy Six never sounded so good.

"Come on, Grace. Wipe that scowl off your face." I start unpacking the food containers onto her kitchen counter.

"I'm not scowling," she replies, getting plates and silverware. "I'm trying to figure out how this happened. It was supposed to be my treat!"

I hang my head to hide my amusement. She's really cute when she's miffed.

"Never gonna happen, Sweet Peach. You're with me, I pay. Always, no arguments."

"Absurd macho behavior." She huffs.

"I'd prefer to think of it as gentlemanly."

"But I'm supposed to be thanking you for all your help! It's perfectly acceptable to let me pay." She places the plates on the counter with a loud thud.

I glance over at her, noticing her cheeks are flushed. Her lips keep moving, but I tune her out and take a quick glance around. Once I spot empty counter space, I swoop down and pick her up, sealing my mouth over hers. She gives a little squeal as I take a few steps and sit her on the space, slipping between her knees. My hands grip her hips lightly as I continue to kiss her until she gives in.

"You really want to fucking argue over who paid for dinner?" I say into her mouth.

Her hands glide up my chest to rest on my shoulders. "Yes," she mutters.

I slide her closer until we're flush against each other and deepen the kiss, letting her know there is no room for argument. Desire simmers in my veins.

If she gets this worked up over fucking take-out, I'm going to be in trouble. I saw a little of her saucy side with Logan, but when it's directed at me, it's more of a turn on than a threat.

Slowly, I end the kiss but don't let her go. "Get over it, Grace, and accept it."

Her eyes meet mine and soften, turning a lighter shade of violet. "Thank you, Nick. I appreciate it."

"You going to pitch a fit every time I buy you dinner?"

She reluctantly shakes her head.

"Jesus, babe, what kind of guys have you dated that would ever let you pay?"

I can tell I struck a nerve and instantly regret my question.

"My last date, Pledge, was a struggling artist and didn't have much money."

My stomach turns at the mention of her 'last date', even more so at his manners. "You dated a guy named Pledge?"

Her face starts to heat up, and she nods. She surprises me when her lips twitch, and she starts to giggle. "He wasn't really the dating type."

"I don't know the guy, and he sounds like a tool."

Her giggles grow into full blown laughter, and she shakes against my chest. "He was! My grandpa shot his taillight out!" she rasps.

The laughter is infectious, and soon, I'm chuckling along with her. She peers up at me, her eyes shining.

"It's a long story, but let's say he never spoke to me again."

"Good." I slide her off the counter and set her back on her feet. "One less asshole to compete with."

We make our plates, still laughing, and I follow her to sit at her dining table. "So what happens next now that the reset is done?" I ask before taking a bite.

"We'll open on Thursday for a few limited hours. Each artist has been invited to see the displays. Logan has a press plan that goes into action on Thursday as well. Then, on Friday night, we have a cocktail party planned for an exclusive showing. Monday, we open to the general public."

At her mention of a cocktail party, my subconscious tells me to push for more. "What kind of cocktail party?"

"The kind where Logan and I schmooze with our loyal clientele and hope for new business. We put on our biggest smiles, work the rooms, introduce the artists, and promote the gallery."

"Is this your first time doing one of these?"

She looks at me regretfully, shaking her head. "It's my second. I did one last fall after a reset then had to get back to school. It was a quick trip."

Her statement came out more as an explanation, a guilty explanation. I reach over and lay my hand on hers, squeezing lightly. "You don't need to feel bad, Grace. We've already established you came to Miami several times. As much as I wish you'd have called, I understand. Second chances, remember?"

Relief washes over her face as she nods. "Nothing we've ever done has been as big as this showing. I'm extremely nervous and excited at the same time. When I think of it, I feel a little queasy. My hope is that it goes well. Logan's been on his own for a while, and I want to pull my weight. This is my chance to really show him I can."

She puts her fork down and takes a sip of her wine. I notice her hand shaking a bit, and her words sink in. Her expression changes to one of unease and apprehension. Her easygoing attitude disappears as self-doubt takes over.

I move both our plates and scoot my chair closer to hers. She looks at me in confusion until I bend and pluck her into my lap, wrapping an arm around her waist to keep her from tumbling over.

"W-w-what are you doing?" she stutters.

"I'm putting you in my lap," I point out the obvious.

"I can see that, but why?"

"Because you were too far away."

Her eyes start to soften in the way I'm growing to understand. "And I want you in my arms when I tell you that without a shadow of a doubt, you have nothing to be worried about. Friday night will be incredible. I'm an idiot when it comes to art, I'll be the first to admit it, but you make it interesting. Your enthusiasm and knowledge make even the most ignorant want to know more. As for Logan, he knows how hard you've worked. When I walked into that gallery today, he had pride written all over his face."

"Really?"

"Absolutely. I wouldn't lie to you."

She seems to think about this for a second until a small grin forms on her lips. "Thanks, Nick."

"So is it invite only?"

"We sent out the invitations weeks ago." She bobs her head rapidly. "We actually have a few people begging to get in at the last minute."

Disappointment digs in until I catch the twinkle in her eye as her lips twitch.

"Begging, huh? That's too bad. I'd love to come. Know any way I could get into this elite event?" My arms circle her waist, and she leans back, shaking her head while trying to keep a straight face.

"It's going to be hard, very hard. I can't think of a way to get you in, unless…" She taps a finger against her mouth as if she's thinking hard.

"Unless?" I bend into her, my lips brushing along her neck.

"Unless you wanted to be my date."

My heartbeat quickens as my plan starts to work. "That sounds like a real hardship. I'll have to check my schedule," I tease her, nipping lightly on her earlobe.

"I understand if you're busy, but—"

"Sweet Peach, there's no place I'd rather be on Friday night. The thought of being your date is the best offer I've had in a long time."

Her face lights up, and she throws her arms around my shoulders. "You may regret that when you're bored out of your mind."

"There's no way I could be bored."

"Charmer."

"Only with you." I lean in to kiss her, pulling her close and forgetting about our food.

She's all I need for now…

Chapter 9

Grace

I try to swallow the moan, but it doesn't work, and instead, the sound comes out as a strangled croak. Nick's encouraged by the sounds, and both his hands skim up my sides as he deepens the kiss. I arch my body into him, tightening my hold on his hips, which swivel into mine with the added pressure.

His erection rubs against my core, and we both groan at the same time. He tears his mouth away from mine and drops his head to the side, resting it in the crook of my neck.

"Holy fucking shit, I can't get enough of you," he pants.

My stomach does a full twist as I try to catch my own breath. "You say that like it's a bad thing."

He lifts up enough to see my face and moves one hand to cup my chin. "It's a very, very good thing… I'd even say it's dangerous."

"Dangerous?"

His eyes turn into the most beautiful shade of liquid blue, and he scans my face, running his thumb across my lower lip.

"Yeah, Sweet Peach, dangerous. One week, that's all it's taken for me to go from curious to crazy."

"Crazy?" I question in a whisper.

"When I asked Shaw to find you, I was curious, wanting to see you again, talk to you, get answers and see how you were doing. That curiosity turned into so much more the second my eyes landed on you last Thursday."

At his words, an electric thrill runs through my body. "Where does the crazy part come in?"

He doesn't answer, leaning in to kiss me lightly. Too quickly, he jerks up and leans all the way back, bringing me with him into a sitting position.

"I should probably go."

My mood falls, not wanting him to leave. I glance at the table and the half-eaten plates of food, blurting out, "We didn't even finish dinner."

He looks behind him and back to me with a smirk. "I got distracted."

Heat creeps up my neck and chest, thinking about how we ended up on the couch. What started as what I thought was a normal kiss became heated, and he quickly relocated us from the table to the sofa. One kiss turned into two and quickly escalated into a full blown make-out session. It's easy to lose track of time when Nick Bennett has you pinned under him.

I don't want him to leave. I want him to lay me back down and continue to kiss me like I've never been kissed. I'm more alive than I've ever felt in my life. The feelings from this morning return, and I try to tamper down the lust running through my veins.

"Grace?" Nick angles his head so it's directly in my line of sight. "You okay?"

I snap out of my thoughts and focus on his beautiful face. "Do you have to leave?"

His face takes on a new expression as he shakes his head. "Not if you don't want me to."

"I don't want you to."

His face breaks into a wide smile. "Then I'll stay."

His phone rings before I can say anything else, and he fishes it out of his pocket. The ring tone is familiar, but I can't place the song. "I need to get this. It'll only be a minute," he tells me.

I shift to get up and give him privacy, but he yanks me back into his lap.

"Hey," he answers the call.

A male voice comes through so loud I can hear it clearly.

"Nicky, I've done the best I can, but Bizzy's clued in. She knows something is up with you. You need to talk to her."

"Shaw, I'll call her tomorrow, promise."

"You better. She's about to climb the walls."

"I don't know why. I spoke to her this morning."

"Yeah, but you've been home from Indy for days, and she's on my ass, saying you're different. Even my best methods of distractions aren't working."

I feel like a complete creep eavesdropping, even if Nick has me in a super hold, and I can't help overhearing.

"Fuck, Shaw, I don't need that visual. And not to get into your business, but if you can't distract her, you must be doing something wrong."

I can't stop the giggle that escapes, and I slap my hand over my mouth, figuring Shaw hears me.

"Fuck you, Nick! It's that damn ESP or voodoo shit you two have going on."

Nick's eyes land on mine and turn warm. He seems to be thinking about this and grips my thigh. "I'll take her to lunch tomorrow and explain everything."

"Maybe you can explain it to me, too."

"I don't think I need to explain it to you, Shaw."

There's silence followed by a loud roar of laughter. "Son of a bitch, you have until tomorrow."

The line goes dead, and he slides the phone back in his pocket.

I try to think of what to say. I have a sneaky suspicion the call was about me. He tags me in closer and rests his chin on my shoulder.

"What are you thinking, Grace? I can't read your face."

"I kinda heard all that."

"You'd have to be deaf not to. My brother's a loud mouth."

"Was it about me?"

"Yep."

"Is Bizzy upset?"

"I wouldn't say she's upset, just curious."

"About me?" I repeat.

"Sort of, but since she doesn't know about you, she's more curious about me."

I stiffen in his arms, not liking where this is going.

"Hey." He slides a hand up to massage my neck, gently turning my head to face him. "Whatever you're thinking is most likely wrong. She doesn't know about you because when I asked Shaw to find you, I also asked him to keep quiet until I could talk to you again, find out more about you. I had no idea what your life was like, and I wanted to learn on my own. I wasn't hiding you."

Some of the tension eases from my shoulders as I understand what he's saying. A flashback of last Thursday runs through my mind, when he asked me if I was seeing anyone. It's hard to believe it was only a week ago he walked back into my life. "And now?" I ask, holding my breath for his answer.

"And now, you better get ready because Bizzy is a force of nature. As soon as she finds out you're back, and we've reconnected, she's going to be unstoppable."

I start to get nervous. What if she doesn't approve? Surely, she knows how I disappeared and never returned his calls. If anything, it was extremely rude, regardless of the circumstances. She's his best friend. She could hold a grudge.

"Your face is scrunching again, which means you're probably thinking the wrong way."

"Does she know about me disappearing and never returning your calls?"

"She knows a little. I played it off, pretending it didn't matter even though it did."

My gut rolls with another round of regret. "Ugh, she's going to hate me."

"She'd never hate you, especially when she hears you're back."

"What are you going to tell her?"

"I'll tell her the truth, but it won't be necessary. She'll see it written all over my face. We kinda share a weird sense of understanding."

"The voodoo ESP?" I repeat Shaw's words.

"Yes, I guess you could call it that. Have I ever told you about how Bizzy and I met?"

"No, but I'd love to hear it." And I would. I'd love to hear anything about Nick's life. In all my following him through the years, Bizzy has been pictured but nothing said except a few mentions of his volunteering and commitment to childhood cancer. But she's an Oncology Nurse so that seems logical.

He surprises me by standing, balancing me in his arms. "Let's clean the kitchen then we'll have story time."

"Aren't you hungry?"

His eyes take on the same shine from earlier today in the gallery, and I gulp, a small tremor running through me. "Forget I asked. It'll make a great midnight snack." I lean in and run my lips across his.

He shifts so I'm forced to straddle him, linking my legs around his waist as he walks us to my kitchen.

"I've always been a fan of midnight snacks," he says against my mouth.

The small tremor from earlier returns, and this time, I shudder in in his arms. He notices and gives me an approving wink.

I'm pretty sure he can read my thoughts by the way he's staring at me, but I can't seem to care.

"You survived cancer together?" My voice breaks saying the word. My head fills with images of a fourteen-year-old boy fighting for his life.

"We kicked cancer's ass. Together, we were a great team. Neither of us ever gave up hope. We encouraged each other on our darkest days and celebrated the smallest victories."

"She sounds like an amazing person. I had no idea of the depth of the friendship."

"A lot of people can't understand. She declared we were best friends. No question, no arguing. That was it. We've been pretty much inseparable ever since. Our families were already close, but now that she's married to Shaw, we're truly a blended group."

I clutch his shirt tighter and try to burrow deeper into Nick's chest. He lazily rubs circles on my arm and kisses the top of my head.

"That's one of the most beautiful stories I've ever heard."

"So why are you crying?"

"Because I can't imagine the heartache and worry. Your families must have felt so helpless."

"Yeah, but you want to know something? Throughout the years, the bad memories have faded, and I remember things with a more open perspective. Don't get me wrong, it sucked—the chemo, the tests, the waiting... all of it—but when we both hit remission, we were on the road to full recovery. I had her, and she had me. It's been that way for over ten years. That's why people think we have the voodoo ESP, because we can pretty much feel when the other has something going on."

I start to feel sick again, knowing the bond between Bizzy and Nick is almost too much to think about.

"Look at me, Grace." He tries to lift my chin, but I press back, not wanting him to see my undoubtedly splotchy face.

"What if she doesn't like me?" I say my fear out loud, not able to stop myself.

He tries again to lift my face, but I fight him, wiggling so my butt is now between his legs and my arms are wrapped around him like a vice.

My new position lasts a millisecond before I'm flying back on the sofa, and his body comes over mine. I'm now forced to let go of him. He positions himself with his back to the couch and pulls my body as close as possible. When I raise my eyes to his, I suck in a deep breath. He's staring at me, his eyes full of determination.

"She's going to like you, Grace. She loves me, and she wants me to be happy. You make me happy."

"I make you happy?" My stomach starts to do a twisty-turny motion as my skin starts to prickle.

"Babe, I've never dated in my life. The only girl I ever wanted to date slipped through my fingers and ditched me. For years, no one has even turned my head. My life has been football and family, and I've been fine with that. But the moment my eyes landed on you at the foundation dinner, things changed. You're almost all I think about. For days, I've had to force myself to concentrate on the field. Then today was pretty much torture, leaving you at the gallery, especially after getting my first taste of you."

The skin tingling intensifies all the way down to my bones. Each of his words seep into my skin, and I fight to control my racing heart.

"I didn't ditch you," is the first thing that comes out of my mouth.

His eyes crinkle, and his lips start to twitch. "You ditched me."

"I didn't."

"Sweet Peach, you did. And for two years, it was not at all funny. But now that we're here, you're in my arms, and we've moved past it, we can joke about it."

"You've never dated?"

"Are we going to dissect everything I said sentence by sentence?"

"Maybe."

"Okay, well, did you hear the part about today being torture and getting my first taste of you?"

"It's slowly processing."

He starts to laugh, his chest shaking against mine. "Take your time. I'm not going anywhere."

"I haven't really dated either." Why I tell him this is a mystery.

He cocks an eyebrow, and I remember the brief conversation in the kitchen earlier.

"Pledge wasn't dating material, and the only reason I invited him to the event at home was to try to dissuade the town nosy nellies from setting me up. There was nothing between us. That decision backfired. Other than him, my life was pretty busy with school and home obligations."

His eyes scan my face, and he licks his bottom lip, pressing me closer to his side. "Does it make me a total asshole that I'm pleased with this piece of information?"

"No."

His expression grows serious, and he leans in closer until his lips are at my ear. "Good, because as of this morning, that changed."

I want to ask him more, but when his mouth starts to kiss along my jawline, my mind goes blank.

Chapter 10

Nick

Shaw was right; Bizzy was on a full out mission. I didn't have time to call her and invite her to lunch because she is ringing my doorbell at seven forty-five in the morning. I get a glimpse at my alarm clock right as my phone starts to ring.

"Biz, you okay?" I answer groggily, still half-asleep.

"Yes, I'm at your door."

"So you're the crazy one ringing the doorbell at this ungodly hour?"

"Um hmm."

"Why don't you use your key?"

"Because I didn't know if you were alone."

"When have I ever had someone spend the night?"

"Are we really going to discuss this right now? I'm standing out here!"

"Use your key. I'll be right out."

She disconnects, and I hear the beep of my alarm when the door opens. There's a rustling and the sound of running water. I say a silent thank you that she's making coffee.

There's an ache between my legs, and I groan, remembering the dream I was in the middle of. Grace was wrapped around me, naked, as I moved inside of her. She was moaning low, whispering my name, and I—

"Nicky, take your time. I'm going to make you some breakfast." Bizzy's voice interrupts my thoughts, and it's like ice water on my throbbing cock.

I throw my legs to the side of the bed, standing, and wince at the pain in my lower back. That's going to suck at practice today. Slowly, I walk to the bathroom and brush my teeth, wash my face, and run some water through my hair. Then I prepare myself for the inquisition.

When I get to the kitchen, Bizzy is in the middle of whisking eggs and dancing around in her scrubs. Her face breaks into a smile when she sees me, then she puts the bowl down and comes straight to me. The first thing she does is cup my chin, roaming her eyes over my face, then leans in for a hug.

This is something she's done since we went into remission. We both need this reassurance that we're okay.

"Morning, Biz." I kiss her temple and step to the coffee maker, pouring us both a cup. "You just get off work?"

She nods, picking up the bowl, and starts whisking again.

"Well, this is a nice surprise, but I was going to call you today and take you to lunch."

"I couldn't wait any longer. I had to see you, talk to you." She cuts straight to the chase, giving me an all-knowing look. Her grey-blue eyes shine with unspoken questions.

I take a sip of my coffee and mix hers the way she likes it. Once I hand it to her, I hop up on my island and tell her what she wants to know.

"I've met someone. Actually, that's not true. I've reconnected with a woman I met a long time ago. She's recently come to Miami, and I ran into her. We've been spending some time together this last week. That's why I've been a little busy."

She sets the bowl back down and leans against the counter, watching me, waiting for more.

"She's pretty special, Biz. I can't explain it, but I'm interested in her. She's amazing."

I stop myself from gushing more because, even if it is Bizzy, I need to keep some of my pride. The room remains quiet, and I feel the heat of her stare. Finally, she speaks.

"Grace Monroe."

I snap my head, my eyes narrowing. "How'd you know?"

"Because I remember... everything." Her tone is snippy.

"Things weren't as they seemed. It was a long time ago."

She opens her mouth right as the door opens and Mathis and Shaw walk in. They both half-wave in greeting as if this is a normal everyday thing.

"Did I agree to have a party and miss the invitation part?" I grumble.

"No, but when I found out my wife wasn't coming straight home after her shift and instead was heading over here to cook breakfast for your sorry ass, I invited myself." Shaw shoots me an evil glare and goes to Bizzy, drawing her into a kiss.

I turn my head, not wanting to lose my appetite before the food is cooked. Mathis slaps me on the shoulder, also avoiding the over the top public affection between Shaw and Bizzy.

"I was on shift last night and overheard Biz telling Shaw she was coming over. So I called him and picked him up. No way we were missing this." He moves to a barstool to sit. "Besides, I'm starved."

Bizzy gives a little squeal, and I turn to see Shaw now has her in his arms.

"Stop that shit!" I bark.

Bizzy breaks their kiss and glances at me apologetically. She scoots down his body and goes to the fridge, grabbing more eggs.

"Did we miss anything?" Mathis asks her.

"Yes and no. I've discovered that Nicky is seeing a woman he met in college briefly. We were about to dive into the details, so I'd say you're just in time."

Her eyes dart between Shaw and Mathis, waiting for their reaction. When neither of them even flinch, her face starts to heat up. She places the eggs on the counter and puts her hands on her hips, glaring. "Why aren't either of you surprised?"

Mathis takes a gulp of his coffee to avoid answering as Shaw starts to back away from her. I bite the inside of my cheek to keep from smirking.

"I'll ask again... Why aren't either of you surprised?" This time, her question is accusatory.

"Bizzy, I may have mentioned Grace to them." I try to appease her.

"When?"

"LastweekwhenIthoughtIsawherandneededhelpfinding her." I say it so fast even I can't understand.

Big mistake.

She crosses her arms and gives me an icy glare. "Did you just say last week when you thought you saw her and needed help finding her?"

I nod, slipping off the counter and moving away from her reach.

The room is silently still, each of us waiting for her to blow. She takes a few deep breaths, throws her head back to the ceiling, and exhales loudly. Then she steps back to the counter and starts breaking more eggs into the bowl.

"I'll deal with you all later, but now, we have more important things to discuss." Her voice is controlled, but even I'm worried about what 'later' means.

All heads turn to me, waiting for what's next.

"There's not a lot to tell. She had a death in the family and left school. During the last two years, she's lived at home, finished school, helped her brother open an art gallery, and is now living here. Easy story."

What I think is a good explanation obviously doesn't quench their curiosity.

"That story fucking sucks. I need details. Did you think I'd accept that?" Bizzy starts to bang pans on my stove.

"What do you want to know?"

"Everything," all three of them answer in unison.

I think about glossing over the details and instantly decide against it. So I settle next to Mathis on a barstool and start talking. They listen intently as I explain everything that's happened since last Thursday. When I get to last night, I skim the part about making out with Grace like a teenager on her couch until two a.m. when I forced myself to leave.

Bizzy stares at me in awe when I stop talking. Her eyes are glassy, and I start to get nervous.

"Bizzy, don't—"

"You really like this girl."

"Well, yeah."

"No, I mean you like her, like her."

"Yes," I repeat, unsure why she's harping.

She twists to Shaw. "Can you get us an invite to the opening tomorrow night?"

He pulls out his phone, and I know he's about to perform his 'Shaw Magic'." There's a two-second chance I can stop this.

"Wait!" I throw my hand up. "Don't do it."

"Why?" There's a trace of hurt in Bizzy's tone. "Don't you want us to meet her?"

"Of course, but this is our first official date. I know her, and she's already on edge. If she knows you're coming, she'll be even more anxious. This is a big night for her, and I want it to be perfect."

"I can understand that, Biz. Maybe another time would be better." Mathis throws in his support.

"Maybe they're right, baby. It's still new, and all of us showing up may be overwhelming," Shaw agrees.

She chews on her bottom lip and nods, giving in. "Okay, but soon. I can't wait to meet her."

I give a little sigh of relief that went so well. Bizzy can be relentless if she wants.

"So it sounds like getting in her space is working out for you." Mathis punches my shoulder jokingly. "Glad to know we don't have to appeal a restraining order."

"Ha ha ha," I mumble as Bizzy serves our plates.

Once everyone is seated, I think of the perfect way to introduce Grace.

"Hey, Shaw, I need a favor."

When I explain what I want, Bizzy gives a loud cheer, clapping her hands and dancing in her seat. Mathis chuckles as Shaw assures me it's no problem.

Now I need to tell Grace… and get her to agree.

The gallery is quiet when I walk in. Grace and Logan are nowhere around. After a few seconds, Logan comes from the back with a smirk on his face.

"Hey, Six." He greets me with a quick handshake then locks the door behind me. "Perfect timing. I'm pretty sure Grace is about to blow her top."

The hair on the back of my neck stands, and my body goes solid. He notices and laughs, slapping me on the shoulder. "You want to date my sister? Come see what you're getting yourself into."

I follow him to the back office, and as we approach, I hear voices. Grace is sitting on one side of Logan's desk with the phone in the middle. She looks panicked when I walk in then shoots Logan an evil eye.

"Did you hear me, Grace Rae?" An older man's voice comes through the speaker.

"Yes, Grandpa. I heard you."

"And I don't want those electronic ones either. I want the kind I can hold in my hand and show off. Everyone in town wants to see."

"Grandpa, I'm a little busy right now. Can't you please pull them up on your iPad?"

"Hell no! How can I brag about my grandchildren's fancy gallery with an iPad? Besides, I'm not nifty on those gadgets." He huffs.

"Now, you're lying. I know for a fact that you are nifty. If you weren't, how could you be a part of the fantasy league with Logan and Dad?" With each word, her accent changes, becoming more southern.

It's one of the sexiest things I've ever heard, and I have to fight getting hard.

"Don't get smart, girlie! I want pictures."

"Okay," she relents, running a hand through her hair. "I'll take care of it this weekend."

"One more thing."

"What?" she asks, exasperated.

"Don't wear any of those coochie cutters tomorrow night. It's tacky."

Her eyes bulge, and she swings her head back and forth between the phone and Logan. "What did you say?"

"Those coochie cutters. You know those short shorts that cut into your—"

"GRANDPA! Where in the world did you learn that phrase?" Her face is completely red, shading darker by the second.

"Todd Chrisley."

Logan lets out deep chuckle then tries to cover it with a cough. Grace is grasping the edge of the desk with white knuckles and shaking her head.

"When the hell did you start watching *Chrisley Knows Best*? Didn't we talk about these programs? They're not really reality."

At this point, Logan is doubled over holding his stomach. I'm trying my best to hold in my own laughter.

"Peach Princess, this Todd guy has a good leash on life. I find myself relating to a lot of his situations. Did you know—"

"No, I don't know… and I never will," she cuts him off.

"Well, take my advice and don't wear any coochie cutters tomorrow night."

"Stop saying coochie!" she shouts.

"All right, Peach Princess, calm down. I was only trying to help." He starts laughing.

"Grandpa, I love you, but I need to go."

"Wait! We haven't even gotten to talk about your new fella. Logan says you're dating a new guy. He even says this guy's decent, makes a good living, has a good job, and seems to be a family man. Gotta say, I'm pleased to hear this after that thug Pledge."

A strangled sound escapes her as she slices her eyes back to Logan. He stops chuckling immediately. Her eyes flare with irritation then start to shine. She crinkles her eyebrows and purses her lips, then a look of mischief crosses her face.

"Oh, did he? Logan says I'm dating a new fella, huh? Well, Grandpa, I think he's probably trying to avoid telling you all about his new girlfriend. Her name is Melanie, and she's a doll. And for some reason, she's crazy about him. You may want to tell Mom there might be white dresses and wedding bells in the future."

The air is sucked out of the room, and Logan's face goes white as a sheet, all humor gone. He almost looks sick.

There's a slapping sound followed by a robust laugh. "Well, I'll be damned! Wait until I tell your parents. Carl and Sharon are gonna go through the roof. Your mama's been itching for you two to find some good people in your lives. They worry about you being so far from home."

"Yep, tell Mama. Melanie's definitely good people."

All questions about me are gone, or at least temporarily forgotten, as he declares he needs to go. She tells him she loves him and disconnects with glowing satisfaction on her face.

"How could you?" Logan chokes out.

"Seemed like a good way to get him off my back." She shrugs nonchalantly.

"Payback is hell, Grace. Remember that." He leaves in a huff, and I feel kinda sorry for him. If their mom is anything like mine, she's going to be calling in about five minutes.

She gives me a shy smile. "Sorry you had to witness that."

I go to her, plucking her out of the chair and planting a quick kiss on her still smiling lips. "It was the highlight of my day."

"Your day must have been really boring then," she jokes.

"Actually, the day was perfect, because technically, it started with you in my arms until two a.m.," I whisper in her ear.

She shivers against me, and I nip on her earlobe before stepping back and taking her hand.

"How was the *rest* of your day?"

"Good. Bizzy showed up before eight with my brothers close behind her. We ate breakfast while they grilled me about you. About ten minutes after they left, my mom called wanting to know all about you. Then I went to practice, watched a few films, and now I'm here."

Her relaxed expression disappears. "Me? What did you tell them?"

"I told them the truth. Without giving up your grandma's secret, I told them why you went home and what you've been doing the last few years. I explained we're spending time together. I had to stop Bizzy and Shaw from crashing tomorrow night."

"What?"

"They're anxious to meet you, Grace. I made it known this morning that I'm into you."

"You're into me?" she asks so innocently my heart squeezes.

"Sweet Peach, you remember last night when I said curiosity led to crazy?"

She nods slowly.

"That crazy means crazy about you."

"Oh my God," she breathes out in a raspy tone.

"So I held them off tomorrow night, seeing as it's our first official date. But all bets are off after that."

She holds my stare, and I swear she's holding her breath, too. I press her closer. "I want you to come to my game on Sunday. Shaw is getting you and Logan into his company suite."

"Isn't that for business and family?"

"Yes, and my family will be there."

She remains still, staring at me. Uncertainty and apprehension are written all over her face.

"Say you'll come."

"I'll come."

"They're going to love you, Grace. I've told you this already."

"But isn't it a little fast? We just started seeing each other."

"Hell yeah, it's fast, but I'm not worried about that."

Her stare changes, and her eyes start to glow liquid lavender. Then she tells me exactly what I've needed to hear.

"I never forgot you. I've followed you since the day I left school. The draft, your career, your life… Big or small, I didn't care. I wanted to know," she blurts out, and my chest tightens at her admission.

To some guys, this news may be inconsequential, but to me, it answers so many unspoken questions I was hesitant to ask. Even knowing the circumstances, I wondered if she thought of me. She didn't walk away that night and leave us behind. Her life was turned upside down, but she didn't forget me. My pulse races as the gravity of her confession sinks in.

Something in me changes. I may have said I was crazy about her, but the feelings start to magnify. My hands go to her head, my fingers threading through her hair as I tilt her face to mine. My mouth crashes down on hers as I try to convey how much this means to me without using words. She sinks into me, her own hands sliding up my back and gripping my shirt to hold on.

As I kiss her, all thoughts of lost time fade away. None of it matters anymore.

Now, I think about how much fun it's going to be making up for lost time.

Chapter 11

Grace

I float around the gallery in a haze, humming as I wipe down the frames and display cases once more before tonight. The last few times we've had a reset and opening, my nerves have been frazzled, but today, I'm completely calm. Maybe even excited.

Nick and Logan are right; this is our best display to date. Everything is perfect.

There's a rustling in the back, announcing Logan's arrival, and I head to the office to try to smooth over his irritation with me. He barely glimpses up as I walk into his office.

"Hey," I chirp a little too happily.

"Hey," he grumbles.

"Are you still aggravated with me?"

"For what exactly? Outing my non-labeled relationship with Melanie to Grandpa? Or for the fact that I had to talk to Mom last night for forty-five minutes explaining it's new, I'm not going to propose, there are no wedding bells and white dresses in the future, and you must have been dropped on your head as a child?"

"I'm sorry, Logan." Really, I'm not, but an apology is the best way to ask for forgiveness.

"Are you?" He pins me with his eyes, and at this moment looks so much like our dad, I crack.

A giggle escapes, followed by another until I'm covering my mouth and trying to hold back.

"You think this is funny?"

"Kinda, I mean, you started it by telling Grandpa I had a new 'fella'. Do you know how awkward it was for Nick to overhear that?"

"Must not have been too embarrassing, considering I walked in here and you two were going at it like you needed to get a room."

"We were not!"

"Whatever, as Grandpa would say, you were playing a fierce game of tonsil hockey."

"Please don't ever say that again!" My humor slips away as heat creeps up my cheeks.

Satisfaction crosses his face, and he sits down, opening his laptop.

"I know a way to make you forgive me."

"Get married and get Mom off my back?"

"How about an invitation to come with me to the Miami game on Sunday? Not only that, but we'll be in Shaw Bennett's corporate suite."

His eyes widen as his fingers stop in the middle of typing. He can't disguise the excitement on his face. "I suppose that would be one way to help me overlook your little prank."

"I'll get more details this afternoon."

He nods as the front door beeps. I give a small wave and go to see who's here, since we are technically closed.

When I round the corner, I freeze. My heart plummets as I come face to face with Bizzy Bennett and another woman. Their eyes land on me, and Bizzy's mouth breaks into a wide, blinding smile.

"Grace Monroe." She walks to me with her arms extended and embraces me warmly, like she's known me forever.

"It's so good to see you." She lets go but stays close, keeping her hands on my arms.

I'm still stunned speechless, taken completely off-guard.

"Shit, Biz, let the poor girl go. You're scaring her to death," the other woman pipes in, and Bizzy takes a full step back.

I take a good look at the other woman and then look back to Bizzy, suddenly feeling very plain in my casual outfit.

Finally, I find a voice and try to smile, hoping it doesn't appear pained.

"Bizzy," I force out.

"Hi, I'm Claire." Her friend offers a hand, and I shake it feebly.

"I'm Grace."

"God, don't I know it. You're all I've heard about the last twenty-four hours. Lucky for you, I was able to wrangle this one down and wait for a decent hour to ambush you." She points at Bizzy. "If not for me, she'd have been here the second you opened the doors."

Bizzy throws her a dirty look and turns back to me. "Please don't pay attention to Claire. She has no couth. We're thinking of putting her in finishing school to learn some manners."

Claire huffs, reaching out and swatting Bizzy on the shoulder. Tension starts to ease, and I try to relax. "It's nice to meet you," I direct to Claire. "And it's nice to see you again," I tell Bizzy.

"Grace, you look wonderful."

"So do you."

"Jesus, it's like I'm staring at Mila Kunis except for the eyes… Has anyone ever told you that?" Claire blurts out.

"Maybe once or twice," I reply shyly, unsure exactly how to answer. I have heard this before, but I don't see the resemblance.

Bizzy rolls her eyes and mouths 'finishing school'.

My lips twitch until I can't hide my grin.

"I'm sorry to barge in here today, but I couldn't help it. You've been on my mind since yesterday morning. I couldn't wait until Sunday to see you."

"What she means is she's nosy, she's intrusive, and she wasn't *going to* wait until Sunday," Claire tells me.

"Claire! Why the hell did I let you tag along? You're ruining this!" Bizzy stomps.

"Because I'm your best friend."

I observe the two of them glaring and decide immediately I love Claire. But I should probably try to intervene so this doesn't become weird.

"It's a very nice surprise." I direct my statement to Bizzy. "How have you been?"

Right as she opens her mouth, Logan joins us. "Who do we have here?"

"This is Bizzy Bennett and her friend Claire. This is my brother, Logan," I introduce them.

Bizzy's mouth remains hanging, and Claire's eyes are bugging out as she takes in Logan.

"Ladies." He dips his head in their direction, giving me a side-eye. I shrug with a look that lets him know I'm surprised they're here, too.

"Umm, hello, nice to meet you," Bizzy almost stutters and elbows Claire, who mumbles the same.

"I'm going to grab something at the café. Would y'all care for anything?"

I ask for a tea, but they decline, watching him closely as he leaves.

"Holy shit, if I wasn't ridiculously hot on another guy, I'd jump your brother," Claire announces with no shame.

"I'm totally obsessed with my husband, but I agree, your brother is gorgeous," Bizzy agrees.

"Yuck!" I do an exaggerated body shiver.

We all laugh, and the mood in the room lightens.

"So you probably know Nick told us about you two," Bizzy tells me.

"He mentioned it."

"I'm personally thrilled."

"You are?"

"Of course, why wouldn't I be?" She crinkles her eyebrows in confusion.

"I guess I was worried about what you may have thought about—"

"Stop." She throws her hand up. "Don't even go there. You lost someone close to you. Nick explained the situation and the circumstances. I'm sorry for your loss."

I search her face for any sign of apprehension, but all I find is kindness. "Thanks."

"I'm really excited for Nick, Grace. I've never seen him the way he was yesterday morning. He may have tried to act macho around Shaw and Mathis, but I saw right through his act. He's in deep."

"I'm not sure about that. We just started seeing each other." I try to stop the butterflies dancing in my stomach. He's been pretty frank about how he feels, but I don't want to give anyone the wrong impression, especially if this goes south and he changes his mind.

They exchange a look I can't read, and the butterflies stop dancing and turn to lead. My throat goes dry.

"I think we should probably warn her now. She seems clueless." Claire talks to Bizzy as if I'm not standing three feet away.

"It may be better to let it play out." Bizzy also ignores my presence.

"Nope, I believe in the sisterhood. Better to stick together."

"But he's my best friend. He should get to do this his way."

"Biz, give it up. You came here on a mission."

At the term mission, my stomach rolls.

"I did not!"

"Yes, you did, and now we've tweaked the girl to the point of horror. Look at her face."

Both their heads swing to me, and I try to remain calm. Bizzy's face fills with concern, and she gives me a reassuring smile.

"Grace, we don't mean to freak you out. It's all good, promise."

"What's all good?"

"Well, Claire and I have decided if Nicky's anything like Shaw, you're not simply seeing each other. You're together—together."

"Yes, time doesn't mean much to them," Claire adds. "One week could equal one month, one year, one decade..."

"I'm not sure I follow." My conversation with Nick from last night comes crashing back to me, but this is somehow different, hearing it from their perspective.

"Do you know anything about Shaw and me?" Bizzy questions.

"A little."

"Well, here's the timeline... We went away on a Thursday. I thought it was a friendly trip, tagging along to relax while he worked. He was sneaky. Thursday night was normal, even though the signs were there. By Saturday night, we were sleeping together. Monday when we returned, we were a couple. He didn't do slow. He skipped over the concept, claiming we'd wasted enough time. I tried to convince him to wait, and he gave me one week before we went public. Then he blew the lid off my plan."

"Yes, but didn't you know each other for a long time?"

"That didn't matter. When the romantic relationship started, all bets were off. He was ruthless. I see the same thing with Nicky."

"Oh yeah, I agree. The fancy opening tonight, a public date. The game on Sunday, meeting the clan. Grace, your timeline is the same. Get ready." Claire ticks off the events on her fingers, raising an eyebrow at me.

"Ummm, we haven't slept together yet." Don't ask me why I tell them this, but it seems appropriate since Bizzy shared her details.

"Oh, that doesn't matter. Give it a few days," Bizzy states matter of factly as if discussing my sex life is a normal occurrence.

"We don't have the history you and Shaw did."

"That doesn't matter either. I knew he was interested years ago, but it was nothing like I witnessed yesterday."

"He told me he's crazy about me," I announce, not thinking that I'm sharing this with his best friend.

Her expression goes soft, and she gives me a sweet smile. "There you go. Don't fight it. He's one of the three best men I know, and I want him to be happy."

The sincerity of her words sink in, and I totally see exactly what Nick was talking about. They share something so deep and beautiful yet so open.

"I want that, too," I whisper, overcome with emotions.

"Well, okay! Now that we have that out of the way, can you show us around this place? I want a VIP tour," Claire breaks in, coming to link her arm through mine. "I'm not an art girl, but maybe you can help me with that."

Bizzy and I don't talk about Nick again as I lead them around showing off the work and explaining the artists. Logan returns with my tea and gives me a loving kiss on the forehead before locking himself in his office.

It's obvious by the expression on his face that he knows how much this means to me.

"Grace, we're going to be late to your own shindig," Nick yells from my living room.

I breathe in and out a few times, looking at my reflection and second-guessing my dress. It's times like this I really wish I had close girlfriends. They'd be able to tell me if my choice was too much. Self-doubt creeps into my head. This is by far the most provocative dress I've ever owned.

I chose a tea length violet halter dress that has a plunging neckline. The 'V' cuts down almost to my navel. I made sure the material was generous enough to completely cover my cleavage since I'm unable to wear any sort of bra. The saleslady was the one who convinced me this was the perfect dress. Once I explained the occasion, she wasted no time.

Surprisingly, my mom agreed when I sent her pictures that this was the perfect choice. She reminded me that I'm not in Thomasville, and this is appropriate for Miami Beach. She also reminded me that I might be part business owner with a ton of responsibility, but I'm also a twenty-five-year-old woman and need to act it.

I slide into my strappy sandals and fluff my hair once more, ready to face Nick.

He's sitting on the sofa sipping a beer when I walk into the living room. He stops, his bottle midway to his mouth when he sees me. The air in the room changes as his eyes rake up and down my entire body twice. He's quick, setting the beer down and getting to his feet.

"Don't move." Slowly, he walks to me, his eyes locked on mine with each step. The heat of his gaze coats every inch of my flesh.

"Turn around." His voice comes out rough.

I do as he asks, twirling once. When I face him again, he grabs my waist and yanks me to him, crushing his mouth to mine. My knees go weak as his tongue outlines my lips and gently slips inside. I'm thankful he has a tight grip when I grow dizzy and lean into him for support. He breaks the kiss but keeps his lips pressed to mine in a way I've come to love.

"You are fucking breathtaking. The sexiest fucking thing I've ever seen in my entire fucking life."

"That's a lot of fucking."

"Have you looked in a mirror? I can assure you there's more fucking where that came from. You're not leaving my side tonight. Looking the way you do, I'll be in trouble." His eyes can only be described as smoldering as his words singe my skin.

I make a mental note to send the saleslady and my mom flowers and vow to trust them the next time I have an event.

"God, you even smell perfect." He kisses across my cheek to my ear. "Exactly how late can we be and Logan not kill us?"

"Any other night, we'd be safe, but tonight, he may murder me," I say breathlessly as he nibbles gently on my earlobe. Then I think the wrath of Logan may be worth it if Nick keeps it up.

"We can't have him murder you on the night of our first official date. I have plans for us."

"You do?"

"Oh yeah." He backs away, linking my hand with his. "So we'd better go."

My conversation with Bizzy races through my mind.

"Ummm, we haven't slept together yet."

"Oh, that doesn't matter. Give it a few days."

"Grace?" Nick squeezes my hand.

"Yes?" I snap back to reality.

"You okay?"

"Absolutely, why?"

"You seemed to check out for a second. You lost all focus. I've noticed you do that a lot."

Oh my God, this is so embarrassing. I really need to get control over my thoughts. "My family calls it Grace Space…"

"Is Grace Space good?"

"It can be. I honestly don't even know it's happening."

He stares at me a beat then kisses my temple before leading me to the door. The gallery is the last thing on my mind as I wonder what plans Nick has in store.

No amount of planning could have prepared me for the turnout and response to the event. This is by far the largest crowd we've had, and the best news is, the guests are buyers. Logan and I have already sold over a dozen pieces, large and small.

True to his word, Nick hasn't left my side all night. He's been recognized by almost everyone, but to my surprise, they have been respectful of his space. A few of the men have tried to talk about the upcoming game, but Nick has expertly answered the questions and turned the focus back to the purpose of the evening.

I've always considered the gallery to be spacious, but I'm thankful to Logan for setting up tables outside. They allow for people to stay and mingle and thin out the crowd. No one seems to want to leave. Socially, this is the place to be on a Friday night. At least, that's what the reporter in the Arts and Entertainment section of the Tribune reported this morning, and it rings true.

"Sweet Peach, I'm very proud of you," Nick whispers in my ear from behind, his arms resting on my waist. "This is quite a showing."

Goosebumps rise on my arms, and I lean into him comfortably. "You helped," I point out.

"I took directions from the boss. That's not too much."

I want to argue with him, tell him this would have been a much more painstaking process without him, but Logan appears at my side with three glasses of champagne and a huge smile on his face.

He offers two of them to Nick and me then clinks glasses with nothing but a wink. There's a bright flash, blinding me momentarily. When my eyes focus, I recognize the cute young man who arrived with a reporter earlier.

"Chad, you better have gotten my good side, or I'll never invite you back," I tease him.

"Miss Grace, I'm not sure you could take a bad picture." He flirts like an expert.

"Flattery is the best way to ensure you're always welcome here."

"I'm telling the truth. Don't you agree, Six?" He peeks at Nick with so much admiration, my heart swells. He's star-struck.

"Oh yeah, buddy. Grace definitely doesn't have a bad side. Every part of her is gorgeous."

Now it's my turn to swoon. It's one thing for Nick to whisper sweet words to me when we're alone, but to announce it to a stranger—and media member—is big.

"Mr. Monroe, can I get a few of you and Miss Grace together?"

Nick steps back while Logan and I pose for a few shots. When he's done, he thanks us and moves into the crowd with his camera raised, but not before a few words of praise to Nick.

One of our largest clients approaches us with an inquiry about a few pieces, and I mouth to Nick that I'll be right back as I follow Mrs. Shields to answer her questions. He gives me a quick kiss on the cheek, tucks a stray hair behind my ear, and brushes the rest of my hair over my shoulder. The intimate gesture sets my heart racing.

To my surprise, Mrs. Shields not only wants information, but she also wants a full display section for the holiday season in her home. Logan explains the process, and I listen intently, my own pride overflowing at my brother's keen business acumen. He doesn't skip a beat as he rattles off the next steps, promising that we'll handle everything after the waivers and contracts are reviewed. By the time he's finished, Mrs. Shields is glowing with excitement.

I excuse myself, promising to be available for the install at her house, and thank her before walking around to make sure the rest of the guests are okay. When I round the corner, my feet stumble to a halt. Nick is leaning against the wall, still holding two glasses of champagne with his arms crossed. A beautiful brunette is standing close, talking to him. I watch as he says something to her, and she takes it as an invitation to step closer, invading his personal space. She arches until she brushes her chest against his crossed arms.

The air around me changes as jealousy bubbles inside. Nick's face snaps to mine, and his eyes widen as he searches my face. Then a cocky smile crosses his lips, and he puts the glasses down on the podium behind him and strides to me, completely ignoring her. She spins around to watch as he approaches me. The last thing I see is shock on her face before Nick pulls me into him and lays his mouth on mine.

"I missed you," he draws out in his sexy voice. "That may be the last time I let you leave my side tonight. How'd it go?"

I'm about to tell him about my conversation with Mrs. Shields when there's an exasperated sigh behind us.

Nick exhales with irritation and twirls us, tucking me to his side and dropping his arm to my waist. I'm now facing the busty brunette, whose earlier flirty demeanor has changed. She's staring at me with a dismissive glare.

"Nick, I wasn't quite done with my story," she snips.

"Sorry, Shannon, I was distracted." Nick leans down and runs his lips along my hairline.

"Who's your friend?" She doesn't try to hide her disapproval.

"This is my girlfriend, Grace Monroe. Grace, this is Shannon," he tells me, tightening his fingers into my hip. I'm momentarily stunned at him introducing me as his girlfriend.

Our eyes meet, and I fight to keep standing at the expression on his face. His eyes are dancing with happiness, glowing the bright blue I love.

"Monroe, as in Monroe Gallery?" Shannon sneers.

"That's me," I confirm with a short nod.

"Logan did mention his baby sister was coming to Miami."

"You know Logan?" I question her.

"Yes, I'm Shannon Rails," she answers confidently, flipping her hair over her shoulder and poking her chest out.

I remain quiet, tossing the name around in my head, trying to recall if Logan has mentioned her. Nothing comes up. The silence stretches, and her face grows more and more agitated.

"From '*Shannon Says*'," she finishes, as if this will clear up any confusion.

I still have no clue who she is. Nick starts to shake, then coughs, covering his chuckle. "Shannon runs an online blog," he explains to me.

"Oh, that's interesting." I try my best to sound sincere, which is a waste of breath. Her eyes cut to Nick, and she crosses her arms defensively.

"It is hardly just an online blog. It's a social entertainment platform covering the most popular and exclusive events in Miami. I have thousands of followers who rely on my news coverage." She stops short of stomping her foot.

"Well, it's a pleasure to meet you, Shannon." I try to pacify her oncoming hissy fit. "Thank you for coming tonight."

Her eyes slice back to me, clearly still offended by the 'blog' comment.

"Yes, nice to meet you, too. I'd love to chat with you further."

I stupidly assume she'd like to discuss the gallery, seeing as it is why we're standing here. "Sure, call me on Monday and we can schedule a time. I have a full calendar of upcoming events and even a sneak peak into next year."

Her face twists uncomfortably as she processes my words. Then she starts to shake her head with a cynical laugh. "Oh, that's fine, but I'm more interested in your relationship with Nick Bennett. My followers are going to want to know exactly how you landed Sexy Six."

Nick goes stiff beside me, a low growl escaping him. "Shannon, Grace is a respectable business owner. She's not going to be a sleazy piece of gossip for you. Our relationship is private. Our personal lives are personal. Leave it alone."

She glares at him, and her lips tilt in a scary grin. "Whatever you say, Sexy. See you around." She leaves without another word to me and struts outside.

"Sweet Peach?" Nick cups my chin, bringing my face to his. "You okay?"

"She's a piece of work."

"She's a spoiled little rich girl whose daddy has bankrolled her hobby in order to keep her happy. He's a prominent CEO in banking and doesn't know how to say no. He uses his position of power to keep her happy. I've had many run-ins with her little act, and it's easier to ignore her than tell her to fuck off. I did that once, and Shaw almost had a coronary."

"Why, does Shaw like her?"

"No, he hates her ass, but it was poor timing on my part. I was about to do a public bullying campaign with a few other players, and it looked shitty to have me telling a woman to 'fuck off'."

"I think I'll conveniently forget I offered to chat with her, and I'll explain it to Logan to stay away, too."

"Probably a good idea."

He's about to say more when we're interrupted by another couple. This time Nick knows them and steps away from me, embracing the woman gently. There are a few words exchanged before Nick turns to me and introduces me to one of the team doctors and his wife.

Like with Shannon, Nick introduces me as his girlfriend, but this time, there is no judgment, only smiles of approval as he keeps me close.

I glance over my shoulder to see Logan eying me with a supportive smile. He raises his glass in appreciation, and I tip my head in acknowledgment.

Every bit of apprehension I've been carrying around dies.

I can do this.

Scratch that. We can do this, and we can kick ass every step of the way.

Chapter 12

Nick

I hold tight to Grace's hand the entire drive back to her place as she replays the events of the night. It sounds like she and Logan had an extremely successful evening. I'm not surprised when she mentions she had to remove her glass sculpture from the display because of endless inquiries to purchase it. She tries to act blasé about it, but I can hear the tinge of excitement, knowing others loved the piece as much as she does.

"I told you it was incredible and one of a kind," I remind her.

"Yes, it's surreal, though, that people may actually want to buy my work. I'm sure every artist goes through this."

"You've never sold anything before?" This piece of news surprises me. She may not have made a lot of money, but I'd think she'd have sold something in her own gallery.

"I have, but not a glass piece. Since it's my passion, it's where I'd like to focus once I'm comfortable."

"Comfortable? What's going to make you comfortable?" I angle into a space and park, twisting to face her. There's a light glow from a street lamp that barely illuminates her face, and I see her chewing on her bottom lip. I squeeze her hand, encouraging her to look at me. "Grace?"

"I'd feel more confident if I could get more training, learn more techniques, and maybe have a sponsored mentor to help guide my designs. Some people have the talent to do general pieces, but I want to create on a more grand scale."

"So do it."

"I'm trying. I've applied for a program, an internship or apprenticeship of sorts."

"That's great." I reach to unclick her seatbelt and cup her chin, trying to bring her mouth to mine, but she stops me with a hand to my chest.

"I wasn't even going to apply, but Grandpa and Logan insisted. It's a highly coveted program that only accepts a small percentage of applicants based on a number of factors. I'm not getting my hopes up."

"They'd be lucky to have you."

"Well, I'm not so sure, and I'd most likely have to leave Miami for a few months."

The air is sucked out of my lungs at her statement. Leave Miami? She just got here. Hell, I finally found her again. I'm not ready to let her go. Pretty sure I'll never let her go.

Her breath hitches, and I realize I've got a death grip on her hand. "Sorry." I release it and lean back. "Where would you go?"

"Well, it depends. There are some phenomenal renowned artists in the Pacific Northwest, maybe New York, Chicago, Vegas. It all depends."

Hearing these locations, my chest settles. They aren't so bad. "All within a few hours on a plane."

"Yes, but there's some guilt since I just got here and started carrying my weight. There's a lot to do, and I'm so excited. It's like my life is really starting. Not to mention, there's yo—"

She stops herself, but not in time. Even in the darkness, I can tell she's blushing. Without a word, I'm out of the truck and at her door in less than five seconds. She squeaks when I lift her and wiggles as I rush to her elevator. The nighttime security guard gives me a sideways glance, not questioning us. She hides her head in my neck, holding tight.

The ride up, I mentally tell myself to try to calm down. My heart's racing so fast I can feel the pulsing in my veins.

"Keys." I balance her weight in one arm and hold out my palm when we get to her door. She hands them to me, and I let us into her apartment, kicking the door shut and heading straight to her couch. I say a silent thanks she left a lamp on, so I don't trip over anything.

Gently, I lay her down and position myself on my side, pressing her close, making sure not to crush her.

"Say it, Sweet Peach… Finish your sentence. Not to mention what?" I'm desperate to hear what she was going to say.

Her eyes start to shine brightly as she inhales deeply. "You." She exhales. "Not to mention you."

I close my eyes and drop my forehead to hers, an unfamiliar sensation burning through me. Whatever it is, I know it has everything to do with Grace.

"Be assured, I just found you again. I'm not letting you go. If it means I put my ass on a plane to Oregon, Washington, New York—wherever the fuck you are—I'll do it. So don't doubt that for a second. You get this opportunity, we'll make it work."

"Nick—"

I shut her up with a kiss, sweeping my tongue over her lips and then slipping it into her mouth, going deep. She frees one hand and slides it up my chest to my neck and holds me in place, meeting me stroke for stroke until I'm forced to break away for air.

"Would you like to stay here tonight?" she asks breathlessly.

"Thought you'd never ask." I nibble on her bottom lip. "I'd love to."

She smiles against my lips and starts kissing me lazily, gliding her hand up my neck until she's scraping her nails lightly against the stubble on my cheeks. At the same time, her leg starts to slide up, her knee wrapping around my waist. My dick grows painfully hard as soon as our hips are flush together.

Her thigh tightens, and I feel the point of her heel digging into the back of my leg. Images of her naked with nothing but those sexy fucking shoes flash through my mind, and I groan into her mouth. My cock starts to throb as I picture her thrashing under me as I fuck her until she's screaming my name.

Desire starts to flame to the point of explosion, and I slip my fingertips up her thigh, under the material of her dress until I reach soft lace. Slowly, I trace the edges of the lace and slide my hand beneath it, feeling nothing but the silky smoothness of her skin.

I deepen the kiss as my hand gently explores her until I slide my fingers along her heat and circle her clit with my thumb. Keeping my thumb in place, one finger slides into her easily, her muscles contracting. She arches her back while at the same time letting out a whimper. It's the sexiest fucking sound I've ever heard in my life, and my stomach coils as my dick starts to twitch.

Please, God, don't let me fucking blow my load like a teenage boy. I pray silently but don't dare stop my movements, adding another finger and thrusting them slowly as her breathing starts to pick up. She bucks her hips into my hand twice, tearing her mouth away from mine and throwing her head back, panting. My lips trail up the curve of her neck and around her jawline until reaching her earlobe.

"You feel so fucking good, Grace. I want to see you come for me." My thumb presses into her clit once more as I scissor my fingers. Her body tightens, and in a split second, she cries out, my name on her lips escaping in a strangled murmur.

The heat of her pussy gripping my fingers, the feel of her slickness against my hand, and the sound of my name is too much. My balls tighten, and warm liquid starts to slide down my dick. I press harder into her side to try to stop the eruption at the pit of my stomach.

I still, taking deep breaths, and lift up, my eyes locking with hers. She gives me a shy smile, her cheeks flushed and her lips slightly swollen. Her eyes are glossy and a deeper violet than I've ever seen. At this moment, she's more breathtaking than ever.

"Fucking perfect."

"Nick," she breathes out, her voice raspy.

I reluctantly remove my hand and use my knee to push myself up, bringing her with me until I'm sitting and she's straddling my lap. My hands wrap around the back of her head, fingers flexing in her hair. She leans into the touch, her eyes fluttering closed.

I stare at her for a few seconds, caressing her scalp and taking the time to regain my control. As much as I want her, tonight is not the night. There's something I want to do first, and unfortunately, that requires a little more time.

I kiss the underside of her jaw then squeeze her tightly, taking both our weight as I stand. When I get to the door of her bedroom, I gently place her on her feet and frame her face.

"I'm going to get my bag out of my truck and lock up, but I'll be back in a few minutes. Get ready and I'll meet you in bed.

Her eyes crinkle in confusion.

"Trust me on this. There's nothing more I want to do right now than to tear this dress off you, throw you on the bed, and run my tongue over every inch of your skin. My whole body is on fucking fire for you. I've never wanted anything as badly in my life as I do right now." I tilt my hips, hitting her stomach and flexing my still hard cock into her. "Feel what you do to me? This is all you, Grace, but I'm using every ounce of restraint to wait."

"Why?" Her voice is small and laced with doubt. Disappointment shows on her face.

Any other time, with any other woman, I'd have them under me in less than two minutes, not really caring about more than a few hours of fun. But not with Grace. This is so much more. I knew that the second I saw her again.

"Whatever you're thinking, it's wrong."

"But if you want me, why are you holding back?" It's obvious the question makes her uncomfortable, and I think about what an ass I'm making out of myself.

"Because you mean something to me."

"Isn't that good? You mean something to me, too."

"That didn't come out right. You mean more than something to me. This is where the trust me part comes in."

The words hang in the air, and I hold my breath, watching her process them. Finally, she stretches up and brushes her lips across mine.

"I trust you, Nick." There's a flash of sincerity that quickly turns into a wicked gleam. One of her hands moves between us and scales down my abs, stopping at my belt, where I'm still bulging in my pants. Her fingers draw a large circle around my groin, purposely pressing against my head. The touch is light but still one of the most erotic things I've ever felt. My stomach rolls, the familiar need for release from earlier returning. I clutch her hand and bring it to my mouth, kissing her fingertips.

"Sweet Peach, get ready for bed."

I back away and adjust myself as I go to my truck. A memory from last year pops into my head. I'm finally beginning to see exactly what Shaw was trying to explain to me.

I'm never going to survive. Or, should I say, my poor dick is never going to survive. It twitches against my stomach, aching as Grace unknowingly grinds her hip into my groin. She's sprawled halfway across my body, her hair covering my shoulder, her arm across my chest, and her warm breath coating the skin on my throat.

The slickness of her nightgown continues to torment me, just as it's done all night. Knowing the material is the only thing separating me from the silky smoothness of her skin against mine is its own form of torture. I'm a man who can appreciate the allure of a woman's lingerie—the silk, the satin, the lace… the way it hugs curves and teases a man to the edge.

But Grace Monroe in this nightgown has the ability to drive me to the brink of madness.

I try to think about dirty, sweaty, nasty men filing into the locker room and the stench after a brutal day of practice.

Anything to mask the desire searing through my body. It starts to work, until Grace hitches her knee and it grazes my balls. The ache increases.

I should scoot out from under her, go to the bathroom, and take care of this once and for all. Jerking off to the thought of her in bed begins to sound better and better. I fondly remember the way my name sounded coming from her mouth as I watched her come undone for me. Then the mess I faced when I got ready for bed.

As I feared, I may have escaped a full explosion, but the sight and feel of her were too much. It was a first for me, coming in my pants. I cringe at the thought, but my dick comes completely alive, twitching over and over.

Yep, I'm going to the bathroom now. It's the only way.

I slide one leg to the ground and try to dislodge her body without waking her. She mutters something in her sleep, and her arms fall down, her hand resting on my lower stomach. A hiss slips through my lips, and I go still.

Her heartbeat quickens against my ribcage, and I know she's waking up.

"Morning." I kiss a few times along her hairline.

"Good morning. What time is it?" Her voice is full of sleep and comes out hoarse.

"Not sure, but I think it's still pretty early."

She sighs, nuzzling deeper into my chest. "One week could equal one month, one year, one decade…" she mumbles.

"What's that?"

"Hmmm, something Bizzy told me yesterday is beginning to make sense."

"Babe, are you still asleep? You've lost me."

She raises her head and scoots back enough for me to get a good look at her face. I'm momentarily frozen at the sight. I've gotten used to being stunned by her beauty, but this is different. No words come to mind as I stare at her and decide I want to wake up to this every morning.

"Didn't you know? I thought she'd have told you."

"Who?"

"Bizzy, she came to visit me yesterday."

My heart starts racing, and I'm torn between aggravated and relieved. "Did she now?" I ask, trying to hide any reaction.

"Yes, is that okay?"

"Depends… I guess I'm not surprised. I should have guessed she wouldn't stay away and wait until Sunday to reacquaint herself. Seeing as you're in my arms the next morning, she didn't chase you away, so I'd say, so far so good."

"She loves you."

"She does, and I love her."

"She's a special person. I can see why you're so close."

The hair on the back of my neck starts to prickle. This could go either way. I know Bizzy would never be ugly to Grace, but I also know how far her protective streak reaches.

"Want to tell me what she said?"

Grace gives me a rundown of their visit, but nothing seems out of the ordinary.

"So what's this one week could equal one month stuff all about?"

Her face starts to get splotchy, and my curiosity grows.

"Grace?" My hand tightens on her hip.

"Actually, it was Claire who used that phrase. She was trying to make a point, saying that time doesn't seem to matter to the Bennett brothers."

At the mention of Claire, I start to get anxious. "Claire was there, too?"

Grace nods. "She was, and I really like her. She's actually very funny."

I relax because this is true, but Claire can be a little saucy and a lot mouthy. There's no telling what she will say.

"She is. Claire is a great person. She's a bit crazy, but we all love her."

"I'm glad they came by. I mean, at first, it was weird, but it broke the ice before the game tomorrow. It's nice to know I'll be walking into friendly faces."

I knew she would be nervous about meeting the crew tomorrow, but I didn't think about exactly how intimidating it could be. I make a mental note to do something nice for Bizzy and Claire.

My phone starts to ring, and I reach to the ground, fumbling for where I dropped it last night. My new ringtone for Shaw fills the room, and Grace starts to giggle.

"You better have a fucking good ass reason to call me this early on a Saturday morning," I tell him, scooting up to a semi-sitting position. Grace tries to back away, but I hold firm, bringing her closer to me.

"Yeah, lover boy. How about, your ass is plastered all over the internet in a lip-lock with a certain brunette, identified as Grace Monroe."

"Damn, that was fast."

"Are you surprised? Want me to read some of the headlines?"

"Is it necessary?"

"Not really, pretty standard stuff. But when I say plastered, I mean it. People, TMZ, US Weekly to mention a few. Even '*Shannon Says*' has a small piece."

"Yeah, we need to talk about her. She was at the gallery last night. She's going to dig. I insulted her when I explained to Grace she ran a blog. You'd have thought I called her a bottom-feeder."

"She is, in a way."

"Maybe, but I wouldn't call her that to her face. I have some manners."

He starts to chuckle at the same time Grace giggles. I forgot she could hear our conversation.

"Well, thanks for using restraint. Do you want us to make any type of comment?" he asks.

"Nope, I introduced Grace as my girlfriend. That's self-explanatory."

"Perfect. That would be my stance, too, but I wanted to give you the option. You need to be prepared, though. The notifications started at dawn. You and Grace are high news today and probably will be until something more interesting comes along."

"How pissed is Gail?" I ask from experience, knowing she was the one who received the first notification on the wires this morning.

"She's fine." His voice breaks, the reception going fuzzy. Bizzy's voice is muffled on the line, and I start to feel uneasy.

"Shaw… what aren't you saying?"

He doesn't try to hide his amusement. "Let's just say you aren't the highlight of this story. Your girlfriend is getting quite the response."

"What the fuck does that mean?" Grace scrambles away and grabs her iPad, flipping it open and typing. I wait for Shaw to answer, watching her at the same time.

My stomach drops when her hand flies to her mouth and she shouts, "Oh my God!"

"Talk to you later, Sexy." He disconnects, and I lean across the bed.

The instant my eyes land on the two pictures side-by-side, possession and jealousy burn in my blood. Grace is a goddess. There's no other way to describe her. She's pressed close to my front, one hand threaded through her hair, as I kissed her. Her legs, her hair, the dress… she's a walking Sex Siren.

"We look like we're making out in public!" she screeches.

"That's the least of my worries. You have attracted half of the male population in Miami with these shots. Hell, probably more than that considering these are everywhere."

She pounds on the screen, pointing at our kiss. "Do you see this?"

Apparently, she's not worried about my statement. "Yeah, I see it. Did you hear me? I'm going to have to fight off—"

"NICK, get serious! I've never been associated with A-listers before. I didn't know anyone caught us kissing." Her voice goes to a high pitch, and I fight back the laughter. She leers at me and narrows her eyes. “This is not funny!”

I take the iPad from her and toss it to the end of the bed, then I tug her close, trapping her under me. “It wasn’t funny at first glimpse when I realized you are now going to be dubbed a sex symbol with those fucking legs in that dress, but watching you freak out about a kiss makes it comical. I’m glad they have a shot of you in my arms. Maybe it will keep some of the vultures away.”

“Nick!” Her screech becomes muffled when I bury my head in her neck, kissing a trail to her collarbone.

“Hmm?” I mumble.

“Are you taking me seriously?”

“Not especially. I have other things on my mind.”

“Should we talk about this?”

“Nope, we should stop talking and go back to how I should have started the morning. Kiss me.” I balance on an elbow and cup her chin. “Forget about everything but this.” I skim my lips over hers. “Forget the phone calls, the press, the pictures… I want you to remember nothing but waking up in my arms.”

Our eyes meet, and I watch whatever she was thinking start to melt away. “How do you do that?”

“What?”

“I don’t know how to explain it, but somehow, you calm me. My mind was racing, thinking about those pictures and being the object of hordes of gossip, but when you looked at me like that, it disappeared.”

There’s so much I want to say, but my head screams that it’s too much too soon. So instead, I grin and kiss the tip of her nose. “It’s part of my charm?”

“Don’t get cocky.”

“I’m not cocky. I’m needy, and right now, I need a kiss from my hot as shit girlfriend who is far too sexy for her own good. We have about three minutes before both our phones start blowing up with this, and I’d like to spend that three minutes kissing you.”

Her face relaxes, and a small smile forms. "Well, when you put it that way—"

I don't let her finish before I lower my mouth and slide my tongue between her lips. She doesn't put up a fight, welcoming me and following my lead.

Less than two minutes later, our phones start ringing, but neither of us moves to answer them.

Chapter 13

Grace

"MAMA! You have to quit calling," I hiss into the phone and search for somewhere to hide. I duck behind a large tree in the corner and shift my overnight bag that is digging painfully into my shoulder.

"This is the last time. I promise," she lies. I know from experience, Sharon Monroe is keeping a list, and every time a new question pops into her head, she writes it down and calls, wanting instant answers.

"What do you need now?"

"Why are you whispering?"

"Because I am in a hallway and I don't want Nick to hear me."

"Ohh, is it fancy?" She couldn't care less of my situation.

"Yes, Mom. He lives on the twentieth floor of a luxury high-rise. It's very fancy. Now, can I go? I promise to call you tomorrow before the game."

"I only need a minute."

"Mom, I don't think you understand. I'm hiding behind a decorative palm tree, slinked up to a wall. If someone walks out, they will think I'm a stalker. Can I PLEASE call you tomorrow?"

"It's not every day that a mother finds out her only daughter is dating a famous football player. I'm still upset I had to learn this from the internet. So no, you can give me a minute of your time."

Guilt… I'm convinced my mom has mastered the art of guilt. It's not so much her words but how she uses them—a touch of hurt, a dash of accusation, and the wounded tone that works every time. Even Logan crumbles when Mom pulls out the guilt card.

"One minute, Mom, then I have to go."

"Word has spread fast. Our phone is blowing up. The latest is Mary Cobb. She wants to know if you are going to bring Nick with you to the fall festival. Says if so, she wants to have a little parade. Went as far as to ask for a special invite to lunch to meet him and bring her family."

I want to hurl at the thought. Leave it to my town to make a circus out of this. "First off, I'm not sure Nick could or would come to the festival. Let's remember he plays professional football for a living, and that usually means every single weekend. Secondly, absolutely no parade. And lastly, you can tell Mary Cobb to keep her meddling, nosy, good for nothing questions to herself. It is none of her business who or what Nick and I are doing. If she gives you lip, you remind her about finding her granddaughter with her skirt around her waist with the last guy I invited to an event."

"Grace Rae!" Mom tries to sound offended, but her giggle gives her away.

"Mom, you know it's true, and that's your way to shut her up. Remind her of Pledge, and she'll back off."

Now my mom is outright howling into the phone.

"Can I go now?"

"Yes, darling. I won't bother you again, and I'll keep your grandpa from the phone, too. But I had to share with you the gall of Mary. Thought it might add some humor to your night."

"Love you, Mama." I disconnect and take a deep breath. Realization hits me. That wasn't my mom using her powers of guilt; that was her way of knowing exactly what I needed to ease the nervous anxiety of coming to Nick's for the first time.

I'm not paying attention and give a little shout when I bump into something solid. Immediately, I smell the familiar scent of Nick and know the solid wall is not actually a wall. His arms encircle my waist, and I peek up, praying he didn't hear any of our conversation.

No such luck. His lips are twitching.

"How much did you hear?"

"Enough to know you've ended my dreams of having a parade and that Mary Cobb's a meddling, nosy, good for nothing with a granddaughter who sounds like a slut. But I should probably thank her for exposing Pledge for the asstool he was."

"So you heard it all?" I mumble, pounding my head on his chest.

"Not yet." His hands gently rub my lower back.

"Well, you heard most of it."

"I didn't hear you invite me to the festival. I may play professional football every weekend, but if I got an invite to this festival, I'd do my damnedest to get there."

I snap my head up with my mouth hanging open, and then I check his forehead for signs of a fever. He has no idea what he's saying. "You want to come to a dinky festival in Thomasville?"

"Are you going to be there?"

"Yes, Logan and I are kinda expected to be there."

"Well, then yes, I want to come."

"I'm afraid you'll be swarmed, and no one will respect your privacy."

"Why don't you invite me and let me worry about the rest?"

"And my family is crazy. They have no boundaries."

He starts to walk backwards, taking me with him. "I know about crazy families with no boundaries. Tomorrow, you get to meet mine."

"Yes, but this is different. South Georgia and South Florida might as well be two different countries. Crazy down here has its own level of sophistication. Thomasville crazy is a different world."

"I can't wait to experience this level of crazy." He leads us into a door and kicks it shut when I'm cleared.

"You seriously have no idea what you're in for."

"You're killing my ego here, Sweet Peach. Don't make me invite myself."

"I'm trying to save you from potential mayhem. These people remember you from your college days. Wanting to throw a parade is the tip of the iceberg. The second you step foot into town, we'll be bombarded."

He stops us, sliding his hands low until they are cupping the cheeks of my ass. He squeezes lightly, giving me a sexy grin. "I'm not worried about that, Grace. If you're there, I want to be there. I want to be anywhere you are, and it seems like a perfect time for me to meet your family. I'm not making any promises, but I'll try my best to be there. So now, are you going to invite me?"

Like this morning, he calms my nervous thoughts. The idea he wants to be with me regardless of the madness he's going to face is almost incomprehensible, but the determination on his face says it all.

He doesn't care. He wants to come home with me.

"Nick, would you like to come home with me for our town's annual fall festival? My family will be there and would love to meet you. It's in four weeks."

He smiles triumphantly and nods. "I'd love to come. I'll talk to Shaw and work on it. Shaw can make miracles happen."

I throw my arms around his neck and bury my face in his chest. "The miracle will be if you make it out unscathed and still talking to me," I mutter into his shirt.

In two moves, he swipes the bags off my shoulder, dropping them at our feet, and picks me up, this time moving forward.

I tilt back to ask him what he's doing, but the words die on my tongue when I catch sight of the view behind him. My eyes wander everywhere, taking in the grandeur of his condo. Floor to ceiling windows with views of the ocean, high ceilings, and incredible architectural design are the basic layout. An enormous, plush sectional sofa faces an equally enormous television mounted on the wall. There are no separating walls; it's all one large space, with a hallway off the kitchen, which I assume leads to the bedrooms. This is a showcase.

There are some personal touches scattered throughout the space, but besides a few pictures and knick-knacks, the walls are bare. My artistic mind blows up with the possibilities of prints that would look terrific.

I'm cataloging my current inventory in my brain when he sits us down and starts to kiss along my jawline. My thoughts become fuzzy as his lips travel down and across my collarbone, sucking lightly on the curve of my neck.

"Your place is incredible." The words come out raspy and low.

"Thanks," he rumbles against the sensitive skin.

"I've never seen anything quite like it."

"Ummhmm..." His hands start roaming, finding their way under my shirt and up my back. He presses forward until I fall into him and grab onto his shoulders for support. "Can we maybe talk about my place later?"

"I was just commenting on its beauty."

"There's something much more beautiful on my mind right now. I've been waiting for you all day. The smell of your skin, the taste of your lips, the feeling of having you wrapped around me... that's what I'm concentrating on."

I'm stunned speechless as his hands explore my sides until they capture my breasts and start to massage gently. He doesn't move my bra but skims his thumbs lightly over my hardened nipples, circling them at the same time his mouth trails up my neck. He's no longer kissing me but teasing me by lazily licking in the same circular rhythm as his thumbs.

Without real skin contact, he's sending a blazing sensation throughout my body. Each nerve ending comes alive, and I turn off my brain and allow myself to feel.

I tighten my grip on his shoulders and flex my hips down at the same time. His rock hard erection slides between my legs, and I bite my tongue to keep from moaning.

In less than five minutes, and while still fully clothed, he has me hotter than I've ever been in my life. I crave his touch and arch my chest into his hands, silently asking for more. He reads me easily and slips his hands under the material of my bra.

Exactly like last night, at first contact, a thrill shoots up my spine, and I can no longer remain quiet, whimpering at the touch. The scruff on his face rubs along my cheeks as he moves his mouth to mine and starts to kiss me, slowly at first, teasing me. The sexual tension grows as the air thickens.

An aching need takes over, and I break away, tearing my shirt over my head and stripping out of my bra, so he has full access. His hands lower to my ribcage, his eyes taking in the sight of me. When his gaze meets mine, he's fighting for control.

Without taking his eyes from mine, he skims one hand up my ribs until he's cupping me. His tongue darts out, tracing my nipple, then he sucks it all the way into his mouth. My body responds involuntarily, arching further into him, encouraging more. Our eyes remain locked as he does the same with the other side. The erotic sight becomes too much, and I can't take it, my head falling back, moaning into the room.

With each swirl, lick, and suck, my insides twist and burn, needing more. Losing patience, I grind my hips roughly and tighten my knees at the same time, making full contact with his cock.

He gives an approving growl and at the same time bites down harshly. Something inside me snaps, and I slide my hands up to grip the back of his neck, holding on for my life. My body rocks against his, my hips never losing contact. A coiling tightens in the pit of my stomach then starts to unravel, traveling everywhere through me.

He swivels his hips twice, and I can no longer hold back. I give a panted whimper as I come apart, pleasure igniting everywhere. I barely hear his voice but feel a rumble vibrate against my chest as he goes still.

Neither of us moves, his hands still clutching my breasts, as we regain our breath. My heart thunders in my chest to the point I know he can not only feel it, but probably hear it, too.

The fog starts to clear, and I realize what has happened. No longer clouded with lust, I let go of his neck and bring my hands to cover my face.

"No way, Sweet Peach." He quickly turns, twisting us so I'm pinned beneath him on the couch. I have no strength to resist when he lowers my elbows down and traps my palms to his chest. "No hiding from me."

"I can't believe that happened," I admit, knowing my cheeks and face are flushed from more than the orgasm.

"Why the hell not?"

"I just dry humped you on your couch!"

"You weren't alone. I was with you every second."

"You were being sweet and sexy. We were starting to make out, then I practically... practically..."

"Turned sexy into fucking hot? Gave me the first taste of your perfect tits? Not to mention, I came in my shorts the second you did?"

Our eyes lock, and the heat from his gaze awakens something inside me. All embarrassment fades, and I wrangle my hands free and frame his face. "We have a thing for sofas, huh?"

"Fuck yeah, we do, and if you won't pitch a mammoth-size hissy fit, I'm buying you a new one as soon as possible."

"Why? I love my sofa."

"I didn't say we were getting rid of it, because it holds pretty fond memories, but I'm six-foot-four. Your sofa is built for much smaller people. I can't even lay fully out with you, much less other things."

At the mention of other things, my stomach does a full flip. I move my thumbs to rub over his lips. "We could always go to the bed." I love the flame in his eyes as he understands what I'm suggesting.

"Oh, babe, we're going to go to the bed, the kitchen, the dining table, everywhere and anywhere... You can bet on that." He flexes his hips into my thigh, proving he's still hard. "But for now, I need to get cleaned up and take my girlfriend to a proper dinner. Then we have to come back here and get ready for game day. I have a very specific regimen I follow."

"Regimen, huh?"

"Yeah, and tonight, it includes round two. Maybe this time I won't mark you."

I peer down to see his bite mark surrounding my nipple, his teeth marks indented into my skin. "I think I like it," I admit. "It's pretty hot."

"Jesus Christ, I'm going to come again if you don't stop."

He turns serious as he pushes up and stands, offering his hand. My eyes go immediately to the spot on his shorts, and I burst into laughter, unable to help myself. He looks down, adjusts himself, and scoops me into his arms.

"You think it's funny that you've reduced me to a fifteen-year-old boy with no self-control?" He starts walking toward the hallway I noticed earlier.

"I wouldn't classify you as a boy, but it is hilarious."

He stops at the door of what I assume is his bedroom and lowers his mouth to my ear, nipping on my earlobe before he speaks. "Laugh all you want, Grace, but I promise you soon, you'll see exactly what happens when I have no self-control."

Chapter 14

Grace

"Ready for this, Gracey Pacey?" Logan jokes, elbowing me gently. "Big step today."

"Shut up, Logan. I'm already frazzled. Can't you be supportive?"

"I'm here, aren't I?"

I slide my eyes to him and roll them in a huff. "Please, you would have killed me if I came without you."

"Someone had to be here to witness the legendary Peach Princess of Thomasville meeting Sexy Six's parents. This will go down in history. It's my job to report the specifics."

"If you don't stop antagonizing me, I'll throw you over this railing!" I point to the banister behind us.

"But it's so fun."

"I'm never, ever—" I don't get to finish my sentence before my name is called.

Bizzy is standing in a doorway, waving rapidly with a welcoming smile. Shaw is behind her, his hands on her shoulders possessively, but his eyes are locked on me.

"Bizzy and Shaw," I murmur to remind Logan, quickening my steps.

"You're finally here." Bizzy shifts from Shaw and embraces me tightly. "I've been watching for you. Everyone is *so* excited you're here," she whispers and gives me an extra squeeze before stepping back into Shaw.

Logan introduces himself to Shaw; then it's my turn. I swallow hard and extend my hand, hoping he can't see through my nervous smile. "Hi, I'm Grace. I've heard a lot about you."

He drops his eyes to my hand then raises them to mine. A bead of sweat slides down my back as seconds pass. He completely shocks me by sidestepping Bizzy and getting into my personal space. His arms wrap around me as his lips brush my cheek. "You have no idea how nice it is to meet you, Grace."

His voice is smooth and deep, sending a different kind of chill up my spine. I hug him back, having to balance on my toes not to face-plant into his chest. Just like Nick, Shaw is much taller than me.

The moment is interrupted when a loud screeching comes from inside the room. "We're waiting! Let her go! Damn, Shaw, you're as bad as Biz." I recognize Claire's voice and feel Shaw tense before moving away.

"She's very mouthy," he starts to explain, causing me to laugh at the same term Nick used.

"I already met her and really like her."

"God help us all."

Logan steps to my side and bends to my ear. "You got this." His words fuel my confidence, and I square my shoulders, turning to the room. The instant I step inside, I'm swooped into a hug from Claire then introduced around.

When I meet Maria and Seth Bennett, there's no denying the Bennett brothers got their looks from their parents. They immediately make me feel comfortable, reminding me a lot of my own parents.

The conversation is easy as they ask Logan and me about the gallery and comment on the local write-up in today's Arts Section. Logan tries to play off their praise, but I know he's beaming inside.

Mathis joins us and stands close, swinging an arm over my shoulder. "You ever been to an NFL game before, Grace?"

"Actually, no. This is my first."

He clutches his chest and gasps. "You're kidding!"

Shaw comes to my other side, looking at his brother as something passes between them. I'd swear Shaw's lips twitch as he jerks his chin.

"Well, since it's your inaugural game, I think we need to give you a special present. Make this day memorable…" Mathis goes on and glances at Claire.

She smiles big, walking over with her arms behind her back. When she gets to us, she hands me a bag. "This is for you."

All eyes are on me as I accept the gift. Bizzy's face is a slight shade of pink, and her lips are pursed together. I can't tell if she's upset or about to laugh.

I dig in and pull out an official Miami team jersey and squeal. "Oh, wow! This is so great!" I hold it up to show everyone then toss it on over my tank top. It swallows me, but I don't care.

"Don't get any ideas, Logan. This belongs to me," I tease, knowing he's got to be biting back jealousy. But when I catch his eye, his face is dancing with humor.

I glance down, smoothing it out. There's no chance to ask what he's smirking about because there's a loud rumbling noise behind me.

"What the hell are you wearing?" Nick's voice booms, and I jump to find him standing in the doorway looking disgusted. He's partially suited up in his football pants, but waist up, he's wearing a tight tank top, outlining every ridge and muscle.

"Hey! It's my new jersey. Isn't it awesome? Your brothers gave it to me."

His eyes dart between Shaw and Mathis, and a muscle in his jaw starts to tick.

"Sweet Peach, take that shit off." This is not a request but a demand.

I'm stunned by his rude behavior.

"Nick, what's gotten into you?"

"Grace, get that shit off of you," he repeats.

"Absolutely not!" I snap back.

There's a split second of silence then an eruption of laughter from everyone in the room except Nick and me. A large black man steps from behind Nick and comes into the room with an enormous smile spread across his face.

"I personally think that shit looks great on you," he tells me then hustles to the side as Nick's arm comes out to punch him.

He's very familiar, but there's no time to think of his name before Nick stalks to me and raises my arms. In one swoop, he's torn the jersey over my head and tossed it. Logan gets a fast catch before it hits the floor.

"Nicolas!" Maria scolds him unconvincingly.

"I don't see anything funny," he tells no one in particular.

I'm frozen in place, trying to figure out what the hell is happening.

"You may not find it funny, but it's fucking hilarious." Shaw slaps Nick on the shoulder.

"Bizzy." Nick tips his head to her, and she hands him another bag similar to the one Claire handed me earlier.

He rips it open, takes out another shirt, and tugs it over my head, not bothering to put my arms through. Then he inspects me with a look of satisfaction. "Much better."

"What the hell is wrong with you?" I hiss.

"You are not wearing Jarvis's jersey, babe."

"Jarvis? As in Eddie Jarvis?"

"That's me." The guy who walked in with Nick raises his hand in the air.

Another round of laughter rolls through the room, and it hits me. I look at the jersey Logan has confiscated and is now wearing proudly.

"Oh my God! You are an idiot!" I try to swat at his chest, but my arms are still inside the jersey, and I realize I resemble Cousin It.

I arrange myself properly and notice the number six now on my chest. Nick sweeps my hair over my shoulder and bends, lowering his mouth to my ear. "I may be an idiot, but you will never wear another man's name on your back." He wraps his arm around my waist and lifts me up to him, kissing me gently.

"One damn week!" Claire announces to the room, and I start laughing against Nick's lips. He chuckles, too, glancing over my shoulder at her, then cuts his eyes to Shaw and Mathis.

"You guys are assholes."

"I'd be careful who you're calling an asshole considering I got your ass up here before the game," Shaw tells him.

"What are you doing here?" It occurs to me he should be on the field warming up.

"I had to see you," he answers with no reservation, clearly not caring who hears.

"More like he was making me crazy in the locker room, wondering if you'd arrived yet." Eddie comes to stand beside us. "By the way, let me officially introduce myself. I'm Eddie." He takes one of my hands, bringing it to his mouth. Before his lips make contact, it's jerked away and Nick growls.

"Hands and lips to yourself."

This gets another round of laughs.

Eddie flashes a blinding smile and winks at me. "Six, we better go before Coach has a coronary."

"Yes, you had a ten-minute clearance. Any more than that and I'll have to answer to your whole coaching staff. They think you're doing a surprise drop-in for Mom's birthday." Shaw taps his watch. "You need to get down there."

"Crenshaw Bennett! You did not lie on my behalf." Maria props her hand on her hip.

"Mom, it wasn't really a lie. Your birthday is next week," Nick points out. "Besides, desperate times call for desperate measures." He slices his eyes back to me.

"Save the sweet talk for after we win this game." Eddie jerks his head to the door and waves goodbye to the group.

Nick threads his fingers in mine and leans over to kiss his mom on the cheek before leading me a few feet away. The crowd all yells their good lucks, except for Maria and Bizzy who both scream, "Be careful," at the same time.

"I hope you kick ass out there," I tell him when we reach the doorway.

"Always, babe, but it's even sweeter to know the prettiest girl in Miami is here today."

"Charmer."

"Only for you."

"I'll be screaming."

"Oh, I have no doubt about that. Before this day is over, you'll definitely be screaming."

He looks at me with such raw heat, my skin starts to burn. There's no missing the meaning behind his words; he's not referring to the game. Suddenly, I feel exposed, knowing everyone is watching as he stares at me with fire in his eyes.

"I think I finally understand the meaning behind Sexy Six, seeing you in my number with my name on your back."

"Stop." It comes out in barely a whisper.

"Tonight, I want you back at my place."

"Okay."

"Kiss me. I have to go."

Without hesitation, I lift my mouth to his and close my eyes. His tongue sweeps across my lips, and I open slightly, giving him access. Too quickly, he ends the kiss and pecks my cheek then disappears.

There's a breathy sigh behind me, and I swallow hard, paste on a smile, and turn to face an entire room with knowing looks.

"You are kidding me!" I say a little too loud, which gets a chuckle from Seth.

"That was clearly pass interference! Is the ref blind?" Bizzy joins, jabbing her finger in the direction of the field. Shaw clamps her hands and gets in close, kissing her forehead. Then I watch as he says something only she can hear, and she melts into his body.

"Can you promise me that you'll never be that sickening?" Claire plops down, handing me a drink.

"Nope, I think it's sweet."

"Of course you do," she rumbles.

The quarter ends, and the teams run off the field as halftime starts. Mathis motions to Logan and walks up to Shaw. They give a quick wave, explaining they'll be back in a while.

Seth and Maria mention going to visit friends in the stands, and the other people in the suite all go in different directions. I met a few of them earlier, most of them from Shaw's office.

"Finally, we have a few minutes alone." Bizzy sits on my other side with a beer, clinking it to the rim of my glass. "How's your first NFL experience?"

"The best. I never expected it to be so fun," I reply honestly.

"It's a lot more fun when you have someone to root for."

"I agree." Claire nods furiously. "But let's get to the good stuff."

Both of them look at me expectantly. "What?"

I take a large swallow of my drink and hold back a cough when the liquor burns down my throat. I'm learning that Claire pours with a heavy hand.

"Don't 'what' us. We want the deets. Obviously, something happened between Thursday and today. Nick has never come up to a suite before a game, and he pulled out the possessive card the instant he saw you wearing Jarvis's jersey. Not to mention the kiss in front of everyone." Claire smooches her lips and makes a loud smacking sound.

The warm and fuzzy feeling returns as Bizzy makes her own kissing sound. "The kiss was classic."

"We haven't slept together yet," I blurt with no hesitation.

Smooth, Grace.

"Not long now," Claire surmises. "If today was any indication, you're in for a treat when you get home."

Bizzy gives a twinkly giggle until she snorts, nodding again.

I don't know what comes over me; maybe it's the alcohol, maybe it's the atmosphere, but whatever it is, I decide to open up to these girls. "Actually, he won't have sex with me. We've come close, but he somehow stops us. We've spent the last few nights together, and he never lets it go too far. It's a little unnerving."

"He's waiting." Bizzy lays a hand on my arm.

"On what?"

"Today."

"Today?"

"It was important to him for you to see this, be here watching him play, meeting his family... He may be Sexy Six to most of the world, but he's old fashioned and traditional. He cares about you."

"Fucking voodoo ESP," Claire mutters.

"I care about him, too. I can't believe how much in such a short period of time. Usually, I'd never, ever be talking about this. We just reconnected. Does it make me a hussy that I want him to have sex with me?"

"No," both reply at the same time.

"I told you, I slept with Shaw almost immediately," Bizzy reminds me.

"But you'd known him forever," I counter.

"I slept with Mathis two days after meeting him," Claire announces.

My and Bizzy's heads both snap to her so fast my neck cracks.

"You what?" Bizzy chokes out. "How didn't I know this?"

Claire shrugs her shoulders and takes a drink. "I didn't tell anyone until now. It's happened a few times, but then he told me we had to stop."

"When?" Bizzy's face goes pale.

"It happened the first time when he came to visit Nick at school, the weekend you introduced us."

"Why didn't you tell me?"

"Because I thought it was a one-time thing, but then it happened the next few times we saw each other."

"Why'd he tell you it had to stop?" My curiosity runs wild.

"It was a huge coincidence Mathis was doing his residency at the same hospital Bizzy and I got job offers. According to him, there was too much at stake. He was starting his career, and the way we were connected through Bizzy was high risk, so he ended it."

"Were you into him?"

"Yep, totally crazy about him. I had heart-shaped glasses on, but there was no way in hell I was going to tell him that, so I agreed and we went back to being friends. It's been a few years now, and we get along great."

"I can't believe this!" Bizzy mumbles. "I mean, it makes sense, the way he looks at you."

"He's super hot… All of them are," I say, hoping not to offend.

"Oh, yeah, Mathis is totally hot. That's one reason it's so hard to stay away. I had too much to drink at Bizzy's wedding and told him the same thing."

"Oh my God, what did he say?"

"He didn't say much, because I jumped him, and we fucked like animals."

Bizzy gasps, and I look between them, waiting for an explosion. Claire seems unfazed.

"I had to show him what he was missing. Now, the ball is completely in his court."

"You are my new hero," I say in awe.

"Enough about me. Let's go back to you. Tell us more about this heavy petting. I agree with Bizzy; tonight's your night." Claire effectively changes the subject, but not without Bizzy giving her a look that plainly reads *'we'll be discussing this situation about Mathis later'*.

Claire gets another round of drinks, and I commence telling them about my weekend with Nick. I give them detail-by-detail about Friday night and Saturday morning. Bizzy groans when I mention Shannon and her blog, telling me Shaw already told her what Nick shared. When I get to the part about Nick overhearing my conversation with my mom, Claire starts to cackle. Lastly, I tell them about last night.

"He took me to this Cuban restaurant for an awesome dinner. Everyone seemed to know who he was but didn't intrude. We had an amazing dinner, talking, laughing, and joking about stupid things. It was so natural. Then he took me back to his place, and we went to bed. There was some fooling around until he stopped. Then nothing—absolutely nothing. No more fooling around, no more making out. We shared some really hot and heavy moments until he tucked me to his side to fall asleep. I woke this morning, still curled up next to him. We had a light breakfast, and he walked me to my car. I didn't speak to him again until he came up here before the game."

When I'm done, Bizzy's eyes are shining, and she has a dreamy glow on her face. "He's taking a trip home with you. That's so awesome." For a second, I think she may cry.

"Told you, girl. One week, one month… all that jazz. Time doesn't matter."

"I hope so," I admit, knowing the intensity of my feelings toward him.

"Give me your phone." Claire holds her palm out, and I drop it into her hand.

She tells me as she programs in her and Bizzy's numbers, then calls her own phone so she has mine. "Let's meet for dinner on Tuesday night. I have a feeling there will be a lot to discuss."

The suite starts filling back up as the third quarter starts. Logan, Shaw, and Mathis return, explaining they went to the tunnel to try to find out what the game plan was for second half. Logan acts cool, but I can tell he's enjoyed every minute of the game so far.

After several more cocktails, the girls and I alternate between watching the game and gossiping. I almost fall out of my chair when Bizzy tells me the story about her and Shaw. My heart physically hurts when she explains that he has a baby with another woman who tried to split them apart while they were dating. I'm not sure I could survive what she did. Even more surprising is the love that shines through when she talks about her stepson, Brayden.

Shaw must overhear her gushing because he looks at her, his own face growing soft, and his eyes dart to her stomach. She starts to blush and explains they are trying for a baby of their own now. Then the conversation takes a turn when she replays the events from Labor Day, when Mathis and Nick snuck on their boat and crashed their romantic getaway weekend to the Keys.

It's my turn to howl as she gives blow by blow of the debacles, including the fact she unknowingly made a sex tape.

The rest of the afternoon flies by, and I can't remember ever having this much fun. Not to mention the fact that Miami wins the game. This easily goes down as one of the best days of my life.

Chapter 15

Nick

I hear the water turn on and off in my bathroom as I hang up my suit jacket and wait impatiently for Grace to finish. If I had it my way, she'd be naked by now, but somehow, she slipped by me the minute we got here and locked herself in the bathroom.

After every win, I ride a high for hours, energy pulsing through my veins. But tonight, there's a different energy driving me. Anticipation seeps into my bones, needing only her.

The door opens, and when I see her, my body goes solid. Thoughts of peeling her out of my jersey vanish as I stare at her in a short teal nightgown with orange lace covering her tits.

My team colors have never looked so sexy.

She strolls to stand in front of me, swaying with each step and keeping her eyes pinned to mine.

"You're wearing my colors."

"I am. Thought it would be appropriate if you won."

My fingers glide across her collarbone and to the base of her neck where her pulse races.

"You look incredible."

She runs her hands up my chest until reaching my neck then rises up to kiss me. My own hands move to the back of her head, my fingers tangling in her hair as I deepen the kiss.

Our passion ignites the second her chest presses against mine. I turn and walk us backward until her knees hit the bed and she falls, bringing me with her. It takes all my self-control to tear away and see her face.

"Are you sure?" I pant.

She nods, smiling seductively, and starts to unbutton my shirt. The instant her fingernails graze over the skin of my stomach, things turn frantic. My clothes go flying. When I'm in nothing but a pair of boxers, I lean back over her and kiss her again, this time with urgency.

Her ankles lock around my hips, and she grinds into me, moaning into my mouth. My cock swells, and the familiar sensation coils in my stomach.

Fuck if I'm going to come in my pants again. I break away from her mouth and place open-mouthed kisses down her body until I'm kneeling in front of her. The matching teal panties are the only thing in my view. What's underneath the silk has the power to be the end of me.

Sex has always been natural for me—a release, a thrill. But tonight, it feels foreign because of the depth of intimacy. This will never be just sex with Grace. The chase is over. Grace will finally be mine… completely and undeniably mine.

My mouth starts to water, and I slip the panties off slowly, prolonging the hunger threatening to unleash. I throw them over my shoulder and take the time to savor seeing her laid out beautifully before me. Gently, I spread her legs and kiss my way up, paying attention equally to each leg and feeling them tremble against my lips. When I finally reach her center, I nuzzle my cheeks back and forth, using my stubble to heighten her arousal. She grows wetter, and sexy sounds fill the room. I can't take anymore and finally stroke my tongue along her slit and suck hard.

"Oh my God!" Grace bucks into me, her fingers scoring through my hair and digging into my scalp.

Her taste coats my tongue, and I growl, increasing my speed. With each lick and suck, I become addicted, savoring her. I alternate between fast and slow, licking a pattern over and inside her, craving more. She thrashes against my face with tiny whimpers, her knees locking on my neck right before she screams again.

"Nick!" her legs quake as she lets go and goes limp.

If it wasn't for the throbbing between my legs, I'd stay here all night, doing nothing but licking her, just to hear my name like that over and over.

But I can't do it. There's a primal need brewing inside, needing only one thing, and that's to be inside Grace.

I reach into my nightstand and get a condom then kiss my way back up her body, this time taking the nightgown with me. She lifts her arms to help me, and I toss it aside, letting it join the other clothes scattered around the room. Then in one swift motion, my boxers are gone and my mouth closes in on her nipples, sucking each one until she starts to shiver.

I lift her and crawl back, laying her out over the full length of the bed, and cover her body with my own.

Her eyes move to the condom then back to me with appreciation. She takes it from me and opens it, rolling it on so slowly my dick starts to ache.

"Look at me, Grace," I demand roughly.

Her hair is spread across my pillows, her face flushed and her eyes shining. I'm going to remember this for the rest of my life.

"Wrap your legs around my waist, baby, and keep your eyes on mine."

She does as I ask, aligning us perfectly. I sink into her wet heat, feeling every single inch as she welcomes me. Her eyes flutter closed when I'm all the way inside. The vision burns into my brain as I start to move. She arches her neck and back, angling me deep, and lets out a purr of approval.

Slow and gentle fly out the window at the sound, and I start to surge in and out. Her eyes fly open, smoldering with desire, which pushes me harder.

In a flash, I'm back on my knees, this time with her folded around me. Every part of our bodies are touching as I pound into her from below.

"Nick," she cries out, throwing her head back and thrusting her chest up.

"Let go," I say as I bite down lightly on her nipple.

She clenches hard as she starts to come, bringing me over the edge with her. Sparks of electricity shoot off as I empty myself into the woman who holds all the power over me.

I wait for panic to set in, but all I feel is really fucking great.

"Wake up, Sweet Peach." I skim my hands down her side and love the goosebumps that rise at my touch.

She burrows her face deeper into my pillow, turning so the sheets fall to her hip.

She's completely naked, and it takes all of my control to stay at her side and not crawl back into the bed.

"Fuck it." I strip my shorts off and slide in, cradling her to me. One of my arms slinks around her waist, while I use the other to prop my head up and watch her. She's fallen back asleep, letting out a dreamy sigh every few breaths. The sound touches me deeply as I remember last night.

From the first sight of her naked body to the sound of her screaming my name replay in my mind.

I was right to wait, wanting to introduce her to my world before taking our relationship to the next level. Fuck if it wasn't hard, but it was worth it. Every single second since I saw her across that room was worth it.

I knew sex with Grace would be something else, but it was more than something.

Mind-numbing, heart-stopping, body-shaking... It was everything.

Over and over again, I couldn't get enough, and she didn't care. She was right with me, stroke for stroke, push for pull, scream for moan. Remembering her against the shower tile has me hard and aching. My dick throbs for more, rubbing against her lower back.

Last night confirmed all my suspicions. She would now and forever be the only woman I'd ever want.

Fuck! Nick Bennett has officially become a pussy-whipped sucker. Grace Monroe has sunk me.

As if she can hear my thoughts, she starts to stir, wiggling her ass against my straining dick. She lets out a little laugh and covers her hand on mine at her waist.

"Morning." Her voice is laced with sleep as she rolls into my chest.

"Morning." I kiss her forehead.

"Hmm, what time is it?"

"It doesn't matter."

Her eyes flutter open and lock with mine. I suck in a breath at the sight of her violet eyes focusing on my face. She's fucking gorgeous anytime, but waking up in my arms, she's breathtaking.

"What's that smell?"

"I made you breakfast."

Her face lights up.

"You did?"

"Yes." I lower my lips to hers and steal a quick kiss. "My trainers always tell me how important rehydration and food are after a game. It's important to refuel your body."

"Well, it sounds like I should be serving you breakfast. You're the one who had a game yesterday."

"Maybe, but I like the idea of refueling your body."

Her eyes heat up, and she reaches to my neck, pulling my mouth back to hers. This kiss turns heated, and soon, I have her under me, her legs latched around my hips, our naked bodies tangled together.

She curves her body into mine, my dick finding her slickness easily. My plan to feed her in bed flies out of my head. She's taunting me, teasing me with no words. It's useless to try to stop when she adjusts her pelvis and, at the same time, scales her nails down my back. I slide in, moaning into her mouth as she takes me all the way. Her thighs tighten, and I feel the muscles contract, squeezing my cock. Red-hot sensations shoot up and down my spine and settle in the pit of my stomach.

The last twelve hours have been nothing less than incredible. After having Grace for the first time, I've been insatiable. At one point, I bit my tongue so hard I tasted blood as I emptied into her, listening to her shout my name. Sometime between the bed and the shower, we had a conversation about ditching the condoms. It was totally her decision. I tried to be the responsible one, Shaw's voice nagging in the back of my head about the importance of safe sex. But when she rationalized about being on the pill, we agreed. There was no more hesitation.

Now, my stamina is nonexistent as her warmth sucks me in. My balls constrict, ready to blow again. This can't happen.

I don't move, breaking away from her mouth and bracing on my elbows to get a good look at her. The edges of her lips are pink from my scruff, and her eyes are now filled with a blazing passion.

"Babe, you can't do that."

"Do what?"

"Tighten, squeeze, contract—whatever the hell you're doing. It's been a hell of a long time since I had morning sex, and never bareback."

Her eyes fill with understanding, and a sly, sexy smile spreads wide. My sweet Grace's eyes start to twinkle as she completely ignores me. Her body tightens on mine, and she surges her hips up, crushing her hipbones to mine.

Then she does it again, clenching so tight my balls start to pulse. There's no way I'm going to make it. The pressure is building with each small movement, diminishing my willpower.

"Grace—"

"Let go." She repeats the words I've said to her over and over.

"Not without you."

"It's okay."

"Fuck no," I grind out. "This is not a solo mission."

"We'll see about that."

I'm so lost in my head, I don't realize until too late. She twists, forcing us to our side, and then I'm on my back. Her hair falls in a curtain around us right before she lifts, sitting astride me. I'm momentarily stunned until she starts rocking.

"Grace!"

"Want to know a little secret?" The sly smile returns. "I've never had morning sex. Daytime sex—yes, nighttime sex—yes... but never morning sex."

A sense of possessiveness I've never known before washes through my body, and a growl escapes. The thought of her having sex with anyone other than me sears my blood. I take a deep breath to tamper down the fire, which only slightly works.

I surge up, taking her in my arms and pressing my forehead to hers. "I'm a pretty easy-going man, Grace, but the thought of you with anyone else makes me violent. I'm going to erase any memories before me."

Her eyes lock with mine, and she stills. "You want to know another secret? No man has ever gone down on me before. No man has ever gotten me to come multiple times. And no man has ever, ever taken the time to worship me as you have. So you've already erased any memories before you."

With those words, the fire dies, and I'm back in her trance. Slowly, I start to move below her, keeping our faces close. What started out as fast and furious becomes a slow dance. Together, we find a rhythm, and exactly like last night, it is perfect.

She starts to whimper, moving more urgently, and the tingling in my spine returns. I thrust deep and watch as her eyes flutter closed. The only sounds in the room are our pants until she shouts my name, coming apart in my arms and taking me with her. My vision blurs as I release, raising my head to hers, and feeling every pulse inside her.

Our hearts race together, both of us clutching tightly. Finally, I get my breathing under control and kiss along her neckline.

My thoughts from earlier return. Grace Monroe has definitely sunk me.

Chapter 16

Grace

"No, I'm not kidding. He was crotchety all weekend. If he wasn't a guy, I'd swear he had PMS. In all my years of knowing him, he's never been so grouchy. I thought he was going to pummel Shaw when Shaw mentioned scheduling a business meeting and staying an extra night in New York," Bizzy explains. "Which would have been convenient since the meeting was with the marketing executives of the new athletic line he's endorsing."

"He didn't mention that." I sip my wine, trying to hide the fact that this little tidbit pleases me. I shouldn't be happy with the information, but it's nice to know Nick missed me as much as I missed him while he was in New York last weekend.

It's been almost a month since Nick and I started seeing each other, and with the exception of his travel, we haven't spent a night apart. He's had back-to-back away games, and both times, it was ridiculous how we acted. I knew he didn't like being gone because he told me repeatedly, but I was miserable.

Hearing Bizzy tell me he was grouchy excites me a little too much.

To say being with Nick has changed my life is an understatement. The gallery is busier than ever after the press coverage of the reset. Logan and I have sold more pieces than ever before, and we have people from all over the state calling to schedule private appointments. We learned that Mrs. Shields's network and outreach is huge. She's bragged to everyone about the display we will be doing in her home, which prompted other socialites to want similar set ups. Not to mention my new escalated status as Sexy Six's girlfriend.

But it's not only Nick that has become a permanent fixture in my life; it's the entire Bennett clan, including Claire. Maria and Seth surprised me at the gallery one day, insisting on taking me to lunch. Mathis and Shaw came in, running an errand for Bizzy and purchasing a collection of pictures Bizzy wanted to get Maria for her birthday. A weekly girls night dinner has become standard, too.

Tonight, we decided to meet early and ride into the game together. It worked out perfectly that Miami plays Thursday night this week, because Nick, Logan, and I leave tomorrow morning for Thomasville. It's a coincidence he is not playing this Sunday since we'll be out of town. If the season schedule wasn't already made, I'd totally believe Shaw can make miracles happen.

Claire snaps her fingers in my face, jarring me from my thoughts.

"Sorry." I glance between her and Bizzy, who are both staring at me questioningly.

"She's in la-la land." Bizzy assumes correctly.

"My family calls it Grace Space," I tell them both. "It's happened for most of my life. My grandma coined the term."

"Grace Space is much classier than la-la land."

Bizzy's phone rings, and her face lights up. She answers, dropping her head and speaking softly as Claire motions to the waiter for our bill.

I check my own phone and see a message from Nick from about ten minutes ago.

Nick: Coach is confiscating all our phones. Some shit about getting our heads in the right place. New England has beat us the last three meetings, and he's pissed. See you after the game. Plan on celebrating all night long.

I shudder in my chair, feeling his words. He doesn't have his phone, but I send him a reply anyway.

Me: All night? Think you'll be up to it? If you're too tired, I'll do all the work...

"Rodney is here. Shaw says traffic is awful," Bizzy tells us, slapping down her credit card before I can reach for my wallet.

"God, I love your overprotective husband. It's awesome to have a driver for our girl's nights." Claire sucks down the rest of her drink. "And I don't have to be at work until Saturday, so I'm definitely letting loose tonight."

"You know, Mathis, Nicky, and Shaw all split the cost. It's not only Shaw," Bizzy informs us.

This is news to me but not a surprise. The more I learn about Shaw, the more I understand Nick is a lot like him. And who am I to complain if I have a designated driver for GNO?

Claire slices her eyes to Bizzy but doesn't say anything as we get up to leave. This has been happening a lot since Claire's confession at the game. Bizzy has called me several times, explaining she's on a mission to push Mathis into admitting his feelings for Claire. She's convinced that Claire and Mathis belong together and is pulling out all the stops. She says Shaw is hesitant to get involved but is not discouraging her.

Of course, Shaw doesn't say no to her. Ever.

I tried to talk to Nick about it, too, wondering if he knew anything about why Mathis was resistant. He replied with, *"I'm not really concerned with my brother's love life,"* and that was the end of the discussion.

Rodney is in front of the restaurant, holding the car door open when we exit. Each of us greets him with a hug and get into the back to find a chilled bottle of champagne waiting. Claire takes no time pouring us a glass as we head to the stadium.

The whole way, we talk about our plans for the weekend. The closer it gets, the more excited I become to introduce Nick to my family. I'm still nervous about his star status and the locals descending on my parents' farm once they learn Nick is there. Mom assures me she's been able to keep his presence quiet. The actual festival will be trickier, but we'll deal with that on Saturday.

Shaw was right. Traffic is awful, and we barely make it to the suite before kick-off. Shaw is waiting at the door with a scowl on his face. The instant he sees Bizzy, he visibly relaxes.

Then he turns the scowl to me and raises an eyebrow. "Did Nick get a hold of you?"

"Yes, I sent a text."

"He wants me to get you to the player's entrance after the game. Regardless of the outcome, he'll have to speak to reporters. Bizzy and I will wait with you."

"What about me?" Claire asks.

"Mathis is taking you home." He says it so naturally, as if we should have known.

Bizzy's eyes grow wide, and I can practically hear her squealing in her head. She gives me a quick wink but doesn't dare say anything.

The suite is packed when we enter. I wave at the people I met last time and see Maria and Seth seated with Shaw's boss and a woman I don't know. Claire whispers that the woman is Gail, Shaw's assistant. When her eyes meet mine, she smiles warmly.

Mathis joins us, standing close to Claire. This wouldn't normally strike me as unusual since they are friends, but it's the expression on his face. He does a full body scan of her, and his eyes grow stormy, landing on her short skirt.

It's then I notice the Bennett Boys all have a similar glare. There is no mistaking he's finally seeing the big picture. Maybe Nick said something to him, but whatever it is, I know the look is packed with promise.

The game starts, and it doesn't take long for New England to score, sending a groan through the room. We all turn our attention to the game as Miami's offense takes the field. Nick runs out, and the crowd goes wild. The familiar music starts and the Jumbo-Tron flashes his picture as the crowd starts chanting, "Sexy, Sexy, Sexy."

The cameras zoom in on him, and his face fills the TV screens around the room. He adjusts his mouth guard and scans the field. His eyes then sweep upward. Seth and Maria both jump out of their seats waving wildly, and Seth points over his shoulder at me.

Nick gives a chin jerk and closes his eyes. When he opens them, a mask of confidence is in place as the line gets in formation.

The exchange was no more than five seconds, but those five seconds said so much. My heart flutters in my chest rapidly. It may have been brief but doesn't go unnoticed by our little group. Shaw and Mathis glance at me then each other, communicating without words.

I don't have time to think about it once the ball is snapped and Nick goes into action.

Tonight, there are servers who keep our drinks refilled as we watch Miami fight to get ahead. By the time halftime comes, the game is tied. I'm mentally exhausted from shouting.

Mathis and Shaw leave again, presumably going to the locker room.

"Whew, I think I'm going to pass out." Bizzy comes next to me, fanning her face. "I don't do well with these close games."

"I do feel a little sick to my stomach."

"There's another half to go. Buck up, you lightweights." Claire shows no signs of nervousness.

My phone vibrates with a text. "You girls want to take a little trip with me?"

"Sure, where?"

"My brother's 'friend' Melanie is here with some people. She wants to meet up." I use air quotes to emphasize the word friend.

They know a little about Melanie. I've told them about Logan's tight lips on their relationship. I don't pry, but I know they are spending more time together. She's been around the gallery a few times, and I haven't missed the way he looks at her.

"I love going into the stands! But we'll definitely need refills." Bizzy motions to the server, ordering us another round of drinks.

Since this is only my second game ever, I have no idea where I'm going and have to rely on Bizzy and Claire to get us to the right section. Melanie is watching and waves enthusiastically when she sees us.

I do quick introductions, and Melanie motions for the seats, explaining her friends are gone for a while. "Isn't this an exciting game?"

"I'd be a little happier if Miami was winning. It's kinda nerve-wracking," I tell her.

"Oh, I'm sure they're going to pull out a win. So how's the skybox?"

"Awesome, although it's a little intense. I like these seats."

"You've never been in the seats before?"

"This is only my second game."

"Oh my God! You have got to stick around for a while. Get the whole experience. I'm sure the suites are nice, but there's nothing better than being here for the action." She whips out her phone and starts typing. "I'm telling my friends to take their time. You girls are welcome to stay here until they get back."

"Cool! I miss being with the common folk." Claire sits back casually, propping her feet on the seat backs in front of her.

"It is really fun down here," Bizzy agrees, tipping her drink to Claire.

We fall easily into conversation, talking about work and my upcoming trip home. Melanie's face fills with surprise when she learns Nick is coming home with me, but she recovers quickly, changing the subject.

By the time halftime is over, I'm feeling no pain with the alcohol running through my system. People file back into their seats, and the energy in the stadium grows. Claire and Bizzy get up and start to dance when the music booms through the air. Melanie and I join them, screaming as the team blasts onto the field.

The instant my eyes find the number six, a rush of excitement runs through my body. Nick's head is down. He focuses on the ground as his coaches surround him, pointing at clipboards.

Claire waves down a vendor, getting us all a beer, when the whistle blows and the game restarts. With each down and catch, the fans around us become increasingly rowdier. Nick throws a pass that Eddie Jarvis easily catches in the end zone.

The stadium goes wild, the four of us included. We scream and join in the high-fives, dancing in circles like idiots. The only people not celebrating are the five people sitting directly behind us in New England gear.

Whatever was said in the locker room works because, by the start of the fourth quarter, Miami is leading by three touchdowns. Melanie's friends still haven't returned, so we stay put, rallying with the other fans. The excitement is electrifying, my voice is hoarse, and I'm having the greatest time.

Then it happens. Nick's linemen leave a hole open just enough for a defender to get through, and he plows Nick to the ground so hard, I swear it rocks my bones. Bizzy and I scream at the top of our lungs but not loud enough to drown out the group behind us.

In unison, they shout, "TIMBER!"

I whip my head around and catch one of the women giving me a smug glare.

Nick gets up with the help of a few players and shakes his head a few times. Bizzy explains that's his way of clearing his head. He gets back in the formation, only to throw the ball out of bounds on the next play. And the next one, too.

Miami's forced to punt, which only fuels the assholes to start jeering.

New England has no luck, and the second Nick's back on the field, the heckling starts again. I'll give it to them; they're ballsy, sitting in a sea of orange and teal. The three men of the group quiet down, but the women keep going.

"Sexy Six my ass! More like sloppy six!"

"How about pick six!"

I lose my cool and turn to find the woman standing behind me with a wicked gleam in her eye.

"What the hell is your problem?" I yell at her.

"What? Can't take a little ribbing. Your quarterback is overrated and sloppy."

The area around us goes silent. Bizzy growls loudly, taking the woman's eyes from me to her.

"Do you two girls got a crush on the Bennett boy?" She glances at her friend who's openly smirking.

"I'd watch it, lady. Sit back in your seat and keep your mouth shut. You don't want to mess with this," Claire advises her, moving her hand between us all.

She ignores the warning and drops her eyes to my shirt, looking between mine and Bizzy's chests. "Isn't that cute? You're both wearing number six." At this point, two of the men in their group step in and try to get the women to sit down. They refuse.

The game goes on behind us, but my focus is now on these two women. Alcohol fuels my courage, and I square my shoulders and stand tall, full of attitude. "It just so happens that I do have a crush on the Bennett boy. He's my boyfriend. And this woman is actually a *Bennett.*"

She glares at us and then at her friend before fake-sneezing, calling 'bullshit', and tossing her full cup all over me. The stench of rum and coke fills my nose, and I scream.

Claire shoves me aside, shaking her beer and spraying it all over the two women.

There's a round of screeching, and both women lunge down. A slap stings my face before I feel the excruciating pain in my scalp. Someone yanks my head forward, and I thrash out, meeting flesh. I can't breathe as bodies crush me from each side and yelling commences. Bizzy gets me free but knocks one of the men, that's trying to pull his friend free, in the mouth.

"You bitch!" I hear while flinging my fists out.

"Don't call my friend a bitch!" My adrenaline skyrockets.

An all-out brawl is going on, and I keep hitting until I am ripped away, my feet no longer on the ground.

"Ma'am, stopping fighting me." I twist into a body and notice he's a police officer, and all the girls are in the same stronghold.

The crowd has gathered around, trying to help clear the area, but I sink into him. "She started it," I say weakly, sounding like a dumbass.

I've never been in a fight before, ever. Logan and I may have wrestled a few times, but that's it. Mortification sets in, and I hang my head as the officer places me on the ground and leads me away.

We are ushered down ramps and through what seems like a mile-long hallway before the officer sits me on a cold concrete bench. I finally look up and see Melanie, Bizzy, and Claire with me, each with their own police escort.

None of the men say anything before walking away and shutting the door.

We hear the women and men we fought arguing on the other side of the door.

I'm quiet, trying to process what the hell happened, and praying this is a bad dream. The silence is broken when Claire starts laughing. Bizzy and Melanie join her, and soon, I'm doing the same. Tears roll down our faces until I can't breathe.

"That was phenomenal!" Claire fist punches the air.

"I can't believe that happened." Melanie holds her waist, wiping her eyes. "Now what do we do? Are they sending us to jail? Do we get to ride in a paddy wagon? I've always wanted to see the inside of one."

This sets off another round of laughter until I fall over, clutching my side.

"Unlikely, I think this is a sober cell. Nicky told me about them," Bizzy explains.

"So what happens next? Should we call Shaw or Mathis?"

Claire and Bizzy look at me like I am stupid. "Hell no!" they say at the same time.

"We call in reinforcements." Bizzy slides her phone out of her pocket. "Maria. She'll save us."

"I'll call one of my friends, too." Melanie does the same.

Any apprehension I had about Bizzy calling Maria vanishes when I hear Maria's laughter through the phone.

"She's going to sneak out and come get us in a few minutes. No worries." Bizzy hangs up.

Melanie's friends tell her the same, so we all settle in and wait. There's a dim roar from far away, and guilt sets in. Nick expects me to be watching him, not sitting in the dungeon of the stadium in sober lock-up.

"I'm sorry I lost my cool, guys. It was highly unlike me," I apologize.

"Wipe that damn frown from your face right now. Those bitches started it, and besides, they deserved it. Who acts like that? Trailer Trash, that's who. This was some of the most fun I've had in a while," Claire says.

The three of them agree with a nod. As we wait for Maria, Claire insists on reenacting the entire scene from start to finish, sending us back into a fit of giggles.

Which is exactly how we are when the door flies open. But instead of Maria standing there, we are faced with four very unhappy men.

Logan's eyes are trained on Melanie.

Shaw's on Bizzy.

Mathis's on Claire.

And Nick, still in his uniform, sweaty and filthy, is staring at me with fire in his eyes.

No worries, my ass. Where the hell is Maria?

Chapter 17

Grace

Nick's silence is killing me. I think I'd rather be back in the sober cell than have to endure this torture. The few times I've tried to talk to him, he's looked at me blankly but not responded.

It's been almost two hours since he stormed into the cell, picked me off the floor, and dragged me behind him to the player tunnel.

He talked over my head and told Shaw, *"keep her there, and for fuck's sake, keep her out of trouble,"* then he disappeared into the locker room. Bizzy tried to scoot close to me, but Shaw had her pressed possessively to him. Irritation radiated off his body, but she kept assuring him she was okay until he calmed down. Then he told us why Maria didn't come to our rescue.

Apparently, Logan showed up with Melanie's friends to surprise her. They were told we had been hauled away by the cops, who informed him we couldn't be released until after the game. Shaw had already been called by the Director of Security, who knew Bizzy, and was on his way to the dungeon. That's where they all ran into each other.

Since they couldn't get us out, they waited for Nick to finish the game. According to Shaw, Nick was getting violent on the field. He didn't share more, saying Nick would fill me in.

Bizzy didn't seem disturbed, but I was freaking out inside. I'd never seen Nick pissed. He did the after-game interview, answering a few questions, but then cut it short and came straight to me.

He turns into his underground parking garage, and I decide to try again. "Don't you want to take me home?"

He parks and gets out without a word. I stay seated, wondering what to do now. I'm startled when he swings open the truck door and reaches in, picking me up easily, and stalks to the elevator.

The whole ride is continued silence, and I start to feel sick. He holds me up by my thighs, keeping his face stoic. His cologne fills the area, and I drop my head to his shoulder, inhaling deeply.

"I'm sorry, Nick, if I embarrassed you. I understand if you want to cancel—"

"STOP!" he roars, setting my nerves more on edge.

Nothing else is said until he lets us into his apartment, going straight to his bathroom and sitting me on the vanity. I'm scared to look at myself, knowing I resemble a train wreck.

He finally locks eyes with me, and my breath catches. One of his hands slides across my right temple, where he presses lightly, and I hiss at the sting.

He steps back, moving both his hands to my collar. I jump as he rips the jersey in half, sliding it off my shoulders and throwing it aside. His eyes never leave mine as he reaches behind me and turns on the faucet.

Tears finally prickle my eyelids when he wets a cloth with warm water and starts to rub lightly over my face, neck, and shoulders, stopping when he reaches my wrist. He repeats the action on the other side and leans in to kiss my temple.

Then he finally starts talking.

"Third and eight, the play is set up. Jarvis and Gade are ready for me. The score is ours. We've practiced it a thousand times. I'm getting ready, and then I feel it. Not the energy, not the chanting—no, I feel you. For some reason, I glance up and see a scuffle in the stands. I think to myself, *Grace is fine, Six. Stop being a pussy*. Then I see a man butting heads with a woman. Your head bounced back, your hair flying, and I knew. My heart stopped beating. I saw red. Furious, murderous rage filled me. I went through the motions, calling the play, throwing the ball, but I never saw Jarvis make the touchdown because, when I turned back, the cop had you in his arms."

"Nick—"

"Grace, I'm a laid back guy, but I've never wanted to fucking pummel someone so hard in my life. I found a guard, told him to use his mic, walkie-talkie, or fucking telepathy, but whatever it was, find SHAW!"

"Nick—" I try again.

"I finished the game and went straight to Shaw, Mathis, and Logan on the sidelines. They talked me down from going into the sober cell next to yours and strangling anyone. The thought of you hurt was my undoing."

"I'm sorry," I repeat, swallowing hard. "Let me explain."

"You were defending me. There are dozens of witnesses who found the cops to tell their side of the story. The super fans, those who follow me regularly, recognized you and Bizzy and told them you were innocent."

"Really?"

"Yes, baby, dozens."

"They were being awful. I couldn't stand for it. Then one of the women started—"

"Sweet Grace, why do you think we make Bizzy sit in the box? Claire? My mom? It's because of the tempers flaring. I learned a long time ago to take the heat."

"I couldn't do it."

"The thought of you standing up for me is admirable, but don't ever fucking go head to head with anyone. I'll lose my shit."

I open my mouth to argue, but his lips crash to mine. This is a kiss unlike we've ever shared before, and I melt into him, letting him have control. All my arguments die as he scoots me to the edge of the vanity, rubbing his erection against my center.

He moves his lips to my cheek, neck, and collarbone, leaving me panting before stopping and stepping back. His face fills with disgust. "I love rum and coke, but the stench on you makes me sick. I need to bathe you."

He sheds his clothes on the way to his massive tub. I force myself to remain seated even though I want to leap down and strip him myself.

Finally, he comes back and places me on my feet, undressing me.

"I'll apologize now, but you may have trouble walking tomorrow."

My text from earlier comes to mind. "So I don't need to do all the work?"

His eyes flare. "Never."

"You going to carry me?"

"Yes, I'll carry you everywhere, if only to keep you out of trouble."

He steps into the tub, sits carefully, and situates me directly on top of him. He pours shower gel into his hands and gently starts washing me. Slowly, his hands roam over my body, leaving a trail of warmth.

His eyes slice to mine when I swivel my hips, purposely grinding on his erection.

"Take it easy, Grace. The images are still fresh. I'm trying to control the urge to find those assholes and pound someone's face in."

I lean forward, kissing along the column of his throat, growing more boldness than I ever have before. Grinding back and forth, I align us perfectly and slide down until he's fully inside. "Baby, I'm fine. Safe and sound, with you. If you want to pound something, I'm right here."

His expression changes, growing more heated, right before his lips form a sexy, wicked grin.

"Definitely not walking tomorrow."

"I'm counting on—" I don't get to finish my thought because he shuts me up with his mouth and starts to move.

Water sloshes everywhere, but I'm too far gone to care.

I twist in my seat, trying unsuccessfully to cross my legs. Even in the plush seats in first class, I can't get comfortable. Nick chuckles beside me and takes my hand, bringing it to his lips and eyeing me hungrily.

I shake my head and mouth '*stop*'.

He leans in, whispering, "Want to join the mile high club?"

"Are you insane? There's no way we'll both fit in that small bathroom."

"We can try." He wiggles his eyebrows, causing me to giggle.

My abdominal muscles burn in protest. Nick may have wanted me to have trouble walking, but I'm having trouble functioning. Almost every part of my body is sore.

Deliciously sore...

"Mind if we switch seats for a few?" Logan speaks over my shoulder, talking to Nick.

Nick agrees, kissing me on the cheek before trading seats with Logan.

"Are you furious with me?" I ask, afraid of his reply. This is the first time we've spoken since last night. He was already in his seat when we boarded the plane.

"Hard to be too mad when your boyfriend gets us into first class."

"He's kinda big to sit in regular seats."

"Lucky for us."

"So are you mad?"

"Not really, I was understandably upset and worried. It's not every day your sister gets in a brawl at a football game with opposing fans."

"I know this is going to sound juvenile, but it wasn't my fault."

"I know, Melanie explained everything. So no, I'm not furious."

"How is Melanie?"

"Well, besides the fact that I got the cold shoulder for almost the full night, I'd say she's the one who's pissed."

"Why?"

"Some fucking girly bullshit I'll never understand. Apparently, it hurt her feelings to know Nick was coming to Thomasville. She said something about us dating longer than you and Nick and feeling like a fool."

Poor Melanie. “Oh,” is all I say.

“Oh? That’s it?”

“I can see where she’s coming from.”

“Where’s that?”

I try to turn in my seat to face him fully. My body objects to the movement, and I have to settle for turning my head. “Do you like her, Logan? Really like her?”

“Yes, she’s a cool girl. I enjoy spending time with her.”

“I think it goes deeper for her. I can’t say for sure, because I’ve only been around her a few times, but her face lights up when she talks about you, and she gets this expression. It’s hard to explain. It’s a woman thing, but I can see how she would be hurt when she learned Nick was invited and she wasn’t.”

“Bringing her home with me is a huge step.”

“That’s exactly the way I feel about bringing Nick. It makes a statement.”

“Yeah, but you two are crazy about each other. There’s no questioning his commitment to you.”

It always feels good to hear those words, even though Nick has left no room for doubt. Suddenly, I feel sorry for Melanie, because Logan’s obviously not in the same place.

“Maybe you should tell her, Logan. Don’t string her along. A few months of dating isn’t that long, but she’s looking at the future.”

“Shit.” He scrubs his hands down his face. “That’s not exactly what I wanted to hear.”

I pat his arm, giving him a sympathetic grin. “I’m here if you want to talk.”

“Thanks, but dissecting my relationship with my baby sister isn’t exactly something I’m comfortable with.”

“Just let me know. “

“Actually, there’s something else I wanted to discuss with you. Something private.” His voice goes low with a seriousness I haven’t heard in a long time.

The hair on the back of my neck stands up. “What?”

"I know last night wasn't your fault, but it can't happen again. You need to think of your reputation and your future. If word got out that you were in a smack down at a public sporting event, there's no chance of getting accepted to the Art Program."

My heart sinks at the mention of the program. I've been internalizing it quietly for the past few weeks, and the thought of getting in still sends a thrill of excitement through me. But leaving Nick makes my stomach turn. This is not something I'm ready to share with Logan.

"It won't happen again, Logan."

"Promise?"

"Promise. After last night, I may never be allowed to sit in the stands again."

Logan laughs, passing his finger over the bruise at my hairline. "Good, Grace. Glad to know you can behave."

He stands, moving back to his own seat. Nick is at my side a few seconds later with his phone in hand.

"Bizzy has sent me a few messages, the last one saying to check your email."

I log onto the in-flight Wi-Fi and see two emails from her. The first one is her checking on me and making sure we made our flight okay. The second is entirely more detailed.

Grace,

You are already airborne, but I wanted to check in. I texted Nick until he finally replied and said everything was okay. He assured me he wasn't too hard on you.

Thought you'd want to know, it's official. Mathis finally got his shit together. Claire is no longer in the friend-zone. I'm not sure what made him finally step up, but Shaw told me Mathis was a different kind of pissed when he heard we were in trouble. He said, and I quote, "Claire's ass is going to be on fire when I finish with her. What the hell was she thinking?"

So, of course, I called her this morning and woke her up. Mathis was in the background, rumbling up a storm.

Isn't that great?

It didn't even take him a week once he came to his senses.

*Now, the bad news. I don't think we'll be allowed in the stands for a long time. Shaw was completely unreasonable. Nothing I did could change his mind. (*wink)*

I can't wait to hear how the weekend goes. Nick may be playing it cool, but he's very excited. Don't tell him I told you, but this means a lot to him.

I have a shift at the hospital tonight, so I'll be unavailable until tomorrow morning. And we have Brayden for the week, but call me when you can.

Xo

Bizzy

PS- I like Melanie. Let's invite her to our next night out.

I finish reading with a smile on my face. Nick gives me a knowing look, and it's obvious he's aware of Claire and Mathis, too. I want to ask him more, but instead, I snuggle to his side and think about what Bizzy said. Nick's excited to meet my family.

Now, I have butterflies for a completely different reason.

Chapter 18

Nick

"Keep Driving!" Grace hisses from the backseat angrily.

"Who is that?" Logan follows her orders and passes her parents' home, which has several cars in the driveway.

"The red car belongs to that damn Mary Cobb! The others I don't know." As she speaks, her phone rings and she answers, immediately starting in on questions for her mom.

Logan glances over at me and rolls his eyes. "We're going to Grandpa's."

Grace hangs up and huffs, sliding to the middle and leaning over the console. "Mama says they started showing up about thirty minutes ago. Mary Cobb orchestrated an ambush, showing up unannounced, with her bridge club in tow. They brought enough food to feed an army. She claimed she was being neighborly and trying to help out since this weekend is such a big deal. Now, she's perched at the front window watching for us. Mama said she can't get rid of them."

"Good thing she doesn't know our rental car," he replies, annoyed. "Wonder how she planned this one."

"I'll tell you exactly how she planned it. She probably reviewed the latest flight schedule into Tallahassee. Then she calculated the time it takes to drive here. She and her cronies had an agenda. Mama is livid."

"Why doesn't she tell her to leave? Find an excuse to get them out of there?" I think about the times my own mom has had to get out of similar situations.

Grace's eyes slice to mine, and I bite back a laugh. She's riled up, and it's hard to keep a straight face.

"Don't forget my dad is the Mayor. Mama has to finesse this, but she promises they'll be gone within the hour. She'll meet us at Grandpa's house."

The more she talks, the more riled up she gets, and her voice transforms. A southern drawl becomes more and more distinct. It's fucking sexy as hell, and I have to fight reaching over and hauling her into my lap.

The thought of hearing my name come from her lips with that accent, while I'm buried inside her tonight, makes my cock twitch in my shorts.

"We're here!" She slides back as the car comes to a stop then gets out.

A mountain of a man leans against a porch column with his feet planted firm and his arms crossed. His eyes are focused right on me, as if he can see the dirty thoughts that were running through my mind.

Roy Monroe is nothing like I expected. When Grace has talked about her grandpa, she's never mentioned he is a replica of Sam Elliot—Roadhouse style.

I come face to face with powerhouse men with the sole purpose of destroying me, but none of them come close to intimidating me as much as Grace's grandpa.

And I'm not even out of the car yet.

"He's not as bad as he appears, but he's protective of Grace. Word of advice, show him she's important," Logan suggests.

"Well, that shouldn't be hard considering she's become my entire world."

"Good, let him see that. Maybe de-pussify it a little." He chuckles and exits the car.

My door opens, and Grace holds her hand out to me. "Come on."

Be a man, Nick Bennett. You got this. I say silently to myself and take her hand.

Logan is already on the porch, waiting and watching us. He's wearing a shit eating grin, completely relaxed. When we get close enough, Roy steps forward, and Grace drops my hand, jumping into his arms. He squeezes her tightly, flinging her around like a ragdoll.

"Peach Princess," he says affectionately, kissing her cheek.

She takes his face in her hands and does a full scan. It's an exchange I recognize well, since Bizzy and I do the same thing so frequently. She returns the kiss to his forehead then looks at me.

"Grandpa, put me down so I can introduce you to my boyfriend."

He does as she says, and I move quickly, extending my hand to him. "Nick Bennett." I barely get out my last name because his grip crushes my hand.

He could kill me with these hands. The force behind his clutch tells all. Grace is precious, and I'd better treat her that way.

"Roy Monroe." He clutches once more before stepping back and tossing his arm around her shoulder.

She's watching me, biting her lip, encouraging me quietly.

"It's an honor to meet you. Grace has told me a lot about you."

He looks back and forth between Grace and me quietly, his expression unreadable. He does this three more times before responding. Beads of sweat run down my neck, and my stomach knots as I wait for him to speak.

"Yeah, I can say the same thing about you. Apparently, you've been spending a lot of time with my girl."

"As much as she'll let me. It's my favorite thing to do."

This cracks the ice. His face softens, and he leans back down to kiss her head again. "We have that in common. It's one of my favorite things, too."

Grace stares at him with such admiration, I swallow the lump in my throat. Her reasons for leaving school and staying home are glaringly obvious.

God, I love this woman.

Logan coughs right as a truck drives up. I turn to see a gigantic blue F-350 come to a stop and a man in a suit jumps out. Grace squeals and calls out, "Daddy!"

She meets him halfway, and he repeats the same embrace as Roy. Grace was sore already, but now I fear she's going to be black and blue. He puts her down and glances at me with a welcoming smile.

I go to him, already less intimidated. He yanks me into a man hug, slapping my back. I grimace, feeling the sting. He may be less intimidating, but he's no less strong.

"Nick Bennett, I'm Carl Monroe. It's nice to finally meet you."

"You too," I cough out as he slaps me again.

Logan takes mercy on me and steps in. "Hey, Dad."

Grace slides to my side and gives me a sympathetic grin, while rubbing lightly where Carl has no doubt left a hand print.

"It's time for a beer," Roy calls out, and I hear the screen door slam as he goes inside.

"It's the middle of the day," Carl yells to him.

"Who the hell cares? My work is done for the day."

"I'm off for the next three days. I'm with Grandpa. " Logan disappears into the house.

"Might as well join them. Your mom will be here soon." Carl follows the rest of the Monroe men, leaving me alone with Grace.

"They like you," she says with a glimmer in her eyes.

"You could have warned me your Grandpa resembles a lumberjack. I was thinking more along the lines of a feeble old man."

"Don't let him hear you say that, or he won't like you anymore."

"Is it totally inappropriate for me to kiss you right now?" I lean into her, nuzzling along her neckline.

"Probably. How about I take you on a tour of the property later, and you can kiss me all you want?"

I inhale, smelling the mixture of her shampoo and body wash. Memories of bathing her last night come to mind, and I smile against her skin.

"You've got a deal, but I may not stop at kissing."

She starts to giggle, slipping her hand in mine once again, leading me inside.

"It was awful! I almost swallowed my tongue when it happened. Thank God I had Bizzy with me," Grace explains the way she felt when I went down last night.

"Jesus, Grace, he's a quarterback. They get sacked!" Roy shakes his head in disappointment. "Did you think they'd tap him on the shoulder and say, 'give me the ball'?"

She huffs and opens her mouth to argue, but her mom interrupts and agrees with her. They go back and forth, discussing the game, while I enjoy my beer.

The last few hours have been like this, every subject turning into a discussion with Grace and Sharon on one side and the guys on the other. I've sat back and taken it all in until they started in on football.

One thing's for sure; the Monroe men may be farmers, politicians, business owners, and legacies, but they are complete football fanatics. These guys follow the game and have as much knowledge as me. Maybe even more. I knew Logan was a fan, but Grace didn't mention her dad and grandpa were as well.

Grace is sandwiched between her mom and me on the sofa and goes still when her dad mentions the touchdown in the fourth quarter. Logan moves his eyes to me before taking a swig of his beer to hide his smile.

"I must have been in the restroom. I missed it," Graces lies uncomfortably.

"How could you miss it? Six shredded them. He started the play with such power the defense didn't know what hit them. They couldn't cover for shit. Even watching on TV, I could see the intensity in his eyes. The play has been on every sports broadcast all day, and you were in the bathroom???" Carl glares at Grace with disbelief. "The bathroom?"

We never got around to discussing the game last night. It was the absolute last thing on my mind when I retrieved her from the sober cell. The entire drive home, all I could think about was stripping her naked and fucking her until she understood how careless she was. Punishment was my plan.

But when she looked at me in the elevator and mentioned me canceling this trip, my resolve took a different direction. She needed to hear and know exactly why I was so upset. Punishment sex can wait for another time.

Her hand grips my knee, pulling my attention to her face. "I am really sorry I missed the play."

The apology goes a lot deeper. I already know she's sorry for the debacle, but her face is filled with remorse. If we didn't have an audience, I'd find a way to erase that guilt.

"It's fine. I already told you that. If you're interested, we can watch the highlight reels."

"Sharon, did you bring that present I asked for?" Roy gets out of his recliner as Sharon points to the bag on the floor.

He grabs it and hands it to Grace. "Thought you might like this," he tells her and sits again.

She rummages through the tissue paper and brings out a burnt orange sundress. Her eyes gaze around the room, full of suspicion. The mood in the room changes, the air growing thick as everyone watches her. Her mom glances at the ceiling, a dimple popping out on her cheek. Her dad rubs his hands together with the smile of a man who's about to tell a punch line.

"Okay, I'll bite. What's this for?" Grace asks no one in particular.

"I figured it may look nice on you since orange is the new black. You'll be the best dressed woman in the clink," Roy answers with a straight face.

The room howls in laughter, Logan being the loudest. Grace's face turns red, her eyes bulging out. "Logan! You told them?"

"Hell yes, I told them."

"How could you?"

"It was too good to keep a secret. The Peach Princess gets hauled away by the police? Nah, I wasn't keeping that one to myself."

My vision is blurry as tears fill my eyes. I'm trying my best not to laugh but fail miserably. Her family is openly mocking her, her grandpa leading the charge.

"I can't—I mean... Why—?" She can't get her words out, which amuses everyone even more.

"Stop laughing at me!" she finally gets out, but no one listens.

"You!" She twists to me, jabbing my chest. "You better stop now! This is not funny!"

"Sweet Peach, it's hilarious."

"I'm calling tomorrow morning and cutting off your cable!" She points to Roy. "This is ridiculous. First the Chrisley's, and now this. How do you even know about Orange is the New Black?"

"TV has changed a lot over the years, and this old man has time on his hands. I like my shows." He shrugs, not affected by her threat.

"Baby." I drag her to my side. "Laugh it up. Let it go. Your family is teasing you."

She narrows her eyes then finally relaxes, starting to giggle. "Just so you all know, we weren't going to the clink. And it was Logan's girlfriend who was wishing for a ride in the paddy wagon."

Logan's face freezes mid-laugh. He gives Grace an evil glare.

"Welp, I think it's time we head down the road to the house and eat some of the food the nosy nellies of the community made." Roy gets back up and claps his hands together, his eyes coming to mine.

There's something indiscernible written on his face. A knot forms in my gut, knowing I'm not going to like whatever he's thinking.

“But before we do that, let’s get Nick’s things and get him set up in his room for the weekend. Don’t want to be an ungracious host.”

My stomach plunges, and I try hard to remain emotionless. I expected that Grace would be in a different room. But a whole different house?

The room erupts in laughter again, and this time, I’m the target. Suddenly, nothing seems funny anymore.

Chapter 19

Nick

"Grace? Where are you?" I call out from the front room of her parents' home. This house is large, and I wouldn't know where to begin searching for her.

"In the kitchen. Walk straight back."

I do as instructed, while her humming gets louder and louder as I get closer. The smell of sugar and cinnamon becomes stronger, making my mouth water.

As soon as I hit the doorway, I stop dead in my tracks. Grace is standing at the edge of the kitchen island, concentrating on the pie in front of her. My heart starts racing at the sight in front of me. Her hair hangs down in large curls, begging for me to run my hands through them. She's wearing the orange sundress from last night with a large brown belt tightened around her waist, showcasing every curve of her waist and hips. But it's not her hair or her outfit that has my dick throbbing.

It's the fucking cowboy boots... *Cowboy boots!*

Grace is always beautiful, but today, she's given new meaning to the term sexy seductress. Without saying a word or even looking at me, there's a primal urge to have her coursing through my veins.

She glances up with her bright smile that quickly dies on her lips. "Nick, what's wrong?"

"Don't move." The words come out harsh and demanding, and she peeks down at herself then back to me.

"Is there something—?"

I make it to her in two long strides, one of my hands going to the back of her head while the other cups her ass. Her eyes grow wide when I thrust my hips into hers, my cock pressing against her stomach.

"Please, God, tell me we're alone in this house."

"Everyone's already gone. We're supposed to meet them at—"

"Your grandpa, too?"

"Yes, he left—"

I don't let her finish, crushing my mouth to hers while lifting her with one arm. She lets out a squeak that is barely audible over the roaring in my ears. I try to think of somewhere to go, retracing my steps in my mind to the living room.

It's too far. The island will have to do.

Her hands grip my hair as I slide her dress up to pool around her hips and rip her underwear in half. They fall away, and my fingers slip inside, finding her wet.

"Jesus, Grace, you're soaked."

"It was all you."

Pride beats in my chest, knowing I affect her the same way she does me. "I'll apologize now."

"Why?"

"Because I'm about to fuck you hard. Not sure I can be sweet."

Her head jerks to mine, her eyes on fire. "Fuck me then."

The words increase the roaring in my ears, and I fumble with my belt and shorts until I'm free and pushing inside of her.

Heaven... that's what this feels like. Pure heaven.

Her sexy moans fill the room, encouraging me to thrust with brutal force. I picture her leaning over the counter as I pound into her from behind, but I'm too gone to reposition us. She flexes up, bringing her hands down hard on the counter with a thud.

With each stroke, I get desperate for release. We've had sex so many times, and each one has been out of this world. But today ranks up there at the top. I've never been this rough, and guilt creeps in until she starts talking.

"Harder, Nick."

"Grace," I ground out through clenched teeth.

"Harder. Don't stop!"

I'm helpless to stop when she screams my name, clutching so tight my balls ache. I come hard, thrusting as deep as possible and feeling the release running through my veins. My vision goes black, and my head becomes heavy. I drop my face to her shoulder, loosening my grip on her hips.

"I like the boots, Sweet Peach." I finally find my voice. "Thinking maybe you should wear them more often."

"Miami is more stilettos and straps than cowboy boots."

"Let me rephrase. Maybe you should wear them more often for me."

"Is this going to happen every time I do?"

"Oh yeah, if I have anything to do with it." I raise my head, and something on the counter catches my eye. Streaks of pink cover the white surface.

"Grace, baby, I think we made a mess."

She lifts her head and inspects her hand. "I think it happened somewhere between *'harder'* and '*don't stop'*. The pie was a casualty."

I stand, straightening us both, and bring her hand to my mouth. She lays her head against my chest, watching me lick the sweet dessert off every inch of her hand.

"It's almost as delicious as you."

She opens her mouth right as there's banging, followed by a high-pitched, "Yoo-hoo! Anyone here? Sharon? Grace?"

Grace's eyes start to bulge, and she struggles to move. "Oh my God! That's Mary Cobb," she hisses, panic written all over her face.

"Babe, I'm still inside you." I wince when she pushes back on the counter and twists out of my reach. My cock bobs free, the cold air hitting it painfully.

"Put that away. Get dressed!" She points to my dick.

"Are you back here?" Footsteps sound on the wooden floors, getting closer.

"Do something!" She waves her hands frantically. "I'm not wearing panties. I can't face that woman."

"What do you want me to do?" I zip my shorts and make sure my shirt is straight.

"Go stall her! She's probably here to see you anyway. Please, Nick. I'll save you as soon as I find my panties."

I spot the scrap of white on the floor and pick them up, knowing they're ruined. "I tore them off you."

"Okay, well, go introduce yourself and give me a minute to clean up."

"Is anyone home?" Mary is no more than a few feet away, so I tuck the torn material in my pocket and go to head her off before she can enter the kitchen.

"Hello?" I call out, walking to the dining room.

Mary is not alone; she's with who I assume is her granddaughter, the same woman Grace told me Pledge was caught with in the barn. I immediately feel dirty when she openly ogles me up and down then licks her lips hungrily. It's probably meant to be sexy, but she fails. This woman has '*skank*' written all over her.

"Hi, I'm Nick." I go to Mary, offering my hand.

"Nick! So nice to meet you. Sharon mentioned you and Grace were friends." She puts emphasis on friends snidely. "I'm Mary Cobb, a dear friend of the family."

"Nice to meet you, Mary." I try to pull my hand away, which only makes her clasp it tighter.

"And this is my beautiful granddaughter, Sheri Cobb." Mary takes my hand and places it in Sheri's. I grit my teeth to keep from cringing.

Right on cue, Grace's voice sounds behind me.

"Mary, what a surprise! I didn't know you were coming over this morning. Mom already left for the festival. You should have called, and I could have saved you the trip. Hello, Sheri." Grace's southern drawl is back and sugary as ever. There's a bite to her tone.

I'm able to get my hand free, so I step back to put my arm around Grace, folding her close and kissing the top of her head. It's an intimate move, meant to send a message.

Move on, Mary. I'm not just a friend.

Mary's eyes widen then flash with annoyance before she speaks. "Well, we're here now, so why don't we all ride to the festival together."

"That's so kind of you, but we're not quite ready to go yet."

"We can wait a bit. I'm sure Nick wouldn't mind hanging out with us while you do whatever it is you need to do." Mary gives her a dismissive wave. "And besides, you know how parking is a nightmare."

Grace tenses, digging her fingernails into my lower back, then clears her throat with a gargled sound.

"Actually, Nick and I have a designated spot at the Mayor's office, so parking is not a problem for us. But before you go, let me give you your dishes from last night. They're back in the kitchen."

Grace doesn't wait for another retort, turning and heading back to the kitchen. I follow, feeling the heat of her irritation, and mentally tell my dick to calm down. The passive aggressive Grace is another turn on.

She grabs the bag from the sideboard and hands it to Mary, who followed us with Sheri on our heels.

"What in the world happened in here? Is that your mother's famous peach pie?"

"It's the remains. I clumsily dropped it on the counter, so I need to do some damage control."

"Oh, lord, that's awful and will take forever. Why doesn't Nick ride with us? We'll make sure he gets to your parents."

Now, I'm the one getting annoyed. This old bitty won't take a hint.

"That's a great idea. We can show Nick around town. He's got to be bored out of his mind watching you fix your mistake." Sheri steps closer, doing that lip-licking thing again.

A low growl escapes from Grace, and when I glance at her, I brace myself. The claws are coming out.

"Nick, baby, this is that southern hospitality thing I was telling you about. Everyone is always showing so much kindness. Mary and her friends making us a welcome dinner last night, and stopping by unannounced today. Just last year, Sheri was gracious enough to show my friend, Pledge, around the pecan property. He had a terrible problem in his pants, and she helped him out. He was able to release some pressure. It was awfully gracious of her to step up to the plate. I did feel bad, though. Grandpa completely got the wrong idea and shot at him."

"Grace Rae!" Mary sneers.

"Oh, that's not all." Grace squints at me with an evil glint in her eye, her lips starting to twitch. "Pledge called me a month later and told me Sheri was kind enough to give him a gift… the kind of gift that requires a doctor's visit, an antibiotic, and a soothing cream you apply *down there*." She points to my groin.

I know this last part is not true, but Grace pulls it off without a hitch.

"How dare you! That's a lie!" Sheri screams.

"Grace Rae, what has gotten into you?" Mary clutches her neck in horror. "Sharon and Carl would be ashamed!"

"I'm sorry, Mary. What did I say?" There's so much saccharine and sarcasm in Grace's tone, I lose my battle to keep a straight face.

I drop my chin to my chest and laugh quietly.

"We're leaving! I can't believe the way you've treated us." Mary stomps out, motioning to Sheri to follow.

Sheri spins around but stops, eyeing the kitchen island. She looks between us and the pie suspiciously. "That's a fucking handprint."

At this, Grace bursts into a fit of giggles and leans into me for support. I hold her close and hope like hell we have time before Mary gets to Sharon and Carl.

Because I'm going to fuck Grace again. This time, I'll move the pies.

"The dog and pony show over?" Roy grumbles, watching another guy walk away from our table with my autograph and a dozen selfies. "Ridiculous."

"It's okay. I don't mind."

"I do! I'm here to watch football, drink beer, and relax. These fools are aggravating me."

"Everyone aggravates you. It doesn't take much," Logan mutters. "Maybe you should stay home."

"And ruin tradition? No way. Not happening."

"Touché." Logan tips his beer before taking a long gulp. "Besides, with Grace and Six being two hours late, he kept a lot of eager townsfolk waiting."

He doesn't even try to hide the implication behind his statement. Grace was able to cover for us well, explaining to her mother the issue with 'dropping' the pie and Mary's uninvited arrival. Sharon seemed okay, but all the Monroe men clearly weren't fooled.

As a precaution, I sent Shaw and Mathis a message with the exact address of Roy in case he did kill me and bury me in his back yard. Even though every second with Grace this morning was worth it, I was afraid of Roy's reaction. So far, I'm still breathing easy, but the day isn't over.

When we finally got here today, Grace walked me around to the vendors and introduced me to tons of people. I'm used to getting attention, but it wasn't me who these people wanted to see. Grace is loved in this town, everyone referring to her as the 'Peach Princess' and asking about her gallery. After an hour, she brought me to this sports bar, where she explained the men spent most of the day.

It was then I became the center of attention, meeting the men of Thomasville. It was all going smoothly until Roy had enough of the constant interruptions of his football games and ran the last guy off. Grace was right; the Monroes are the aristocrats of this town. Even with Carl being the Mayor, it's obvious Roy holds the most respect.

I peer across the street and see Grace laughing with a bunch of women who appear to be our age. One of them hands Grace her baby, which she cuddles close, kissing its forehead.

My heart swells, watching her interact. A sense of déjà vu overwhelms me, remembering Bizzy with Brayden the first few times. It's a beautiful sight. But with Grace, it's more of a longing. I think about what kind of mother she'll be.

Mother to our children. Our children…

When I learned Shaw was going to be a dad, a sense of panic took over, not only because of his stupid mistake, but because the thought of kids scares the shit out of me. But reconnecting with Grace has changed things.

Now, I know I want it, and it's time I make my intentions known. I clear my throat a few times and sit up straight, inhaling deeply before looking at Roy. He observes me closely, doing the opposite. He sits back, planting his feet firmly on the ground, and crosses his arms.

Carl walks in and shakes a few hands before sitting at the empty seat at our table. He reaches into the bucket of beers, picks one up, and loosens his tie.

"I'm done for the day. Last contest judged. What'd I miss?" He tips his bottle to the screen.

"You're just in time to watch pretty boy squirm," Roy tells him with a sinister grin. "Been waiting for this since you drove up to my house."

Carl whips his head to me, his expression changing. "How long are you going to play football?"

It seems like a weird question, considering I'm about to spill my guts about planning a future with Grace, but I answer honestly. "As long as I can. Barring injuries and the league, I think I have at least another ten years."

Logan whistles low, shaking his head. "Mom's not going to like that."

"So ten years of Grace not coming home for Thanksgiving and Christmas?" Carl goes on.

It clicks then; my team schedule will always have me playing on these holidays. They're thinking about the future, too. I swallow hard, careful of how I answer.

"Jesus Christ, you were laid out by a two-hundred-and-ninety-five-pound lineman the other night. Now, you look like a scared jackrabbit!" Roy fires off, clearly enjoying my discomfort.

"You can visit us. I'll buy us a house big enough for everyone to stay as long as you want."

"Do you want children?" Roy's face remains stoic.

"Yes."

"How many?"

"However many Grace will give me."

"You know I shot at the last man Grace brought home. He was a piece of shit walking. He didn't deserve to breathe her air. I know why she did it. It was clear she didn't have any interest in him, so I took great pleasure in ushering him off my property with a few rounds."

"Not to sound violent, but I'd have probably been in jail after knowing what he did to her. He's a stupid dickhead. Lucky for me, he was long gone before I found her again. But if he wasn't, it wouldn't have stopped me."

All three of them seem to like the response because the mood at the table lightens, Carl relaxing in his chair.

"That's it?" I'm pretty sure these men have been practicing this since Grace was born.

"There're a few things you need to promise me, boy, and I'll take your word as your honor."

"What's that?"

"You'll love her like she deserves. Never hurt her."

"Easy, done."

"There's a peach tree in the back of the orchard. She and her grandma loved that tree. Grace wants to get married under that tree."

Easy again. "Done."

Roy shares a look with Carl, and the hair on my neck starts to pickle.

"Last thing, Grace has dreams, big dreams. I'm aware she gave up a lot to be here with me because she's stubborn and insisted I needed her. She was right, I did, but I've regretted a lot since I lost Kayla. You need to promise me to make her follow those dreams."

"I'm a little lost here. What am I missing?"

"Grace has talent, big talent. She's been wanting to get into this elusive Art Program for most of her life. She's got a good chance to get accepted. Don't let her turn it down," Logan explains.

"Why the hell would I do that?"

"Because Grace loves hard. She'll sacrifice for those around her. My baby girl is in love with you, and the last thing she'll want is to be away from you." Carl's words hang in the air as all eyes stay on me.

"One thing to know about me, Carl, is that I love hard, too. And Grace is no exception. If she gets into the program, I'll make sure she goes."

"We're counting on it."

Chapter 20

Grace

"Delivery for Grace Monroe."

"Right here." I meet the delivery man halfway and take the box out of his hands. "Do you need me to sign for anything?"

"Once I get it all. There's more in the truck."

"More?"

"Yes, more." He goes to the black van and returns with an enormous bouquet of flowers and a picnic basket.

I sign and he leaves before I open the card nestled in the flowers.

Thank you again. The weekend was perfect.

Love,

Nick

I open the box and let out a loud laugh at the new number six jersey. Unlike the flowers, this card is written in his handwriting.

Since your other one was ruined, I figured you needed this for the game this weekend. I'll imagine you wearing it.

Love,

Nick

Flutters start in my stomach as I open the picnic basket and start taking out the items. High-pitched giggles pour out of my mouth as I take inventory. Four bottles of wine, a large fruit and cheese tray, and all my favorite snacks.

It's probably self-explanatory, but I tried to get all the things you love. Think of me while you enjoy. Have I mentioned how much I'm beginning to dread away games?

Love,

Nick

Yes, Nick, you've mentioned this a few times, I think to myself. Truth is, I dread away games, too.

I line up the cards on the counter and re-read them over and over again, my heart swelling at his signature. *Love, Nick.*

There is no doubt in my mind I'm head over heels in love with Nick Bennett. I think I always have been. At first, the feeling petrified me. It was too soon, but now, it feels right.

So, so right.

"Did you change your birthday and not tell me?" Logan comes around the corner, seeing the mounds of gifts on the desk.

"Nope." I gather the cards and slip them into the picnic basket.

"So what's all this?"

"Nick leaves for Buffalo tomorrow morning."

"So?"

"So he wanted to surprise me with a few things." I shake out the new jersey, showing it to Logan.

"Are you kidding me? This is the sorriest show of masculinity I've ever seen."

"Logan!"

"I'm sorry, Grace, but really?" He palms one of the lilies, shaking his head.

"Why are you being so snarky?"

"I'm being real. He's giving the rest of us a bad name."

"Maybe you should take notes. This is called being romantic."

"Romantic my ass, this is bonafide whipped."

"Romantic." I click my tongue on the 'c' to emphasize the word.

His lips twitch, trying to hide his smile. "I'm kidding with you, Grace. I like that he puts that goofy grin on your face, even if he does need to get his head in the game."

"His head will be in the game by the time it starts on Sunday. I can guarantee it."

"Good, you coming over to my place to watch it?"

"Sure. Is Melanie going to be there?" I ask flippantly, trying not to sound too nosy.

"She's invited."

"Want me to call and ask her?"

"Not really. If she wants to come, she will."

"I don't mean to pry, but are y'all on the outs?"

He shrugs, avoiding eye contact.

"Logan, look at me."

He does, his playful mood from earlier now gone. "I don't know what to say. I thought about what you said on the plane, and I do like her. She's a cool girl, and I like spending time together. Do I picture a future? Yes, I'd like to. But I think I hurt her feelings."

"So apologize."

"I tried, but it was a disaster."

"Oh, lord, what happened?"

"She started crying. It was awful."

I try to hold back, but the horror on his face is too much for me, and I burst into laughter. He narrows his eyes, clearly not amused.

"I'm sorry! I really am, but you should have seen your face."

"It was obviously a mistake to try to talk to you."

"No, no." I cover my mouth and force myself to calm down. "I'm sorry. Tell me more. What did you do next?"

"I left her alone."

Now, it's my turn to be horrified. "Logan, your girlfriend started crying and you left her alone? That's terrible. Tears are not the kiss of death."

"I didn't know what to do."

"Well, take a page out of the Nick Bennett playbook and go get her something nice. Surprise her with it. Tell her you're sorry and truly mean it."

He truly looks like a lost boy, so I try to think of something to help him out.

"I got it!" I snap my fingers and turn to the computer. When I find the email, I forward it to his work address.

"Want to fill me in?"

"Yep, when we were at the game, she mentioned wanting to get familiar with the art world a little more, to know about our business since you are so involved. I got an invitation this morning to view some pieces going on display at a gallery downtown. The artist wants us to consider him for next year. I wasn't going to be able to go because it's the weekend I'm going to Jacksonville. You should go and take Melanie. You can show her a little of what we do."

He doesn't seem overjoyed at the idea." I don't know, Grace. That's more your scene. You're better at that."

"Bullshit. You're great. You pulled it all together when I was still in school, and look at the masterpiece we did with both our styles." I wave my hand to the room.

He glances around and starts to nod. "Yeah, okay. I'll ask her to go with me."

"Great!" I jump up and down clapping, completely satisfied with my meddling. I like Melanie, and even if she's not the one for Logan in the long run, I'd hate to see him lose her for being a dumbass.

"And besides, I need to get back into practice. I'll have to be the point person when you're gone."

Confusion hits me. "Gone?"

"Gone for the apprenticeship, or whatever you call it in that program."

Ugh, that damn program. I had to finesse my way through questions from my family all weekend about the waiting process. They're convinced I need to call and follow up since it will start in less than two months. If accepted, I'll have very short notice to get things in order.

The truth is, I'm not convinced it's what I want to do anymore. My apprehension has grown stronger and stronger each day. Thinking about leaving Nick for any period of time makes my stomach roll. But it's not only him. I love my job and my life in Miami. Going away doesn't appeal to me as much now, even if it is only for a few months.

I'm not ready to have this conversation with Logan, so I smile politely and start placing the gifts back into the picnic basket. "I sent you that email. You should call Melanie now and invite her so you can RSVP."

"Good idea."

As soon as he's out of the room, I hug the jersey to my chest and think again about Nick's notes. Then an idea pops in my head, and I grab my phone before I lose my nerve. In order to pull this off, I'll need some help. I find the number and press send, thankful that Nick made me save all his family's contact information.

"Shaw Bennett's office, this is Gail."

"Hey, Gail, it's Grace Monroe."

"Grace dear, how are you?"

"I'm great. How about you?"

"My only complaint is my boss."

I giggle, knowing she and Shaw have an excellent relationship. "You should demand a raise. I hear Shaw's been in a generous mood lately."

"You heard about that, huh? It's quite an extravagance."

"Bizzy came by on Tuesday and showed me. She tried to act nonchalant, but I could tell she was beyond excited."

I'm referring to the brand new car Shaw surprised Bizzy with over the weekend. To me, it was a luxurious, sporty convertible, but Nick explained the 911 C4 Cabriolet is so much more than a 'sporty convertible'. It is a top of the line, specially ordered, high-end car meant to make a statement. He may have known Shaw was buying it, but seeing it was a different story. Bizzy said she swears he started drooling.

"She's always said that Shaw…"

"…has more money than sense." I finish the statement for her, Bizzy telling me the same thing.

"Well, it's certainly a surprise to hear from you. What's going on?"

"That's why I'm calling. I need Shaw to help me with a surprise. Is he available?"

"He sure is. I'll get him."

She places me on hold, and I start to have doubts. This is one of the craziest ideas I've ever had.

My stomach plunges when the noise starts on the other side of the door. Thunderous footsteps fill the room as the men rush in. There's a lot of loud banging, which kicks my already frazzled nerves up a notch.

What the hell was I thinking, runs through my head for the twentieth time since I made the call to Shaw. Then I start to consider how this could go terribly wrong.

This is by far the boldest idea I've ever had in my life.

Please, God, don't let me throw up.

Conversations grow louder as the men shout back and forth across the locker room.

I hear water running as they start the showers, and I realize for the first time how many women would die to be in my shoes—standing less than twenty feet away from an entire football team as they strip down.

Sweaty, dirty, naked men… hmmmmm. My insides start humming for a totally different reason. Sexy, X-rated visions fill my head.

My ears perk up when Nick's voice grows closer. He's on the phone, and I know its Shaw secretly leading him to me. He hangs up right as he opens the door, expecting to meet with a trainer.

The look of shock on his face when he spots me shoots a thrill throughout my entire body. He stops, his eyes meeting mine for a brief second before traveling slowly down, taking in my outfit. I purposely chose the skimpiest skirt I own to go with the jersey. But what sets off the outfit is the shoes. I know I've accomplished the desired effect when he lets out a low whistle.

"Fucking cowboy boots."

The mood in the room changes when he looks back at me. He stays quiet, turning to shut the door and locking it.

Then he spins around, tossing his phone on a chair. His blue eyes pierce mine with dark burning desire.

"Surprise," I croak, my mouth dry from the fierce vibes he's sending.

My knees start to wobble as I take him in. He's shirtless, his torso still shiny with sweat. There are streaks of dirt on his forearms and covering his athletic shorts.

I lick my lips, trying to remember my plan that has inconveniently flown out of my head.

"You came to surprise me?"

I nod and decide to wing it. "I actually came to thank you for the gifts."

"You didn't want to wait until tonight when I got to your place?" His voice is deep and husky.

I begin to feel braver, taking a few steps toward him. "I could have waited, but then I read your note again, the one that said you would imagine me wearing this. I didn't want you to have to imagine it, so I decided to come down here and show you myself."

"Shaw in on this?"

"He told me where to hide, made sure the room was empty, and got you to me."

"That explains why he was being so cryptic."

I close the distance between us, feeling the heat radiating from his hard body. Rising on my tiptoes, I wrap my arms around his neck and put my mouth to his. "This is more of a going away present. Maybe to help ease your dread of road games."

He parts his mouth slightly, sliding his tongue along my lips. "I'm pretty sure your plan backfired. Seeing you in this sexy as fuck outfit, waiting for me, makes me never want to leave you."

His hands circle my waist, hoisting me until I'm completely wrapped around him. My skirt hikes up, pooling at my hips, the cool air on my bare ass sending a shiver up my back. Our eyes stay locked as he lowers one hand, finding the thin string of my thong and snapping it.

"Nick! What are you doing?"

"I think you know the answer to that." He slides a finger into me.

"You have to stop tearing my underwear."

"Stop wearing them when you know you're driving me wild, which is all the time."

"We can't do this." I squirm. "There are people on the other side of that door."

"We'll be quiet."

"We can't," I repeat, my eyes fluttering closed when he applies pressure to my clit.

"What did you think would happen when I walked in here and saw you in this getup?"

"We'd make out."

"Make out, make love, fuck... Call it what you want, but it's happening."

He twists, pressing my back to the wall and shifting his hips, his shorts falling. In one swift movement, he fills me. His face is now masked with undeniable desire.

"Oh my God," I moan, feeling every inch of him stretching me. My head falls back, clunking into the wall.

He kisses me deeply, covering my moans as he starts to thrust. He sucks on my tongue, slowing his movements. His hips start to grind in the same rhythm as his tongue, sending waves of urgency through my veins.

My fingers thread through his short hair, gripping tightly. Without words, I'm begging him not to stop. My body is full of Nick, and I still crave more.

What has he done to me?

Coiling starts low in my stomach and spine, both tingling when he swivels his hips again.

"Please," I plead into his mouth.

He drives faster, giving me exactly what I need. I'm close, so close I break away, knocking my head back into the wall again. My breathing starts to come in pants. His lips skim over my throat, leaving a trail of heat that singes my skin.

"Now, Grace," is all he has to say and I explode, squeezing my eyes tight and holding back a scream.

He lets out his own low moan, pumping once more, then stills. His cock pulses inside of me, each tick hitting my sensitive skin. Neither of us moves as we fight to regain our breath.

I finally come back down from my high, releasing his hair and putting my forehead to his.

"Three minutes, that's all I could hold out." He grunts. "And it still didn't take the edge off."

"But it was a great three minutes."

"You make fantasies come true."

"I'm not the only one."

"Grace, I need your eyes on mine."

I slowly open my eyes, only to be stunned breathless again. He's staring at me with a look I recognize.

It's the look Shaw gives Bizzy.

The look my dad gives my mom.

And the look Grandpa gave Grandma.

I know this look well because, in my mind, I'm retuning it to him.

"I love you, Nick," slips out of my mouth before I can stop it.

His eyes start to shine a crystal blue, and he nips gently on my lips once more. "You stole my line."

"I did?"

"You did. So I need to steal it back. I don't only love you; I'm in love with you. You are my world. If someone asked me who my soulmate is, I'd describe you down to the fucking pink polish on your toes. Every single thing that makes Grace Rae Monroe is what I was put on this earth to love. When I was fourteen and fighting for my life, there were some really hard times. But I'd gladly go through them again and again, knowing that I'd be here with you in my arms eleven years later."

My heart starts to ache, and the damn burst, tears flowing freely down my face. He kisses them away, pressing close.

"Now, we're going to go home and find a bed, so I can show you how I feel. And I can promise you it'll take a lot longer than three minutes."

"Charmer." I smile through my tears.

"Only for you, Sweet Peach. Only for you."

Chapter 21

Nick

Losing sucks.

Losing to Buffalo on the road, then facing the week of scrutiny before another road game fucking sucks.

Coaches, trainers, reporters, and league personnel—all of them want some kind of answers. And they expect me to give them. I've had a week of playing the 'woulda, coulda, shouda' game. Coaches may pretend to shake off a loss with the standard statement, "We're looking forward, not backward," which is a lie.

Because if that were true, I'd be with my family right now in a nice hotel, instead of sitting in this room. Better yet, I'd be with Grace.

"Anything you can add, Bennett?" our defensive coordinator asks.

"Nothing more than I've already told you. Reed Matthews had already graduated when I started on the team. He's quick and has chemistry with the quarterback. Defense needs to be ready."

Eddie and Gade both give me fist bumps, knowing we have the same chemistry on the field. It's also a show of support.

Reed Matthews also played football at FSU, training and learning from the same coaches who taught me. So, naturally, the team has questioned me about his techniques. Since Jacksonville isn't a conference game, this is the first time we're meeting on the field since I was drafted.

Coach finally calls the meeting, reminding us we're under curfew and lockdown tonight.

I press *send* on a text message I've been waiting to send for the last thirty minutes.

We're done. Meet me at my hotel.

SP- On our way! Love you

We all shuffle out, going to our respective rooms to do God knows what until we leave for the stadium tomorrow. An eight p.m. curfew leaves a lot of downtime tonight. Luckily, I'll have my family to help pass the time. Shaw, Bizzy, Mathis, Claire, and Grace all flew in this morning and checked into a different hotel.

Fucking Shaw. This is where the line between brother and agent is drawn. He knew we were going on lockdown and made sure Grace couldn't be a distraction. I was pissed. I wanted her at least in the same hotel, but she agreed with him, promising me a full night of celebration once we got home. I had no choice but to accept the decision.

On the way to the elevator, a group of us pass the restaurant, which is packed with traveling fans. Heads turn, recognizing us, and the shouts start.

"You got this!"

"Get out there and show 'em how it's done!"

"Gunslinger!"

"We love you, Sexy Six!" comes from a chorus of women, and I hang my head, giving them a wave.

On the ride up, there are a few murmurs, but mostly everyone is quiet as we start the mental preparations for tomorrow.

Grace Space pops in my head, thinking about her term for when she spaces out.

"You good?" Eddie pats my shoulder when the elevator opens to our floor.

"Yeah, the family is coming over. We'll probably watch some football, shoot the shit for a while."

"Grace coming?"

"Yep."

"Think she misses me?"

"Not a bit."

"Maybe I'll come down and hang for a bit. Nothing like a pretty girl to get the motivational juices flowing." He flashes a bright smile, wiggling his eyebrows. "Maybe show her the Jarvis—"

"You itching for a fight?"

"Whatever it takes to get you riled up."

"You mention showing my girlfriend anything of yours, I'll show you riled up."

"Good, man, catch ya later." He slaps me on the shoulder again and disappears down the hallway.

I let myself into my room, taking in the dismal surroundings. I hope to God Shaw got something nicer for Grace. I want her to enjoy this trip, because next year, I'm going to demand she travel with me. A lot of the wives do it, so she won't be alone.

I hear them before they even get to the door. Claire is howling in the hallway, singing the Miami theme song off-key. I open the door and step out, noticing the scowls on my brothers' faces. In contrast, all three women are smiling wide.

"What's going on?"

They file into my room, Grace stopping at my side with a short kiss. "I think we've pissed off the Bennett brothers."

"Pissed off is an understatement." Shaw slices his eyes to Claire.

"What happened?"

"Shaw's overreacting and being a jealous twerp." Claire announces.

"Claire, stop antagonizing him," Bizzy scolds her, not hiding her smile.

"Sweet Peach, what are they talking about?"

"Claire joined Tumblr."

"So? Why is that so infuriating?"

"Because she's gotten hooked on the world of Tumblr porn. Since we got in the car to leave this morning, these girls have been locked in the world of social media pornography," Mathis answers in an aggravated tone.

Grace's eyes are shining as she bites her lip, watching my face for a reaction. "You've been watching porn all day?"

"Not all day."

"I'm not going to lie. The thought of you watching other people have sex surprises me."

"Some of it is HOT," she says low enough for only me to hear. "You should see some of the blow job techniques."

My cock stirs, and I wish like hell there wasn't a room full of people behind us.

"And get this! My identifier is 'BennettBabes2017'. Isn't it brilliant?" Claire's proud of herself.

"Once again, why the faces?"

"I'll give you five minutes of being around Claire watching that shit. Then you'll understand," Mathis explains.

I imagine the whole experience was slightly less painful than getting sacked by a mammoth-sized lineman. But the opportunity to remark is too easy. "Maybe she's trying to give you a hint on how to satisfy your woman."

Mathis's mouth narrows in a tight line, his eyes flaring. Claire snuggles to his side, throwing her arms around his shoulders. "I'm very satisfied." She plants a sloppy, lip-smacking kiss on his cheek, and I cringe.

"Enough of that shit."

"I agree. That's why we're getting out of this room before Claire finds a new page to stalk."

"Where are we going?"

"We've got two hours to eat and get you back. Let's go." Shaw takes Bizzy's hand and starts back toward the door.

"Come on, Sexy. We need to feed you and make sure you meet your curfew." Grace tugs on my arm.

I bend to her ear, where only she can hear. "If you were staying here, I could eat all night and not worry about a curfew."

Her eyes light up, and she gives me a little push. "Tomorrow night, I hope you're *starving*."

Oh, she can count on it.

Her scent assaults me the instant I walk into my condo. Most of the spacious area is dark except for the dim lamp next to the sofa, where Grace is sprawled out, sound asleep, under a light blanket.

Quietly, I drop my bag and keys on the counter and go straight to her. She barely stirs when I slide in behind her and curl my body around hers. Her hair's still damp from her shower, and I inhale deeply, taking it all in.

My chin rests on the top of her head, and I close my eyes, completely relaxing in peace. I wasn't happy about not seeing her after the game, but the fact that she'd be here waiting for me when I got home helped me through the after-game obligations.

I was half-expecting her to be waiting naked considering the suggestive texts I received after she was already on the plane. But lying here, with her in my arms, is all I want right now.

That's not right; it's what I *need* right now. Coming home to Grace kept my adrenaline racing long after the last second of the game. She was my win, and at this moment, I decide she needs to be here permanently.

As if she hears my thoughts, she twists into me, her eyes flickering open. "Hi," she says sleepily.

"Go back to sleep." I kiss her lips lightly.

"What time is it?"

"It's really late. Our flight was held up, and then we were faced with excited fans when we departed. I signed a few autographs."

"Sexy Six throws for the best game of his career, outshining every quarterback in the league today."

"You've been watching the NFL Network?" I'd already heard and read what the press was saying. Not to mention the calls from my parents and Grace's dad, congratulating me.

"Yes, I'm proud of you, Nick. You were a showstopper out there today. It was incredible to watch."

I brush some stray hair from her forehead and cheeks, my chest growing tight with her praise. "It was a good day."

"You were beaming at the end of the game. I know you were excited."

"I was, but having a good day puts a huge target on my back for next week. Can't let it get to my head."

Her hands move to my cheeks, and she pulls up, bringing us nose to nose. "You can be humble to the public. I get that, but with me, let's celebrate your talent and skill. Today was a big fat fuck you to all the haters of the last week. It was wonderful. You *are* wonderful."

"You're stealing my lines again."

"Well, get over it and accept it." She settles back down, keeping her eyes locked with mine. "It's like every day I fall deeper and deeper in love with you."

"That's a perfect reason for you to move in with me."

Her eyes grow wide right before she screeches, "WHAT?"

"Move in with me."

"Are you insane? It's only been a few weeks since I've even had shampoo and conditioner in your shower."

"That was your hang-up, not mine, and I'm the one who bought them. I clearly remember you protesting."

"It's way too soon."

"For who?"

"For anyone who has sense."

"Today's win was secondary to coming home to find you waiting for me. I want that every day and every night."

Her eyes dart nervously around the room, and I can see the wheels spinning in her head. She's not convinced. The last thing I want is for her to say no, so I decide to take a different approach.

"Three weeks, Grace. I'll give you three weeks, then we're discussing it again."

"Nick—"

"No." I place a finger on her lips. "And know something… I'm not giving you the three weeks to come up with excuses to say no. I'm allowing you three weeks for reasons to say yes."

"You're being cocky."

"You're being difficult."

"I'm being reasonable."

"I beg to differ."

She quietly glares at me, her eyes full of defiance, sending a challenge.

"Three weeks, Sweet Peach, and we're breaking your lease. You don't like it here, we'll move."

"You're not being charming." She sneers.

"You'll see that's exactly what I'm being once you're moved in. Now, let's talk about how hungry I am and that victory celebration you promised. I think you mentioned something about new blow job techniques." I toss the blanket to the ground and roll on top of her. The irritation on her face dies as I smile smugly.

"Tomorrow, brace yourself, baby, because I perform my best when faced with a challenge. And you just issued me a challenge."

Chapter 22

Grace

"I'm done!" I announce, flinging my hands in the air triumphantly.

"And so am I." Logan puts his drill and level away.

"We outdid ourselves. It looks great." I appraise the art display in the entryway, hall, and great room of Mrs. Shields's home. She's already started prepping for the holidays, so we were under a deadline to get the install done before Thanksgiving next week.

"Let's get out of here. I'll even buy dinner."

"Great! Nick's with the crew for MDN tonight."

"MDN?"

"It's short for monthly dinner night. Bizzy started it a few years ago. It's once a month the four of them get together for dinner alone. Mathis, Shaw, Nick, and Bizzy."

"I'm surprised you're not there."

"It's pretty sacred. But Nick did mention me coming next time. We'll see what happens. It doesn't bother me. I think their traditions are important."

"Let me load the car, and you think about where you want to eat." He gathers the bag of tools while I take a cloth and polish each frame once more.

Mrs. Shields comes in and completes her inspection with approval before we leave.

Once in the car, Logan voluntarily starts telling me about his and Melanie's weekend. The art show was a great idea; she loved it. But more so, I think Logan enjoyed sharing this part of his life with her. From the sound of it, all is forgiven, and she spent the weekend at his place.

I choose a restaurant we both enjoy, and the hostess seats us with her eyes glued to Logan the whole walk to the table. She's glaringly obvious, and I want to burst her bubble that he's taken. The girl can't be older than eighteen.

Let her dream.

She seats us and sighs when he gives her an appreciative, "Thanks."

"We as women really are shameless creatures," I assess, watching her stroll away.

"How so?"

"I don't remember ever outwardly giving a man bedroom eyes. It's like so many women have a honing beacon that sprouts up, and they zone in on men with this *look*. Do they think that look is going to make a man fall head over heels and they'll live happily ever after?"

"Someone's feeling snarky tonight."

"Come on, didn't you notice that hostess sizing you up?"

"Grace, she's still a girl. Did you actually think she had bedroom eyes?"

"Yes!"

He narrows his eyes and slides his menu toward the middle of the table. "Did that girl looking at me truly bother you?"

"I don't know." I shrug. "I mean, it shouldn't, but these last few months with Nick have me seeing the desperate side of women I never witnessed before."

"He's a celebrity, Grace. His face is plastered on billboards, bus stops, and buildings all over the city. He visits with children on the cancer ward. Not to mention, he's got commercials on television for everything from pain medicine to razor blades. He's going to get attention, from men and women."

"Not helping, Logan."

He reaches over and covers my hand with his own. "What's going on in your head?"

"I think I'm feeling insecure. Women are relentless and assertive in their pursuits."

"Have you told Nick this? From where I sit, you have nothing to worry about. He's crazy about you."

"He asked me to move in," I blurt out and brace for him to blow up. Instead, he waves down our waitress and orders for both of us. When she leaves, he focuses back on me.

"What'd you say?"

"I haven't answered him. He gave me three weeks, which is up soon."

"Do you want to?"

"Aren't you going to say it's too soon, or try to talk me out of it?"

"Nope, not my place. I'm not surprised by this. He's completely devoted to you, so if you move in, that's your business. You're doing a month-to-month lease anyway since you're leaving in January."

I wince, welcoming the glass of wine the waitress offers. "I'm still trying to decide if it's too soon. Giving up my own space is scary."

"He seems convinced."

"Yeah, I think he won't take no for an answer. He can be persuasive."

"This conversation just took a turn I never want to talk about." He squirms uncomfortably.

I give a half-hearted laugh and change the subject. "Okay, let's talk about Mom and Dad's visit next week."

"What's there to talk about?"

"Maria and Mom arranged for dinner to be delivered after the game on Thursday night. We're going to the Bennetts'."

"Sounds good."

"That was easy."

"I don't get involved in those plans. I'm trying to prep for Small Business Saturday and the next display."

"I've got some ideas. Want me to tell you now?"

His head does a small shake as he narrows his eyes. Then his expression quickly changes.

"I have a great group of young artists ready to do a small show. I'm thinking in six weeks, at the end of December. That could lead us into February, where we can do a total reset again with a group that contacted me out of South Carolina. It's a little different than our normal styles, but what I've seen so far is beautiful watercolor acrylic work."

I'm so amped up about the upcoming events, I miss the way his face goes tight.

"Okay, Grace, put together a plan." His voice is strained, but I ignore it. Instead, I ramble on about the possibilities.

Then I share with him my invitation to join a Women in Business group, explaining their purpose.

By the time we finish eating, my excitement is at an all-time high.

It's hard to wipe the smile off my face when surrounded by Bizzy, Shaw, Nick, and Brayden. They all dote on the toddler endlessly, and he loves every second of it. At nine months old, he looks so much like Shaw, I have to wonder if he inherited anything from his mother.

"Come on, buddy, come get me." Nick squats and puts his arms out as Brayden scoots across the floor until he gets on all fours and crawls as fast as he can to his uncle. When Nick scoops him up, Bizzy cheers loudly, getting in the little boy's face and smothering him in kisses.

Brayden squeals in delight and wiggles free to do it all over, this time going to Shaw.

"It's amazing how he's changed in the last week," Nick comments, and Shaw growls.

Shaw has made no secret how much he wants full custody of his son, but legally, he has to split fifty-fifty with Brayden's mom, Sasha.

Bizzy shoots Shaw a sad look, then gently steals Brayden, bringing him to her chest and blowing raspberries all over him. It's a heartwarming sight, and I hold out my arms, wanting my own turn.

The little boy has no aversion to strangers, coming to me easily, grasping my hair, and drooling as he tries to put it in his mouth. I catch Nick watching me warmly.

"Do we have him for Thanksgiving?" I ask Bizzy, and she nods.

"My mom is going to be in heaven."

"It's a fight among the moms, so tell her to get in line. Maria sends evil glares to my mom every second he's in her arms. Shaw has to intervene often."

"It'll be fine because Mom is going to be focused on getting to know Sharon. She's beside herself," Nick says, warming my heart.

"I'm going to start dinner." Bizzy gets up and runs her hand through Shaw's hair before heading to the kitchen. He stares after her lovingly.

"That's our cue. I'm taking Grace home." Nick gets up and takes Brayden while helping me stand.

We say our goodbyes, and when we get into Nick's truck, I announce, "I'm in love with him."

"He's a cute little guy."

"Do you think about that, Nick?"

"What?"

"Children?"

"Sometimes. Never until Brayden came along, but now, it doesn't scare me so much."

"Their situation is a shame. They don't seem to think highly of Sasha."

His fists grip the steering wheel, and his jaw goes tight. "She's a raging bitch that almost killed my best friend. None of us think highly of her."

"It was insensitive for me to bring it up. I'm sure the memories are still raw."

"You know, I was furious and terrified out of my mind, but it was nothing compared to what Shaw went through. Knowing now how much being in love can change a person, I'm not sure how he got through it."

"I think they have a beautiful love story."

He opens his mouth to say something, then shuts it, working his bottom lip between his teeth. The last thing I want is for him to be plagued with thoughts of Bizzy in the hospital, so I decide to change the subject quickly.

"How was MDN?"

"You're coming next time. It's decided. I was distracted all night thinking about what you were doing."

"That's silly. I told you I was at dinner with Logan."

"Yeah, but I'm selfish and wanted you there with us."

"We'll see what happens next time."

"Go ahead and mark your calendar. The next one is Tuesday after Thanksgiving."

I want to debate the reasons this should remain a foursome, considering their history, but my heart is jumping for joy.

MDN is a big deal. This is one more step in integrating our lives together.

Of course, when I move in, it'll be a big deal, too.

Chapter 23

Nick

Logan is sitting at his desk, papers strewn all over, and drinking a highball of dark amber liquid when I arrive. He barely glances up when I walk in, motioning to a chair across from him.

"You okay, man?" I choose to remain standing until I know what the hell is on his mind.

"Not really."

My earlier conversation with Grace comes to mind; she said they had a great day. Business was good, and their parents and Roy are flying in Wednesday night to spend the long weekend here in Miami. Everyone is coming to the game on Thursday. Thanksgiving dinner is being catered. Her mom is even coming to the gallery to help on Saturday.

Grace was flying high on cloud nine, but obviously, Logan doesn't share her excitement.

"Not to be a dick, but if you're having a bad day, why'd you ask me to come meet you? Grace is at my place, waiting on me to eat dinner."

He finally looks at me and literally snarls, his lips parting enough to let out a growl. "Grace is waiting on you for dinner, huh? Are we closing in on the three-week deadline where you convince her to live with you?"

Hostility fills the air between us, and anger starts to bubble up. "All due respect, Logan, but that's none of your fucking business."

His eyes start to burn with betrayal. He takes a large swig of his drink and slams it on the desk.

"That's where you're wrong. While you've been busy sweeping my sister off her feet, you've failed to keep your word to us."

"What the fuck are you talking about? I'll warn you now, Logan, you're on your way to pissing me off, and that's not a smart move."

"Pissed off? Pissed off? You think I care about pissing you off? This isn't fucking about you!"

"What the hell is your problem?" I roar, clenching my fist to my side.

His expression changes to complete disgust. "Grace said something last week at dinner that caught my attention. Actually, she said a few things, making plans for December and February, mentioning the Super Bowl, joining a Women's Business Association, shit like that."

"What's the problem with that?"

"December? February? March even?"

"I'm not following you." My anger spikes at his condescending tone.

"Grace is supposed to be in Alaska, New York, California! Not Miami!"

His point hits me hard, understanding washing through me.

She hasn't told him she wasn't accepted to the program.

I sink into the chair and try to think quickly. This is a conversation she should be having, but I can't let her walk into a situation like this. I'd kill him if he directed this type of anger toward her.

"I'd never overstep, because you should hear this from her, but she didn't get accepted. I think it's hurt her more than she's letting on."

His body jolts, physically stilling. "W-w-what?" He draws out the word.

"She didn't get accepted," I repeat.

He lowers his head and blows out a few deep breaths before raising his eyes back to mine, this time with a questioning glare. "Is that what she told you?"

"Yeah, kinda. When I asked her, she replied, 'there's always next year'."

"So she never actually said she wasn't invited to join?"

"Not in those words, but the implication was clear."

"Shit, shit, shit."

"What's wrong now?"

He rubs his eye sockets with the butt of his hands. "She didn't tell you either," he assesses, sliding a small stack of papers my way.

I pick them up, my stomach starting to roll as I read through the first one.

Miss Monroe,

After careful consideration and review of your application, the AIT would like to formally invite you to join our 2017 program.

As you know, this prestigious program is offered to a select group of artists who show accomplishments in areas of not only academia but also community. Your background and references are exactly in line with the type of individual we'd like to have join us.

In the coming days, we will be sending extensive information on the next steps, including location assignments.

Congratulations, and we look forward to having you become a member of our team of esteemed artists.

Sincerely,

The AIT Acceptance Board

I have to read through it twice to truly understand the words.

"She duped you, too," Logan accurately guesses.

"Why?" I look at him, trying to calm the thundering in my chest. "And how do you have this?"

"I made a few calls. My suspicions were nagging at me nonstop. Something wasn't right. Every time I asked her about this, she somehow blew me off, never wanting to discuss the importance of planning. I started to get worried that they'd rejected her, so I did something I swore I'd never do. I decided to intervene."

"Intervene how?"

"I called the board, explaining I was a reference and she still hadn't heard back."

"And they sent you this?"

"They didn't have to. This woman told me they were so disappointed Grace decided not to join them. She told me they were leaving a space open, in hopes she changed her mind before the deadline."

"Logan, I'm going to need you to spit this out. Tell me what I'm supposed to catch onto here. There has to be some mix-up."

"Keep reading." He points to the stack in my hands.

I do as he says, my eyes skimming through each page, noticing for the first time these are Grace's personal emails.

Miss Monroe,

We've had quite an interest in your skills from each of our instructors. After careful consideration of your personal interests, we've decided to send you to work with a group in Seattle, Washington.

More details are attached to this email. We look forward to hearing back from you.

The next few pages outline a syllabus of learning techniques, schedules, and lodging recommendations in Seattle.

There's another email.

Miss Monroe,

After several emails and voice messages, we've yet to hear back from you regarding your acceptance. Please confirm receipt of offer letter and assignment status.

We anxiously await to hear you're joining us on January 7th, 2017.

My own confusion sets in. Why hasn't Grace responded to them? And better yet, why didn't she tell me? My questions are answered as I flip to the last piece of paper.

Dear AIT Acceptance Board,

Thank you for your consideration into this elite and esteemed program, with the chance to work under some of the most respected mentors in my field. This is an opportunity of a lifetime that I deeply cherish.

With that being said, it is with great regret that I decline. This was not an easy decision, as I've loved art all my life. However, I've learned timing is everything. And the time is not right for me.

Please understand that I will forever be grateful for this opportunity and know your acceptance is the greatest and highest recognition I've ever received.

Sincerely,

Grace Monroe

My heart hammers hard, sending a roaring to my ears as I read back through the dates and times. The acceptance came three weeks ago, the day before she came to Jacksonville. She knew the whole trip she'd gotten in, yet she kept it to herself and insisted that I focus on the game.

I think about when I brought up the subject, knowing the time was coming where she should hear something. Holding her tight in my bed, she squeezed me back, telling me there was always next year. Like an asshole, I'd assumed she didn't get in and didn't want to press the issue. But I should have.

Then I look at the last time stamp. Her rejection was sent this morning, two hours after she left my condo where I reminded her my three weeks was up. My plan was to have her agree to move in with me before her parents arrived, so we could break the news over the weekend.

She smiled coyly, not acknowledging my timeline, but I figured I'd gotten through to her. Now I know, reading this, Grace was giving up much more than her apartment for me. She was giving up a chance of a lifetime.

When I glance up, there's a highball of whiskey filled to the rim in front of me. "Peace offering." He slides it closer.

"She lied to me." I take a healthy gulp, feeling the sting as I swallow.

"No, she sidestepped your question. She has a knack for that."

"I didn't want to be insensitive. I should have questioned her harder."

"Nah, because then she would have lied to you."

"How do you know? Maybe I could have convinced her to accept."

"Because she's my sister, and I know she's stubborn."

Selfless is another word that comes to my mind. "She can't do this. I'll talk to her. She's going."

"I owe you an apology. I thought you knew. She tells you everything."

"Apparently not." I finish the rest of the whiskey, this time welcoming the burn.

"What are you going to do?"

My mind is blank with ideas, but I know I have to think of something. "Convince her to go," is all I say.

"She doesn't know I have these emails. I had to backdoor into her email, essentially spying on her, after hearing she turned them down. I needed all the evidence."

"How do you want me to handle that?"

"I'll fess up, telling her I called and learned she declined. For now, I won't mention the emails."

"I'll go home and talk to her tonight."

"Actually, I think you should wait. Let the shock settle before you try to reason with her. She's going to be mad at me, even more furious I've told you. It's smart to wait a few days."

"How long?"

"I'll tell her on Monday. That gives you this week to figure out what you should say."

"You gonna be able to keep your temper down around her? Treat her normally? Because if you pull the same attitude on her, we're going to have a problem. A huge problem."

"Yeah, I actually feel like a dick right now. I assumed you knew and went back on your word."

"Dick move, but I understand. I've been known to jump to conclusions before, too."

The memory of barging into Shaw's office last year and laying him out when he hurt Bizzy springs to mind. She was devastated, and when I learned exactly how deep her fears and devastation ran, I went after him.

"Nick, I'm going to ask you something else. I'm not telling my family anything about this because they'll suffocate her with their meddling. Grace is excited about this upcoming weekend. The game, our families, the holiday—all of it. Don't ruin it for her."

I slice my eyes to his, my hand itching to throw a fist to his face. "You don't have to tell me that shit. I fucking love your sister more than anything."

Fury rolls between us as I wait for his response. If he says something else stupid, I can't be responsible for my actions. He throws his hands in the air, leaning back in his chair.

Smart choice considering I'd like to jump over his desk.

"Get your head together, think about how to proceed, and try to work your magic. I'm here if you need me."

I place the emails back on his desk and leave without another word. I'm not going to need him. I have a week until he approaches her. Seven days of pretending to know nothing and coming up with a way to send her away.

"Run this by me again." Shaw leans back, crossing one leg over the other and strumming his fingers on his knee. It's a move I've become familiar with over my professional life. It's his 'solution seat'. Every word soaks into his brain as he works to find a solution.

I repeat what happened during my meeting with Logan and tell him of my promises to the Monroe men.

"Quite a predicament."

"No shit."

"These are the kind of revelations that make me wonder if he truly did go to law school." Mathis rolls his eyes at me dramatically.

Shaw cocks an eyebrow at him, and I grin, some of the tension in my shoulders easing.

"It's no secret how I reacted when Bizzy told me she was leaving, taking a job in Charlotte. I lost my mind," Shaw adds.

"Totally different situation. Bizzy had her reasons. This is completely different," I argue.

"But I was hurt she didn't discuss it with me."

"You were having a baby with her nemesis! You broke her heart. How is that even relatable to this?" I'm beginning to lose my patience and regret asking Shaw and Mathis to meet with me for advice.

His golden eyes flash with annoyance, telling me to reel it in. Shaw loves his son, but the memories before Brayden were born are grim. He almost lost Bizzy twice, and both were because of Sasha. Reminding him of her heartbreak is the best way to set him off. Luckily, Mathis takes the opportunity to speak up.

"What are the chances you can get her to change her mind?"

"Hopefully, a hundred percent."

"And if she refuses?"

"I'll have to change her mind some way. This is her dream, a dream she shared with Kayla. She's loved art for her entire life, and I can't let it slip through her fingers. It's only a few months, and that's why I can't understand why she didn't talk to me."

"Nick, I hate to point out the obvious, but you need to find out why she changed her mind. Don't assume it's because of you."

I scrub my hands over my face and know Mathis is right. I need to talk to her and find out her reasons, but that doesn't change the fact I have a job to do.

"Let's dissect both scenarios. What if you succeed, and she goes away? You say it'll be at least three months. Let's roll back to the facts." The lawyer in Shaw is back.

"According to the agenda, the program is anywhere from twelve to fourteen weeks, with the option to extend based on different circumstances. Grace really wants to perfect her glass blowing knowledge, so who knows what her end date will be."

"And what will you do while she's gone?"

"Hopefully, get through playoffs and another Super Bowl. Then I'll go to her."

"Does she know this?"

"She will once I talk to her. I'll explain."

"Worst case scenario, you'll be apart for six weeks."

"Doesn't seem too bad."

Mathis and I both swing our heads to Shaw, my eyes narrowing on him. "You didn't make it fourteen days until you moved to Charlotte."

The argument is clear on his face, and I let out a fierce rumble. "Don't you dare say anything you can't take back. I fucking love Grace to the bottom of my soul. She's it for me. Sometimes, the feelings are so strong I can't put it into words."

"Damn, brother, I think you just did." Mathis gives a low whistle.

"That's why I can't take this opportunity away. She deserves the world handed to her, and I'm not going to let it slip away."

"Sounds like your mind is made up. She's going, regardless of her initial decision," Shaw agrees under his breath.

He's right. Hopefully, this will be painless, but my gut is telling me to be prepared.

Be prepared to do whatever it takes to get her to Seattle.

Chapter 24

Grace

Watching my mom flutter around the gallery, talking with the customers, should have me smiling. Instead, there's a weight in my stomach that gets heavier as the day goes on.

Something's not right. I can sense it. There's not one thing I can pinpoint that's out of order, but the nagging feeling is still present. And it started when Nick came home on Monday night.

I expected him to pounce on me, knowing he'd expect an answer about living together. There was no pouncing, jumping, or leaping. Gone was the confident, smug man who'd left me that morning with the promise of getting an answer out of me. Instead, he fixed me a light dinner and took me to bed, saying he was exhausted from practice.

The next night was the same, except this time, he made love to me so tenderly, so sweetly, I cried when he fell asleep. But since my family arrived on Wednesday, we haven't had a chance to be alone. Knowing my family's traditions, he didn't argue when I explained I needed to stay at my place with my grandpa while Mom and Dad stayed at Logan's.

Even after his win on Thursday and our Thanksgiving meal, Nick stayed unusually quiet. He didn't even crack a smile when I served him a piece of the peach pie my mom made that morning.

There is so much happening around me. My parents and the Bennetts hit it off immediately. My Grandpa has declared he's in love with Claire, which had Mathis offering her to him for a week, jokingly. Melanie is back in the picture, too, fully involved with our crew. But my mood is sinking by the minute, my mind swirling with things I could have said or done wrong.

Nick is upset, and I can't figure out why.

"Grace, which picture did you mention to me you loved?" My mom's voice breaks me out of my Grace Space, and

I glance up to see Maria with her. I didn't even notice her come in.

"Let me show you." Anxiety spikes as I walk to the back. This was going to be a gift to Nick when I moved in.

"It's perfect," Maria gushes. "Where would you hang it?"

"In the entryway hall."

Luckily, there's no more time for conversation because another customer walks in and I rush to her, desperate to get away.

The afternoon drags on until I'm delirious with worry. Finally, when Logan takes Mom to his place to meet Dad, I break down and call Nick, ready to get to the bottom of this.

"Hello." His tone is sharp, jarring me.

"Nick?"

"Hey, Grace, what's up?"

"Nothing, I haven't heard from you today. Everything okay?"

"Yeah, I've been busy. Doing some shopping."

"Shopping?"

"Thought about getting a new TV, so I'm at the store."

"Where are you putting a new TV?"

I think about the seventy inch in his living room and the sixty inch already in his bedroom. There's no room for a new one.

"Not sure yet, maybe in the living room, but I need to go. The salesman is in front of me."

"Nick, I think we need to talk. Something is wrong."

He sighs impatiently and muffles the phone before coming back. "Grace, let's talk on Monday night after your parents leave."

"Monday night? Aren't we doing brunch tomorrow?"

"Sorry, I forgot. I'll see if I can make it."

"What the hell is happening here?"

"I need to go. Can I call you later?"

"Yes, Nick, call me when you're not so *busy*." I hang up and stare at the screen.

Then I scream into the empty gallery.

I swipe the hot tears from my cheeks and concentrate on driving. Anger and resentment fill my mind as I think about what Logan has done. How dare he? This is my life, my decision, end of subject. I'm a twenty-five-year-old woman who can stand on my own.

So why do I feel like a child who just left the principal's office?

Because my brother and business partner just scolded me, filling my head with horrible thoughts. And on top of it, he called my boyfriend, exposing my secret. The tears won't stop, so I pull over until I can regain my composure.

The scene from earlier replays in my mind, making me angrier by the second.

"Grace, can you come to my office when you lock up?" Logan called from the back.

I locked the doors, dimmed the lights, and closed down the computer.

"What's going on?" I asked, plopping in the chair and kicking off my shoes. It'd been a long day on my feet, and I thought about the bubble bath waiting for me when I got home.

He turned his phone over and over in his hand, blowing out a deep breath. When he looked up, disappointment was written all over his face. That's when it clicked; he knew.

Seeing no need to dance around the subject, I figured we might as well get it over with. "How'd you find out?"

"I made some calls today. Finally spoke to someone who told me you rejected the opportunity."

"You shouldn't have done that."

"You left me no choice. Every single time I bring it up, you brush it off. Mom and Dad are curious, yet, you blow them off, too."

"So you violated my privacy?"

"Making a phone call is hardly violating anything. Don't be so dramatic."

"Okay, so now you know. I decided not to go. The timing is wrong."

"How can the timing be wrong? This was always in the plan. We've been discussing this for over a year."

I knew he'd be upset when I told him, that's why I'd been avoiding this conversation. But he was clearly looking for more than a simple excuse. I closed my eyes and took a deep breath, ready to defend my decision.

"Plans change. I've changed. Not sure if you've noticed, but I have a new life."

"What you mean is you have a new boyfriend." Sarcasm leaked from his tone.

I straightened my shoulders and glared at him. He wanted an argument; he was going to get one. "Yes, I do have a new boyfriend, but I also have a lot more than that. I have friends who I've come to love. I have the gallery and all the artists. I also have you, and even though you're being a prick, I'd like to think you like having me around."

Shock registered on his face then quickly disappeared. "Of course, I like having you around, but I'm not going anywhere. Neither is the gallery. We'll both be here when you come back. As for you having friends, that's great, Grace, but those are Nick's people. His family. Are you actually going to make a decision this important based on them? If there's no more Nick and Grace, there are no more friends. Don't you see that?"

"That is low."

"Think about it, Grace. If you two split up, whose side do you think they'll be on? I'm sure they'll be around for a little while, but then they'll fade away."

"Why do you think we'll split up? We're in a great relationship!"

I kept the last few days of rejection and fear to myself. It was none of his business.

"Oh, that's right. You're on the accelerated path of becoming a quarterback's wife. A life of luxury and riches. Then, in ten years when he's done, he'll find a new trophy wife."

His statement stung, and I fought the tears that threatened. "Is that what you think of me, Logan? You think I'm with Nick because I want to be a quarterback's wife? Luxury and riches? Am I that shallow to you? If I were to marry Nick, it would be because I love him with all my heart. How dare you characterize my relationship with such disrespect? Is that what you've been thinking all along? Of me?"

He shrugged without an ounce of regret. "I'm looking out for you, telling you what you need to think about. You're so blinded by lust that your judgment is clouded. I'm not going to let you throw away this opportunity."

"Do you think I'm incapable of making my own decisions?"

"When it comes to Nick Bennett, I think you'd do anything."

"You asshole! I told you, I like my life here. This is my decision. Nick is a factor, but he's been nothing but supportive."

He smirked with such venom a chill ran up my spine. "Supportive? Yes, he is. That's why I called him to see if he was in on this decision. Imagine his surprise."

"You didn't." My heart sank.

"He's not too happy."

Getting up slowly, I slipped my shoes back on and turned to leave. I was done with our conversation.

So this was what betrayal felt like? A deep hatred stirred inside me.

"Grace, I'm sorry. This is not how I wanted the conversation to go, but your best interests are always my first priority. You need to think long and hard about your future." I heard him sigh, but I kept walking, never looking back.

My phone rings, jolting me back to the present, a picture of Nick and me flashing on my screen. God, I need him right now.

"Hey, Nick."

"Sweet Peach, where are you?" His concern gives me hope.

"I'm on my way home. Are you already there?"

"No, I'm at my place, but I'll meet you in an hour."

"Okay." I hiccup, the tears threatening again. "Are you mad at me, too?"

His pause is the confirmation I need. "We need to talk."

"You know what, Nick, I've just had the worst conversation of my life with my brother. I'm not in the mood to talk. If you're angry, then stay home. I have my reasons for not telling anyone I declined the program. If you're going to come over and be ugly, I can't take it tonight." My voice cracks, and I start bawling.

"Grace, where are you exactly? I'll come get you."

"Don't bother. I'll be fine."

"Baby, I'm not mad. I'm worried. We'll talk about it in a bit. I need to make a quick stop, and then I'll be there."

"I'm serious, Nick. I can't take anymore tonight. I need you to hold me, to reassure me things are good and my brother is an asshole."

"Maybe tomorrow would be better." His voice is raw, and my heart splinters.

There is no more energy in me to fight. The one person I thought I could count on is turning me down. I know Nick will understand my reasons, but there's no way I can go through it again.

"Okay, call me tomorrow." I hang up without saying I love you.

He calls back immediately, but I hit ignore and get back on the road. I'm done pleading my case.

What's done is done.

Chapter 25

Nick

I bang on the door with brutal force, hearing it rattle on the hinges. Rage pulses through my veins, threatening to explode.

When Logan finally answers, panic sets in. He looks like shit. He doesn't seem surprised to see me. Without a word, he goes back to his office, me following on his heel.

He falls into the closest chair, his body deflating in a heap. "She called you."

"No, I called her, ready to put my plan into action. Instead, I'm greeted with her crying. Actually, that's not right. She was bawling. The only thing she said was she'd had the worst conversation of her life with you. Of course, I was confused, because last we discussed, I was going to be the one to try to make her see reason."

"I fucked up. Fucked up big time. I didn't mean for it to happen, but once it started, the words, the lies just poured out of my mouth so easily. I didn't mean any of them, but still, I said them with such conviction and certainty."

My own panic starts to set in. What lies? This man in front of me looks physically ill. "What did you do?"

As he tells me what happened, my rage from earlier grows with each word. When he's done, there's shame brimming in his eyes, but I can't see past my own fury. My arm jets out, punching him with ravaging force. He flies to the side, the chair going over with him, and I take a step back to try to find some control.

"You told her I'd replace her with a trophy wife? That our friends would dump her? *WHAT THE FUCK WERE YOU THINKING?"* I roar, my voice bouncing off the walls.

"I don't know! It came out of nowhere." He rights himself, smartly staying on the floor.

"Did it come out of nowhere, or do you really believe that shit? Was this your way of expressing your jaded fucking opinion?"

"No, I don't think that. It was all lies. I know you love my sister."

"I don't only love your sister, I cherish your sister, and instead of taking the delicate approach and letting me handle changing her mind, you've now planted vicious thoughts in her head about me. About us. About our future. No wonder she was sobbing."

He stays quiet, shaking his head.

"What did you think you'd gain from that? As each vile word spewed out of your mouth, what was your end game?"

"The only end game I had was looking out for her, which is the polar opposite of what happened."

"You know what, Logan? I had it handled. I was ready to be the asshole, ready to push her away for the sake of this fucking opportunity. But now, I can't be the asshole because you've done it for me. It's been killing me inside, the last six days, watching her light go out as I started putting my plan in place. Our families are bonding and getting to know each other, yet, I stayed back. Our first holiday together, one where I was going to announce she was moving in and start the process of building our lives together. She'd stare at me with so much confusion as I prepared to keep my word to the Monroe men and make her chase that dream. Now, my woman, who is everything to me, is sitting in her house, thinking I'm mad at her. She's all alone while I deal with your bullshit."

"You should go to her. Don't let her be alone."

"Oh, I'm going to her. I'll be in her bed tonight comforting her as she tells me, in her words, what you've said. My job is to take care of her, and if I can't calm her, you bet your sorry ass I'll be back tomorrow, and the least of your problems will be a black eye."

"I deserve that."

"You know what I don't get? Why? Why is this so damn important to you? What do you get out of it? Will the gallery be more exclusive if she does this? Will you be a major player in the Miami art world?"

"Don't insult me." His eyes heat in anger.

"It's better I insult you than kill you."

"Grace gave up a lot to go home. She may have pretended it didn't bother her, but I know she wanted to go away for her MFA. She didn't. I want her to have this, knowing she worked so hard."

"Is this guilt? Because you got to continue on with your life after Kayla died and she put hers on the back burner?"

I know I've hit a nerve when he barely nods. "But there's also her promise to Grandma."

"And that is why I'm going to convince her to get on that plane, because I fucking love your grandmother without ever meeting her. You can go to hell."

"I'm already in hell. I destroyed my relationship with my sister tonight."

"Lucky for you, I'll try to clean up your destruction. But if you ever hurt her again, you'll be out of her life. The things you said could cause irreparable damage to someone."

My fist clenches, ready to go after him again, but instead, I leave him to nurse his eye that's already swollen to only a slit.

I get in my car and think about calling Grace again, but there's too much anger still boiling inside. Her brother has made my job a hell of a lot harder. I expected him to be there to pick up the pieces.

Thinking about what he told her has me speeding toward her house. Unfortunately, I'm going to have to build off that foundation.

Her eyelids start to flutter, eyelashes tickling my chest. I rub my fingertips up and down her arm that's slung over my chest. She lets out a soft sigh.

"Are you actually here or am I dreaming?"

"I've been here all night."

Her head pops up, and the instant I see her face, I want to punch Logan again.

And again…

And again…

Her beautiful violet eyes are bloodshot, remnants of mascara stained on her puffy cheeks. I've seen Grace shed a few tears over the last few months, but never this kind of damage. Slowly, I lift up and kiss each eyelid, willing the swelling to decrease.

"You've been here all night?"

"I tried to wake you up, but you were practically comatose. I was two seconds away from calling 9-1-1 until I found the Benadryl on your vanity."

"I took it hoping it would diminish the effects of crying myself to sleep. I figured it was effective for allergies, so maybe I had a chance. Did it work?"

"I'm not going to lie, babe. You look like you've been crying all night."

"Uggh…" She drops her head back to my chest and curls into me. "I'm sorry I didn't wake up."

"It's okay. Probably for the best. I was pretty livid when I arrived. It took the last nine hours to calm down."

She tenses, her arm across my chest tightening. "Were you livid with me?"

"No, your piece of shit brother. When he called me earlier in the day, telling me about your acceptance, I was irritated."

Lie #1

"I'm sorry."

"When you called me crying, my irritation switched to him, so I went to have a little talk."

"Did he tell you what happened?"

"He did."

"It was awful."

"That's why he's nursing a black eye today."

"You hit him?" She tilts her head, horror written on her face.

"Fuck yeah, I did."

"Well, that's not good."

"I didn't like hearing you cry."

"Did he tell you everything he said?"

"I guess."

"He was so vile and nasty. It wasn't my brother. That was a man I don't know."

Time to get this show on the road.

I lift her arm and roll out of bed, immediately missing the warmth of her body.

"I'm going to make coffee. Meet me in the kitchen." I avoid eye contact. This is going to be hard enough without seeing the evidence of what her brother has already started.

Ten minutes later, she joins me in the kitchen, her face freshly washed and hair in a high ponytail. She's wearing one of my old college shirts that hangs on her. Usually, she'd be completely naked underneath, but today, she's slid on a pair of pajama pants.

I fix her coffee and hand her the mug then walk to the other side of the kitchen. I prop my hip against the counter and start with the obvious question. "Why didn't you tell me?"

"I didn't tell anyone. I needed to process how I felt about it and truly think. After a few days, I realized the level of excitement I should have felt was not there. That's when I knew it was no longer what I really wanted."

"Why?"

"If Logan told you everything, then you know it's because my life has changed. I like being here in Miami. I love my job, my friends, you... things I didn't know when I moved here. If I would have had any idea of the roots I would build, I would have either not applied, or waited a year."

"That's fair, but you did apply, and you need to go."

"I don't want to leave. I've moved on. It's no longer on the table."

"Can it be?"

"Why? Are you saying you want me to go?"

"Yes, I want you to go. I think it will be a good business decision for you."

She studies me for a second, her eyes roaming over my face. I remain still, hoping she can't see through the laid-back façade.

"Business decision? What about us? Won't you miss me?"

Here we go.

"Sure, I'll miss you, but we can meet up when you get back. Then see what happens then."

"Meet up? See what happens?"

"Sure. If we're both still single, we can see where this thing goes."

She stumbles, and it takes all my willpower not to reach out to her.

"This thing goes?"

I sigh unnecessarily and place my mug on the counter, inhaling deeply and praying for strength to get through this. When I twist back around, she's gripping the counter for support.

"Listen, Grace, the timing on this sucks, but I've been thinking about this for a few days. I think we need to take a step back, breathe a little. Slow things down."

Lie #2

She visibly pales, blinking rapidly. "Slow things down. Three weeks ago, you asked me to move in with you. I argued, and you wouldn't take no for an answer. We took this relationship at lightning speed, and now you want to slow things down."

"Yeah, and I see how smart you were to make us both think about that moving in thing. Once I realized what I was asking, it became clear I'm not ready."

Lie #3

"You're not ready? What changed your mind?"

"Let's not do this, Grace. Let's not make it ugly. We've had a great few months. Let's take some time and see what happens."

"What's going on, Nick? Is this because I didn't tell you about the acceptance? Are you punishing me?"

"That's not my style. This is not a punishment. But now that you mention it, when I found out you kept it from me, I was surprised. We'd fallen into a routine where we shared everything. Then I let it go because it was proof we still have a lot to learn about one another."

"I see, so you want to take some more time to get to know each other?"

"I think it's smart."

Lie #4

"And you've been thinking about this since last week. Is that why you've been distant, closed off?"

"I'll admit introducing our families put me on edge."

Lie #5

"On edge? You're the one who insisted we do it."

"I know, and for that, I apologize. My decisions have been a little off lately."

All the color now drains from her face, and she starts to shake. My beautiful Grace stands in front of me, her lips quivering. A lump forms in my throat, threatening to choke me.

"Are we breaking up?" Her voice cracks on the last word, sending me deeper into my own hell.

"If you choose to put a label on it, then yeah."

"This nightmare keeps getting worse. First Logan, now you."

I involuntary cringe at being put in the same category as him, even knowing it's where I belong. She notices, her eyes piercing into mine. I mentally force myself to remain stoic, giving her my best blank expression.

"Tell me, Nick, and be completely honest. Are you doing this to push me away, trying to turn into an asshole so I'll change my mind? Did Logan put you up to this?"

Yes!

I press myself deeper into the counter until I feel a touch of pain. It's the only way I can keep focused on finishing this farce.

"Like I said, the timing sucks. I've been thinking about this before Logan called. My opinion is you should contact that group and see if they'll still take you, but you do what you want. It's your decision and doesn't affect me. I want you in my life, Grace. Taking a step back doesn't mean we can't be friends. Who knows what will happen in the future?"

Lies! Lies! Lies! Everything out of my mouth is a lie. I do know what's going to happen in the future. I'm going to chase you down and crawl on my knees for forgiveness. Then I'm going to marry you and love you for the rest of our lives.

"Why are you here then? Why did you slip into my bed in the middle of the night if you wanted space? Seems like a shitty way to show it."

"Another poor decision on my part. I wanted to talk to you last night, and when I heard you crying over what Logan said, my protective instincts kicked in. He was out of line, and I figured you needed some support."

"So you got into bed with me?"

"Habit." I shrug, trying to drive my point home. "It won't happen again unless you want it, but I figure you're not really a casual sex kinda girl."

"I thought you loved me. How can you be this cruel?"

"I do love you, Grace, but I think I was caught up in the idea of it all. The girlfriend, moving you in, declaring my love… it seemed like the thing to do. But I can't continue stringing you along under false pretenses. It's not fair. This is me loving you."

Her body jolts, her face crumbling. My blood starts to boil with hatred of myself.

"Lies, it's all been lies. None of this was real?"

"I have feelings for you, Grace. That's not a lie. You'll always be my Sweet Peach. Like I said, let's step back and give it time."

"Okay, Nick. If that's what you want," she finally relents.

I have to get out of here before I collapse at her feet. This is by far the stupidest thing I've ever done, and the worst thing about it is she believes me. There was a small part of me that hoped she'd laugh in my face and call me on my shit. But the way she's focused on me tells me I've accomplished my goal. The only upside is that she looks as crushed as I feel.

God, please let her forgive me.

I knock my hand on the counter a few times, trying to act casual about my mood. "I'd better get going. I'll call you later."

"You have MDN tonight," she reminds me.

Fucking monthly dinner night. The same dinner I insisted Grace attend. Bizzy is going to kill me. I deserve it.

"I'll touch base then tomorrow. See how you're feeling."

"Okay."

With nothing left to say, I go to her room and dress, the entire time eyeing her bed. She hasn't moved when I get back to the kitchen, still staring into space.

"Sweet Peach?"

Her eyes fly to mine at the use of her nickname.

"I'll call tomorrow. Let's do lunch or something. Taking things slow doesn't mean we can't hang once in a while."

Her only answer is a nod.

I leave her apartment with so much regret and self-hatred it starts to suffocate me. I've been an athlete all my life, but no loss will ever compare to walking away from Grace.

Chapter 26

Grace

Once I got over the initial shock of everything, I became angry. Then fury turned into sadness, humiliation, rejection, devastation, and every other emotion one person could carry around at once.

The instant Nick walked out, my knees buckled and all my strength gave way. I crumbled to the floor and cried until I was sick. Then I crawled back in bed for the next twenty-four hours, not caring that Logan would be left alone at the gallery. I dissected every word, every look, and every movement from Nick, trying to make sense of it.

Logically, it was too coincidental he decided to end our relationship hours after speaking to Logan. But any way I tried to justify it, I kept thinking back to his attitude and actions the week before. He had started acting different way before he found out. Maybe it *was* just awful timing as he had put it.

Was it?

Regardless, the fact still remained that he wanted space, and I was going to give it to him, even if he was sending me mixed signals throughout the entire conversation.

"I have feelings for you, Grace. That's not a lie. You'll always be my Sweet Peach. Like I said, let's step back and give it time."

Grandma Kayla taught me a lot of things, and one of them was that when things got rough and seemed to spiral out of control, it was time to take a good look at the facts.

And that's why I'm in my car, driving up to my childhood home. Being away from Miami is exactly what I need right now.

My phone starts ringing again, and I regret turning it on after the flight. I haven't spoken to Logan all week, so why the hell does he think I'll answer his calls? Ignoring him is the best option.

A text dings, and I'm pleasantly surprised to see it's from Bizzy, ten minutes ago.

Bizzy: Your voicemail is full. Can you call me as soon as possible?

I park the car and call her, waving at my mom who's waiting on the front porch.

"Grace, where are you?" Bizzy asks breathlessly.

"In Thomasville. Are you okay?"

"Yes! I was rushing to answer before Nick seized my phone."

"Why would he do that?"

"Logan called and said you took off. Then you haven't been answering your phone. We were all worried."

"Well, Logan is a douchebag, and I sent him an email before leaving. I flew home to my parents' for the weekend."

"You're not coming to the game?"

"No."

"Why didn't you tell anyone?"

"Who was there to tell?"

There's a mumbling on her end, then the sound of a door closing. "Grace, I don't know exactly what's happening here, but I'm your friend, no matter what Logan said. Don't shut me out." She sounds so sincere, I feel guilty.

"I'm sorry, Bizzy. It's been a horrible week."

"I know. I've heard. Nick isn't himself. He says you two needed space, which sounds like bullshit to me."

"It's his call. He thinks I lied to him, he thinks I gave up an opportunity for him, and before all that, he freaked out. I'm not the kind of woman who begs for a man to love me, so I'm taking some time to myself."

"He's an idiot. I'll try to talk to him, get more details."

"Don't you have that ESP thing?"

"Yes, but mine is messed up lately. I've been feeling off a lot. I think I caught something at the hospital last week, so I don't even have the energy to fight with Shaw about being overbearing."

I smile to myself, picturing Shaw's irritation at Bizzy still taking PRN shifts at the hospital.

"Anyway, can we have lunch next week?" she asks.

"I'd love to. Pick a day Claire's off and let's do it, but promise me something. Talking about Nick is off limits. I'm not sure my heart can take it."

"Hmmm…" I hear her fingers tapping on the phone. "I promise I'll try. How's that?"

"The best I can ask for. I need to go. My mom is waiting in the cold for me to come in."

"Okay, let me know when you get home. Be safe."

"Bye." I power my phone back off, drop it in my purse, and get out, rushing to my mom's outstretched arms.

"Hey, baby." She hugs me tightly.

"Hey, Mama."

"Let's get you inside."

I let her usher me into the house, tucked close to her side. As I should have expected, Dad and Grandpa are waiting for me in the living room. I take a glimpse around, smelling the freshly baked scent of pie.

Memories assault me, and I lean into my mom, a sob escaping. Then another. I can't stop them, openly weeping, clinging to my mom. The emotions of the last week take over.

She gets me to the sofa where she and my dad crowd me, rubbing my back with soothing 'shhh' sounds. I don't know how long I cry, letting it all out, but a glass is shoved in my hands, and I calm down enough to see the pink liquor.

"What's this?" I stutter, looking at my grandpa.

"Moonshine! Drink up."

My tears start to dry up, and I let out a little giggle before taking a sip. The liquor is strong, scalding my throat and landing in my empty stomach. Grandpa hands me his handkerchief, and I gladly take it and wipe my face. When I've regained my composure enough to talk, I scoot back, laying my head on my dad's shoulder.

"I've had a bad week," I tell them.

"Obviously. Logan said you aren't talking. You left without telling him anything," Mom says worriedly.

"I sent him an email."

"What's going on?"

I glance at each of my family and exhale loudly. "Y'all may want to get comfortable. This is a long story."

I take another swig and start from the beginning. I tell them about falling in love, which they already know, then about the program, the acceptance, my decision to decline, and I finish with the details from Monday night and Tuesday morning.

None of them interrupt; even when my voice cracks and I cry through parts of the story, they listen intently. When I'm done, I raise my eyes to my grandpa first.

He's standing tall, his feet planted firmly, his arms crossed, and a murderous look on his face. I slink back as his eyes pierce into mine. I recognize the stormy gaze and fear for Nick's life.

"Your brother is about to eat shit. When I'm done with him, he's going to regret every vile word he spewed to you." He surprises the hell of out me when he reaches in his pocket, takes out his phone, and slams the front door on his way outside.

"Uh oh," I whisper.

"It's the truth, Grace—Logan was out of line. However, this thing with Nick is certainly surprising, too."

I nod sadly, trying to shove the thought of Nick away. "Are you two mad at me?"

"Hell no, why would we be?" Dad tucks a stray hair behind my ear. The gesture makes my eyes sting again. Another reminder of Nick.

"Because everyone else seems mad that I turned down this damned opportunity."

"But, baby, you explained yourself. The timing wasn't right. You aren't excited. Why do something you're not passionate about?" Mom pats my knee gently.

Dad stays quiet, too quiet. The expression on his face can only be described as pained.

"Dad?"

"Grace, this may be my fault."

"How?"

When he tells me about his conversation with Nick, and making Nick promise to encourage me to go away, my sadness fades and is replaced with resentment.

"You did what?" my mom screeches. "Carl Monroe, I told you to stay out of it!"

He throws his hands in the air defensively, leaning far away from us both. "I only meant for the boy not to hold you back, not to guilt you into staying."

"That 'boy' is a man, the same man who seconds before told you he loved our daughter. I warned you to walk a straight line, to keep your overprotective attitude in check. Grace is a mature business woman. She can make her own decisions."

"It was a friendly talk."

"Friendly talk my ass." She's stabbing the air aggressively, trying to reach his chest. Lucky for him, he's out of range.

I suck in a breath, waiting for her to spit fire.

"Get out and take Roy with you. Both of you go think about what you've done. You can call me in the morning, and I'll let you know if it's safe to come home." She slings her arm in the direction of the door.

"You can't kick me out of my own house," he sputters.

"Hell yes, I can. Maybe you'll learn a lesson."

He stands, running his hand down my arm and linking our hands. "I am sorry, Peach Princess. If I had anything to do with all this, I'm terribly sorry."

"Dad—"

"Nope, nuh-uh, don't be sweet," my mom orders me.

I snap my mouth shut but give my dad a wink before he walks out the door, muttering under his breath.

"I can't believe you did that." I gulp the last of my moonshine.

Mom takes my glass and tugs me off the couch with her. "We're going to do something very long overdue."

"What's that?"

"We're going to finish this moonshine, get drunk, and talk about boys. Maybe somewhere in there we can figure out what to do about Nick, because I can tell you right now, he doesn't want space."

"I'm pretty sure, if I had the energy, I'd throw up right now," I tell my grandpa, moaning into the sofa cushion. "That was one of the most awful programs ever."

"You said that about the last one."

"Because they're all awful. How do you watch this? I think my eyes are bleeding."

"You may want to get that checked out."

"Can you please find something decent to watch?"

"We could watch football." He takes a bite of his sandwich, making my stomach rumble in disgust.

The thought of food mixed with the thought of watching football sends waves of nausea through me. My mom was smart enough to know her limit, but apparently, days of not eating much topped with endless moonshine was my undoing last night. I continued to drink until she hauled me to her bed.

There was a trashcan on the floor and a bottle of water on the nightstand when I woke up at noon. She was long gone, deciding to forgive Dad and attend a christening event in town. When the room stopped spinning, I crawled to the bathroom and cried in relief when I saw the fresh clothes she'd laid out for me.

Taking a shower was an effort, but I made it through and stumbled to the sofa, which is where Grandpa found me a few hours ago. He took one look at me and sunk down in the recliner, happily taking over the remote.

"If you want to watch football, you need to go home," I reply grumpily.

"Nah, I want to spend time with you."

"Can you at least find an NCIS marathon?"

His eyes light up, and he does as I ask, smiling. This was our thing when I lived here. He and I were NCIS junkies. There probably isn't an episode we haven't seen up to this season. This time, he surprises me with NCIS LA, which means hours of enjoyment with Chris O'Donnell, LL Cool J, and Eric Christian Olsen.

I snuggle deeper into the couch, curling a blanket around me, and sigh contently. We watch in silence, except for the sound of Grandpa munching on his chips. For the first time in over a week, I feel at ease. Besides the raging hangover, I'm in a good place.

"He doesn't want space. He wants you."

I should have known the peace wouldn't last long. "He says differently."

"He was too influenced by us. We did that to him. He thought he was doing the right thing. You need to go home and straighten him out."

"Monroe women don't beg." I mimic Grandma's phrase she used so many times during my life.

He looks at me with one eyebrow raised, a smirk on his lips. "No, Monroe women don't beg. But I bet he'll have no problem begging."

"We'll see," I reply non-committedly.

"I straightened Logan out, too."

"Doesn't matter. Besides work business, I don't have anything to say to him either."

"Lick your wounds, Peach Princess, but always mend your fences. Life's too short."

This time when I look at my Grandpa, he's turned serious and a bit nostalgic.

One story I've heard over and over again growing up is that he and Grandma had a hard time when their parents didn't forgive them for eloping. It plagued Grandma almost to the point of depression, and he felt hopeless. She used to say she was going to be okay, that his love was enough, but he wasn't convinced.

He once told me he didn't regret much in his life, and never a day he was married to her. But one regret he did have was the pain their marriage caused.

"Grandpa, this is a different situation with both Nick and Logan. I can't explain how it felt."

"Why don't you try?"

"You really want to know how I felt when my boyfriend dumped me and my brother berated me?"

"Have at it. Let it roll." He spreads his arms wide, flapping his fingers to his chest in a 'give it to me' motion.

So many words run through my mind, but after spilling my guts to my mom last night, only one stands out. "Unwanted. I felt unwanted. Logan wouldn't listen to me, already on the warpath. He wasn't fazed by the thought of running the gallery alone, never once saying I was an essential part of the operations. Then when Nick hit me with wanting space and how we should slow things down, I was defeated."

"I can't speak for Nick, but I suspect he's rethinking his stupidity. He listened to us old men. We're at fault, too, but when I got a hold of Logan last night, I told him to pass along a message to Nick. I told him to tell that man we made a mistake and we were wrong. You have all your dreams right there in Miami.

"As for Logan, we know he's an asshole. He's a Monroe man, and it's a characteristic we carry proudly. But be assured, he'd lay down his life for you. He appreciates and respects you more than he lets on. Once again, I think you'll have an apology waiting when you get home."

"We'll see."

"Listen to your grandpa. I'm right."

He unmutes the TV, putting an end to our conversation. We watch in silence, me snoozing on and off until my parents come home and we all spend the rest of the day together, doing nothing. Our conversations are safe, staying away from anything in Miami. My mom catches me up on all the small town gossip and upcoming Christmas festivities.

I go to bed early, knowing I have to leave at the crack of dawn to return the rental car and catch my flight. When I lay in bed, I think about how coming home was a good idea. Besides my initial breakdown, my head is clearer.

I'll forgive Logan… eventually.

But dealing with Nick is a puzzle. Does he really want space? Does he seriously want to slow down and take a step back after all we shared? Or was Grandpa right? Was his whole spiel a charade in an attempt to keep his damn word to my overbearing family? If that's the case, he needs to talk to Shaw about a career in acting when his football days are over. I may have agreed with him that morning in my kitchen, but I know there's no going back for me.

Thinking about Nick has me reaching for my phone. It's been turned off since I got here. When I power it up, there are a few missed calls, but mostly text messages.

Claire: Just so you know, I miss your artsy ass. This game sucks balls without you.

I love Claire.

Bizzy: Your brother's here at the game with Melanie. I sent him a death glare, but Melanie looks super cute.

Typical Bizzy.

My pulse starts to race when I see Nick's name.

Nick: I heard you took off for the weekend. Have a good time. Let me know when you get home.

Completely bland, devoid of any emotion. No Sweet Peach, no mention of my absence at the game, nothing.

Curiosity gets the best of me, and I Google Nick's name to check if they won the game. The search produces hundreds of results, but the one that catches my eye is from one hour ago. I groan when I see it's a blog post on Shannon Says. I'm tempted to close out of it when the screen fills with a video that resembles a celebration. Stupidly, I press the play button and wait.

The scene starts off with so much cheering and celebrating, it's hard to hear. Shannon flips the recording to her and starts yelling.

"Hey, guys! Shannon Rails here for this special treat for all you Shannon Says viewers. Today, I'm with the Miami football team that has clinched their place in the playoffs with the win today. As you can hear, the celebration is underway in the locker room.

As much as I'd love to keep talking, let's see what's happening with our winning team!"

She flips the image again, and I'm transported into the locker room where people are wall-to-wall clapping and whooping as the team enters. A few guys I've met before, including Eddie, walk into the limelight, dancing and pumping their fists in the air. There's so much noise it's hard to understand anything until the crowd starts chanting, "Sexy Six".

My heart lodges in my throat when I see him. Like the others, he's removed his shoulder pads and is fresh off the field. The tank top he's wearing is visibly drenched with sweat, and he's dirty. Memories flood my mind, and my mouth waters instantly, thinking he's the sexiest man on the earth at this moment.

He gives a few high fives then waves humbly in the air. His blue eyes shine with happiness when he spins in a circle pointing to his teammates.

"This isn't me. This is us!" he yells, and the crowd 'whoops' again. The room starts to quiet when he waves his hands to the ground, trying to encourage silence.

"I'm so proud to be a part of this team for so many reasons. Today is proof that hard work and dedication pay off. When we get our heads in the game and focus, anything is possible. Keep doing what we're doing, and we're headed back to the Super Bowl!"

There's no way to hear anything over the triumphant cries as families swarm the guys and champagne corks pop. Shannon flips the camera back to herself with a wide smile and starts talking about the next three games being important, but with the division records, Miami can't lose their spot in the playoffs… Blah, blah, blah…

My eyes stay glued behind her where Bizzy, Shaw, Mathis, and Claire all give hugs to Nick. He smiles warmly, his face softening when Bizzy whispers something in his ear.

From somewhere behind him, a beautiful blonde bounces in and leaps into his arms. He catches her, his hands firm on her waist. I view in horror as his eyes grow wide right before she plants a kiss on his lips.

This doesn't go unnoticed by Shannon, who steps full into the frame with bulging eyes. *"Look at that, ladies and gentlemen! Maybe Sexy Six has a new good luck charm! Just remember, you saw it on Shannon Says first!"*

Bile rises to my mouth as I click exit and throw my phone to the floor with all the force I can muster.

Logically, I know what I saw can have a hundred explanations, but it hurts no less. I've watched women throw themselves at him for months, one in my own house. But he's always rejected the attention.

Then it hits me full force, and I know I can't do it. Logan was malicious, but he was right. Besides the gallery, living in Miami has revolved around Nick.

I may love Miami, but maybe Miami doesn't love me.

Chapter 27

Nick

I wipe my sweaty hands down my jeans and jump out of my truck, watching Grace through the window. She's on the phone, making notes, and nodding. My heart leaps at the sight. It's been too long since I've seen her in person. It hasn't been for lack of trying. I've texted her, asking to meet for lunch or dinner, but she's continuously rejected me.

Just when I thought I'd go crazy, and I was going to force her to talk to me, she skipped town for two days. Everything has been a blur since leaving her house.

Eight days—that's how long I've been deprived of her.

Eight excruciating days.

My lower back twinges in pain, and I flex to try to work out the kinks. I haven't been able to sleep in my bed since the last time Grace was there, so I moved to the sofa, which fucking sucks. But I'm not going back to that bed until I have Grace with me.

I've gone through the motions. Practices, films, meetings, all of it, trying to appear normal. It's all been an act, but today, it'll be worth it. Grace finally contacted me and asked me to meet her at the gallery today. I've been pacing my living room for hours waiting until I could get to her.

I run my hands through my hair and suck in a deep breath then head straight to her.

She peers up and gives me a small smile when I walk in, finishing her conversation. Logan comes from the back, his lips going tight when he spots me.

We've spoken exactly three times since I left him on the floor last Monday night. None of the conversations have been pleasant. The last was after his grandpa sent a message through him that we'd fucked up.

If that wasn't a kick in the gut. Fucked up wasn't even in the right category of what we did, but it was done. Now, it was time to fix the mistakes.

"Logan, can you lock the front door and meet us in your office." Grace hangs up and motions me to the back.

I eagerly follow, my hands begging to snatch her into my arms and carry her. She steps inside the door and stops, pointing for me to sit.

"Hey, Sweet Peach, it's good to see you." I bend and kiss her cheek, my lips lingering on the soft skin before I go to the chair.

Logan comes in and sits on the corner of his desk looking at her expectantly. "Are you actually going to talk to me now?"

"I've been talking to you."

"No, you've been answering questions and emailing every chance you get. Even from fifteen feet away, you email me."

"There's a reason." She flips her hair over her shoulder and looks between us. Her eyes are clear and expressionless, her face unreadable.

"I asked Nick to join us because I wanted you both to hear it from me. Your ploy worked. It's taken a few days, but I've been able to rescind my rejection, and I'm going to study with AIT. I leave in a week."

All the air is sucked out of the room at her announcement. Logan drops his eyes to the floor, while I stare at her. A week? She's leaving me in a week? That's not enough time to clean up the mess I've made.

"I've obviously had to make some changes to my schedule, but the organizers were kind enough to work with me. You both should know that I'm grateful for the push. It turns out my talents have gotten the attention of some pretty renowned people, and I didn't have to plead for another chance. Thank you both for your faith in me."

"Grace, this wasn't about faith. This was about you, all about you," Logan tries to explain.

"In order to leave you in the best possible position while I'm gone, I've been making calls and scheduling interviews for some help in the gallery. When you check your email, you'll see I've updated both our calendars with interviews scheduled and resumes attached. If you're unhappy with my choices, please feel free to start your own search." She goes on as if he didn't speak. "But I'll be honest; these are the best I've come across. If their interviews go well, you'll have a hard choice because they're all eager to get their foot in the door of an art gallery such as ours. All of them would clean the toilets if we asked, for a chance to learn the business from you. Ultimately, the choice is yours."

"Grace, stop being so aloof. The choice is ours," Logan snaps at her, and I ball my hand into a fist, ready to pound him if he gives her more attitude.

"Whatever." She shrugs and goes to the other side of the desk, careful not to get close to either of us.

She gathers a handful of papers, and my heart dulls to a slow thump. She lifts her eyes to mine again, but this time, there's a fire of righteousness as she aims her words at me.

"One thing I learned from my grandma was to dig deep until you discover the root of the problem. Well, I did my digging and uncovered a string of deceit." She lays out the emails Logan retrieved from her private account. "If I didn't know it already, here's the proof that you two were in cahoots. Why and how, I don't want to know, but your gig is up. I'm aware now that I never stood a chance to explain myself and my reasoning. You both took it upon yourselves to dictate what was best for me."

Oh, fuck! My neck can no longer support my head, and I drop my chin to my chest.

"But I'm not mad. I love you both, and I'm going to follow your wishes."

My head snaps up, my neck cracking painfully, but I stare at her. Hearing her say she loves us give me hope that there is a path to forgiveness. Logan stays quiet, too, his lips in a tight line.

My hope dies as she goes to the door again, her back to us. "In case you haven't figured it out, you hurt me deeply.

Regardless of the motives, I've never felt so inconsequential in my life. But that's over now."

"Logan?" She looks over her shoulder. "I'll be back tomorrow morning. We're moving on from this."

"Nick." She twists enough to speak directly to me. "I'd love if we could have dinner before my trip. It would be nice to clear the air before I get on that plane."

With that, she's gone, leaving me to stare after her with my jaw hanging and my ass glued to the chair.

"Welp, we're both fucked." Logan lets out a loud breath. "That was Grace's way of dismissing us both."

"Bullfuckingshit!" The shock wears off, and my legs find strength, pushing me up. "I'm going after her."

His hand lands on my forearm as I pass, and I growl at the interruption. "Good luck," he says, snatching his hand away.

I ignore him and run to the back door, screaming her name. "Grace!" I throw open the door in time to see her driving away.

Hell no, she's not dismissing me anymore.

I give her the courtesy of knocking twice before using my key to let myself into her apartment. Music blares from her room, the sound drifting through the place. Boxes are stacked neatly along the walls, all labeled with her belongings. Her scent hangs in the air, but otherwise, this looks nothing like her place. It's barren, every picture, knick-knack, and piece of art packed.

An ache pierces my chest. Not only is she leaving, but she's been doing all of this alone. I should have been here, helping her.

"NICK!" Grace shouts, causing me to whirl around. She stands at the foot of the kitchen with her hand over her chest and a look of fright on her face.

Without delay, I stalk to her, lifting her in my arms and pressing her as close as possible. "You've never been inconsequential. You've always been number one," I say into her hair. "Always, Sweet Peach."

She squirms, shoving hard to get away, which makes me tighten my grip. "Let me down."

"No."

"Nick, I'm having trouble breathing."

I loosen my hold, but only enough to shift back a few inches so I can see her face. "I'm sorry."

"Okay." Her response is robotic, without an ounce of sincerity.

"I'll apologize every day of my life if you will forgive me."

Pain flashes across her face while she braces on my biceps, trying to get away.

"Stop fighting me."

"Then put me down."

"No."

"Why?"

"Because I need you to accept my apology with more than an okay."

"What exactly are you apologizing for? We can start with conspiring with Logan and end with you making out with the busty blonde after the game on Sunday."

My arms go weak, and I place her back on her feet before staggering back. "What the hell are you talking about?"

"The blonde that leaped in your arms after the win. It was all over the internet."

"You know I don't look at the internet."

"Well, unfortunately, I did, and the image is burned in my brain. I especially like the part when she leaned in to kiss you so sweetly while everyone stood by smiling from ear to ear."

I vaguely recall Sunday after the game, remembering very little after leaving the field. The only reason I walked into that locker room chaos, instead of heading straight to the press room, was because Shaw encouraged me to be a leader to the team. I knew what he was doing, trying to help lift my spirits by seeing the celebratory mood. But I didn't feel like it. I did my job, and all I wanted was to get to a phone and see if Grace had called.

Looking at her face now, I understand why. The memory comes crashing back.

The girl, the jump, the kiss.

Then me throwing her away as if she was diseased and Bizzy threatening to kill her.

"Grace, it wasn't what you think. I swear to you."

She nods, walking back to her room and turning off her music. I'm on her heel, ready to explain, until I see her room.

Her beautiful room, her gorgeous décor, the bright colors and all her personal belongings… Gone. Packed away, exactly like the living room. Every trace of Grace is disappearing.

It's almost more than I can handle. The overwhelming need to beg her to stay is on the tip of my tongue. She can't leave like this. I can't have this distance between us.

"Grace, that woman is no one. I don't know her name, and after Bizzy threatened her life, Shaw had her escorted from the stadium and banned from the player quarters. She was searching for her five seconds of fame. If she knew anything about me, she'd know I'm taken."

A menacing smile appears on her face as she gives a guttural laugh. "Not anymore. You need space, remember?"

"You have to know I didn't mean any of it. You understand the position I was in."

She tilts her head to the ceiling, and for a split second, I think I've gotten somewhere… until she shakes her head.

"Nick, I really can't do this tonight. I've got a crazy week beginning tomorrow. Let's get together on Saturday when I get off work and talk."

"Saturday, I'm in Denver." Has she forgotten my schedule already? I programmed all my away games into her calendar. Did she delete them?

"When do you come home?"

"Monday."

"That's no good. My parents are flying down to see me off and help me get my stuff into storage. Then I leave on Tuesday."

"TUESDAY? I thought you said a week. Tuesday is six days from now!"

"Tit for tat. It's almost a week." She says it with such blasé, terror sets in.

"No, Grace, it's not tit for tat. It's an entire fucking day I'm losing with you."

"You're welcome to come to dinner on Monday night with my family."

"This shit is ending now, Grace. Quit with the tough act. We're going to dinner tonight. We're talking this shit out. We can do it here or at my place."

"Well, we can't do it here. My fridge is bare, and my dishes are packed. We can go to a restaurant."

"We'll stay at my place." The thought of having her back in my bed thrills me to no end.

"No, Nick, you'll stay at your place. I'm staying here. Dinner is it. Take it or leave it, but whatever it is, be quick. I've got a lot of shit to do, and tomorrow's a big day of interviews."

My sweet Grace has disappeared, and in her place is a woman I don't recognize. But I'll take what I can get. "Dinner it is."

"Give me a minute. I'll meet you in the living room." She rips the hairband out of her hair and disappears into her bathroom, shutting me out.

I leave her alone, fighting every instinct to wrap her back in my arms. I avoid her kitchen like the plague, the thought of going back in there sending a scorching pain to my gut. This apartment is full of too many memories, the good weighed down by the last time I was here.

Then it hits me like a freight train. The memory of last year, in Charlotte, with Bizzy. No matter what Shaw's intentions, he shredded her with his motives.

He thought he was protecting her, shielding her from the situation at hand.

She felt abandoned, alone, and like their lives together were over.

He fucked up.

I've done more than fuck up. I've fucked up to the point of epic proportions. The love of my life needed me to have her back, trust her decision, understand her… believe in her. I let her down.

Thinking quickly, I send a text to Shaw.

I'm in trouble here and need help. Tomorrow morning, your office. All hands on deck, including Gail.

My body starts buzzing as I come up with a new game plan. One thing I know about is the game—the planning, the strategy, the perfectly played execution.

The anticipation of the defense.

The thrill of the score.

I also know, actions are the only thing that matter.

Chapter 28

Grace

"That's the last of it." I drop the roll of tape on my sofa.

"Not everything." Claire points to my room.

"My dad is going to break down the bed on Monday," I explain. "I need somewhere to sleep."

Bizzy and Claire exchange a conspiring look.

"Whatever you're thinking, the answer is no."

"Sorry, we are under strict orders." Bizzy types something on her phone, and immediately, my front door opens. Shaw strolls in casually followed by Mathis.

"What's going on?"

No one responds, but Bizzy directs them to my room.

"Hey, stop that!" I yell when Mathis easily stands my mattress on one side and props it against the wall, doing the same with the box springs.

"The movers will be here tomorrow to get your stuff into storage," Shaw tells me.

"That's not my plan." I stomp. "Don't you dare disassemble my bed!"

He raises an eyebrow at me with a smirk, not phased at my childish behavior.

"Seriously, guys, this is nice of you to help, but it's enough already."

"Grace, stop being stubborn. We're your friends, and we want to help." Bizzy digs in the bag she dropped on my floor earlier and hands Shaw a drill.

He crouches and starts to remove the screws in my headboard, ignoring my death glare.

"If you are really my friends, you'll stop this right now! I'm not staying with Nick!" I shout.

"Told you this wasn't going to be easy," Mathis says to Bizzy, taking the drill from Shaw. "But it's going to be fun to watch him worm his way out of this."

"There is no worming out of anything because it's not happening. Why can't anyone understand that?" I huff.

"Because we're intrusive and slightly inappropriate at times," Claire jokes.

"So you're trying to force me to stay with him by making me homeless?"

"Don't be so melodramatic. If he can't convince you to stay with him, you can sleep at my place," she adds.

"Or mine. I have a guest room," Mathis offers.

"Or stay with us," Bizzy says.

"How about I move into a hotel for the next five days? Or sleep on the floor?" I throw my hands in the air. "That seems like the most logical idea if you guys are seriously taking my bed apart."

"You want to see Nick go crazy, you try moving into a hotel. You want to sleep on your floor, he'll be right beside you. He's pretty determined about this, Grace." Shaw's voice is gentle and kind. There's worry written all over his face. "Please don't leave with all this uncertainty between you two. It's killing him inside."

"Guys, I know he's your brother and friend, but you can't understand what happened. He made his point clear."

"He didn't mean a word he said, and you know it," Claire reminds me. "Nick was put in a bad position, and he reacted stupidly. Men do it. No one regrets it more than him. He loves you deeply, and he's desperate to show you."

"He's beating himself up with regret, Grace," Bizzy says softly. "He needs your forgiveness."

"I forgave him. He apologized, and I accepted. We had a nice dinner last night, where he explained his position, and I told him I understood. End of story. Now he's trying to dictate my life."

"No, he's trying to show you how sorry he is, and he wants to spend as much time with you as possible before you leave."

Suddenly, it hits me, and Logan's words replay in my mind. "That's why you insisted on helping me finish packing, isn't it? Because Nick asked you to?"

Claire catches on first and hisses. "Fucking Logan! Wipe those thoughts out of your head right now, Grace. We are your friends, too. It was my and Bizzy's idea to help you pack because it seemed like a good way to spend time with you before you leave for a few months. And it opens up some free time for you to spend with Nick before you go. This whole thing is a cluster-fuck."

It's on the tip of my tongue to argue, but I'm mentally exhausted with everything going on. Because now, I'm the one lying to everyone. Pretending that I'm still going to Seattle was the easiest way to leave things.

But spending time with Nick is going to make leaving so much harder. There's no way I can explain this to the four people standing in front of me without giving away my secret, so I decide to let it go and stop questioning their motives.

"Where is Nick? He's so adamant about spending time together, why isn't he here?" I ask no one in particular.

"He had an important meeting," Shaw tells me, his golden eyes shining brightly.

"Everything okay?"

"Yes, he's meeting with Shannon Rails. He's going to politely ask her to remove that video from her blog."

"Will she?"

"We don't know. It could go either way, but if she won't, we'll get creative."

The image of the blonde in Nick's arms pops into my head, and I wince.

"Did Nick tell you that Bizzy almost ripped that girl apart?" Claire asks me.

"He mentioned something like that."

"Well, Shannon conveniently edited that part of the video out. It was the best part of the day."

"Hardly," Shaw mutters under his breath, and I catch him eyeing Bizzy unhappily. When his eyes drop to her stomach, I suck in a quiet breath.

No one else seems to notice, but her hand covers her lower abdomen, and I know. She spots me gawking, and her eyes grow wide.

I give her a small headshake and see the relief on her face. It takes all I have to stay standing without jumping for joy. She's been very open about her dream to have a baby with Shaw. Not knowing if she could get pregnant has been on her mind for a while.

Seeing this silent interaction between her and Shaw makes my chest feel like bursting.

Bizzy's pregnant…

I lock eyes with her and try to communicate without words how happy I am for her. She returns a small smile and winks.

My heart swells with happiness at the same time my throat starts to close painfully. I'm going to miss it. I'm going to miss every part of it.

Because when I saw that video…

When I found those emails…

When I figured out what Logan and Nick were doing…

I didn't act rationally. I didn't give anyone time to explain or apologize like my grandpa suggested. Instead, I called AIT and asked for reconsideration. Then I jumped on the first opportunity they offered.

Which means I'm leaving in five days… and not returning for a year.

"Nick, where are we going?"

"It's a surprise." He repeats the same words he's told me each time I've asked.

He lifts our joined hands and kisses the back of mine, not taking his eyes off the road. I stay quiet as we drive, staring out the window and thinking about the day. Bizzy accidentally let it slip about their meeting at Shaw's office, but none of them would share with me exactly what they discussed.

I was extremely uneasy about the whole thing but finally let it go and enjoyed the rest of the afternoon, trying to soak up as many memories as possible. When Nick arrived, I didn't even argue with him when he announced we were leaving. There was no use. It was hard enough to get him to leave me at my apartment after dinner last night.

"Sweet Peach?" He squeezes my hand, bringing me out of my thoughts.

"Hmm?"

"I think I lost you to Grace Space again."

"Sorry, I've got a lot on my mind."

"How were the interviews this morning?"

"They went well. I like the second girl we interviewed. Logan seems to agree. I believe he's checking references tomorrow. If anything, Mom has agreed to stay for a few weeks to help out until he can get settled without me."

"My mom's going to help, too."

"She is?"

"Sure, she's excited, and she has the time. I think she called Logan this afternoon while you were packing."

"Nick, I don't mean to sound ungrateful, but isn't that weird?"

"Why would it be weird?"

So many reasons come to mind, but none of them are spoken when he makes a turn, and I realize where we are. "Oh my God, are we—?"

He gives me a boyish smile, parking in a reserved spot. "We are," he confirms.

"How did this happen? I thought you were banned."

"Shaw took pity on me. Well, that and I got Bizzy involved."

He gets out of the truck, goes to the back, and opens the liftgate, grabbing two overnight bags.

"Are we spending the night?" I ask stupidly.

He doesn't answer, just walks to my door. He takes my hand and leads me to a beautiful boat docked at the end. I giggle when I see the name *Benn Bizzy* painted on the side. I've heard a lot about this boat over the last few months.

As soon as we step on, he drops our bags and takes me in his arms, hugging me close. "I know you are hesitant to stay at my place, so Shaw agreed to let us use his boat the next two nights. Maybe by the time I leave for Denver, you'll feel comfortable staying in my condo."

"Two nights?" My voice squeaks at the question. It was bad enough knowing he'd arranged for me to stay with him. But on this boat, I'm trapped. Even though it's large, it's still close quarters. Too close.

"Yes, two nights. We're going away."

"Going away? I can't go away."

"Sure you can. Logan's handling everything at the gallery. Your apartment is taken care of. This gives us tonight, tomorrow, and tomorrow night together alone. I need this time with you."

Now, panic starts to set in. This is not good. It's only going to make it harder for a clean break when I leave. My defenses will be shattered, along with my battered heart.

"Nick, this isn't a good idea. I'll agree to stay with you at your condo, but we can't go away."

"It's done." He kisses along my hairline, and my heart starts to beat faster.

"What about the movers? They'll be there tomorrow according to Shaw."

"I asked Gail to reschedule for Saturday afternoon, so you could be there."

"Nick, I have far too much going on right now. It's irresponsible."

He leans back and bends a bit, bringing his face eye level to mine. “Grace, we need this. I can’t let you go away with the way things are between us.”

“I told you, I forgive you.”

“You lied. You’re still lying.”

“Don’t you have football stuff to do?”

“It’s taken care of.”

“Nick, please. We can’t.” I’m prepared to beg.

His hands move to my head, his fingertips sifting through my hair and forcing me to keep my face to him.

“Grace, I fucked up, and I know it. I’m sorry for that. But you aren’t leaving Miami with any doubts of how much I love you. It was an act, a charade. It was all lies. Not one word that came out of my mouth that morning was the truth. You are everything to me. If I could go back in time, I’d change everything.”

Hearing his confession breaks the last remaining pieces of my heart. It’s the validation I’ve been praying for, but it’s too late.

“Nick, we can’t be together while I’m gone. Regardless of your reasons, I now agree with you. We should take a step back and see what happens when I return.”

“Not fucking happening. You’re mine, Grace, and when you step foot on that plane, you’ll still be mine. Seattle isn’t that far. As soon as the season is over, I’m coming to you, and until then, I’ll pay for you to fly home every free day you have.”

Pain shoots down my side, and my knees give out. I double over, falling into him. He catches me easily, sliding an arm under my legs and lifting me. He carries me inside and sits, cradling me in his lap as I concentrate on not hyperventilating.

“Baby, I’ll buy a plane if I have to. Nothing is going to keep me away from you.”

This is it. I have to tell him about my change of plans and my rash decision that will likely end any chance of a continuing relationship.

"Nick?" I take a deep breath and raise my face back to his. He's looking at me with such love and concern, I know I've made a huge mistake. "I need to talk to you about my trip."

"Not tonight. Maybe not tomorrow either. This is our time."

I lose my courage and nod, agreeing because I'm a coward.

"Give me this, Grace. Please?"

"Okay, Nick."

Internally, I'm at war with myself, but I'm giving in. Because when he finds out what I've been hiding, he's likely never to speak to me again.

Chapter 29

Nick

It's all wrong.

My stomach and chest both tighten at the same time, forcing me to balance against the railing. The sun beats down as I stare out onto the horizon and think about the woman asleep inside the cabin who's emotionally unrecognizable to me.

Grace is quiet, closed off, hesitant to give me any type of clue what's happening in her head. Maybe it was selfish of me to try to whisk her away for this time alone. She's uprooting her entire life in a few days, and I basically stole her from her responsibilities.

If I was a better man, I'd go inside and pack our things then take her back to Miami.

But I'm not a better man. I'm a bastard, and I'm stealing every minute I can with her.

Last night didn't go exactly as planned. I don't know what I expected, but her falling asleep against my chest fully clothed was not it. Every primal instinct in my body was telling me to rip her clothes off and worship her body until she was thoroughly convinced of my feelings.

Instead, I changed her into her pajamas and slid into bed next to her, never letting go. When the sun started rising, I slipped out quietly and guided us out of the marina.

"Hey." Grace's sleepy voice comes from behind me.

I twist to find her standing in the doorway, watching me with uncertainty. She's so fucking beautiful my heart hurts.

"Come here, Grace." I open my arms, and she comes with no hesitation.

She buries her face into my chest. "Sorry, I fell asleep."

"Don't be."

"Where are we?"

"About twenty miles north of Miami."

"I can't believe I slept through us leaving."

"You must have been exhausted."

"Yeah, I guess," is all she says, snuggling in deeper to my chest.

She lifts her face to mine, and I lay my forehead against hers, inhaling deeply. She smells exactly like I remember in the morning. The hint of mint from our toothpaste, the smell of her lotions mixed with her shampoo… It all surrounds me, and I lock the memory away.

"God, I've missed this," I tell her.

"Me too."

She tilts her face and rises on her toes, brushing her lips across mine. My hands slide down her back, gripping her hips and urging her up. She gives a little gasp, her legs wrapping around my waist. My tongue slips inside her mouth, and I groan at the first taste of her. She gives me full access, opening wider and touching the tip of her tongue to mine.

Familiarity hovers over me. This is us.

My insides light on fire, igniting for her. I try to go slow, but as if she feels me holding back, she deepens the kiss, gliding her hands up my chest and neck until she's cupping my cheeks. Her mouth moves urgently against mine, her thighs tightening as she crawls further up my body.

This is unlike any kiss I've ever shared with Grace. Desperation and urgency pour from both of us as I grasp her hips tighter then slide my hands to her ass. She moans into my mouth, rocking into me at the same time. My dick throbs, pressing painfully against the waistband of my pants.

She shifts, grinding on me until I'm forced to break away from her mouth and growl against her lips. "Grace, you have to stop."

She ignores me, her teeth nipping my lower lip then skimming across my jawline. "I don't want to stop," she murmurs. "What I want is you. Make me forget it all, Nick… all the hurt and heartache."

Ice runs through my veins, the self-hatred returning. I tense, breaking us apart until I can see her face. She braces on my shoulders and looks at me in confusion.

"I love you."

Her eyes start to shine, darting to the side to avoid mine.

"Tell me you know I love you."

She bites on her lower lip as it starts to quiver.

"Tell me, Grace. Yell at me, scream, do anything you need to do. But tell me you believe me when I say I love you."

Her body trembles, but she stays quiet.

Actions, Nick. Take action. My subconscious screams at me until my feet start moving.

I walk us back into the cabin to the bedroom and lay her down, still attached to me. Her eyes finally come back to mine, and I see a level of hurt that causes my heart to slam in my chest.

I brace on my knees and break away enough to slide her shirt over her head. She lays still as my eyes roam her trembling body. My mouth grazes over her lips before moving lower to kiss every inch of exposed skin. Her hands go to my head when I gently suck one of her nipples into my mouth, twirling my tongue in the way I know she loves.

Her calf slides around my thigh, her back arching into me. She lets out a husky whimper when I move to her other nipple, sucking harder. Slowly, I go lower, using my tongue and lips to kiss down her stomach until I reach her hipbones. She lifts up, helping me slide her panties off, until she lies below me completely naked.

My mouth waters to taste her, lick her until she's screaming my name, but I remind myself we have all day. Right now is about so much more than carnal pleasure.

With one movement, I rip my pants off and crawl back up her body. She drops one knee to the side, right as my cock rubs against her wet heat. I swallow hard and lock eyes with her as I slip inside. She gives me another whimper as she stretches with each inch. Her eyes roll back when I sink in as deep as possible.

My mouth skims the column of her throat, kissing until I reach the sensitive skin below her ear.

"I love you, Grace Monroe, more than anything," I tell her over and over again.

She lets out a choked sob, her arms circling my shoulders, and I start to move, rocking in and out of her gently. Her body responds to mine like always, sucking me in, sending a fiery thrill through my veins. But it's not enough. I need more.

My hands slide under her back, scooping her up and leaning back, so she has no choice but to wrap around me fully. Her chest slams against mine, and I feel her heart racing to the same beat. With one hand, I grip the back of her neck tenderly and tip her face to mine. There are unshed tears in her eyes, and she rolls her hips with mine.

"Tell me you believe me."

"I believe you." Her voice cracks, but she doesn't break eye contact. "And I love you, too."

My own emotions threaten to erupt as relief washes through me. "I'm going to love you forever, Grace, and never, ever betray you again."

A flash of something crosses her face, but she drops her mouth to mine before I can question her.

Whatever it is doesn't matter, because she's back in my arms.

"Want to tell me how you pulled this off in less than twenty-four hours?" Grace pops a grape into her mouth, watching me from the couch.

"I had lots and lots of help."

"Does this have anything to do with your secret meeting in Shaw's office yesterday?" She raises an eyebrow expectantly, waiting.

"I knew I had my work cut out for me with a limited amount of time, so I asked for help. It wasn't a secret how upset I was about our situation, and when Bizzy found out what I had really done, she almost became hysterical. Shaw had to intervene, which wasn't pretty, and because he already knew I'd been an ass, she turned her wrath on him. Then when I explained you had reconsidered and were leaving, everyone jumped on board. Bizzy and Claire wanted to help you pack, so it would free up some time. My brothers offered to help, too. Gail scheduled the movers, and I set up the meeting with Shannon.

"The original plan was to have you stay with me, which you figured out, but Bizzy saw how upset it made you, so she called Shaw. She told him to do whatever it took. He called me with the suggestion we take the boat. I jumped at the chance. Bizzy arranged for the boat to be stocked when we showed up. All I had to do was get you here."

"Was this your plan? To drive me far enough from shore that I couldn't escape?"

I finish the omelets and plate them, going to sit next to her. "Not at all. I thought we'd go to West Palm for the day, spend the time away from Miami. More than anything, I wanted to be with you."

A frown forms on her face, and she starts picking at the hem of my t-shirt she threw on when I insisted on feeding her.

"Can we talk about it, Nick? All of it?"

My fork is halfway to my mouth when I freeze, my appetite disappearing. I'm prepared to do anything to win back Grace's trust, but the last thing I want to do is rehash the last two weeks.

"Do we have to?"

"I think we do, in order to fully clear the air."

"I'm an asshole. My actions were despicable and inexcusable. I love you more than anything, and you said you love me, too. That's where we are. Let's not relive it."

"I know, and I don't want to relive it either, but I think you need to hear me out. You may have been a jerk, but you also may have been right. Logan, too, but I'll never admit it to him."

I push both our plates away and haul her across the small space. She gives a little yelp when she lands in my lap.

"Why'd you do that?" she sputters.

"Because I want you surrounded by me whenever you say what you're going to say."

"I did choose you. It wasn't all a lie. I loved my life in Miami, too. Everything was a factor in my original decision, but when I stepped back, it was mostly you. And I wanted you to choose me too. When you didn't, my heart was crushed, but I was prepared to stick to my guns, stay in Miami, and go on without you. Then it was all too much, and when I saw that video, I knew I couldn't stay in Miami and take the chance of seeing you with other women. I chickened out and decided to leave."

"You know she meant nothing to me. She's a no one in my world."

"But it left me with a gaping wound. I needed you to choose me, and you didn't. So in the end, I think maybe you were right about the space thing. While I'm away, we can take the time apart—"

"Stop right there," I cut her off before she can finish her statement. "The last thing I want is space. When you leave here, we're together as a couple. The two of us and no one else. I did choose you. Every mistake I've made is because of loving you so much, but I learned the error of my ways. I'm not losing you again, Grace."

"Grandpa told me to give you a chance. He told me you'd apologize, and I didn't listen to him. I acted irrationally, and now—"

"Shh." I place a finger to her lips then replace it with my mouth, kissing her lightly.

"No, you have to let me finish. This is important."

"No, I don't." I stand, going back to the bedroom.

She opens her mouth then snaps it shut when I stop walking and press her up against wall, grinding my hips into hers.

"We're not going to West Palm. What's most important now is that I go back to making love to you until we have to head back to Miami tomorrow morning. All this shit is meaningless now. We're putting it behind us, not discussing it, not mentioning it again. The rest of the day and night, it's just you and me only."

She lets out a breathy sigh and nods, bringing her mouth to my ear. "Just remember how much I love you when I'm gone."

Chapter 30

Grace

Nick: Call me the instant you wake up, no matter what time.

It's only seven a.m. in Miami, which means it's five a.m. in Denver, but I do as I'm asked and call him.

"'lo," he answers, his voice husky and full of sleep.

"Hi." I burrow deeper into his pillow, smelling the faint scent of him.

"Where are you?" He's fully awake now.

"In your bed. Where'd you think I'd be?"

"Thank God. Shaw and Mathis called and said you girls went out last night. I wanted to make sure you weren't in jail."

"Nick! It was one time, and it wasn't jail. It was a sober cell."

"Whatever, I didn't hear back from you last night and spent half of the night worrying and the other half bugging the shit out of my brothers."

"Nick, I think they were trying to rile you up. I spent the night at the gallery, working on some last minute notes for Logan. Bizzy and Claire stopped by for a minute to check on me, but it was brief. I think everyone had plans. Claire, specifically, was ready to show off her new lingerie. She said Mathis had been working thirty-six hours straight."

"Assholes."

"Besides, I don't think Bizzy's breaking any laws right now, including drinking."

"She told you?" he asks with a mixture of surprise and relief.

"You know?" Now, I'm surprised.

"Yes, it's the most heavily guarded and worst kept secret ever. I went over last week when you were avoiding me to hang out after practice. Brayden was with her, and Shaw was at a meeting. She had to throw up twice in the first hour I was there. I stayed until Shaw got home. The way he went to her, the way he held her, he forgot I was in the room. The first thing he did was cradle her stomach. It was pretty obvious."

"That's beautiful." I picture the scene.

"Well, I was sworn to secrecy, until they hit what Bizzy refers to as a safety zone. Then Mathis told me he knows because he heard from Bizzy's boss that Bizzy's PRN work is changing dramatically. He figured it out."

"So she hasn't told Claire?"

"My guess is Claire knows, but Bizzy and Shaw are waiting to tell the parents."

I start to get choked up, knowing I'm going to miss it all.

"I'm really happy for them."

"Me too, especially after what they went through."

"And considering you and Mathis pretty much raided their baby-making weekend on Labor Day."

"Can we NOT discuss that ever again?"

I giggle, wishing I could see the scowl on his face when he thinks about what he interrupted and what he saw.

"How long were you at the gallery?" He changes the subject.

"'Til about ten, then I came back here and went straight to sleep. I was exhausted."

"Did you get a lot done?"

"I think so. Mom and Dad will be here in a few hours, and I'll spend some time today and tomorrow with her in the gallery going over all my notes. Logan will be there, too, and thanks to you and the girls, I don't have to rely on them to help me pack and move into storage, so we'll have a lot more free time together."

"Are you watching the game?"

"Maybe," I reply coyly, smiling into the pillow.

"My parents' invitation still stands." He refers to his parents' game party this afternoon.

"I think we'll end up at Logan's house. Melanie is doing some kind of dinner, and we promised."

This is all the truth, but I leave out the part about being afraid to see his parents and have them ask a lot of questions.

"Does that mean you're talking to Logan?"

"I never stopped talking to Logan. There just wasn't much to say."

"He loves you, Sweet Peach. Don't leave holding a grudge. If you can forgive me, you can forgive him."

"I have forgiven him, the first, second, and hundredth time he apologized. It's the things he said I can't forget."

"Grace—"

"Nick, do you really want to talk about my argument with my brother?"

"No." He sighs. "I'd like to know more about where you slept and what you're wearing."

A thrill slides up my spine, and warmth spread through me at his tone. "I slept in your bed like you asked."

"And what are you wearing?"

"Nothing," I tell a little white lie, omitting the pink lacy hipsters.

I hear a throaty rumble and the phone shifting before he speaks. "That's the vision I want to think about all day and until the minute I step foot back in Miami. It'll be nice to finally to sleep in my bed again."

It's on the tip of my tongue to say something about him sleeping on the couch, but I refrain. It's another painful reminder we don't need. So instead, I go a different route.

"It's very lonely without you. I dreamed a lot last night, remembering the last time I was here and what you did to me. I woke up curled around your pillow."

Another throaty rumble comes through the line, this time sounding like brutal torture.

"Fuck, Grace, I'm hard as a rock over here."

"Hmmm, such a waste. Maybe I should let you go take care of that," I tease.

"Hell no, you're not going anywhere. We're taking care of this."

"What do you suggest?" I nearly purr, feeling the sexual tension build through the line.

"Grace, tell me about your dream."

"I'd rather you tell me about your dreams."

"Jesus Christ," he hisses. "I've never in my life thought I'd be into phone sex."

"Don't let me corrupt you."

"Holy fuck. Touch yourself, Grace. Tell me how it feels."

"Tell me what to do, Nick. What do you want?"

There's more rumbling on his end, and his breathing picks up. "I'm going to tell you exactly what to do, and I want to hear it all."

I suck in a deep breath, feeling sexier than I ever have in my life. "Okay," I give in to him, needing this as much as he does. My entire body is on fire, needing this touch. Thinking of him, lying across the country, in bed, gripping himself as he tells me what to do, proves he has complete control.

"I'll do whatever you want."

"First, I need you to trace your fingers around your nipples and slowly run them down your stomach…"

"You're finally done, Grace. It's all ready," I say to the empty office and close down my computer, shoving it into my bag.

I take one last look around, checking the printer and making sure I've got everything. Then I walk through the gallery, memorizing its layout, knowing it will be different when I return.

When I get in my car, I send a quick text to my mom that I'm on my way and drive toward their hotel. This is it. Only Mom knows my plans. She's been an integral part of helping me get things together, so I'm comfortable with the transition.

The drive to the hotel and ride in the elevator, I rehearse what I'm going to say with a knot growing in my stomach.

Grandpa throws open the door before I even knock and hauls me into a hug. "Peach Princess!" He twists me around as if he hasn't seen me in forever.

"Grandpa, I saw you last night."

"But this old man needed some love." He places me on my feet and brings me inside where my mom promptly hands me a glass of wine.

I flash her a grateful smile and lay my bag down on the table in their suite.

Dad and Logan come in from the balcony when they spot me. I take a large gulp of my wine and grab a folder out of my bag, going to the barstool by my mom.

"I wanted to talk to you all tonight before we meet the Bennett's for dinner. There's something I need to tell you."

I focus directly on Logan first. "Logan, I've been keeping something from you, not only as your sister, but also as your business partner." I take the top two papers in the folder and walk them to him.

He starts to read and scowls, shock registering on his face. "What the hell is this?"

"I've spoken to a lawyer and had my share of the gallery transferred to Grandpa for the imminent future. If you have something that needs legal attention, he will be your partner. I'll be out of touch for a while. My schedule will be unpredictable, and you shouldn't be left in a lurch waiting on anything."

Logan opens his mouth, but Grandpa beats him to it. "Peach Princess, what is going on? I don't want to be involved with your business. Hell, I don't know anything about your business."

I give him an apologetic smile, having known he wouldn't like this. "I know, Grandpa, but you're a good businessman, and you gave us the money for the gallery. It's only right you have a say. Mom and Dad will be right there to help, too, if you have any questions. It's a family thing."

"Grace, I think you're being a bit overzealous. You'll be gone a few months, and I'll be able to contact you anytime. This was completely unnecessary." Logan tries to make sense of this.

"This is where I apologize to you Logan. I've misled you. I'm not going away for a few months, and I'm not going to Seattle. When I signed on, I had to agree to take what was available. I'll be leaving tomorrow for a year, and instead of Seattle, I'll be going international. My destination is Greece."

The room goes still, and my dad falls to the sofa without taking his eyes off me. Mom's hand comes to my lower back in a show of support.

"Oh my God," Logan repeats a few times with a look of horror. "You can't be serious."

I remain quiet, letting the news settle.

"You can't be serious!" He shouts this time, throwing his arms out in disbelief. "Why?"

"Because I decided it was what I wanted, and I took a good look at my life. Even though you were malicious in your delivery, you were right about so many things. I was living with my head in the clouds. The new friends, Nick, the popularity of the gallery… all of it. I was stubborn enough to stick to my guns on staying here, even if just to spite you. But then the weekend at home gave me clarity in so many ways."

I don't dare mention seeing Nick on the video in the locker room or the fact that this was a rash decision. Instead, I square my shoulders and hold my head high, knowing there's no going back.

"So, I'm following those dreams everyone was so worried about, but this time, the plan changed."

"Did I do this? Are you running away from me?" Logan's voice cracks, and Mom's hand grips the fabric of my dress, her body going rigid beside mine.

"No, Logan, this is all me," I say softly. "I love you, and I hope you will welcome me back with open arms."

"I love you, too, Grace. I don't want to own this business without you. It's as much yours as mine."

I nod, feeling a little relief.

"Does Nick know?"

The relief turns to anxiety at his question.

"No." I shake my head. "I've tried to tell him, but he was determined to avoid the subject. I'm going to tell him tomorrow morning. He deserves to know, and maybe he'll resent me, but he'll know."

"Grace, you can't do that to him. This is going to devastate him," Grandpa tells me with disappointment.

"I know." My eyes start to prickle. "But if it's meant to be, it's meant to be."

My dad leaps off the couch and comes to me, yanking me into his arms. "This is what you want, baby girl? You sure?"

"Yes, Daddy. I'm going to study under one of the finest glass sculpture artists in the world. This woman is a recluse. She spends most of her time in seclusion, but she's agreed to teach me, and for that, I'm excited. And after six months of training, she's going to oversee my creations in her studio." I hiccup into his chest, trying to tamper my emotions.

"That's a damned smart woman," Grandpa says gruffly, his own emotions coming through.

"Everyone, get in here," my mom demands until I feel all four sets of arms around me in a group hug.

"Promise me something." Logan's words are muffled through all the bodies.

"What?"

"Monroe Gallery gets exclusive rights to your first display. Every piece, Grace. Don't you sell one of them without letting me have first rights."

I start to laugh and cry at the same time. "Okay, Logan. You'll see everything."

"I'm so fucking proud of you, Grace, even if you are a pain in my ass."

There are a few chuckles from the men as I cry harder at my brother's words. He's proud of me.

Now, if only I can make Nick say the same.

Chapter 31

Nick

There's a searing pain in my side and pounding thud in my chest as we walk through the airport. In less than two hours, Grace will be on a plane out of Miami. She walks next to me silently, gripping my hand to the point of numbness. She's been like this all morning, staying close and holding me tight. The only time she's been out of my sight was when she went to the balcony to call her family.

I slide my eyes to the side and watch her as we walk. She's unusually pale, her eyes dull and lifeless as she visibly chews the inside of her cheek. I want to ask her to talk to me but don't for the fear she'll break down, and I'll beg her to stay with me.

Because that's what I want is for her to stay.

As we get closer to the security line, her walking slows.

"Nick, I need to talk to you." She glances around nervously and tugs me to a deserted area about ten feet away.

"Sweet Peach, what's going on?"

She lets go of my hand and rubs her eyes with her palms. Her eyes start to pool with tears before she even looks up, but when she does, my heart breaks.

The feeling from the morning on the boat slams into me. Something's very, very wrong.

"I've been keeping something from you."

The first thought that runs through my mind is she's pregnant. Instead of being scared to death, I'm ecstatic. This means I can keep her with me without seeming like the biggest jackass on the planet. Images of her and Bizzy being pregnant together start to run wild through my head. My mom is going to go batshit crazy.

Then I look at her closer and see the same anguish I felt three weeks ago. This isn't a surprise pregnancy announcement. Whatever it is, it's going to gut me.

"I've been dishonest with you. At first, I didn't think it mattered because you wanted your space. But then you came in with barrels blazing, not wanting space. It was too late. There wasn't anything I could do without ruining my credibility, so I tried to stay distant, but you wouldn't let me—"

"Baby, you're babbling. We've gone over this before."

"Yes, but you wouldn't let me tell you. I tried to tell you on the boat, but you wouldn't hear me out."

"You're losing me here, Grace. What is going on?"

"I'm not going to Seattle for a few months. I'm leaving Miami for a year!"

Her statement swirls in my head, not fully sinking in until I see the sheer fear on her face. I have to turn my back and take several deep breaths.

'I'm leaving Miami for a year!' replays over and over.

A fucking year?

I spin back to her with hurt and anger bubbling inside. "Repeat that," I hiss. "Tell me I heard you wrong."

"I tried to tell you. I tried—"

"You should have tried harder. Maybe blurted out the fact that you were abandoning me for a year."

She cries silently, tears streaming down her cheeks. "I'm not abandoning you. You wanted space. You wanted to take things slow. I saw you on video with another woman in your arms. It was all too much for me."

"You know all of that was bullshit! Every single bit of it. So now you're the one punishing me? All that shit these last few days? I busted my ass to make sure you knew how much I loved you. I've beat myself up trying to prove my devotion, but you've known you were leaving me."

"I trie—"

"Tried," I finish for her. "You tried to tell me. I get that. Come up with something new. So you really didn't forgive me? You were stringing me along, trying to hurt me?"

"Hurting you was and is the last thing on my mind. I love you, Nick."

"You love me? You're going to stand here and tell me you love me after lying to me. What was your plan, Grace, to leave again and reappear, hoping we'd have a third chance?"

She jolts, looking like I've struck her. Instantly, I feel shame, but my fury takes over.

Her eyes clear and she straightens, determination on her face. "I thought we'd gotten through that. My grandma died, and I went home. I didn't leave you."

"What do you want from me here, Grace? You've just thrown my world into a tailspin."

"I'm sorry, Nick, for everything. You're right. I should have blurted it out, made you listen to me. For that, I take the blame. But now, I'm going to go. I'll call you in a few days."

In a flash, she kisses me on the cheek and walks away, disappearing into the sea of people going to security.

When I shake out of my stupor, I call her name and search for her. She's nowhere to be seen.

Fuck no, I'm not losing her again.

I take off running to the front of the terminal like a madman. When I get to the Delta Airlines Service Center, the line is fifty deep. I whip out my phone and try calling her, telling her to stay put, that I'm coming, but her voicemail picks up immediately. By the time I get to a ticketing agent, I'm sweating bullets. It's been almost an hour since Grace walked away.

"Can I help you?" the perky agent asks, her eyes scanning over me hungrily.

"Hey, sweetie." I draw out the '*sweetie*' in a way that gets her attention. "I need to surprise a friend who's flying to Seattle. Can you get me on the next flight out?"

She gives me a flirty smile and starts typing. "I see there's a flight leaving in about one hour, which is cutting it close, but if you don't have baggage, I can slide you through security, Mr. Bennett."

She tries to sound sexy, but it makes my skin crawl. I try to hide my disdain by fisting my hand so hard my nails dig into my palm. If flirting with this woman will get me to Grace, it'll be worth it.

I peek at her name tag and swallow hard, pasting on my signature smile. "Carli, I'd love to be on that flight. Can you see if the seat next to Miss Grace Monroe is available? If not, can you upgrade both seats to first class?" I slide my Amex across the counter.

She types some more, scowling as she starts pounding the keys. "Mr. Bennett, there is no Grace Monroe on this flight."

"There has to be some mistake. I just left her off at security."

"No mistake, she's not on the flight to Seattle, or any of our connecting flights into Seattle."

I think fast, knowing I helped check her bags in at the Delta counter earlier. Taking a deep breath, I try to calm my racing heart. For the first time in my life, I use my celebrity status, knowing I'm desperate.

"It's really important I find her. Can you please check again? Her name is Grace Rae Monroe, birthdate June eighteenth."

Carli types some more, her face growing serious with each tap. "Mr. Bennett, I'm sorry, I can't give you any more information."

Motherfucker! Grace is in this airport, and I'm getting to her. I think fast, tapping the credit card nervously on the counter. Sweat slides down my neck and back knowing I'm running out of time.

"Mr. Bennett?" Carli jerks me from my thoughts. "I found a Grace Rae Monroe on an international flight. Destination Athens, Greece through Atlanta."

Fucking Greece? Grace is going to Greece?

"Get me to Atlanta."

"I can get you to Atlanta, but I can't get you to her. The flight she's on has already boarded, and by the time I get you there, she'll be airborne to Greece." She gives me a sympathetic smile.

I hang my head in defeat. My temper fucked it up this time.

"Thank you, Carli." I back away and walk impassively to the parking garage.

Somewhere along the way, a few people recognize me, but I don't acknowledge the shouts and calls for autographs.

Now what?

My doorbell buzzes for the fourth time, but I don't move from my lounger, where I stare aimlessly at the computer screen that's tracking Grace's flight to Greece. One hand holds my phone and the other a bottle of Johnny Walker.

Voices grow loud inside my condo behind me, and I groan into the night, cursing loudly.

Why do I give these fucking people keys to my place?

"He's out here!" Mathis yells backwards, finding me on the balcony.

Immediately, people crowd around me, Bizzy scooting in and wrapping her arms around my shoulders. She bumps my hip until I make enough room for her to lay out beside me.

"We heard," is all she says.

"Bad news travels fast."

Someone tries to remove the bottle of Johnny Walker from my grip, and I growl until Grandpa Roy's face appears in front of mine.

"Rude not to share." He takes a swig directly from the bottle and eyes me warily.

"Not feeling very hospitable." I return his glare.

"She didn't tell you."

"She told me half, I freaked, she ran… I went after her. But then I couldn't get to her." I surmise the story in two sentences.

"Stubborn ass granddaughter of mine."

I give a strangled laugh. "She said that. On the boat, she said she should have listened to you. At the time, I didn't understand. Something about letting me apologize."

"Did she tell you anything?" Logan pulls up a chair, followed by Shaw, Mathis, Carl, and Sharon.

"Jesus, how many of you are there?" I twist my head and search my condo to see if my own parents are lurking in the shadows. Bizzy gives a small giggle and places her head on my chest.

"She didn't tell you." Logan reaches for the bottle from Roy. I watch as the rest of my JW disappears into Logan's mouth.

"I'll tell him." Carl leans his elbows on his knees, eyes piercing into mine.

He repeats the events from last night and the extent of Grace's opportunity in Greece. Apparently, Logan went to work today and spent every hour researching the artist Grace will be studying under. This isn't some measly opportunity to gain credentials; this is big time. Grace could be famous in her industry once the year is over.

Bizzy gently takes my phone, handing it to Shaw, then does the same with my computer to Mathis. I start to argue, but Shaw shoots me a warning look, his hand flexing into a fist. He's not happy about Bizzy being draped around me, but he won't dare say anything.

"She loves you, Nick," Sharon tells me gently. "Unfortunately, she has a lot of the Rae and Monroe traits. Regardless of the opportunity, she wasn't going to back down once she committed. Now, we need to figure out how to make this right."

My head pounds, and the need to be alone overwhelms me. "Is everyone always this meddling?" I ask out loud.

"Always," everyone responds.

I lay my head back and close my eyes, picturing Grace the night she showed me the small glass sculpture of the peach tree she created. Her face lit up with so much happiness that I know this is where she needs to be.

Memories of the last three months flash through my mind, and I hold tight to Bizzy, needing her more than ever. She doesn't let go, finally whispering in my ear, "You have to go to her."

I snap my eyes open and zone in on Shaw. "I need you."

"I'll do what I can do. It'll be tough. You win the next two games, you'll have twelve days between season and divisional championships. You can skate out for four days max. "

"Consider it done. And plan any interviews online or phone."

"This has to stay completely confidential. One-hundred percent, no one can know their star quarterback is jet-setting across the globe, especially before the biggest games."

"We'll help any way we can. Circulate his name around the art community. Take a few candid shots then leak them so people think he's still in town," Logan offers.

"And I'll even take Shannon Rails to lunch, feeding her snippets about Nick's preparations for the games," Bizzy suggests. "I can't stand her, but she'll be able to spread the word he's in his zone."

"I'll be here, too, coming and going, so no one catches on he's not in his condo." Mathis remembers the local paparazzi staking out my place last year.

My head starts to clear, feeling the support around me. My phone dings with a text, and Shaw tosses it to me.

Grace is finally responding to my text from hours ago.

SP: I love you, too, Nick. Sorry I disappointed you.

I don't respond in front of all these people. Instead, I start working on my game plan.

Two wins plus one week, and I'm going to her.

Chapter 32

Grace

Greece is breathtaking.

Beautiful, ancient, classic. Everything about Athens has been more than I can imagine. The days bring so much joy and adventure, traveling around the city to different places and experiencing the culture. I've met with so many artists, browsing through their work.

It's the nights that kill me. I lay in my bed wondering what's happening at home, both in Thomasville and Miami.

The holidays were the hardest, missing Christmas at home. I received several e-cards from Mom and Dad, Bizzy, Claire, and Maria with gifts cards, which made me laugh because I did similarly. All my shopping was online this year. The only personal gift was the picture in the gallery I wanted Nick to have. Logan delivered it and promised me it was hung exactly where I wanted it.

My biggest surprise came from Grandpa Roy in the form of a Netflix gift card and a note to start watching some of his shows. I did, emailing him nightly how ludicrous they were, then admitting I was hooked

I rang in New Years alone, then spent the next day streaming the Miami game, watching Nick and Miami win another game in a row. I sent him a text of congratulations, and he replied thanking me. That was the extent of our communication—a few texts throughout the weeks, none of them mentioning the state of our relationship.

I expected more anger when he found out where I was, but there was none. His message was sweet, kind, and encouraging.

Sweet Peach, your family told me about this chance of a lifetime. Now, it's my turn to say kick ass. I'm sorry for the way I acted in the airport. When the shock wore off, the words I should have said finally surfaced. So I'll say them now.

I love you, Grace.

What happens next may be a mystery, but never doubt how much I've loved you since the day I saw you again.

You have a whole bunch of people rooting for you, and we're all proud.

That was three weeks ago, and so far, neither of us has called.

My life here is getting easier, but every day I regret my immature actions. Who knows how things could have ended if I'd only talked to Nick? There are too many what-ifs, and all of them are my fault.

The only thing I have to look forward to is next week when I start with Doni. I didn't understand why she demanded that I come to Greece early before we started our training. But now it makes sense. She wanted me to get acclimated to my surroundings and prove I wasn't going to run back to the states homesick.

My stomach growls, and I glance at my watch, deciding on an early dinner. Then I'll be home in time to watch one of the stupid shows I've become addicted to and text Grandpa before I go to bed.

It's only a seven hour time difference, but with no social life, I find myself in bed by ten most nights.

The little café I've grown to love is less than a block from my studio apartment, and when I walk in, the waitress waves for me to sit anywhere. If given a choice, I always choose a table in the corner with a view of the street that's private enough I don't feel stupid sitting alone. Today, I luck out and sit, setting my iPad on the table.

I order my usual and open my email, covering my laugh when at least a dozen are from Logan. My waitress gives me a wink when she brings my water, knowing my routine. Carefully, I answer each one, reminding him that next week, my availability will decrease.

A throat clears loudly, and I glance up to find a handsome man wearing a kind smile holding out a cup to me.

"Hello," I say.

"It's a shame for a beautiful woman to be sitting alone. I was hoping to buy you a cup of coffee and join you." He has a strong Grecian accent, but his English is perfect.

"That's very nice of you, but I'm working on a few things, so I'm not much company." I point to my iPad in explanation.

"It's a shame to work on such a beautiful night." He gestures to the window, and I see night falling, with the sun setting on the horizon. It is a beautiful scene, and I decide it won't hurt to have a little company tonight.

It's harmless to talk to a local while eating my salad. And besides, human interaction sounds nice.

"You're right." I close my iPad and motion to the other chair. "Please sit."

He does, sliding the cup my way.

I take it politely and smile.

"You're American?" he asks, sitting back casually and crossing his legs.

I notice immediately how nicely dressed he is, the black suit with stark white shirt, tieless and relaxed. Memories of Nick walking into the gallery after the Indy game in a similar outfit assault me. The day reruns through my head, and I have to breathe deeply to stop my heart from racing.

"Yes, I'm American," I manage to answer.

"Where are my manners?" He leans over the table, offering his hand. "I'm Nicolas."

At the mention of his name, a squeaky cough escapes, and his eyes drop to my mouth.

"I-I-I'm sorry," I stutter, trying to gain my composure and lifting my hand. "I'm—"

"Taken," a harsh growl answers for me at the same time a large hand lands on Nicolas'.

The voice sends a shockwave all the way to my toes. I jump back in my seat and snap my head to find Nick standing there with a murderous glare aimed at the man sitting in confusion across from me.

"Nick," barely comes out in a whisper.

Both men look at me, but I only have eyes for the man standing at the edge of my table.

There's an uncomfortable silence as both men stare at me until I leap out of my seat and onto Nick. He stumbles before catching me, both arms circling my waist possessively.

"Are you really here?" I mumble into his neck.

"I'm here, Sweet Peach."

I lean back and grab his face, locking eyes with him. "How?"

"It's called an airplane." He flashes a cocky grin.

"But how'd you find me?" I clarify.

"I've kept tabs on you since you landed in Athens. Your favorite places to shop, eat, visit, all of them; I've even been watching these stupid fucking shows in tandem with you and Roy."

"You're kidding!"

"On that part, I wish I was. But I'll admit that Chrisley guy is growing on me."

"Oh my God." I clutch him tighter, bringing his mouth to mine. Then I proceed to kiss all over his face. "I can't believe this."

"Baby, I'm not opposed to PDA, but I think people may be actually filming this."

I twist to find all eyes in the café are on us, a few phones zoned our way. Nicolas is no longer at the table, but instead is leaning against the front door with a small smile. He waves then leaves.

"Does this mean you don't hate me for leaving? You're not mad at me anymore?" I focus back on Nick.

"Never."

"Why haven't you called? God, Nick, I've been so ashamed of not telling you my change of plans, and so confused about the state of our relationship."

"There's a lot we need to talk about, but not here."

I scramble down and reach for my things.

"Miss Grace, this is for you." The waitress hands me my food packaged in a to-go bag, and I hug her.

"Thank you." I slip money in her apron and squeal when I'm hoisted in Nick's arms.

"If you take a right at the corner—" I begin to give him directions.

"I know where you live, Grace. I've already been there and had your landlord let me in." He stalks down the street expertly.

"I can walk."

"Fuck no, I'll get us there faster. And quick warning, Grace, seeing you with that man has me in a mood."

His eyes burn with heat, desire, and hunger. An all-over body tremble runs through me, and I give him a seductive grin.

The last few weeks… hell, the last few months evaporate from my mind. Nick is here, with me, and I'm going to take advantage of every second.

A craving takes over, and I curl into him, licking along his cheek until my mouth is at his ear.

"Your moods don't scare me."

"More," Nick orders, thrusting deep and pinning me to the wall with his body.

"I can't," I whimper, clinging to him.

"More."

His movements slow, rocking in and out of me. He slides his hand between us, circling my clit while sucking hard on the tendon at my neck. Each stroke rubs deliciously inside my already hypersensitive flesh. I find enough strength to squeeze my core as tight as I can, feeling the constriction everywhere.

"Fuck, Grace, stop that shit." He's panting, his arm muscles starting to bulge.

"It's too much." Black spots cloud my vision as the boiling starts at the base of my stomach and spine.

There's nothing gentle about this. He owns me, every part of me down to the two orgasms he already demanded I give him as he drove into me relentlessly. This is raw, unfiltered sex, reminding me exactly why I belong to him.

"I'm going to fuck you until you promise to never flirt with another man." He drives deep, licking along the curve of my neck and cupping my ass with brutal strength. The sensations are too much. Every nerve ending in my body is on fire, scorching me from the inside.

"I promise," I yell into the room, squirming wildly.

"Promise you will never leave me again."

"Never." My voice grows hoarse as I chase my release.

"Promise you're mine forever."

"Forever."

He slams into me twice more, his groans vibrating against my chest. He lets out a roar, and I feel his cock thicken then start to pulse.

My ankles lock around his hips, trying to gain some balance as there's a fiery rush. Then I'm free-falling into darkness, pleasure pouring out as I fly apart, screaming his name.

I go limp, unaware of any more movement until my back is on the bed and Nick collapses on top of me, careful not to crush me. Our slick bodies stick together, neither of us moving as we fight to catch our breaths. Dazed, I open my eyes to find him staring, his bright blue eyes shining with love. "You okay?"

"Define okay."

"Did I hurt you? I don't know what came over me, but the minute we hit your door, I was unstoppable."

"Hmmm, I think it was hot."

"Well, then hopefully, you'll still think it's hot when I tell you what I planned before I mauled you."

"What?" I go on alert, bracing for anything.

"It's over. Whatever song and dance we played is over. You're mine, Grace. No more miscommunications, no more secrets, no more lies."

"Okay."

"I'm always going to have your back, Grace, on every decision you make from this day forward. Do you know why?"

Without knowing what he's going to say, I know my life will forever be altered. This is more than rough sex declaring I'm his.

"Why?" I croak, emotions swirling inside.

"Because I choose you. And I'll follow you everywhere you go to chase the dreams you and Kayla had. I. CHOOSE. YOU."

He repeats my tearful words from the morning on the boat. I was right. At this moment, my life is defined. There's no warning, and I can't hold back the wail. "My grandma would l-l-l-love you!" I choke out.

He rolls, bringing me with him until I'm cradled to his body.

"I certainly hope so, Grace, because we're naming our first daughter Kayla."

Another round of sobs come, this time with lots of giggles in between.

Chapter 33

Nick

We should have stayed in bed. Then I wouldn't have to share her. But staying in bed meant I couldn't follow through on the last step of my plan, so it was my idea to come to the market and let her show me around. Her eyes lit up with excitement when she started to describe the people she'd met while she roamed the streets the last few weeks, getting accustomed to the culture.

She's curled to my side with my arm slung around her shoulders, pointing out different places, when a man jumps in front of us, scaring the shit out of me. Possessively, I tuck her behind me, glaring at the man whose eyes grow wide at my sneer.

"Nick, it's okay. I know this man. He runs the pottery shop on the corner." Grace runs her hand up and down my arm reassuringly. "He's harmless."

I grumble and sidestep, allowing her to speak to him. While they chat, I eye the grocery on the corner Grace's landlord told me about. I listen to them for a minute, and when I decide he's safe, I lean down and kiss her cheek.

"I'll be right back. Don't go far."

"Where are you going?"

"To get a few things." I jerk my chin to the store, and she nods, going back to her conversation.

I easily find what I'm searching for and am back by her side in less than ten minutes. The man breaks into a wide smile this time, giving me an approving look, even as I guide Grace away.

The driver I hired for the day is waiting on the corner and greets us with a grin before taking the bag from me and opening the door. I slip a piece of paper in his hand then slide next to Grace in the backseat.

"What are you up to?" she questions.

"It's a surprise."

"When did you have time to plan a surprise? You've only been here for a day."

"This is a few weeks in the making."

She frowns in confusion.

I outline her lips lightly, kissing a trail behind my finger. "All those nights I wasn't calling you, I was researching."

"I wish you would have called," she grumbles.

"I couldn't, babe. I had to stay focused, and I knew if I heard your voice, I'd blow this whole thing out of the water."

Her face goes soft, because she now knows the story of what happened the day she left. She knows about the ambush on my balcony and the help from our families to get me here without alerting anyone locally that I was out of the country.

"I guess I can forgive you since it was such a good surprise." She winks and cuddles next to me with a dreamy sigh.

Our driver starts talking, pointing out different areas of the countryside, and explains some of the agriculture. The ride is over an hour, and Grace engages with him, asking about the people and the land, soaking it all in. She explains a little about her home and their methods of farming, comparing techniques.

I watch her with such pride and awe that my heart swells.

She's so smart, so beautiful, and so fucking mine.

When he drives through the gates of the winery, she squeals, wiggling in her seat. "Is this you or Gail?" She eyes me suspiciously.

"It's all me. Promise." I cross my heart.

A hostess meets us at the large wooden doors, offering to take my bag, and mouths *'I got it'* while Grace is distracted. We join a tasting already in progress, while my body starts to hum in anticipation.

Finally, we're encouraged to enjoy the grounds, and I take Grace's hand leading her to the spot I have chosen. Since I discovered this winery online, I memorized the path.

I make sure to watch her face closely when the tree comes into view. She gasps, stopping and twisting to me.

"How did you do this?"

"Planning."

I lead her the rest of the way, pleased with the way the hostess organized the lunch I bought. The wine is set up on the side, along with a small fire pit to help fight off the chill in the air. Everything is as I instructed.

"This is so amazing."

I glance around at the surrounding area. Trees are already harvested for the season but still have some greenery, and the grounds are well landscaped. If the weather holds out, this is exactly what I pictured.

"You hungry?"

"I could eat." She flashes a suggestive smirk.

My cock stirs, liking her implication. "Food, Grace, I need to feed you."

"Spoil sport." She lowers herself to the blanket, and I pour us a glass of wine before joining her.

She scoots between my knees, leaning her back to my front, and sighs loudly. "I'm going to have a hard time when you leave."

"Me too, but I'll be back in a month."

"A month is a long time."

"A year is a long time, but we're going to make it work."

"Yes, but I can't help thinking of everything I'm going to miss. Will it be the same when I return?"

"Absolutely. My parents are already planning to visit us this summer. Your parents are coming in May. Mathis and Claire are talking about a trip. Logan's dying to get here when you have pieces to show. The only people who won't be able to travel are Bizzy and Shaw, but that's because Shaw is an overprotective idiot."

She sits up and turns, her eyes wide. "Wait, your parents are coming?"

"Hell yeah, once I move here, it may be hard to get them to leave."

"You're moving here?" she shrieks.

"Of course, I'm moving here as soon as the season ends. What did you think when I said I was coming back in a month?"

"I thought you were coming to visit. What about football?"

"I choose you, Grace. That means I'm with you. I may have to go back and forth a few times until training starts, but otherwise, I'm here.

"Shaw's already working on finding me a training facility to work out. Gail is looking into finding a decent place for us to live."

"Place to live?"

"Baby, I don't want to have to face your landlord every morning after what she hears coming through the walls. We need privacy."

Her cheeks start to flush, and she nibbles on her bottom lip. "Good point."

"And while I'm playing ball, you'll be creating masterpieces. We'll figure it out as we go. I'll fly you home every weekend if you want, and during our times apart, we'll become experts at phone sexing."

Her face now grows red, but there's a glint in her eye. "Experts."

"But before I leave here, I need something from you. You can say no, but I pray to God you don't."

"I'll do anything you ask."

"Marry me," I breathe out, knowing what I'm facing.

She sucks in a deep breath, staring at me in shock.

"And I'm not asking you to marry me in a few months, or even a year. I'm asking you to marry me today, right here under this tree."

"Today? Here?"

"Right here."

I see the wheels in her head start spinning as she thinks about what I've said. "What about our families and friends?"

"We'll do it all again for them. We'll have another ceremony in the peach orchard, under your favorite tree, and then the big celebration. But today, it'll be only for us."

I reach inside her purse and easily find the box I slipped in this morning while she was in the shower. Pushing back to my knees, I kneel before her and flip it open.

Her eyes grow wide, and she gasps, her hand flying to her mouth. "Where did you get that?"

"I went to the gallery before I left and told Logan I was bringing it to you." I gently lift the glass figurine of the peach tree she made in remembrance of Kayla. "Take a closer look."

She takes it from me, turning and inspecting it closely. The instant she spots the ring I've placed on one of the branches, she lets out a yelp, her eyes flying to mine.

I remove the ring and take her hand, sliding it on her finger. "Will you marry me, Grace?"

Her hand starts to tremble as she looks between the ring and me. She doesn't make a sound as her lips quiver.

"I'm going to be Grace Bennett."

That's all the confirmation I need before I haul her to me and kiss her everywhere.

She starts to laugh, her chest vibrating against mine. "Are we really getting married today?"

"Hell yes." I get my phone and send a text, then stand, bringing her with me.

"Is it even legal?"

"No, but we'll work out the specifics when I come back. This is for us. I couldn't leave here without having you as my wife. It may not be legal on paper, but it'll be legal in my heart."

Her eyes start to shine again. "Charmer."

"Only for you."

The owner of the winery comes into view, a wide smile on his face.

"Who's that?" Grace whispers.

"That's the man who's going to marry us."

"You had all this planned out."

"Even down to our wedding buffet." I wave my hand at the assortment of food on the blanket.

"I'm so in love with you, Nick Bennett." She rises on her toes and kisses me quickly.

"It's a good thing because you've stolen my heart twice in my life."

Nothing more is said as the man joins us and explains the commitment ceremony.

Legal or not, from this day forward, Grace will be my wife.

Grace climbs back in bed, curling into my side with a smug grin.

"What's on your mind?"

"There will be tears of outrage when the women learn that Sexy Six is off the market." Grace holds her hand in front of our faces, the diamond sparkling bright.

"Sexy Six has been off the market for a while."

She lets out a content sigh. "How do you want to handle this?"

"Handle what?"

"Telling people."

"That's your call. I'm following your lead."

She props up on an elbow, bringing her face to mine. "Nothing can be more magical than yesterday, but I do want a ceremony at home."

"Talk to your mom and plan it. Everything you want."

"July. I'll have some time in July to come home."

"Perfect."

The alarm on my phone goes off, and Grace falls backward with a groan.

"Babe, it's time."

"Don't say that. Let's pretend it's yesterday and go back to celebrating our nuptials."

"As much as I'd like to do that, planes don't wait for men to have sex with their wives."

"They should!"

"It doesn't work that way."

She rolls back to me, throwing her arms around my waist with such force I grunt. "What will happen if I don't let you go? I could chain you to the bed."

I grin at the thought. "If you want to chain me to the bed, I'm game, but in about two days, we'd have a very pissed off Shaw banging on the door with threats to kill me."

"Humph, that sucks."

"I agree, but it's my deal."

"Does it make me a bad person that a small part of me wants you to lose the divisional game next weekend, so you can get back here sooner?"

"It doesn't make you a bad person, but be careful who you repeat it to. I have a whole city relying on me."

"Fine! I don't want you to lose. It was a selfish reaction."

"Come here." I lift her to me, placing my lips on hers. "Be assured that every minute of every day that I'm away, I'm thinking of you, even on the field. But you've got a lot going on. Spend your days learning and your nights planning our wedding. Before you know it, I'll be back here."

She grins against my lips, slipping her tongue along the seam. Her hand trails down my chest and stomach until she slides her thumb over the tip of my dick. It starts to throb as she skims her fingernails down slowly.

Lust and desire build in her eyes, turning them a deep shade of purple. My body responds, heating at her touch. I'll never get enough of this woman. The insatiable hunger boils so hot it's never-ending. We've had more sex in the last few days than I've had in my life, and still, I can't wait to be buried inside her again.

Her grin turns wicked, and she slides lower, keeping her eyes locked with mine. She licks her way down until she's kneeling between my legs, her tongue circling my crown.

"Planes may not wait for sex, but what about a quick going away present?" Her voice hums against the sensitive skin, causing my cock to twitch.

My eyes close at the sensation, knowing exactly what's coming next. "Yes," is all I get out before she sucks me in deep.

I should tell her we have time because I set the alarm early with exactly this in mind, but I'm lost to all coherent thoughts.

She'll figure it out soon enough.

Chapter 34

Grace

Doni may be a crotchety, foul-mouthed, irritable woman, but for some reason, she's taken to me. She's not only a gifted artist and teacher, but she's also funny, witty, and downright brilliant. The first time I showed up at her studio, I was scared to death. She gave me one look, turned her back, muttered under her breath something about a southern belle, and told me straight up I was in for six months of hard work.

Then she proceeded to work my ass off with no mercy.

And I loved every second. During that time, she's become one of my favorite people in the world.

My days are spent working with Doni, and my nights spent Face-timing with Nick, watching Netflix with Grandpa, and alternating between calls and texts with Bizzy, Claire, and Mom. Once Nick returned to Miami and told everyone we were engaged, the floodgates opened.

Bizzy and Claire apologized endlessly about being aloof for my first few weeks in Greece, explaining they were scared they'd ruin Nick's surprise visit. It was easily forgivable, especially since I had to make my own apology for leaving without being honest with everyone.

All was forgiven, and I started planning a wedding.

Nick and I decided to keep our 'marriage' quiet and personal. Maybe one day we'd share what we did, but for now, the special memory was ours.

That is until Doni got me highly intoxicated, and I told her the story one evening. Her fortress crumbled that night, and she started showing her softer side. But I soon learned that was only for me. She was still extremely harsh to anyone else we came in contact with, which was a lot of people once she started taking me to the local galleries that sold her pieces.

There is still so much for me to learn, but I have confidence she's going to give me the best hands-on education anyone could ask for.

Because of this special relationship, she wiggled her way into coming with me today to pick up Nick from the airport. Why she wanted to come is a mystery to me, seeing as she's a recluse who doesn't like crowds and most of the time doesn't like people.

"You know you can wait in the car," I tell her the third time she complains.

"No," is her only reply.

"Suit yourself," I shrug and lean against the information desk, watching the large screens for arriving flights.

The instant Nick's flight status switches to landed, my body starts to buzz with excited energy. "He's here!" I reach for her hand, needing the support.

"He's here," she repeats, giving me a short squeeze.

Time slows as I scope eagerly for him. The baggage area starts to fill with travelers, but Nick is nowhere. Finally, I spot him leaning casually against the escalator railing, his eyes burning into mine.

My feet take off running toward him. He's barely off the escalator when I jump into his arms, squealing wildly. His lips are everywhere, kissing my neck, throat, chin, and cheeks until they land on my mouth. I hold on to him for dear life, pouring four weeks of love into the kiss. He returns the same, until there's a stinging on my back, forcing me to break away.

"You're acting like a fool! Get down!" Doni continues slapping at me until I dislodge my legs and slide down Nick's body.

"Sorry," I half-heartedly apologize, not meaning it.

There's a collection of sighs around us, and I realize we've gained an audience of mostly women.

"Eat your heart out, bitches. He's mine," I say quietly, but not quietly enough. Doni's eyes narrow right as Nick starts to laugh.

"Nick, this is Doni. Doni, this is my Nick." I introduce them.

Nick steps away and surprises me by embracing her. I try to warn him to stop because I fear for his safety, but the words die in my mouth when she hugs him back with a kiss on the cheek.

"What the hell?" I spout, completely stunned.

"Relax, Sweet Peach, Doni and I are friends," Nick says coolly.

"But Doni doesn't have friends. She doesn't even like people."

"She likes me." He pecks her one more time and tugs me back to his side, leading us to the baggage carousel.

"I don't know what to say or think about this. How are you friends?"

"Grace, for weeks I've listened to you babble about this guy. Not to mention he's been in touch," she tells me in her deep Greek accent.

"Been in touch?"

"Doni helped me out with our living arrangements."

"Living arrangements?"

"Did you transform into a parrot? What's wrong with you?" Doni scowls at me. This is the woman I know, not the one hugging Nick warmly as if they are long lost friends.

"I'm confused. Can someone please explain?"

Nick lifts my chin gently to him. "I emailed Doni and asked her to help me find somewhere to live. She knew someone who was renting."

"I thought we'd do that together." I pout.

"Baby, we'll look at the place tomorrow. If you don't like it, we'll start over."

It doesn't matter if it's a one-bedroom shack on a pig farm, I know I'll love it because we'll be together.

"I'm sure it's perfect," I say, dropping my attitude.

Nick sees his bags and goes to get them, leaving me with Doni.

"He sure is a beautiful specimen. You've chosen well."

"Do I need to worry about you trying to steal my husband?"

"Thirty years ago, I'd have tried, but it would be useless. That man only has eyes for you."

"Isn't he perfect?" I gush.

She looks at me with an unusual shine in her eyes. "He's put this smile on your face, so full of love that you're glowing. For that, he is perfect, Grace."

I act fast, wrapping my arms around her quickly, and then jump back before she can swat me again.

Her scowl returns but fades when Nick joins us with his suitcases and takes my hand possessively.

"I'm going to take you ladies to lunch then steal my wife away for a few days for a proper reunion," he tells her.

For the second time today, I almost fall when she lets out a loud laugh.

Who is this woman?

I let it go and don't ask, because the only thing I can think of is what Nick has in store for a 'proper reunion'.

Nick kisses me hard, swallowing my scream as I come apart. His hips swivel again, causing me to whimper, and then he groans, tearing his mouth away. My vision is spotty, unable to focus when I try to open my eyes.

"Never again going that long without you." He skims his mouth to my ear. "Never."

"Never," I agree, still clutching him.

"Goes without saying, I missed you."

"I missed you, too."

He nuzzles into my neck, nipping lightly at the skin with small whispers.

"I have something for you," I tell him when I regain my full voice.

His head pops up with a smug grin. "You ready to go again, Sweet Peach?" He thrusts his hips, proving he's still hard. "Gotta say, thought you might need a few minutes after the last one."

"Cocky much? I meant I actually have something for you."

"Does it require me moving?"

"Yes." I push on his shoulders.

He rolls to the side, moaning as I slide away and go to my bag on the dresser. He holds the sheets out for me to get back in bed and promptly positions me so I'm straddling him. His chest is gleaming with sweat, and his hair is tousled from my hands running through it. My mouth goes dry at the sight, and I almost forget my mission.

"Babe, the way you're looking at me says you *are* ready to go again." He bucks up.

"Give me a second. I'm enjoying the view."

He links his hands behind his head and gives me another cocky grin. "Take your time. I'll enjoy the view, too." His eyes roam up and down my naked body, heating as they go.

Shakily, I open the small box in my hands and remove the ring. "I bought this for you last week. When I saw it in the window, I fell in love with it. You don't have to wear it now if you don't want."

He brings my hand closer, silently inspecting the cobalt and platinum ring. It literally jumped out at me as I passed that window. Buying Nick a ring was going to be a challenge because, in my head, it had to be unique and masculine—something different than a traditional band. This was it, and I hoped he felt the same way.

"If you don't like it—"

"Put it on me." He lays his palm flat against my stomach, locking eyes with me as I slide it on. When I hit the base of his finger, he curls our hands and knifes up, touching his lips to mine. "I love it," he says softly.

"It reminded me of you."

"I'll wear it with pride."

I bite the inside of my cheek, trying to think of a way to bring up the next subject delicately. "Do you want to talk about Sunday night?"

"What's there to talk about?"

"We haven't really discussed it, and I know how much it meant to you."

"We lost. It happens. It's only a game."

"It surprises me you're so calm about it. The Super Bowl is a big deal. You've been working toward this the entire season, maybe even your entire life."

He twists, adjusts the pillows, and then scoots to lean on the headboard, the whole time keeping our hands joined. When he gets settled, he has a gleam in his eyes. "Grace, did you watch the after game interviews?"

"No." I shake my head. "I was too upset for you."

"Well, let me see if I can explain this without sounding like a pompous asshole. I won the Super Bowl last year as a second-year quarterback. It was my year to be on fire. I knew it walking onto the plane last year that we would bring the trophy back to Miami. It was 'there'. Everything clicked. This year, it didn't. We fought hard, but in the end, they were a better team. We have next year, and the motivation is there. Our team will take some time to let it settle, and when we hit the field again, we'll use this as motivation."

"I can't believe you're so calm."

"Losing you hurt a million times worse than losing that game. There will always be another game. That's why when the reporter asked me what I was doing next, I told her the truth."

"The truth?"

The gleam in his eyes starts to dance, and he swirls my diamond ring around my finger. "The truth. She expected me to say something along the lines of going home and watching the tapes until I found my errors, or expending all my energy in the offseason to correct those errors. Instead, I told her I was coming to Grace Land. That's what was on my mind. So when I left Houston, I left the game behind, ready to get to you. And this ring you've given me means so much more than a Super Bowl ring."

We stare at each other for a few seconds. So many things come to mind to say, but none of them can equate to the way my heart is bursting. This man has always had the ability to take my breath away.

"Did you actually say you were going to Grace Land?"

"I did. Only a few people in my inner circle actually know what that means."

"The tourism in Memphis probably skyrocketed with fans."

"Maybe, but you're the only fan I care about."

"Sexy Six is off the market." I giggle.

"Sexy Six is hitched. Gone for good. No other woman will ever turn my head."

"Charmer."

"Only for you. Now, can we get back to our reunion? Because tomorrow we've got a house to look at. While my wife's learning to make masterpieces, I've got to get us moved. Then I give it one week tops until our families are calling about visiting."

"One more question."

"Grace!" He throws his head back, rolling his eyes at the ceiling. "We've got the rest of our lives for questions. You're straddling me, naked, tormenting me with your body. There are much more important things to do right now." He rocks his hips again.

"Tell me about the house you found, and I promise to hold all further questions until it's you who can't walk tomorrow."

This gets his attention, and his head snaps up, determination on his face.

"The house is on the edge of Doni's property, with enough room for us to have guests. She may be a recluse, but she likes the idea of having us close. It's ours as long as we want it."

I know this house. It's quaint, charming, and exactly what I would have picked.

"It's all so surreal," I whisper, the weight of the last few months evaporating.

"Three years in the making, and finally, we're starting our life together the way it should be."

A lump forms in my throat, and my eyes start to tingle. "Don't make me cry."

"As long as they're tears of happiness, it's okay."

"Delirious happiness," I correct him.

"I'm going to give you everything in my power to make you happy always."

"You already do."

Epilogue

Nick

5 Months Later, July, Thomasville, GA

I stare at the enormous field that separates Roy's house from Carl and Sharon's. Masses of people are cleaning up from our wedding celebration last night. Tents are being lowered and tables stacked and loaded into vans. It's hard to believe that less than twelve hours ago, this place was packed with hundreds of guests. The people of Thomasville will be talking about that party for years.

Grace and I decided to have family only at the small ceremony under the peach tree. That family now includes Doni, who traveled with us with a surprisingly great attitude. The only outsider was the family minister, and he beamed with pride when Grace and I exchanged vows. He mentioned Kayla a few times, which brought tears from the women. Even Roy wiped his eyes a few times.

At six forty-five, Grace Rae Monroe officially became Grace Rae Bennett. In my mind, it happened on that day in January at the vineyard in Greece, but now the world knows.

The vision of Grace walking to me on her dad's arm will stay in my mind until my last dying day. Her violet eyes stayed locked with mine with every step. It was very traditional until I slipped the band on her finger. What happened next was out of my control. I hauled her to me and kissed her until my lungs burned from lack of oxygen. Time stood still, and it was just me and her until Shaw nudged me to acknowledge the minister.

Perfect… it was all perfect.

Then we got back to the reception and all hell broke loose. Grace was hijacked by almost every man in attendance. Shaw and Mathis were laughing their asses off, but there was nothing funny in my mind. When Eddie Jarvis moved in to kiss her cheek, I saw his life flash before my eyes.

Again, my brothers found this hilarious.

That was it. I was done. Grace was no longer moving more than six inches from me for the rest of the night.

I found great pleasure carrying her away from the reception to the waiting car as she sputtered incoherently and the crowd cheered. Our hotel was an hour away, so I had plenty of time to make it up to her.

Oh yeah, it was perfect.

"You're here early." Roy joins me on the back porch.

"Grace wanted to help her mom with the brunch. We came by to pick up Bizzy and Shaw. Grace disappeared upstairs to help Bizzy while Shaw loads the car."

"Bizzy going to make it back to Miami without having that baby?"

"She's not due for six weeks."

"Could have fooled me."

"That's why it's great to have a doctor in the family. Mathis is pretty much on call twenty-four-seven nowadays."

He crosses his arms across his chest in the signature 'Roy' stance. I wait, knowing he has something else to say.

"I need to apologize to you for the position we put you in." His statement shocks me. I was assuming we'd never mention it again.

"It's done. I'm the one who made the stupid decisions. Thank God she forgave me fully," I tell him honestly.

"She's happy. My Peach Princess is the happiest I've ever seen her. Thank you for that."

"That's my life goal, her happiness. 'Til my last breath."

He smiles, gripping my shoulder affectionately, our little heart to heart coming to an end.

"I'll see you at brunch. I'm going to go spend some time with Claire before she leaves me again for your brother."

"The offer still stands. You can have her if you want her!" I call to his back as he goes inside.

"Are you trying to give Claire away again?" Bizzy comes around the side yard, waddling toward me.

"No one will take her."

"She may get a complex one day."

Bizzy tries to keep a straight face, but we both laugh at the same time.

"Okay, she'll never get a complex," Bizzy admits.

"What are you doing out here?"

"I needed to talk to you for a minute alone." She comes to stand in front of me, taking my hand in hers. She spins my ring until it's at my knuckle.

"What are you doing?"

"I noticed the tan line on your finger the other day, but I didn't get a chance to ask you about it."

"Tan line?" I know exactly where she's going with this, so I avoid meeting her eyes.

"Nicky, look at me."

When I do, I'm busted.

"I knew it! You got married in Greece!"

"Yeah, we did, but we'd prefer to keep it quiet. A lot of feelings may get hurt."

"But you couldn't tell me?" she asks in a wounded voice.

Now I feel like shit. Bizzy hurt is one of my undoings, but Bizzy pregnant and upset could kill me, so I decide to tell her the truth and hope she understands. "Biz, it was something between us. When I went to Greece back in January, I wasn't leaving her there with any doubts about the level of my devotion. It was a commitment ceremony."

Her eyes start to shine, and she pounces on me, her large stomach hitting me first. I grunt, stepping back at the force.

"I'm so happy for you!" she cries into my chest.

Relief washes through me that she's not crying for another reason.

"Thank you." I kiss the top of her head.

"When I have this baby, I may beat your ass, but for now I'll be excited."

"You may have that baby today if you bump me like that again," I tease her and then yelp when she pinches my side.

"Don't be a shithead. I'm perfectly fine."

It's not smart to argue, so I grumble again.

"I can't wait until Grace is pregnant. You'll see that your little remarks aren't very cute."

"I can't wait either, and I'll gladly eat my words when she's as round as you and waddling like a duck."

"OOOWWWW!" I scream at the pain of her nails pinching harder.

She starts to laugh loud, bending and holding her stomach. Then she starts to snort.

Seeing her hold her stomach, full of a life she's craved for so long, hits me hard. I tug her gently back into me, laying my chin on the top of her head. "I love you so much, Bizzy, and I'm so happy for you and Shaw."

She hugs me back and raises her face to mine. "I love you too, Nicky."

"So now that you've exposed my secret and you don't hate me, can I ask a favor?"

"Yes."

"Can you help me speed up brunch, so I can steal my wife back to the hotel and get started on making babies and seeing Grace waddle like a duck?"

"Ugh! Don't be so crass. There are some things people don't need to know."

I wiggle my eyebrows, sending her into another round of giggles.

"Yeah, I'll help you. Let's go wrangle up this group, so we can have the world's quickest brunch."

"And that is why you're my best friend."

"You've got your own wife now. Think you can let go of mine?" Shaw's irritated voice comes from behind me, and I purposely pick her up and step out of his reach.

Right then, a jab kicks my stomach. "What the hell was that?" I put her down gently and glare at her with fear.

"The baby kicked you." Bizzy rubs where her stomach is visibly rolling. Shaw is at her side in an instant, his hand taking the place of hers.

"That's right, baby girl, you have permission to beat up on Nick anytime you want." Shaw talks to her stomach, and she gasps, her mouth dropping open.

"Shaw!"

My knees start shaking as I realize what he let slip. "Girl? Baby girl?"

"It was supposed to be a surprise!" Bizzy shrieks.

"Baby girl?" I repeat stupidly.

"Yes, we're having a girl," Shaw confirms proudly. His face glows as he continues to palm her stomach.

"Nick, you can't tell anyone else. We wanted to surprise everyone," Bizzy begs.

"So I wasn't the only one hiding something?" I cock an eyebrow at her.

"Who's hiding what?" Mathis comes out, takes one look at Bizzy and Shaw, then says, "Oh, the baby girl."

"You knew, too?" Bizzy's face starts to turn pink.

"I saw the sonogram, Bizzy. I'm a doctor."

"Oh yeah." She bites on her lip. "That makes sense."

"Where's Grace?" I scan over his shoulder and see her walking toward us. She comes to me and nuzzles into my side, wrapping her arms around my waist.

"We probably should go. Logan called and said he and Melanie are about to go crazy. Mama is in a tizzy."

"I agree. I can't leave Claire alone too long with your grandpa. I think he's serious about wanting to steal her," Mathis mumbles.

"You afraid of a little competition?" I goad him.

"It's not the competition. It's the fact Roy's been known to shoot people off his property."

Grace starts to giggle and buries her face in my shirt. "It was one time!"

"I love that story!" Bizzy starts bouncing, and Shaw grabs her in his arms, terror written on his face.

"Stop that!" he orders, holding her in place.

I'm not the only one who thinks she's going to jiggle this baby out.

Mathis starts laughing while shaking his head.

I look at the people I love most in the world with Grace attached to my side. My heart is completely full.

I lay my lips to the top of her head and speak low enough so only she can hear. "Thank you, Sweet Peach."

She raises her face to me, her violet eyes glowing brightly. "For what?"

"For choosing me, giving me this."

She smiles sweetly, knowing exactly what I mean.

2 Weeks Later

"I can't believe this!" Grace gushes, spinning in a circle with her hands spread wide. Her face is pure awe, and I breathe a sigh of relief. It's taken months of private calls, secret emails, and tons of help, but I've finally been able to pull it off.

Grace now stands in her own studio, equipped with the best that money can buy. She will now be able to create her sculptures in her own space when she moves back.

"This had to cost a fortune!"

I scoop her into my arms and twirl us both. "Don't worry about the money, Grace. When you come back from Greece, I wanted you to have a place of your own. I even had a bedroom set up in the loft, so if you're working late nights, we'll have somewhere to stay."

"You've thought of everything."

"I figured, since I couldn't give you a honeymoon until spring, I could give you your wedding present now. Even though it'll sit empty for a few months, it's here when you come home."

"Home," she repeats with a smile.

"Home, with me."

"How'd you do all this?" She braces on my shoulders, her face shining bright with excitement.

"I had lots of help, but Doni was essential in making sure I ordered the right things. Actually, I ended up handing over my credit card and telling her to handle the ordering."

"That sneak! So the whole time she was on my case, working me to the bone, she knew about this?"

"At least since March."

"I love it!" She leans in and lays her mouth on mine, tracing my lips with the tip of her tongue until I part them. Our tongues swirl together, slowly at first until I grip the back of her neck and angle her head to go deeper. Her hands scrape along my shoulders until she reaches my face and holds it tightly.

The kiss turns wild, and her legs lock around my stomach, forcing me to reposition so my hands are holding her ass.

Fifteen stairs. If I can get to the staircase, there are only fifteen stairs until I can lay her out on the bed. I start moving, and she tears her mouth away.

"Wait," she says breathlessly. "I have a surprise, too."

"The only surprise I care about is under this dress." I nip at her throat and keep moving.

"No, wait, this is important." She clutches at my jaw and brings my face to hers.

"I'm not leaving. Well, actually I am leaving to get our things, but then I'll be back."

This stops me. "Sweet Peach, you're babbling. "

"I'm not staying in Greece. I'm coming home. There's no way I could be there the next four months. I'd die without you for that long."

"What about Doni and the program?"

"She's coming with me. While you were conspiring with her to build me this studio, she knew she'd be here, too. She's going to come to the States for a while."

"Son of a bitch, you're kidding."

"No! She's going to rent an apartment and continue to help me. While she's here, she's going to travel, too. It's going to be great."

"So you're going back for how long?"

"A week or two. I'll close out some projects and pack my things. I should be here for the last preseason game."

"When did you decide this?"

"That's the irony. I was trying to decide how to tell Doni I couldn't fulfill my time in Greece. The thought of missing everything happening in Miami was tearing me up inside. Doni actually suggested we come here together. I was worried about where we'd work, but the whole time, she knew you were doing this for me! She's been playing us both."

"Sneaky little woman."

"I was going to tell you this morning, but you distracted me. Then you insisted we come here."

I start moving, making it to the staircase in three long strides. Grace squeals loudly when I get us up the stairs, to the bed, and drop back, bringing her with me.

"So you're coming home?" I ask, needing to hear the confirmation again.

"Yes."

"Fucking great. Now, we can get started on my next plan."

I rock up to a sitting position and strip her dress over her head easily, my eyes going to her naked chest.

"Next plan? What is that?"

A low rumble escapes as rational thoughts fly out of my head. The only word I can form is 'waddling'.

Grace sucks in a deep breath as understanding hits her. "Waddling?"

I nod, still focused on her sitting astride me in nothing but bright blue lace panties and strappy sandals.

"I can get on board with waddling, but let's make a deal."

"Anything."

She smiles seductively, arching her chest into mine and bringing her mouth to my ear. When she whispers what she wants, I break into a wide grin.

"You got it, Sweet Peach."

I'm confident down to my bones, this is one promise I can deliver.

Grace

6 Months Later

Confetti falls in the air as the field is swarmed with people. Shaw holds on to both my and Bizzy's arms protectively as he maneuvers us through the crowd. Mathis and Claire follow closely, cheering loudly.

When we finally reach the stairs to the stage, my eyes find Nick instantly. He's surrounded by players, all of them screaming and a few crying openly.

"Go to him," Shaw tells me, urging me forward.

"Aren't you coming?" I glimpse at them over my shoulder.

"Not this time. This is for you. We'll be right here."

I open my mouth to argue, but Claire and Bizzy both push me away, waving me to go.

I climb the steps, my stomach in knots of excitement. Nick spots me and leaves the huddle of men, racing to pick me up.

"We did it!" he screams, kissing everywhere he can.

"Y'all did it!" I shout back over the noise.

He looks over my head and jerks his chin at our crew before stalking across the stage to where the reporters are firing questions. It's all a blur as the commissioner gives his speech and the coach and owner accept the trophy, and then all eyes fall on Nick. He's still holding me close as he accepts the MVP award again then immediately hands it off to his team.

It's wild, loud, and crazy, but none of it compares to the excitement I'm feeling.

"I held up my end of the deal, Sweet Peach," Nick says so only I can hear.

"As did I."

His eyes grow wide with shock, and I take the opportunity to dig the piece of paper out of my pocket. He turns to shield us and takes it from me.

"Congratulations! Should I call you MVP or Daddy?"

He doesn't answer, staring at the sonogram. When he raises his eyes to mine, they're shining with unshed tears.

"I've haven't cried since I was fourteen years old, but you've brought me to my knees. When I didn't think I could love you anymore, you prove me wrong. Three years, eleven months, and five days. "

A lump forms in my throat and I fight back my own tears.

The crowds start roaring again, and then the chanting starts.

"SEXY! SEXY! SEXY!" gets louder and louder until he's forced to hand me back the picture, kissing me quickly and turning to the fans. We're swept to the front, and a microphone is shoved in his face.

He can't hide his emotions this time, his voice cracking as he praises the teamwork that made it possible to win this game.

The entire time he speaks, he never lets me go.

And I know, he never will.

Acknowledgements

First of all, to my readers—A huge, overwhelming, and enormous THANK YOU for your support of Sexy Six. There was so much excitement leading up to this release that I felt it every day as I worked on this story. You have so many options for your reading pleasure, and I hope this leaves you with a satisfied smile.

To my family—There was a time we didn't know how this would go, but you drove me with endless encouragement and support. Hopefully running away from home in order to get organized won't become a habit. I love you!

My Team—Lisa, Melissa, Nita, Kendra, Becky, and all my beta readers… you should be awarded for your patience and talents. I hope you know how much I appreciate you.

There's a group of women who help guide me every day with smiles, laughter, and advice. You know who you are, and I'm a very lucky person. Thank you for inviting me into your groups, your pages, your hearts and giving me courage when needed. It is my hope that I do the same. I look forward to many more releases with you by my side.

Bloggers—Our Indie community is driven by readers who rely on your promotions, recommendations, and knowledge of authors and their books. Thank you for allowing me to be a part of this.

FTN Girls—Always keeping it real.

CATB— I love #grouptherapy

For anyone I missed, I say this every book… I suck, but I love ya!

Meet the Author

Ahren spent her formative years living in an active volcano, where her family made collectible lava art. She studied rock collecting at the Sorbonne in France, which is where she met the love of her life—her pet pig Sybil. She returned to the States and started writing. She is happily married to a guy who used to live under a bridge whom she met while pole-dancing.

Now, meet the real me. I'm a wife, mother, and full-time Human Resource Specialist. Living on the Florida coast, my family spends a lot of time at the beach, which is my favorite place to get lost in books.

For more information, including all Ahren Sanders books, please visit www.ahrensanders.com

Author Links- Keep in touch!

Facebook: www.facebook.com/authorahrensanders
Twitter: @Ahrensanders
Instagram: www.instagram.com/Ahrensanders
Amazon : http://amzn.to/1eejSKy
Mailing list: http://bit.ly/1RrWAR4
Bookbub: https://www.bookbub.com/authors/ahren-sanders
Website: www.ahrensanders.com

Other Books

Surrender Series:

Surrendering (Surrender #1)
Surviving (Surrender #2)
Salvation (Surrender #3)

Finding Our Way Series:

Finding our Way
Staying on Course
Finding our Course (Duet)

Bennett Brother Series:

Hotshot (Shaw & Bizzy, Standalone)
Sexy Six (Nick & Grace, Standalone)
Heartthrob (Mathis & Claire, Standalone)

Standalones:

Reed's Reckoning
Smokescreen
Finn
Trixsters Anonymous
Fat Cat Liar

Made in the USA
Coppell, TX
10 September 2021

62142459R00195